THE WOLF'S LOVER

First edition. January 19, 2018.

Written by Samantha MacLeod.

For my dad, who taught me how to build a fire and gut a fish, and who never once told me I should consider law school.

Love you, Dad

FAIR WARNING

W elcome, reader.

Thank you for joining Karen on her adventure. This book, *The Wolf's Lover*, is a stand-alone novel. As such, it can certainly be read and enjoyed by itself.

The Wolf's Lover is also, however, part of a larger universe. If you'd like to know how Vali's father, the Norse god Loki, met his wife Caroline, that story begins with *The Trickster's Lover*[1].

Also, please note that this story contains graphic depictions of sexual acts, suggestions of sexual violence, dubious consent, grief, loss, mental illness, and self-harm. This dark urban fantasy is not intended for readers under 18.

Still interested?

Then, please, do join me. Karen McDonald is in Yellowstone National Park right now, and the sun is just coming up.

---

1.   *https://www.amazon.com/Tricksters-Lover-Erotic-Loki-Romance-ebook/dp/*

   B01K352QNA/ref=sr_1_1?ie=UTF8&qid=1498491200&sr=8-

   1&keywords=trickster's+lover

CHAPTER ONE

I dreamt of him again.

My heart raced as I blinked in the claustrophobic pre-dawn gloom of my single-person tent. A long, slow shiver rippled through my body. I pushed my palms against my eyes, trying to convince myself the trembling was just my arms and legs responding to the low temperature. Even in August, the nights in Yellowstone National Park are cold.

I pulled on my fleece and jammed my knit wool hat over my head before unzipping the tent's door. The first rays of sunlight were just hitting the crowns of the lodgepole pines across the meadow, and the sky beyond the trees shimmered in delicate cerulean. I fumbled out of my tent, stood, and stretched, pressing my knuckles against the small of my back as I gazed across the vast willow and sagebrush expanse of the Lamar Valley.

"Somewhere out there," I whispered to myself, "are the wolves."

Yawning, I reached back into the tent for my grizzly bear spray. My bear spray canister was bigger than a beer can, with the same gleaming silver finish. The safety latch glowed in the dark, which was simultaneously reassuring and deeply disturbing. I'm here, the glowing safety latch declared all night long. Just in case a 1,500 pound grizzly bear decides to rip open your tent like a sardine can!

I clipped the bear spray canister to my belt before walking to the tree where I'd hung my food and supplies. The bag was undisturbed, with no tracks in the vicinity.

"Thank God," I sighed.

My frozen fingers made untying the rope and pulling out my stove a somewhat clumsy affair. A shrill, metallic jangle filled the clearing as I pulled out the instant coffee packets, and I frowned. I hated going into the backcountry with a cell phone, and I could have sworn I'd turned the damn thing off before I buried it at the bottom of the bear-proof supply canister. The phone fell silent for a moment, then started ringing again. With a sigh, I fished it out of its waterproof bag and swiped the screen.

It flashed the name *Diana*. Weird. I hadn't talked to Diana in weeks.

"Hello?" I said.

"Good morning, Karen," Diana's voice filled the meadow. She sounded disturbingly cheerful. "You're in the park!"

I blinked. "Uh, yeah, I hiked in yesterday. How did you..? Did I even send you my itinerary?"

Diana made a noncommittal grunt. "There's a storm coming," she said. "How were your dreams?"

"Fine," I lied. Full of running and sex, but that was none of her business. "Did you have some news about the wolves, or something?"

"The moon's gibbous. Good for dreaming. And the park's a thin place. Just thought I'd check."

I pinched the bridge of my nose and took a deep breath, ignoring her hippie-dippy blathering. That kind of talk was exactly why the rest of the biologists at Montana State University thought I was wasting my time talking to Diana.

"And you have some news about the wolves?" I asked again.

"The wolves are exactly where they were yesterday," she said, somehow managing to sound condescending. "It looks like the Leopold pack is about twelve miles west of you, bedded down."

"Thank you."

Diana is not a scientist. She lives alone in a log cabin on the eastern side of the park, just outside Cooke City, with an ungodly array of computer equipment and satellite dishes. She spends her time tracking the wolves. All of her time, as far as I can tell, with the possible exception of hunting season. God only knows how she supports herself. She doesn't seem much like one of the trustafarians who live in Bozeman, running tiny art studios that are open for six hours out of the week while they live off of the dwindling fortunes of some wealthy distant relative, but she must have some secret source of income.

"Oh, and a few of the regular wolf watchers spotted that male," Diana said, just as I was getting ready to hang up.

"Where?" I grabbed my notebook.

Every wolf in Yellowstone National Park is under surveillance. They're microchipped, they're radio tagged, we have their DNA samples on file. We know who their parents are. We know who their grandparents are.

Last month Diana called to say she'd spotted a new wolf. I told her this was impossible. A new, adult wolf in Yellowstone would've had to migrate down from Canada. In the twenty plus years since wolves were reintroduced to Yellowstone, this has never happened.

"He's near you," Diana said. It sounded like she was smiling.

For a heartbeat I had the disconcerting feeling she was about to say something like, *In fact, he's right behind you.* The hairs on the back of my neck prickled, and I turned around. There was nothing behind me but lodgepole pines.

"I'd say he's about five miles west of you," she said. "Moving slowly. Ambling. He's alone."

I scribbled in my notebook: *5 miles W, lone.* "This is fantastic. What direction was he heading?"

"Toward you," Diana said, with that same smile in her voice. "I'd say you'll see him today. If not, then tomorrow."

"That might be the most unscientific thing you've said all morning," I told her. And then I remembered the gibbous moon comment.

Diana laughed. "I like you," she said. "You take care."

"Thanks," I said. "I like you—"

But the line was already dead. I sighed and slipped my phone into my pocket as I carried my supplies back to the campsite. Once I'd balanced the delicate silver tripod of my MSR stove on a flat slab of granite, I attached the fuel bottle, twisted the knobs, and lit the gasoline. The cool morning air filled with the hiss of the stove. I put a pot of water over the delicate blue flame and filled my titanium mug with instant coffee mix.

And I tried not to think about my dreams.

I always had strange dreams when I was camping, but these had been disturbingly vivid. They were Yellowstone dreams, filled with the rotten egg sulfur smell of the hot springs and the cold chatter of snowmelt over stone. But there had been something odd too, some acrid, burnt smell in the air, something that made me want to run through the pines and sagebrush flats. Something that made me want to run to him.

I hadn't dreamt of him in years. Not since that horrible winter in my early thirties when I was living with my parents, examining the shattered fragments of my life. He had appeared in my dreams then, tall and handsome, with his wild, dark hair falling down his back in waves. For months he was my constant companion while I slept in my parents' log cabin, in my childhood bed. At the time, I assumed my subconscious was trying to convince me to stay alive.

But last night I dreamt of him again, for the first time since I'd moved to Montana. In my dream, I had stood in a meadow of tall grass and wildflowers, purple penstemon and indigo lodgepole lupine and delicate shooting-star columbine, surrounded by aspen trees, whose pale green leaves trembled as he approached. My dream lover, his body lean and muscular, his high cheekbones and riot of dark hair exactly as I remembered. He'd smiled at me with his golden eyes. Our bodies came together without words, without thought, his hips pressed against mine, his lips—

I shook my head to stop that train of thought. Even here, by myself in the backwoods of Yellowstone, my cheeks flushed and burned. I hadn't had dreams that sexy in years. Shit, I hadn't had sex in years. I assumed that part of myself had just dried up and gone away, atrophied from lack of use, another casualty of the divorce. After all, it had been, what, almost four years? Yes, nearly three years living in Bozeman. One year lost. Equals four.

The stove hissed and sizzled as the pot boiled over. I grabbed the silicone hot pad, pulled the pot of boiling water carefully from my precarious tripod stove, poured water into my instant coffee, and sat back to watch dawn unfold over the valley.

After coffee and a breakfast of instant oatmeal, it was time to deal with the rest of my gear. Our tracking equipment was heavy, so I'd only packed in part of it. My graduate students Colin and Zeke would bring the rest later today, and then we'd really start working.

I inspected the tranquilizer gun and loaded the darts, smiling as I remembered my father cleaning his hunting rifle in the living room. After that, I set up the tiny satellite dish and the receiving antennae, turned everything on to make sure it was still working, and turned everything off again to save battery life.

Once I'd run all the equipment checks and recorded everything in my field notebook, it was finally warm enough to pull off my wool hat. I ran my fingers through my hair, listening to the grasshoppers warming up in the buffalo grass as I pulled out my binoculars and glassed the sagebrush across the valley. Nothing moving out there. Yet.

My phone gave a sharp ding. I jumped, jarring the view through the binoculars. A new text from Zeke appeared on the screen.

Boss Lady. Headed 2 Canyon w Colin. Losing cell. ETA 12:30.

Before I could even groan, my phone dinged with another incoming text.

PS. Colin driving - don't flip UR lid

"You're in the canyon now?" I yelled at my mute phone. "That's almost a hundred miles away!"

Damn it all, I told them to be in the park by noon today at the very latest. They'd never make it here by twelve-thirty, even if they drove fifty miles over the speed limit, which I wouldn't put past Colin and Zeke.

"Ugh, when am I going to find a grad student who's not a complete fuck off?" I asked the empty meadow as I shoved the phone back in its waterproof bag. Just for good measure, I kicked the dirt in front of me.

Five miles west of you, Diana said this morning. *Moving slowly.*

I picked up my daypack, the water bottle, and a bag of granola bars. Then I headed west.

The area to the west of my campsite was tough traveling, full of burned, fallen trees from the fire of '88. I walked slowly, picking my way around and over the downed pines and scanning the forest edge for movement. I found it disturbingly hard to focus, despite two cups of instant coffee. I tried to watch the ground for scat or tracks, but my mind kept sliding back to last night's dreams, to my imaginary lover's strong body and soft lips.

I balled my fists in frustration. Even if I wasn't distracted by my stupid dreams, it wasn't like I could accomplish anything this morning anyway. If I was lucky, I might be able to spot the Leopold pack. Maybe. But I couldn't tranquilize a wolf by myself, and it was highly doubtful I'd get close enough to make any meaningful observations. I leaned against a fallen tree and tilted my head to the sun, enjoying the quiet. Being in the backcountry always made me feel like a kid again, playing by myself in the woods behind my parents' house.

The soft murmur of running water teased me, beckoning from somewhere close by. I turned to my phone, expanding the topographical map I'd downloaded. It looked like I had almost reached a tiny tributary of the Lamar River. I grinned. It was just past noon, and there was no way Colin and Zeke would make it to the campsite for another full hour, at least. And, in the direct sunshine, the day was almost hot.

"Well," I told myself, "if I'm not going to accomplish anything, I might as well take a bath."

The little creek was cold and clear. I followed its gentle meanderings, twisting in and out of clumps of willows and threading my way around downed logs, until I found a clear, pebble-lined pool. Perfect.

Out of nervous habit, I looked around with the binoculars before I took off my shirt.

"You're being ridiculous," I told myself as I slipped the binoculars back into their leather pouch. "This is backcountry Yellowstone. You're seven miles from the nearest road, five miles from the nearest trail. No one is going to see you naked."

Still, I stepped behind a big willow bush before slipping out of my pants. Once naked, I folded my clothes and stacked them on the grass near my daypack, making sure the gleaming, silver canister of bear spray was within easy reach. The pool was clear and so still I could almost make out my reflection in the shifting surface. I plunged my arms in the stream, disrupting the image.

The water was freezing cold. It may have been snow this morning, melting off the high shoulders of Druid Peak. I pulled my arms out, took a deep breath, and decided I'd better do this quickly if I was going to do it at all. I stepped in up to my thighs, gasping before I crouched low enough to dunk my head under the icy water.

I exploded out of the stream a heartbeat later, falling back onto the grassy banks and laughing. I spread my arms, soaking up the bright August sunlight for a few minutes before grabbing my little plastic vial of biodegradable soap. Nothing in this universe smells quite like Dr. Bronner's soap, and soon the scent of willows and grass and running water was drown out by an odd combination of peppermint and eucalyptus.

I rubbed the soap through my hair, down my arms, and over the curve of my breasts. My body tingled with peppermint and the memory of the cold water. It made me think of last night, and the feel of my dream lover's lips against my skin. He'd spent a long time kissing the inside of my wrist as his hand moved down the curve of my stomach—

"Stop it," I muttered, shaking my head. "What is with you today?"

I gave my arms a final scrub of peppermint eucalyptus soap before stepping back into the stream. It felt even colder this time around. Quickly, I rinsed the soap off my arms and chest. Then I crouched down and leaned back. Holding my breath, I dunked my head under the icy water and ran my fingers through my hair, shaking out the soap.

My chest tightened with the sudden, unshakable conviction that I was no longer alone.

A jolt of panic surged through my body, and my eyes snapped open. I saw only dancing sunlight on the underside of the ripples. I stood up cautiously, blinking as cold water ran down my face. My clothes, soap, and bear spray were all still stacked neatly on the bank, just out of reach. Very slowly, I turned toward the opposite bank.

There, standing so close I could have spread my arms and touched him, was the lone wolf.

He stared at me with golden eyes.

CHAPTER TWO

I took a deep, slow breath. He was a magnificent specimen. His coat was a rich, shimmering black with a distinctive pattern of grey around his eyes and muzzle. He must have been at least 40 inches at the shoulder, and maybe 140 pounds. Huge. Wolves are not meant to live alone, and lone males are not always healthy. But this wolf—

Was standing right in fucking front of me. A fresh spike of adrenaline surged through my body as my latent survival instinct finally overrode my scientific observations.

The wolf displayed no signs of aggression. His ears pricked up, indicating friendly interest. His tail hung at his back, reflecting a bored ambivalence toward the presence of a naked woman in the stream.

But his gleaming golden eyes were fixed on me.

My jaw clenched as my teeth began to chatter. The water was damn cold, and I couldn't stand thigh-deep in it much longer. I desperately wanted to turn and lunge for my bear spray, but I was afraid to break eye contact with the wolf. If I moved, I could be perceived as a threat. And if a strong, healthy wolf perceived me as a threat... well, I wouldn't have much of a chance.

The wolf tilted his head to the side. His eyes seemed to sparkle with, what? Curiosity?

Stop anthropomorphizing, I told myself. You're a scientist, for fuck's sake. I hugged myself as I began to shiver. My hand splashed the surface of the water, very gently.

The wolf's eyes shifted to my hand. Then they traveled the length of my body, back to my face. He'll be afraid of human voices, I realized. He'll bolt if I talk.

"Hello," I said, making my voice as soft and gentle as I could manage through chattering teeth.

The wolf didn't bolt.

"I am not a threat," I said, feeling ridiculous.

The wolf's eyes shifted, moving from my body to the pile of clothing and gear on the far bank. I watched as his gaze settled on the gleaming silver canister of bear spray.

"I wouldn't use that against you." As soon as the words tumbled from my mouth, I knew they were true. I could never use that on a wolf.

He turned to me again, fixing me with his golden eyes. It was an unusual eye color for a wolf. Still, these seems familiar somehow. My body trembled violently, and I lost the thought.

"I n-need to get out," I said, trying to keep my voice low and gentle. "The water's t-too cold."

The wolf didn't move.

I forced myself to crouch low in the water until I reached the opposite bank. The wolf's eyes flickered as I eased myself slowly out of the water. For a heartbeat, I felt absurdly aware of my fat thighs and stretch marks. I stretched my pale legs slowly in the warm sunlight, then held still, frozen in the strange gaze of the wolf's golden eyes. The glassy water of the little pool separated us, but that wasn't much of a barrier. An animal that size could easily jump over the water, rip out my jugular, and feed for a week.

The wolf raised his snout and sniffed the air. I froze. His gaze traveled the length of my naked legs and up my torso.

"Well," I whispered, "it's been nice meeting you."

His golden eyes met mine, and I forgot to breathe. Grasshoppers sang from the meadow; the sweet trill of a yellow warbler drifted across the water. The wolf's eyes narrowed. My heart hammered against my chest. Then his head turned downstream, and he vanished into the willows.

My shoulders slumped in relief. A series of violent trembles lanced through my body. I pulled my legs to my chest, rocking back and forth as my teeth clanked together. When the shivering finally subsided, I pulled my clothes back on, snapped my bear spray canister to my belt, and told myself I was an absolute fucking idiot to get naked in the backcountry. Finally, I pulled out my notebook, checked my GPS, and recorded the coordinates.

My fingers trembled, leaving a long streak of ink across the top of the page.

"Did that just happen?" I whispered.

I glanced at the opposite side of the stream. Willow bushes swayed in the breeze. Insects buzzed and fluttered in the bright sun, and somewhere, deep in the lodgepoles, I heard the incessant thwack-thwack-thwack of a hairy woodpecker. I ran my fingers across the page as if I could erase the ink smear.

Visual confirmation, I wrote, under the GPS coordinates. *Male. Black. Large - 140 lbs? 40 in? height*

I paused again, looking across the water.

Golden eyes, I wrote.

IT WAS ALMOST FOUR in the afternoon when I finally heard Colin and Zeke approaching the campsite. I had done everything I could possibly think of without their equipment, and I'd resorted to watching a mule deer graze through my binoculars for entertainment.

"Hey, Boss Lady," Zeke called. His Southern twang echoing across the clearing.

I watched the mule deer raise her head through my binoculars before turning to greet them.

"It's about damn time," I said, coming to my feet. "What took you—"

My voice died in my throat as I turned to meet them. Zeke, an enormous, burly man wearing an enormous, burly backpack, gave me a wide smile, showing off his broken front tooth. He had a swollen black eye that looked painfully fresh.

"Zeke, what the hell happened to you?"

He shrugged in an offhand manner as he set his backpack down. "Oh, living," he sighed.

I turned to Colin, who was just walking into the campsite. How those two were best friends I would never know. They shared an intense, almost destructive love for the outdoors, everything from backcountry skiing to technical rock climbing, but that seemed to be the only thing they shared. Colin was a small, almost delicate, introvert from Idaho while Zeke was enormous, outspoken, and aggressively Southern.

"You know anything about that, Colin?" I asked.

"I'm afraid I've been sworn to secrecy, Professor McDonald," he said, raising an eyebrow.

"Did it have anything to do with the Bar-muda Triangle?" I asked.

Both boys just grinned as they started to unpack their backpacks. I rolled my eyes, but they didn't notice. Sometimes, I was half tempted to hit the dive bars in downtown Bozeman just to tell everyone the legendary Ezekiel Dills also happened to be brilliant and could run a computation analysis faster than anyone I'd ever met. It made me wonder what he could do if he didn't spend so much time drinking.

Well, I supposed if he wasn't also drinking and bar-brawling, Zeke would probably be doing research for one of the serious big names at MSU instead of working for me. With a sigh, I settled back to watch the boys set up their tents. This was our second summer working together, and our second Yellowstone research trip. Zeke and Colin seemed as comfortable in the backcountry as they were in our lab and, I had to admit, I was grateful for both of them. Even if they were four hours late.

I got the satellite tracker up and running while Colin set up an elaborate camp kitchen with two stoves and three lightweight plastic cutting boards.

"It looks like the Leopold pack moved closer," I told the boys as I squinted at the satellite readings. "They're maybe three miles away."

"Sweet," Colin said.

He was bent over his MSR stove, stirring a pot of something that already smelled like an Italian restaurant. Among his many other talents, Colin was a fantastic camp cook. He had already unwrapped two loaves of homemade French bread, and it looked like he'd actually backpacked in a thermos full of ripe tomatoes. Probably from the garden he'd planted behind his shoebox-sized graduate student housing condo.

"Zeke, I think he's trying to outdo our cooking," I said.

"Can't be done," said Zeke. "Nothing beats Dinty Moore beef stew."

I wrinkled my nose. "You brought Dinty Moore?"

"Oh, not only that," Zeke said, with a wide smile.

Zeke's broken front tooth made him look slightly deranged, and the black eye wasn't helping matters. Last month he told me he broke his tooth in a bar fight, and I hoped to God that wasn't the watered-down version of the story. I assured him the graduate student health insurance plan would cover a dentist, but I think he actually liked the look of the chipped tooth.

"Tonight, Boss Lady, for your drinking pleasure," Zeke said.

He reached into his massive backpack and pulled out a six pack.

"Is that beer?" I said. "Zeke, did you just backpack a six-pack of cheap beer over seven miles?"

"Wrong on both counts, Miss Boss," he said, grinning. "First, this is not just any beer. This is the champagne of beers."

He handed me a can of Miller High Life. It was warm.

"And second," he said, reaching into his backpack and pulling out six more beers, "I carried twelve."

COLIN SERVED US A DINNER of spaghetti with fresh tomato sauce, homemade bread, and a spinach salad with balsamic vinaigrette that was, hands down, the best backcountry meal I've ever had. It made last night's solitary dinner of freeze-dried beef stroganoff look downright pathetic, and I told him so. Colin shrugged off the praise, as usual.

"So," I said, once the dishes were done and we'd settled into a post-dinner round of warm, well-shaken Miller High Lifes. "I saw a wolf today."

They were instantly all business. I omitted the part about being naked and in the water, but left the rest unchanged. They wanted to know everything: height, weight, what direction was he heading, where was his pack?

"Hey, hold the phone," Zeke said, suddenly. "You were how close to this thing?"

I smiled. "About as close as I am to you."

Colin whistled. Zeke slapped his leg and cursed into the gathering darkness.

"I know," I said. "Crazy. I've never been that close to a wolf before."

And then I fell silent as I remembered that wasn't exactly the truth.

IT HAD BEEN FOUR YEARS ago, in late November, and I was at my parents' house. I was living there, although none of us actually called it "living." But I'd been there since May, and I wasn't showing any signs of moving out.

To be honest, I wasn't showing many signs of doing anything.

It was a dismal day, almost cold enough to turn the steady patter of raindrops to bullets of ice, and I'd borrowed my dad's old, blue pickup truck to drive to town. I had to fax the final paperwork for the divorce back to my lawyer in Chicago, who had emailed me the form that morning. Barry had already signed it; his firm, confident signature sat snugly on the bottom left hand side of the paper. It was a little smudged, but that was from my parents' printer. Nothing else.

This Certifies the Dissolution of a Marriage, it said.

I signed it in the car, in the Kinko's parking lot, the windshield wipers frozen in their half-way position. My hand shook. I held the certificate under my jacket to protect it from the rain, and my cheeks burned with a sudden rush of shame as I handed it to the middle-aged woman behind the counter, even though it was hidden behind an official and reasonably boring cover sheet.

"Will that be all, deah?" she asked, stretching out the last syllable and dropping the hard -r sound. It had taken me years to learn to pronounce the -r at the end of a word. I nodded. The dingy gray fax machine sucked in the dissolution of my marriage and spat it back out.

"Looks like it went through," she said, and she handed the stack of papers back to me.

I threw the papers on the passenger seat of my dad's truck and took a deep breath. I looked down at my left hand, but of course I'd stopped wearing the wedding ring months ago. I felt like I should do *something*: cry, or cheer, or call someone on my phone. Instead, I sat in the cab for a long time, watching the sleet hit the windshield.

Finally, I decided to head back to my parents' house and stop at Plourde's on the way for a milkshake. And I'd throw the paperwork in their trashcan.

The headlights of the truck flashed across a "Now Hiring" sign in the dusty front window of Plourde's, the little ramshackle building that served as our town's gas station, post office, sandwich shop, and grocery store. The ceiling was decorated with a wide assortment of items made out of beer cans; Budweiser bird feeders, model airplanes, and moose sculptures all jangled as I closed the door behind me.

As I counted out two dollars in quarters to pay for my milkshake, I asked for a job application. The teenager behind the counter handed it to me without a word, and it went in the passenger seat, right where the divorce paperwork had been that morning. The divorce paperwork that was now lying in a sleet-filled trashcan next to a gasoline pump.

"So," I said that night, over dinner. "It looks like Plourde's is hiring."

My parents shared a brief, worried look.

"I bet it would pay more than the GED class I'm teaching now," I said, picking at the food on my plate. Dad shot a moose that fall, and I was already sick of moose roast.

"Karen," Mom reached for me, putting her hand over mine. "All those years at Northwestern. You earned your doctorate, after all—"

I glanced away, staring at the gaudy fleur-de-lis Orleans crest over the fireplace. But I didn't turn quickly enough to miss the expressions that flickered across my mother's face; fear, concern, and a bone deep disappointment that made my numb chest twist in on itself.

My dad coughed to clear his throat. "Karen, honey, could you go out and get some firewood?"

"Sure, Dad," I said, pushing my chair back from the table.

The night was brisk, hovering on downright cold, although the sleet had stopped falling at dusk. The front porch was loaded with firewood, firewood I'd neatly stacked in all my copious free time, when I'd gone from not really helping my dad in the two bays of McDonald's Auto Repair at the end of their driveway, to not really helping my mom in the house, to not really completing my applications for an real job at an actual university. One that would use the doctoral degree I'd spent the better half of a decade earning.

I ignored the wood on the porch and walked to the far stacks, the stacks in the trees, figuring I might as well give my parents some time to talk about me. As I bent low to pick up a few stray pieces of wood, I had that strange, unshakable conviction that I was no longer alone.

When I looked up, I saw the wolf.

He stood between two pine trees, so close I could almost touch him. He was a massive animal, and in the darkness he looked entirely black. He turned his head to one side; his cool, golden eyes glinted in the dim yellow glow of the porchlight.

"Holy shit," I said, stumbling backward.

My words broke the spell between us. The wolf turned and fled. Dropping the wood I'd collected, I backed toward the front porch. My hands shook as I opened the front door.

"I just saw a wolf," I said.

My parents stared at me, their mouths identical O's of shock and disbelief.

"There aren't any wolves here," Mom said, shaking her head.

Dad cleared his throat and pushed back from the table. "I've never seen a wolf here."

"It was a wolf," I insisted. "I spent five years studying coyotes in Chicago. I know the difference between a wolf and the other canidae."

Dad came to his feet and grabbed the flashlight. "Where?"

Together we walked to the end of the row of firewood. I pointed between the trees, and my dad shone the flashlight on the ground. The wolf's tracks were clearly visible in the light coating of sleet shimmering on the duff beneath the pines.

My dad whistled once, long and low. The prints were as large as my hand with my fingers outstretched. I stared at them in amazement; I'd half expected there would be nothing, that I had imagined the entire encounter.

"Where did he come from?" I asked.

My dad shrugged. "I'd imagine they come down from Canada."

"Does this mean there's a pack?" I said, half to myself. "I mean, they're not like coyotes. They're social animals. One wolf wouldn't move alone, right?"

"I don't know," my dad said, turning to me with a smile. "Someone should study that."

CHAPTER THREE

I shivered in the gathering darkness. Crickets started to sing from the sagebrush as the light faded from the pale blue sky. Colin and Zeke had made quite a dent in the twelve Miller High Lifes, and they were completely immersed in a heated discussion about the various merits of different brands of climbing ropes. Thankfully, they didn't seem to have noticed their doctoral advisor just completely zoned out. I zipped up my fleece jacket and hunched my shoulders against the growing chill in the air.

Dad was right, of course. Seeing the wolf that night sparked something in me I'd thought had died after the divorce. I borrowed Dad's old Chevy pick-up the next morning and drove two hours to the University of Maine to have lunch with Professor Leclerc, who studied raccoons in Acadia. By the time we'd finished our sandwiches, he offered me a postdoctoral position in his lab. And, by the time the snows retreated and the lilac bushes along the side of my parents' house flowered, I'd been hired as a professor of wildlife biology at Montana State University, specializing in tracking the wolf population in Yellowstone.

And that night was also when my dreams began.

Almost every night after I saw the wolf behind my parents' woodpile, I met my dream lover, tall and muscular with golden eyes, long, dark hair, and never a hint of clothing to obscure his mouthwatering body. Sometimes we talked, but mostly the dreams were just sex, an explosion of pure animal lust and pleasure, our bodies coming together and falling apart, over and over. Between my dream lover and my return to the world of scientific research, that November in Maine was the month when my life began to feel like it might actually be worth living, after all.

I hadn't thought about the wolf encounter behind my parents' cabin in years. In fact, I actively tried to avoid thinking about my time in Maine. It was embarrassing. None of my peers at Montana State had spent an entire year depressed and living with their parents. None of them had even gotten divorced.

I stood and stretched. "I'm going to check the satellites and then call it a night, boys," I said. "Remember, we get up with the sun."

Zeke gave me a salute. Colin just smiled.

It didn't take long to align the satellite dishes and find the Leopold pack on the glowing screen of my iPhone. The wolves with radio collars weren't moving, so I assumed the rest of the pack had also bedded down for the night. I imagined them curled in the grass, tails over their noses to conserve warmth. The alpha female, 259F, successfully reared four pups last year. I could picture them all: two gray pups, one black female, and a deep, dusky male with white markings. All of them skinny with long legs.

But what would happen when they met the lone black wolf?

Sometimes lone wolves are accepted into a new pack. Sometimes they even become the alpha, although that thought gave me a sick feeling in the pit of my stomach. The current male alpha of the Leopold pack, 457M, was young, strong, and kind of a jerk. The lone black wolf was bigger, but I thought any fight between 457M and the new wolf would be a serious confrontation. Maybe to the death.

"And that's how nature works," I muttered. "It's my job to observe, not to get attached."

Still, I wondered where the black male was now. Did he know he was close to another pack? Did he know he was close to us? A shiver ran down the back of my spine.

Was he still close to us?

Slowly, I turned around, looking for the gleam of golden eyes in the fading light. There was nothing behind me but lodgepole pines, their shadows pooling and gathering beneath them as the last of the light left the sky. I took a deep breath and shook my head.

"I'm starting to lose it," I whispered, glancing up to make sure Zeke and Colin weren't watching me talk to myself in the dark. It was definitely time for bed.

SUNLIGHT.

Spring sunlight.

But it's not springtime, my brain insisted. It's August. And I'm in Yellowstone. I rubbed my eyes and the aspen grove came into focus. Wildflowers bobbed in the gentle breeze.

"Dreaming," I whispered. "Of course, I'm dreaming again."

I took a few steps. The aspens' heart-shaped leaves rustled above me. Their speckled white and black trunks shimmered in the sunlight, making it difficult to estimate distance. But I knew exactly where I was going, and it only took a handful of steps to find our meadow.

My breath caught in my throat when I saw him. He stood in the middle of a small clearing, the wildflowers reaching to his knees. He was staring into the sky, completely naked. His dark curls tumbled to the middle of his back. He wasn't exactly my type, some distant, rational part of my brain realized. I'd always ended up with nerdy, intellectual guys who wore smaller size jeans than me.

But my dream lover was different. He was muscular, enormous, and wild. Something about his eyes and the way his body moved spoke of raw animal strength and barely contained power. What the hell was my subconscious doing, inventing him?

He turned as if he'd heard me, and our eyes met. His face lit with a smile that made my heart stutter. Maybe not exactly my type, but damn, he was gorgeous. That smile could rival the summer sun.

His muscles rippled in the dappled sunlight as he crossed the meadow. He didn't stop in front of me, didn't even bother with a greeting. Instead, he wrapped his arms around my waist and pulled me to his chest, kissing me deeply, hungrily. My body surged with heat, and I opened my mouth to him.

"I didn't think I'd see you again," he growled into my neck, his breath warm on my skin.

I laughed at the absurdity of his statement. How could my own dream lover be surprised to see me?

He sighed into my hair. "I've missed you."

"I saw you last night," I said, giggling as his hips pressed into mine.

"Oh, but it's been a very long day." He ran his face along my neck and I closed my eyes, pleasure rippling through me in slow waves as his hands traveled my back.

"You always wear clothes," he sighed.

I frowned and looked down. Yes, I was certainly wearing clothes. Black polypro pants and a maroon silk turtleneck. The same outfit I wore as I climbed into my sleeping bag.

"Huh. Guess I don't have much of an imagination," I muttered.

My dream lover tilted his head and raised an eyebrow. "They are...nice clothes," he said.

I snorted and pulled out of his arms long enough to yank my shirt over my head.

"This place used to be different," I said as I stepped out of my pants. "It was—"

"Pine trees, correct? And a bed of moss." He pulled me into his arms. Now the heat of his arousal pressed directly against the soft skin of my stomach. I shivered as he ran his fingers up my back and along my neck. He smelled good, musky and wild, with a hint of sweetness. Like clover flowers, or honey.

"There was a stream, too. Do you remember?" he asked.

I smiled. I did remember the stream in the pine forest, the setting for all those dreams that had left me panting and drenched with sweat, my limbs hopelessly tangled in the sheets of the narrow twin bed in my parents' house. We washed in that stream, sometimes, or drank from it, like wild animals. I turned to tell my dream lover what I remembered, and his lips pressed against mine. I opened my mouth to welcome his kiss as my body melted against his chest. His fingers gently pinched my nipples, and I moaned into his mouth.

He pulled away grinning, then dropped to his knees before me. His hands wrapped around my ass as he pulled me close. "Damn, I missed your taste," he growled.

He ran his tongue over the crest of my sex and I gasped. I plunged my fingers into his hair as my hips rocked against his mouth.

"Oh, God, yes," I said.

My dream lover was always crazy about giving me oral; some nights that was all we would do. *Because apparently, I don't have much of an imagination,* I thought, before his lips and tongue became so distracting I could no longer think of anything.

My body burned against him, the pleasure rolling through me in great, red waves, making my legs tremble until I lost all sense of balance; the only thing holding me up were his strong arms around my waist, cupping my ass. He moved slowly inside me, his tongue tracing circles around my clit, his animalistic moans of pleasure against my legs sending shivers through my entire body. My eyes closed, and I rocked my head back, the muscles in my abdomen tightening—

"Mmmm, you're close," he murmured, pulling back.

I whimpered. The air in the aspen grove felt almost cold against my suddenly exposed flesh. He raised his hand to my sex, tracing it with his thumb, and my body trembled so violently I would have fallen if he hadn't braced his shoulders against my legs.

"I want to keep you there," he said. "Just about to come."

He turned to kiss the inside of my thigh as his thumb circled my clit, pressing hard enough to make me shudder, but not hard enough for release.

"Y—Yes," I said.

The entire aspen grove spun around me. I closed my eyes, my body aching, my hips straining against his hand. I couldn't think, couldn't speak. His lips moved over my thighs like butterfly wings, covering my skin with light, chaste kisses as his fingers teased my clit. I tried to ask him for more, but my mouth had forgotten how to form words.

"I love doing this to you," he said. His breath was hot against my skin.

I moaned, my fingers sinking into his hair as if it were the only thing keeping me from floating away. His kisses traveled across my hips, tracing the edge of my dark pubic curls. One of his fingers slipped inside me, then another, and I whimpered. His thumb was still tantalizingly soft and delicate. I pressed my hips against him, my entire body resting against his strong shoulders.

"More," I gasped. "Please!"

His thumb dropped away, and he pressed his mouth between my legs, his tongue devouring my clit, his fingers moving deep inside me. The energy he'd so carefully built exploded like firecrackers through my body, blinding me with a hot, red flood of pleasure. I came so hard I screamed. My legs collapsed, and I folded into his arms.

For absolutely no reason, I started crying. No, not just crying. I sobbed in big, ugly, choking gasps. My shoulders shook as I tried to hold back the flood of hot tears. Dream lover said nothing. He just held me, running his warm, strong hands over my back until I could pull myself together.

"Oh, damn, I'm sorry," I stammered, wiping my eyes with the back of my hand. "I'm so sorry."

"It's no problem." He smiled at me like I didn't just totally lose my shit in his arms. "Do you want to talk about it?"

My shoulders relaxed. Of course, my dream lover would say the exact right thing. "Honestly, I don't even know why I just...why I...Shit, I'm sorry."

He kissed my forehead. "Are you feeling better?"

I took a deep breath. "Yeah. Actually, I am."

It was true, and it wasn't just about my body. This was as relaxed as I'd felt in years. Honestly, it was as relaxed as I'd felt since I stopped dreaming about him every night.

"Good." He leaned back, pulling me with him until we were both resting on the wildflowers, our naked chests pressed together. "Then let's do it again."

PUFFY CUMULUS CLOUDS chased each other through the pale dream sky as I lay on my back, panting in the tall grass. Satisfaction swirled through my body, as if sexual contentment was washing over me in languorous waves. Damn, I hadn't felt this way in—

"What are you thinking?"

I shifted somewhat, meeting my dream lover's golden eyes and slow, lazy smile. It felt good to think I'd put that dreamy expression on his gorgeous face.

"Nothing," I said. "Just trying to remember the last time I felt this good."

He laughed softly, then reached to tuck a stray hair behind my ear. "That's what you used to say."

"Really? I don't remember that."

"Tell me, are you still studying..." His forehead creased. "Those little dog things? Like wolves, but more annoying?"

"Coyotes," I said. My cheeks were starting to ache from smiling so much. "And why would you know that?"

"I remembered. I wanted to remember everything about you."

With a sigh, I let myself collapse back onto the sweet-smelling grass. I felt too damn good right now to question my own ridiculous dreams.

"No, I'm not," I said. "For your information, I'm studying wolves."

He leaned over my chest, his eyebrow arching. "Oh, really? And what have you discovered?"

"Well, last year my big genetic study was published in *Nature*."

His forehead creased again. "Is that...Should I be impressed?"

I laughed until my chest ached. Apparently my subconscious thought I needed a lover who'd never heard of *Nature*.

"Yes," I said, once I'd finished gasping for breath. "Damn straight you should be impressed. Although I'm kind of worried they picked my article as their token woman scientist, or because wolves are such great clickbait."

I'd never told anyone those fears, not even my parents. And I sure as hell hadn't mentioned them to anyone at the university. Relentless self-promotion was part of the tenure process.

My dream lover just laughed and leaned over to kiss my neck. "I see you're still doubting yourself."

His words sounded odd and tinny, as if we were talking over a phone line and not lying naked next to each other in the grass. I sat up. My vision swam. His beautiful face blurred, and the entire aspen grove collapsed around me, drifting away in thick ribbons of white smoke.

CHAPTER FOUR

My sleep-clouded eyes slowly adjusted to the blue-tinged gloom inside my tent. "Shit," I whispered. "Dawn already?"

I already missed my dream lover so much it hurt with a low, dull ache deep in my chest. The last thing I remembered was lying next to him on the grass, my head in the hollow of his neck, our fingers laced together over his chest as I told him...something. Something boring and trivial about the *Nature* article, if my foggy early-morning memory could be trusted. And of course, my dream lover was listening like he actually cared, and asking questions, and interrupting me with little kisses across my neck and shoulders.

I groaned and tried to stretch in the tight sleeping bag. My entire body felt worn out and sore. Sitting up in the sleeping bag, I slipped my hand between my legs. *Damn.* My underwear was drenched. It was enough to make me think I really had spent all night fucking someone.

"Get a grip, Karen," I muttered. "You haven't gotten laid in half a decade."

I ran my fingers through my hair before unzipping the tent door. Nothing stirred in the campsite, so I grabbed the pots and pans and started banging them around outside Zeke and Colin's tents. Colin emerged with a smile on his face, and Zeke eventually stuck his head through the door, scowling under the wool hat pulled low on his forehead. At least his black eye looked a little better after a night's sleep.

"So," I said, trying to keep the breakfast discussions quick and professional, "our original goal is to monitor the Leopold pack. If we can, we want to tranquilize and radio-collar at least one of the new pups."

Colin smiled at me over his second mug of instant coffee. "But there's a new wolf in town," he said.

"Right." I smiled too. "If we do see the lone black male, he becomes our first priority. If we could get an intact DNA sample from him, we might be able to determine his origins. And that would be— Well, I don't need to tell you that would be huge."

"Roger that, Boss Lady," said Zeke. He'd just finished a four-serving packet of freeze-dried scrambled eggs. By himself.

"Okay," I said, coming to my feet. "We'll triangulate around the valley. Let's get moving."

After half an hour of hiking, I paused to unscrew my water bottle and glassed the far side of the Lamar valley one more time. Nothing. I pressed the button on my walkie-talkie.

"Colin? Zeke? You boys see anything?"

Static crackled as Colin's soft voice came over the line. "Negative. Nothing on my end."

Zeke's voice boomed through a second later. "Not a thing, Boss. I'll keep moving my ass."

I shook my head, stretched, and took a few deep gulps from my water bottle. After another twenty minutes of trudging through the sagebrush, my walkie-talkie crackled to life and Zeke's voice roared from the receiver. Singing. It sounded like *Freebird*, but it was so loud and pathetically off key I couldn't be certain. I jumped as a snowshoe hare shot out from under a fallen tree, startled by the noise. There was a moment of silence before the walkie-talkie exploded with Colin's laughter.

"Boys, boys," I said, pressing the TRANSMIT button. "I'm not sure singing Lynyrd Skynyrd is the best use of our grant-funded research equipment."

"Roger that, Boss Lady," Zeke said. The line fell silent, and then his voice crackled again. "Do you think the National Science Foundation would prefer Guns N' Roses?"

I snorted a laugh as Colin's voice came over the line, clipped and urgent. "Karen," he said. "Get the tranq gun. Headed your way, north-northwest."

My fingers trembled as I pulled the tranquilizer gun off my shoulders and loaded a dart. I couldn't see anything yet, so I grabbed my binoculars.

It was the black male.

Something must have startled him; probably Zeke, from the direction he was running. I took a deep breath and brought the gun to my shoulder. I was raised hunting; I could make this shot. I held my breath as the black male wolf zig-zagged through the sagebrush and across the low grass. I led him just a touch with the barrel of the tranquilizer gun, waited until he was close enough to make out the golden glint of his irises, and then squeezed the trigger.

The wolf yipped in alarm. A wave of guilt curled my stomach when I saw the bright red dart sticking out of his flank. He took off again, running away from me this time, although it took no more than a minute for his steps to falter. He disappeared from my sight along the creek as the walkie-talkie erupted with cheering.

"Hell of a shot, Boss Lady!" Zeke called over the walkie-talkie.

"I saw him go down," said Colin. "In the willows by the creek. Headed over now."

"Me too," I said.

I jogged across the flats. The wind picked up against my back, and it smelled like rain. A quick glance toward Druid Peak revealed churning, dark cumulus clouds, promising an afternoon thunderstorm. We'd have to work fast; the tranquilizer only subdued the animal for about twenty minutes. Where did this wolf come from? Canada was the most likely option, although that would be one heck of a long walk, all the way across Montana—

I was almost to the tall willows lining the creek when I saw Colin. His face was bizarrely pale, and my heart started racing as I sprinted the last few feet to reach him.

"Colin?" I panted.

"You'd better see this," he said.

He took my hand and led me around the willow bushes. There, on the soft, green grass next to the river, was the body of a naked man.

A bright red tranquilizer dart stuck out of his left thigh.

CHAPTER FIVE

D imly, I realized Colin was still holding my hand. I turned to him, opened my mouth, and closed it again. Then I turned back to the man on the grass. He was completely naked, lying on his stomach among the wildflowers. The grass hid his face, but his body looked strong, young, and healthy. And in ridiculously good shape, I realized as I followed the lines of his muscular legs to the curve of his—

I shook my head, trying to focus on the tranquilizer dart sticking out of his thigh. Damn it, I was not here to check out his ass. But there was something disturbingly compelling about his naked figure, something almost familiar. As if I already knew how his skin would feel under my fingertips. How it would taste.

I cleared my throat. "Colin..."

Colin's hand twitched against mine.

"I shot a wolf," I said. My voice sounded very small, as if it were coming from far away.

"Yes," he whispered. "I saw it. You shot a wolf."

I shook my head and squeezed my eyes shut, picturing the black wolf running through the sagebrush. Remembering how he yipped when the dart hit his flank.

I opened my eyes. The man was still there.

There was a soft beep as Colin pressed *transmit* on his walkie-talkie. "Zeke," he said. "Get over here. Bring the first aid kit."

Zeke's voice came over the transmitter. "What happened? Boss Lady stab herself with a tranq dart?"

"Just get over here," Colin snapped.

My backcountry first aid training was slowly percolating through the layers of shock and disbelief swaddling my brain. I dropped to my knees next to the man. Carefully, I brought my fingers to his neck. His skin was warm under my fingers, his pulse strong and regular.

"He'll be in shock, once he wakes up," I said. "We'll need a sleeping bag, or something."

I pulled my backpack off my shoulders and brought out my rain jacket. It wasn't much, but I stretched it over his torso before turning to the tranquilizer dart. A small trickle of blood leaked from the spot where the dart had sunk into his skin. I took a deep breath, wrapped my fingers around the smooth metal of the dart, and yanked it out of his leg.

He didn't even flinch. I stared at his thigh. This was a shallow puncture wound; I needed to apply steady, even pressure. I tossed the dart to the grass and pulled my sleeve over my palm, pressing my hand against the bloody hole in his leg. After taking a deep breath, I turned to Colin.

He hadn't moved. He was staring at the naked man in the grass with an expression that was almost wounded, as if the man's very existence was an insult.

"Colin," I snapped. He shook his head, bringing his eyes to my face. "We're going to need a sleeping bag."

He nodded.

"I need you to get a sleeping bag," I said, speaking slowly.

"Okay."

"Do you have a rain jacket? In your backpack?"

Colin nodded.

"Leave it with me, please. He's going to be in shock."

Colin pulled a bright red and yellow North Face jacket from his backpack. He stepped very carefully around the naked man and placed his jacket on the ground next to me. His hands trembled. The wind picked up again, rattling the leaves on the willow bushes. This time the scent of rain was unmistakable.

"I don't think we have much time before the storm," I said. "How quickly do you think you and Zeke can get a tent over here?"

"We'll do it," Colin said.

"Good."

But he didn't move. His eyes focused on the tranquilizer dart in the grass, the one I'd just pulled from the man's thigh.

"Colin! Go!"

He shook his head a final time and nodded, turning to leave the willow grove on unsteady legs. Once he was out of sight, I took a deep breath and looked at the naked man whose skin was warm under my hands. His body was exquisite. His muscular chest rose and fell with his breathing, my rain jacket barely hiding the dark hair scattered across his pectorals. I fought the insane urge to run my hands down his chest, to feel the rasp of his hair against my palms.

"Karen, focus," I muttered.

I tore my eyes away from him and looked at the sky. Dark thunderheads churned over Druid Peak. I checked my watch. It had been almost thirty minutes since I shot the tranquilizer dart. This would be the time we'd need to call it, to get away before the animal woke. If this were a wolf.

Slowly and carefully, I pulled my palm off the stranger's thigh. There was a small bloodstain on my sleeve, but his leg had stopped bleeding. I reached for Colin's rain jacket to wrap around the naked stranger's chest.

"You shouldn't be here," I whispered as I leaned over him. "And you really shouldn't be so damn familiar."

The wind gusted as I wrapped Colin's rain jacket around his chest, and for a second his scent overwhelmed me. Musky and wild, with a distant hint of sweetness, like honey and clover flowers. I rocked back on my heels, trembling.

"Oh, shit," I said. "It's him."

My heartbeat roared in my ears as I forced myself to lean over his chest until I could see his face. His high cheekbones, his soft lips. His long, dark hair.

He was, without a doubt, my dream lover.

His beautiful face looked almost peaceful with his eyes closed and his hair spread across the grass. The wind picked up again and I grabbed Colin's jacket, wrapping my arms around his back and chest to keep the thin fabric from blowing away. A strand of dark hair fluttered across his lips and I brushed his mouth with my fingers, pushing the errant hair behind his ear.

His golden eyes flickered open, following my arm until he met my gaze. I felt his heartbeat quicken under my fingertips.

"It's okay," I said. "You're okay."

He said something guttural and strange in a language I did not understand. Then he shook his head and tried to pull himself up to sitting. He slipped, and I reached for him, wrapping an arm around his back before he could fall. He shook his head again, his hair falling in his face. I shifted my weight, supporting his body with mine.

"You're okay," I said again. "There was an accident. But you're going to be fine."

He took a long, shaky breath, and his golden eyes met mine again. "You," he whispered. And then he smiled.

He had a gorgeous smile, like daybreak in winter, sunlight over snow, and it made my body surge with heat. I didn't need to move much to press my lips against his. His mouth opened to mine, and his familiar tongue entered me, exploring me. He ran his fingers slowly down the back of my neck. My body trembled in his arms. *Karen McDonald,* some tiny, distant part of my brain whispered, *what the fuck are you doing?*

I jumped back, pulling away from him. "I'm so sorry," I stammered. "That was completely unprofessional. You—are you—"

He raised his hand to trace the curve of my cheek. "My woman," he said.

I opened my mouth to disagree and then thought, under the circumstances, I might just let that one slide. His thumb lingered on my bottom lip, and I fought back the urge to pull his finger into my mouth.

"Why do I feel like I'm drunk?" he asked.

"Oh. Right. I, um, shot you. With a tranquilizer gun."

"You did this?" His grin widened. "I knew you were special."

My heart gave an absurd little flutter at that, which I tried to ignore. "I'm sorry. It was an accident, and you might feel a little, uh, strange. For a few hours. But you'll be fine, I swear."

"But where are the trees?"

"The trees?"

"Our trees," he said, frowning. "Where are our trees?"

He thinks he's dreaming, I realized, with a jolt. Dreaming of me, in the aspen grove. I reached for his arm, wrapping my hand around his wrist. His heartbeat raced under my fingertips. "What's your name?" I asked, trying to distract him.

"Name?"

Electricity surged through my body as he grinned at me. Oh, God help me. It was impossible, totally fucking impossible, but he really was my dream lover.

And I was not dreaming.

"I'm Karen," I said. "Karen McDonald. What's your name?"

"Names?" He sighed, rolling his head back in a wide circle. "Funny. We already know each other so well, without names."

He tilted his head and gave me a wide, predatory smile that made me slick with heat. "I'm Vali, my Karen McDonald. Vali Lokisen."

Still smiling like he fully intended to devour me alive, he grabbed my waist and pulled me into his lap. His cock twitched against the seam of my pants and I whimpered, my body burning, my hips rocking against his. Karen, no, I told myself. Zeke and Colin—

"I don't think—" I said, but he pressed his lips to mine and all my concerns faded to dull background noise. My mouth opened for his hungry tongue, his hands traveled down my back, and I stopped worrying about the tranquilizer dart or the approaching thunderstorm or the sheer impossibility of someone existing simultaneously in my crazy sex dreams and in the backcountry of Yellowstone—

My walkie-talkie exploded with static. Vali jumped, and I fell from his arms into an undignified heap on the grass.

"Boss Lady!" Zeke's voice crackled through the receiver. "Do you copy? You're freaking us out over here."

Vali scrambled to his feet, his eyes scanning the horizon. "What in the Nine Realms was that?"

"It's okay," I gasped.

My breath caught in my throat before I could say more. He was a very attractive, very naked man, and the hard curve of his erection was quite distracting. I clambered to my feet and faced him, reaching for his arm.

"I'm so sorry. About the tranquilizer. About everything. You're going to be fine. It's all going to be—"

"I am dreaming, am I not?" His voice was sharp, his eyes hard.

"Uh, no. I don't think so."

Thunder rumbled over Druid Peak.

"But how are you here?" Vali demanded. "How am I awake? How did you do this?"

"I—I don't know. I tranquilized a wolf. A black wolf."

"Karen, you cannot do this." His voice dropped and his eyes grew wild. "He'll find me."

The first serious crash of thunder echoed across the Lamar's sagebrush flats. Vali leapt from the clearing, disappearing behind the willow bushes.

"Wait!" I called after him. "Vali, wait!"

The light dimmed, and the temperature dropped as the storm descended. I raised my hand to shade my eyes as I pushed the willow branches out of my way, but I didn't see him.

"Hellloooo!" The cool wind carried Colin's voice across the valley.

I turned and saw Colin and Zeke trotting through the sagebrush. When I waved, they broke into a sprint, running toward me. Zeke wore his enormous orange backpack.

"Where's the wolf?" called Zeke.

"Where's the man?" called Colin, simultaneously.

Both of them stopped, turning to stare at each other, and the rain began to fall. I walked over to them, handing Colin his rain jacket. The second I raised my own jacket over my head I realized it smelled like him, like my dream lover Vali, sweet and wild.

Oh, shit.

That just happened.

My head spun, and I dropped to my knees, crouching on the grass, watching raindrops pool along the hood of my jacket. Colin and Zeke sat down next to me. Crouching near the ground, with the sky dark above them, they both suddenly looked very young. And they were looking to me. They expected me to make this all better.

"What the hell happened here?" Zeke asked, staring at the red tranquilizer dart on the trampled grass.

I reached out, putting a hand on Colin's arm and Zeke's knee. "I don't know what just happened," I said. "I—honestly, I don't even know what to say. But I can tell you what we're going to do."

They both turned to me, the exact same expression on their wildly different faces.

"We're going to leave it here," I said. "We're going to just leave all this crazy shit right here. We can come back to it—maybe someday we'll even understand it—but right now, we're just going to stand up and walk away."

I stood up.

"We've got four more days in the field," I continued, "and we have a ton of work to do. We're not going to let today ruin the rest of the week."

Zeke nodded as he came to his feet. Colin took longer, and when he stood his face was ashen. He struggled to pull his eyes from the spot where he'd first seen Vali. Where he'd been expecting to see a wolf.

"We're scientists," I said, gently. "That doesn't mean we have all the answers. But it means there are answers, and someday we might even find them. Right, Colin?"

Colin shook his head, slowly bringing his eyes to my face. "Yeah," he said. "Answers. Right."

We were all very quiet as we walked back to the campsite, in the rain.

The thunderstorm didn't last long, perhaps only half an hour, but rain while backpacking is an epic pain in the ass. Everything was drenched: the cooking gear. My clothes. The backpacks. And, thanks to my suggestion to bring a sleeping bag for Vali, my sleeping bag was now also soaking wet.

"You had to bring my sleeping bag," I muttered.

"It was the closest," said Zeke, with a shrug.

We spent the afternoon setting up our tracking gear, monitoring the Leopold pack, and stringing up a clothesline between the pines to hang our wet gear out to dry. I even spread my sleeping bag on a big, south-facing granite boulder, although I didn't really have much hope the last few hours of August sunlight would be able to dry it.

It was almost time for dinner when I stood up from the satellite dish, stretched, and slipped my cell phone into my pocket. Colin and Zeke were again debating merits of various brands of climbing ropes, which I took as a good sign. I walked through the woods for about ten minutes, aimlessly, until I realized I'd come back to the little stream where I took a bath yesterday. Where I'd seen the huge, black wolf.

I shook my head and pulled the phone from my pocket, dialing Susan, my best friend in the entire state of Montana.

"Hey, Karen?" she answered. "I thought you were in the park?"

"Yeah, I am in the park. Listen, I need to call in that favor."

I BOUGHT A HOUSE AS soon as I moved to Bozeman.

Actually, I bought a house before I even moved to Bozeman. As soon as I accepted the full tenure-track position, Assistant Professor of Wildlife Biology at Montana State University, I was on the phone with a real estate agent. I flew out one weekend in May, looked at half a dozen little houses on the artsy, affordable southern side of town, and then signed my life over to the bank to purchase one.

My neighbors were Susan and Bob. Susan was tall and strong, with long, curly brown hair, the kind of woman who wore sensible shoes and chopped her own firewood. She worked as an adjunct Spanish instructor at MSU during the winters and a park ranger in Yellowstone during the summers, and I liked her immediately. Her boyfriend Bob, however, was short and perpetually twitchy. He was, as far as I could tell, a marijuana dealer, and possibly also some kind of fishing guide. I wasn't crazy about Bob, but I loved Susan, and I was desperate to have normal friends again, so we shared a few cookouts and potlucks that first year.

Then, in July, Susan found herself with a few unexpected days off from her post at Old Faithful. She decided to drive back to Bozeman and surprise Bob. Bob was absolutely surprised to see her. So was the naked woman in their bed. That night Susan moved in with me. We lived together for almost three months, until she found a little apartment above an art gallery on Main Street.

"Anything you need," she told me, as I helped her move into her new place, "you just call. I owe you one hell of a favor."

MY CELL PHONE WAS SO quiet I pulled it away from my ear to make sure I hadn't dropped the signal. "Susan? You still there?"

"Yeah, sorry. Still here. What's up? You okay?"

Not really, I thought. I just shot someone with a tranquilizer gun. Or I'm losing my fucking mind. Either option was pretty shitty.

"Listen, do you have access to the hiker's records?"

"You mean the ones at the trailhead?" she asked.

"Yeah, where you have to sign in with the name, date, and number in party. Do you keep those electronically or what?"

Susan laughed over the phone. "Karen, this is the Forest Service. Of course, we don't keep those electronically."

I made a face, even though I knew she couldn't see me. "This is going to be a pain in the ass, then. Is there any way you could search the hiker records for someone named Vali Lokisen? Probably in the Lamar valley, but I guess he could have come from anywhere."

There was a pause on the line.

"Yeah, I can do that," Susan said, finally. "But, I've got to tell you. Those hiker records are a joke. I mean, most people don't even fill them out. Especially if they don't want to be found."

"I filled it out," I protested.

"Did your students?"

I thought of Colin and Zeke, rolling into the parking lot four hours late, loading up their backpacks with twelve cans of Miller High Life. "Probably not," I sighed.

There was another pause before Susan's voice came through again, lower this time. "I can check with the police, if you want. Discreetly."

"Thanks."

"What was the name again?"

"Vali Lokisen."

"Appearance?"

"Tall," I said. "Strong, athletic. Long, dark hair."

"Clothes? Backpack?"

I felt my cheeks going red. "Uh, no," I stammered.

Susan laughed. "Trust me, you'd be surprised how many people get naked in the backcountry."

"Yeah," I muttered, remembering my bath in the stream.

"When you get back to town, you'll tell me what this is about, right?"

"Of course." Just as soon as I can think of a way to explain it that won't make me sound like a nutcase. "Thanks again."

"I'll text you if I find anything. You take care."

CHAPTER SIX

I was back in our meadow, that beautiful clearing surrounded by aspens. The tall grasses bowed and danced in a gentle breeze, their heads heavy with seeds. The grass parted before me as I walked, smelling aspen leaves and the soft, delicate perfume of penstemon, lodgepole lupine, and columbine.

"Dreaming," I whispered. "I'm dreaming again."

A shiver danced up my spine, and I turned. Vali was watching me from the trees. He was tall and lean and naked, his muscular body moving silently through the dappled light. His long, wild hair fell to his back in a riot of curls.

"Hi," I said, feeling a little ridiculous.

His golden eyes followed my movement. "Karen."

"Vali."

He tilted his head, watching me closely. "Are you a..." He made a sound like rocks tumbling in the back of his throat.

"A what?"

"A sorcerer. Sorceress. A witch."

I almost laughed, but there was no humor in his eyes or the hard lines of his face. "No. Vali, no."

His eyes narrowed. "You're not the first to seek me out, in dreams."

That stung. My back stiffened.

"I'm not a witch," I said.

"Then how did you do it? How did you break the prison?"

Frustration burned deep in my chest. It felt dangerously close to anger. "I don't even know what you're talking about, Vali. I shot a wolf."

He crossed his arms over his chest, raising an eyebrow. "You...shot me?"

"Look. I'm a scientist. I study wolves. And, yes, sometimes I shoot them. With a tiny little dart. It puts them to sleep for about thirty minutes, then they wake up, and they're just fine." I realized my hands were trembling and crossed my arms over my chest, imitating his posture.

"No one has ever broken the prison," Vali said, his voice so low he might as well have been talking to himself. "It has held for centuries."

"What prison?"

The hint of a smile played across his full lips. "My prison. I've done terrible things, Karen McDonald. The wolf's body is my cage."

I shivered. "Where are you now? I mean, when you're not dreaming?"

"Back in my cage. Where I belong. I'm only free in my dreams. It's what keeps me from losing myself completely, although I often wonder whether that's mercy or just another form of torture."

He turned away, staring into the trees. "If I had any magic at all, if I could give any credit to my family's name, perhaps things would be different."

His voice died, and my heart ached. He looked so desperately unhappy. I walked to him without thinking, wrapping my arms around his waist. His body stiffened in my arms.

"You're beautiful," he said. His voice carried no emotion; it was a statement of fact. "Beautiful Karen."

I whimpered, then brought my hand to my mouth.

"You are hurt?" Vali asked.

I shook my head. Vali tilted his head to one side, examining my body. I looked down and realized I was again wearing what I'd worn to bed that night: long underwear pants, a polypro shirt, and wool socks. Not exactly sexy.

"You're crying," Vali said. He brought his hand to my face, gently brushing my cheek.

"I—It's just—It's been a while since anyone called me beautiful."

Vali smiled, but his eyes were dark. For some reason I didn't want to hear what he was about to say, so I stood on my toes, pressing my lips to his.

Vali kissed me, softly, then pulled away. "Beautiful Karen. We can't."

He took a step back, and my heart burned with frustration and adrenaline. "But we're dreaming!" I yelled. "Look around us! These flowers don't even bloom at the same time. Columbines are late summer, and that pasqueflower is early spring..."

My voice trailed off as he took another step away from me, toward the edge of the trees. He's leaving, I realized. I am babbling about wildflowers, and he's leaving.

Vali shook his head, and his long curls swirled around his shoulders. "I'm sorry. Karen, I'm not safe. And I won't put you in danger."

He turned. His body vanished soundlessly into the aspen trees. I called his name and heard nothing, not even an echo.

I woke up in my tent, blinking in the darkness, with silent tears streaming down my cheeks.

"Fuck," I hissed, pressing my palms against the heat of my cheeks. "I can't even meet a guy in my dreams."

My fingers trembled as I unzipped the tent door for the thousandth time that night. But this time, I finally saw faint traces of pink in the velvet sky above the trees. Thank God. Sleep had been impossible since Vali ran out of my dreams, and I'd spent the rest of the miserable night alternating between staring at the roof of my tent and wishing I could still believe Vali was just the product of my overactive imagination and long-neglected libido, and trying not to sob so loudly I woke up Colin and Zeke.

I clambered out of the tent, stretched, and walked to Colin's and Zeke's tents to shake them. Colin muttered a sleepy, "Right away," before climbing out to start boiling water for his coffee. Zeke ignored me until Colin threatened to unzip his door and dump a water bottle into his sleeping bag.

"God, where do you find these barbarians?" Zeke asked, scowling at Colin as he crawled out of his tent.

"Get your breakfast quick, boys," I said. "The pack is headed toward the hoodoos, and we're following them. We can be set up by ten, and have the entire afternoon to search for fur and stool samples. Maybe we can even find some wolves before we have to leave tomorrow."

"And they say science isn't glamorous," Zeke said, rubbing his face.

BY THE TIME I REMEMBERED to check my phone for a message from Susan, we were in the hoodoos, an especially bizarre part of the park. All of Yellowstone is weird in its own way, but his part of Yellowstone is especially strange. The landscape is dotted with cylindrical, dark volcanic spires several stories tall, rising from the sagebrush and lodgepole pines like ancient stone sentinels. It was just past nine in the morning; we'd moved quickly. Zeke and Colin hiked fast. I didn't want to show weakness in front of two people who were technically my employees, so matched their pace, even if it left me panting and exhausted. At least I was too distracted by my aching legs and burning lungs to dwell on my dreams.

I leaned against one of the crumbling dark hoodoos and gasped. "Hang on. I've gotta check my phone."

"Sure thing, Boss Lady," Zeke said. He didn't even sound winded. Show off.

"You guys can set up the satellite," I panted as I slipped my phone from its waterproof bag in my pocket. There was one new text from Susan.

No luck, it read. *Not in trail records & nothing from police. No Vali, Valley, Val, Vince - nada.*

Thanks anyway, I texted back. I went to return the phone to its case when it dinged again.

Sure thing, Susan wrote. *You will tell me what this is about??*

Of course, I wrote back. I'd have plenty of time to come up with a plausible story before I saw her again. My phone dinged again, and I glanced down.

The goods are odd, Susan wrote.

I laughed, then covered my mouth, hoping the boys hadn't heard. There was just no diplomatic way to explain that joke to Zeke and Colin.

About a week after Susan moved in with me, we walked together to Main Street to get burgers and a pitcher of beer. Susan was holding up pretty well, given she'd just broken up with her boyfriend and moved in with a total stranger, and I was feeling good, too. After all, I'd survived a divorce, got hired as an Assistant Professor, and even made a friend in Bozeman. We raised our pints to each other, sitting in a sidewalk cafe in the long evening sunset, and I told Susan hey, who know? Maybe I'd meet Mr. Right here in Bozeman. After all, weren't there four men for every one women in Montana?

Susan laughed and laughed at that. "You know what they say in Alaska?" She finally asked, wiping the tears from her eyes. "Well, it's true in Montana, too. The odds are good, but the goods are odd."

After a few horribly awkward first dates with Montana men, I decided Susan was right.

Yes, I texted back. *Goods = odd.*

"You ready, Boss Lady?" Zeke called.

"Coming," I said, turning off my phone and putting it back in the waterproof case.

CHAPTER SEVEN

Once I left the boys and began canvassing on my own, the hoodoos started to bother me, as if the surreal landscape was tugging at my subconscious. For some reason, I kept thinking about Diana. *The park's a thin place*, she said. That's how it felt right now, as I slipped between stone pillars of ancient ash, looking for the quick, dark bodies of the wolves and trying not to think about what happened yesterday. Everything felt a little *thin*.

"Karen," Colin's calm, measured voice crackled over the walkie-talkie. "We're in luck. I can see the Leopold pack."

"On my way," I said, turning north-northwest, toward Colin.

"I've got a clear shot on one of the pups," he said.

"Take it," I told him.

There was a pause. I held still, listening. A distant yip echoed through the valley. I jogged up a small rise and spotted Colin hunched over next to a twenty-foot tall hoodoo spire. Then I saw the wolf he was watching.

He'd shot an adolescent, one of last year's pups from the alpha pair. The dappled gray female. The young wolf was sprinting across the sagebrush, but her steps were starting to waver. As I watched she slowed, swayed on her feet, and then fell.

"You got it, Colin!" I called.

I jogged over to him, pressing the button on my walkie-talkie. "Wolf down," I said. "Zeke, get over here ASAP."

"Roger that," said Zeke.

"Please stay a wolf," I whispered as I jogged through the sagebrush. "Please. Please. Please."

The young, female wolf lay on her side in the sagebrush with her eyes rolled back in her head. Her breathing was deep and relaxed. She was beautiful, with a dappled gray coat and white paws. The red of a tranquilizer dart stuck from her right haunch.

"Thank God," I whispered under my breath.

Colin sighed behind me and I turned, watching relief play over his usually reserved features.

"Right," I said, pulling off my backpack. "Everything like it's supposed to be. Now. To work."

Zeke joined us a few minutes later and bent over the wolf's body with his equipment without saying a word. I took blood samples and affixed her radio collar while Colin and Zeke measured the young female's paws, her incisors, and her weight. She looked strong and healthy. She'd made it through the most dangerous part of puppyhood, this little one. With any luck, she might have pups of her own next spring.

"That's thirty minutes," I said, tearing my eyes away from the wolf to double check my watch. "Colin, you got a fur sample?"

Colin nodded at me, grinning.

"Zeke, did you finish with her paws?"

Zeke gave me a thumbs up.

"Let's call it, then." I ran my hand gently over the wolf's side. Her fur was soft and warm under my hand. "Thank you," I whispered.

"That was nice work," I said, once we'd gotten several hundred yards from the wolf. "Let's split up again. Maybe we can get one more before it gets dark."

Zeke and Colin both grinned as the headed off in opposite directions. They always seemed excited about field work, but this was different. This was relief. Relief to be doing something normal, I guessed.

We canvassed the hoodoos for another two hours, collecting fur and stool samples. I'd stopped to rest on a fallen tree and eat some M&Ms when my walkie-talkie crackled to life again.

"Karen, Zeke, you'll want to see this." Colin sounded serious, almost grim. "Get to high ground. Look east, north-east."

I climbed a small rise and brought my binoculars to my eyes. The bottom dropped out of my stomach.

It was Vali.

Vali and the Leopold pack alpha, 457M, faced each other in the dusty shadow of a truly massive volcanic spire. The two wolves circled each other, the hair on their haunches sticking out in all directions. Both had their tails up and straight out, demonstrating extreme aggression.

Fuck! 457M was a young alpha, and he was an asshole. Last year Diana and several of the wolf-watchers watched him kill 322M, a male who challenged him for pack leadership. 322M was the first wolf I'd ever tranquilized. I attached his radio collar. And 457M killed him. I bit the inside of my lip as my stomach churned, something bitter rising in the back of my throat. It was my job to observe, not to interfere.

But it's my job to observe wolves, I thought. And that's not a wolf.

That's Vali.

I dropped my pack and ran toward the wolves. When I was close enough to hear them growling, I stopped and raised my tranquilizer gun. Vali and 457M were baring their teeth now, snarling and growling as they spun around one another. The rest of the pack had gathered under the lodgepole pines in the distance, watching. If Vali won this challenge, they might accept him as their new alpha.

Or they might all try to kill him.

"Fuck," I whispered as I watched the wolves through the sight on my tranquilizer gun. It was useless. I was too far to get a clear shot, and they were moving too quickly.

Give it up, Vali, I thought, desperately.

457M made the first move, lunging for Vali's haunches. Vali leapt sideways, gracefully avoiding 457M's jaws. Then he spun so quickly he was just a blur of sleek, black fur, and he caught 457M's shoulder in his jaws. 457M pulled away with a yip. Vali's mouth bristled with 457M's pale gray hair.

457M spun back, growling fiercely. He was smaller than Vali, but his ears pricked forward, and his teeth were bared. He showed no signs of submission. He lunged for Vali again, and this time I heard his teeth clack together as Vali again leapt out of reach. Vali's growl grew louder.

Vali reared back and lunged for 457M. There was another yip as his body collided with 457M, but 457M was small and fast, and he backed away before Vali could pin him. I saw blood on 457M's shoulder, and blood on Vali's muzzle.

I raised the tranquilizer gun again. If 457M lunged again, I'd have a clear shot. My finger trembled. What if I accidentally hit Vali? What if he became human again? Wolves usually fear humans, but what about a naked, tranquilized human in front of an entire hungry, aggressive pack? The two wolves began circling again, growling and snarling, bared teeth flashing in the late afternoon light.

Vali raised his snout in my direction and hesitated.

Me, I realized with a sick ripple of fear. He was smelling me.

457M lunged forward, catching Vali's neck in his jaws. Vali screamed as 457M pinned him to the ground.

"No!" I bellowed, running towards the two wolves.

I lowered my tranquilizer gun and pulled the trigger. The shot went wide, missing both wolves. Vali screamed again as 457M's jaws closed around his throat.

I reached in my pocket and grabbed my cell phone in its waterproof case. I threw it as hard as I could. It hit 457M in the abdomen. He yowled in pain and shock, raised his head, and growled at me, a threat deep and low in his throat.

Vali shot up, standing between me and 457M.

There was a flurry of movement in the lodgepole pines. The rest of the Leopold pack scattered, running from the screaming human who just interrupted a battle for dominance of their pack. But 457M did not run. He stood and glared at me, his pale eyes full of rage.

Vali growled, baring his teeth. I crouched low and grabbed the first rock I could find, throwing it at 457M. It glanced off his shoulder. He yipped, his eyes now confused.

"Get out of here!" I screamed, waving my arms wildly. "Get the fuck out of here!"

From somewhere in the distance, the rest of the Leopold pack began to howl, calling for their absent alpha. 457M's ears pricked as he heard their voices. He looked again at me, then at Vali, before turning and sprinting away, his tail level. Not submission, that tail said. Not surrender.

"Oh, thank God," I panted. My body started to tremble, and for a moment I worried my legs were about to pitch me face first into the dirt.

Vali turned his enormous black head toward me. His lips curled back, showing his white teeth. They were streaked with blood. I stepped backward, and Vali followed me. His growl built, coming from deep in his chest. I held my hands up with my palms out.

"It's me," I said, staring into his golden eyes.

I did not see recognition.

I've lost my mind, I thought. I've lost my mind, and this is how I die. I stepped backward, stumbled against something hard, and fell on my ass. Vali was so close I could smell him; he still smelled like the man in my dreams, wild with a subtle, irresistible sweetness. He was so close his growl felt like low thunder in my bones.

"It's me," I said again, my voice jagged. "Vali, it's me."

He stepped over my body, his giant paws resting on either side of me, his hot breath smelling of blood. He breathed deeply, running his snout along my body. His fur prickled against the soft skin of my neck.

Then he leapt over me and was gone.

Something was hissing and buzzing. No, it was forming words. It was—

"Karen! Karen! Come in!"

It was Colin, over the walkie-talkie. I pressed the button and brought the walkie-talkie to my lips. No sound came out. I coughed and tried again.

"This is Karen," I stammered.

Someone yelled behind me, and I turned to see Zeke running across the meadow. I tried to stand, winced, and waited for him to join me. He whistled once, long and slow, as he came to his knees in front of me.

"Colin told me a black wolf turned into a ripped, naked guy yesterday," Zeke said. "That was him, wasn't it? That was the wolf who turns into a dude?"

I opened my mouth, blinked, and closed it again. Then I nodded.

"Damn, Boss Lady! He must have one fuckin' nice ass! I mean, 457M could've gutted you like a fish. He could've torn your throat out just like walkin' in the park. Hell, he could've decapitated you in—"

"Thank you, Zeke," I said. "That's enough."

Colin jogged up to us, panting. "You okay?" he asked, his cheeks flush against his pale face.

I nodded again, hoping they wouldn't notice how violently my arms and legs were shaking. "Thank you. Yeah, I'm okay."

Zeke whistled again. "That's gotta be the single motherfucking dumbest thing I have ever—"

"Zeke, that's enough!" I shouted. Then I grinned at their shocked expressions. "And don't you ever do anything that stupid!"

Colin started to laugh. Zeke joined him, and then we were all laughing, laughing so hard we doubled over in the late afternoon sun, in the spot where I had almost died.

"Oh, Boss Lady," Zeke said in his thick Southern drawl. "I will never do anything that epically D-U-M-B, I promise you."

I shook my head. It felt good to laugh. It felt good to be alive.

"Listen," I said, "if we go back to Montana State and tell everyone I shot a wolf who turned into a human, or that I got between two males fighting for pack dominance...Look, I'll never get tenure, and you guys will never get your degrees. So, let's just leave those parts out of our reports, okay?"

Zeke nodded. "What happens in the backcountry of Yellowstone, stays in the backcountry of Yellowstone," he said, with great solemnity.

We all started laughing again, laughing hard. Zeke and Colin pulled me to my feet, and I clapped my arms around their shoulders. They were both significantly taller than me, so we must have made quite the sight, walking together through the hoodoos. If any golden eyes were watching.

CHAPTER EIGHT

I opened my eyes to the bright spring sunlight of the dream forest. Our dream forest. Smiling, I walked through the tall grass and wildflowers. It only took me three steps to reach the clearing in the aspen grove.

Vali was in the meadow. He was naked, of course, and pacing among the wildflowers, his long strides fast and angry. He froze when I stepped into the sunlight.

"That was foolish," he growled. "And unnecessary."

"Nice to see you, too," I muttered.

He crossed the distance between us, grabbing my arms. His grip was so hard it almost hurt.

"You don't understand," he snapped. "I'm dangerous!"

"So I've heard."

"Yet you don't seem to listen!"

Anger flared in my chest. "You know who else is dangerous? The other alpha! Vali, I've seen him kill challengers!"

Vali snorted. "So?"

"So he could have killed you!"

"You think that animal could have hurt me?" His fingers tightened, sending a bolt of pain down my arm.

I tried to pull out of his grasp, but his fingers were unyielding. "Oh, you arrogant jerk!"

"I'm arrogant? You put your life in danger, and for nothing!"

God, I wanted to smack his handsome face. "Nothing! You think getting a wolf off your jugular is nothing?" I was screaming now; I couldn't stop myself. "You're lucky I was there! He would have killed you!"

Vali barked a sharp, bitter laugh. "I've never needed help, and I sure as hell didn't need it today."

His golden eyes flashed. I felt the heat of his naked body, inches from my chest. Damn it, did he have to be this handsome? I narrowed my eyes, trying to ignore the heat surging through my body, making me slick between my legs.

"He had you pinned," I growled. "By the neck."

Vali growled, deep and low in his throat. "You. Don't. Understand! I can't always control myself. Not like that. Not as a wolf!"

His muscles tightened, and he tilted his head, running his cheek along my hair, smelling me. His body hummed with energy. Vali's dark curls fell back, exposing the tanned length of his neck. There, just above his collarbone, was an angry red oval of shallow puncture wounds.

"Oh, God, Vali!"

His back stiffened and his breath hissed sharply. "Don't!"

"That's where he bit you!"

"I said don't!" Vali shoved me backward. "No help! I've never needed help. I don't need help!"

I took one stumbling step back and hit an aspen tree. Its coarse bark bit into my shoulders as Vali's chest pressed against my breasts, his golden eyes burning into mine. I felt the wild pounding of his heart through my thin turtleneck. Shit, he was gorgeous. My nipples strained against my shirt and my sex pulsed with hunger.

"You could have been hurt," he growled. "You could have been killed. I am dangerous!"

His lips pulled back in a snarl. Anger and arousal surged through my body, drowning any remaining rational thought.

"Me!" I barked a laugh, raising my lips until they were almost touching his. "You were the one getting hurt, damn it! I saved your life! Don't you dare tell me you didn't need help!" I shifted in his arms, pressing my hips against the heat of his erection.

Vali turned away, releasing my arms.

"I could have killed you," he hissed, his voice a low rumble.

I ran my fingers up his neck and threaded them in his hair. "But you didn't," I said. "I'm right here. I'm not hurt."

"Karen," he moaned. His body shuddered. "If you had...If I'd..."

"You're not so dangerous," I whispered, pressing his face closer to mine.

His pulse raced under my lips; his hands trembled around my arms. I arched my back, rocking my hips into his and pressing my breasts against the hard muscles of his chest.

"I mean, what are you going to do, Vali? Fuck me to death?"

He moaned, deep and low in his throat. His back stiffened and his hips crashed into mine, slamming me against the tree.

"Damn it, Karen," he snapped.

The trunk shuddered as he let go of my arms and grabbed my pants, pulling them apart down the middle. The fabric gave way with a loud, long *rip*. My mind had time to register shock - that wasn't possible, no one was that strong - before he picked me up by my thighs, wrenched open my legs, and shoved me against the tree. The rough bark dug into my shoulders and hips. His cock pressed against my slick entrance. I moaned.

"Vali..." I pleaded. I couldn't think anymore, couldn't speak. My body was burning against his, every part of me aching to be filled.

"Oh, damn, Karen, you can't—"

His words cut off as his lips found mine, crushing me in a bruising kiss before pulling away to rub his face along my neck. His breath hissing hot and fast over my skin. His body trembled above mine, his stiff cock pulsing against the lips of my pussy, and I moaned a wordless plea, over and over.

With a moan that may have been pain, Vali thrust into me so hard and fast it took my breath away. I gasped, and my body clenched around him as his hips drove me into the tree trunk. The wood groaned in protest, and gentle green aspen leaves fell all around us. I linked my ankles around his back, moaning in rhythm with his thrusts. Electricity sparked and surged through our bodies.

Vali bit me, hard and low on my neck. I yelped and flinched. The sudden burst of pain faded almost as quickly as it had appeared, washed away by the waves of heat surging between my legs. He bent over me and bit me again, lower, almost on my collarbone. This time there was no distinction between the pleasure and the pain, and when I cried out, his name flew from my lips. He pressed his mouth to mine, swallowing my cries as his body surged against me, both of us wild with desire and need.

I came so hard my head crashed against the tree as every nerve in my body fired, my mind obliterated in a red flood of ecstacy. Vali's body slammed into mine as my head reeled. His breath was shallow and uneven, and his thrusts lost their earlier rhythm. He moaned my name as he came; his cock spasmed deep inside me as his hands clenched my thighs.

My head fell onto his shoulder and I wrapped my arms around his shoulders, reluctant to let him go. Slowly and softly, he began kissing my neck. I gasped as I felt his cock twitch inside me, stiffening. I arched my back, ready to offer him more, but the rough aspen bark bit into my shoulders. I hissed in pain and pulled away.

Vali pulled back, his eyes wide. "Are you hurt?"

"No. No, I'm fine. More than fine. Just...the tree is maybe not the most comfortable place."

He ran his face along my neck once more and sighed as he lowered me to the ground. My legs trembled when my feet touched the grass. Afraid they might give out altogether, I leaned against the hard muscles of his chest.

"You were foolish today," he said.

I closed my eyes, breathing him in. "Yeah. Probably. But it was my fault you got pinned."

"What do you mean?"

"You smelled me, right? When you were fighting. You hesitated, and that's when 457M attacked."

"Four-fifty... what?"

I smiled and met his eyes. "The other wolf. The male alpha. We call him 457M. Scientists assign the Yellowstone wolves numbers, not names."

He laughed at that, and my heart surged. He had a beautiful laugh, like clear water flowing over stones. "So, what's my number?"

"Well, you're not exactly a wolf, are you?"

Vali's forehead creased, and his eyes darkened. He turned away, revealing the tight oval of puncture wounds on his neck where 457M bit him this afternoon. His dark hair fell across his high cheekbone, and he looked so sad my heart ached. I stood on my toes, kissing him. He sighed as my lips moved across his chin and down his neck.

"Beautiful Karen," he said, his voice rough. "I only meant to reprimand you, to warn you to stay away. But I couldn't—I couldn't stop myself."

"I'm not complaining."

His arms tightened around my waist. "It was not well done. I apologize. It's... it's been a long time since I had a lover."

I laughed, feeling the rise and fall of his chest brush my nipples. "It's been a long time for me, too."

Vali's body relaxed. He kissed me again, running his fingers through my hair. I leaned against him as I watched the distant clouds in the light blue dream-sky. I was leaving Yellowstone in the morning, and damn did I ever want to ignore that fact.

But I had to tell Vali. I owed him that much, at least.

"I leave tomorrow," I whispered, blinking against the sting of tears welling under my eyelids.

Vali sighed. "That's probably for the best."

"Do you think...even if I'm not in the park...could we still..?"

"I don't know."

"I want to keep seeing you," I pressed. "Please, Vali. I lost you once, when the dreams stopped. I don't want to lose you again."

Vali's eyes darkened again, and he turned away. His heart hammered under my cheek.

"I don't care if you're dangerous," I said. "I mean, you can't be dangerous here, right? Not in our dreams?"

Vali brought his hand to my cheek, caressing me softly, almost like a child. "I would very much like to keep seeing you," he whispered. "Here. Where I can be sure you're safe."

"Good," I said. Despite my frantic blinking, a tear escaped my eye and slid down the curve of my cheek.

"But, Karen, please. You must promise me you won't seek me out, not outside of dreams. Not as a wolf. If I hurt you—"

I kissed him, cutting him off. "I promise," I whispered.

He gasped as my fingers traced the inside of his thighs.

"Now, let's stop talking," I said.

"SOMEONE IS CALLING you," Vali said, as we lay curled together in the crushed grass of the meadow.

I wrapped my arms tighter around Vali's strong chest, burying my head in the curve of his neck. "Ignore them," I muttered.

"You can't," he said. His voice was sad, and already distant...

My eyes snapped open and I shot up. The tent was shaking around me.

"Boss Lady!" Zeke called. "You alive in there?"

Shit!

"Jesus H. Christ," I yelled, squinting against in the bright sunlight filtering through my tent's fabric. "What the fuck are you—"

I blinked. Bright sunlight?

"Well, it's past eight in the morning," Zeke drawled from outside the tent. "Seeing as how you usually wake us up at ass-crack-o'clock, Colin and I thought you might have died in there."

I heard the two of them laughing as I sat up and rubbed my eyes.

I was naked. Shit again. I did not sleep naked. Not in the backcountry. Not even in my own bedroom. What the fuck happened to my clothes? I reached across the tent and rummaged in my backpack until I found underwear, a pair of shorts, and another polypro shirt. I got dressed as subtly as I could. Then I brought my fingers to my neck, pressing gently. Ouch. There was definitely a sore spot where Vali had bitten me. In my dream.

"That's not possible," I muttered.

"What's that, Boss?" Zeke called.

"Nothing!" I yelled. "Pack up the equipment!"

I tied a bandana around my neck and hoped to hell it would cover the bruise, because there was no possible way I could explain waking up with a hickey. Once I felt at least halfway presentable, I slowly unzipped the tent door. Colin and Zeke stared at me, looking quite amused.

"I'm really sorry about that," I said, running my fingers through my greasy hair.

"Pleasant dreams?" asked Zeke, with just enough of a smile to worry me.

"Hey, I'm still your boss," I said. "And besides, what happens in the backcountry of Yellowstone..."

Colin and Zeke laughed, and the world began to feel slightly normal again.

"Pack up," I said. "We're headed back to civilization this morning."

None of us, I noticed, looked particularly happy about that fact.

"LET'S STOP FOR WATER," Zeke said.

He stepped to the side of the trail and slipped off his pack. He didn't even sound winded, which was totally not fair. My shoulders and back throbbed, and my feet sang with blisters. I felt completely exhausted, as if I really had spent all of last night fucking Vali. And maybe I had. I shook my head to stop that train of thought. These past four days had been crazy enough.

"Here?" I asked. "We're almost to the parking lot."

Colin nodded. "Here's good," he agreed, taking off his pack.

I was too tired to put up much of an argument, so I just nodded. I worried that if I took off my backpack I'd never be able to force myself to put it on again, so I leaned against a lodgepole pine instead of sitting down with the boys. The air was still and warm, filled with the buzz and hum of grasshoppers and the smell of sun-warmed sagebrush in the valley.

"That was a weird trip," said Zeke.

I suddenly understood why he'd wanted to stop. Colin nodded, looking back over the trail, almost as if he expected to see Vali following us. Of course, I'd been looking back over the trail all morning.

"We're going to leave it here," Zeke said, handing me his water bottle. "Right, Boss Lady?"

I drained the water bottle and nodded.

"Yup," I said. "We're going to leave it here."

CHAPTER NINE

M y front door stuck shut.

"Great, I guess it rained here, too," I muttered, carefully jiggling the key and pressing my shoulder against the top of the door frame—the part that swelled shut after every single storm. The part I kept meaning to sand down, if I ever had a freaking half an hour to spare. My stupid door finally swung open, almost knocking me off balance. I stumbled into the hall table and heaved my filthy, smelly backpack onto the living room floor.

It looked like Susan had watered my houseplants and collected my mail. A tiny stack of envelopes waited on the table, just under my fingers. I sighed and sorted through them. Credit card offer. Open a bank account with us and get a free shotgun. Have I considered switching my car insurance?

The penultimate letter made my stomach drop. That plain white envelope. That tight, neat handwriting and the subtly pretentious return address sticker, a gold embossed Barry R. Richardson, Ph.D. 237 Monticello Place. Evanston, IL.

Well, of course. It was almost the end of the month. And Barry R. Richardson, Ph.D. is nothing if not punctual. I ripped open the envelope and found the check. No note, no card, just the check, which had been folded in half and slipped into the white envelope. As per usual.

I told Barry I didn't need alimony payments anymore. I had my own job now, thank you very much, as a tenure-track professor at a respected research institution. I told him two years ago I was no longer interested in receiving monthly checks from the world's foremost authority on the role of dragons in medieval literature, the great Professor Richardson. He responded with some half-hearted email about the complications of renegotiating the divorce settlement, and I'd let it slide. My fingers trembled as I unfolded the check. This was as close as we'd come to speaking in over a year, my fingers on the paper he'd touched a week ago.

"Damn it, Barry, I don't want your money," I said, but my voice sounded feeble, even to me. I imagined ripping up the check, stuffing the tiny paper flecks into the garbage.

"But first," I said, placing the check delicately on the table, "a really long, really hot shower."

That night I stood in my bedroom and stared at my closet with my arms crossed over my chest. I didn't have a single sexy outfit in my entire goddamn house. I hadn't even owned much lingerie when I was married, and most of that had just made my ass look huge and my boobs look saggy. When the neat little boxes of my married life arrived at my parents' house, I threw away anything remotely intimate, leaving me with a nighttime wardrobe that consisted entirely of flannel pants and tank tops.

"Karen, you're being insane," I told my reflection in the bedroom mirror.

I wasn't even certain that what I wore to bed was what I wore in the field with Vali. Maybe, if I just concentrated hard enough, I'd show up in a black lace corset. I smiled as a slow tingle of arousal moved through my body. Damn, I couldn't even come close to explaining who Vali was or how the dreams worked, but that mystery didn't seem to dampen my libido. I pulled on a tight white T-shirt and my very best underwear and climbed under the covers. My clean sheets felt so good after a week in the wet sleeping bag that I almost moaned in pleasure.

"I'm ready for you, Vali," I whispered.

I closed my eyes and tried to will myself to sleep, but it did not come easily. Those clean sheets soon felt too hot, and I kicked off the cover. My house seemed full of strange noises after so many nights in the backcountry; the refrigerator kicked on and off, traffic purred outside my windows, and the pipes gurgled and trickled. Without the moon and stars overhead, my bedroom seemed too dark, almost claustrophobic. I was idly debating pitching my tent in my own backyard when sleep finally took me.

My dreams were strange. At first, I was falling, and then I ran through the aspen grove. The blue sky above was mottled with clouds, the grass dotted with wildflowers, but I couldn't seem to find our aspen grove. Every turn led me back to where I had started, a strange, dark forest where the trees crowded so close together they felt like the bars of a cage.

"Vali!" I screamed. "Vali, can you hear me?"

For one horrible moment I almost thought I heard a response, some distant, echoing cry. I bolted toward it, but the further I ran, the more the trees closed in around me, their leaves snapping in my face, their twigs snagging my hair. The dream shifted, and I found myself back where I'd started, my legs trembling and my chest heaving as I screamed Vali's name over and over. There was no further response.

I blinked open my eyes, forcing myself awake. My lungs still burned from sprinting through the dream forest, and the backs of my hands and arms felt raw with scratches. For a heartbeat, before the glowing blue numbers of my alarm clock came into focus, I thought I might still be dreaming.

It was four in the morning. Just fucking great.

Grumbling, I tossed the covers off and wrapped myself in my ratty old blue robe. Falling back asleep was going to be impossible. Might as well answer my bajillion emails.

By the time the sun rose over Bozeman, I'd finished an entire pot of coffee and my empty inbox was a thing of beauty. Amber, our department secretary, sent me a cryptic email two days ago about a "message" she had for me. Of course, she couldn't just send me the message; Amber was not one to miss the opportunity for drama.

"Please don't be a message from Barry," I said to my kitchen as I washed out my coffee pot.

I packed up my laptop and filled the back of my Subaru with all the transmitting equipment we'd used in the park, ready to return it to the lab.

"Please not Barry," I whispered as I drove toward campus. "Anyone but Barry."

AMBER WAS ON THE PHONE, laughing shrilly as she leaned over the hundreds of baby pictures decorating her desk. It sounded like our department head had a huge, public argument with his rival in the math department, and she was giving someone on the other end of the line a blow-by-blow recap. She waved her hands at me, hung up the phone, and launched breathlessly into a painfully detailed description of exactly everything I'd missed. I nodded, smiled, and tried not to look too anxious.

"And you had a message for me?" I asked as soon as she paused for breath.

"Oh, you got a call from Stanford," Amber said.

"What?"

"Yeah, someone at Stanford wants to talk to you. Something about the wolves."

"I don't know anyone at Stanford," I said.

"Hold on, I took a message. It's in here somewhere." Amber bent over the chaos of her desk, shifting staplers, Post It notes, coffee mugs, and picture frames. "Oh yes, here it is. Professor Laufeyiarson. And there's the number."

"Thanks," I said, taking the paper and edging out of the office.

I rattled my office door open, dropped my laptop into the pile of course requests covering my desk, and sat down.

"A collaboration with Stanford would be huge," I whispered, fingering the note from Amber.

But who the hell was Laufeyiarson? Wildlife biology is a pretty small field, and I was almost positive the only person at Stanford who studied predators was Garcia. I dialed the number as I pulled up Google, typing in *Laufeyiarson Stanford* and clicking the first link.

Stanford's website loaded as the phone rang. I blinked at my computer screen. Laufeyiarson was a woman. A young woman. And she studied...I squinted to be sure. Norse mythology? What the actual fuck?

"Hi! This is Professor Caroline Laufeyiarson," a cheerful voice said on the phone.

"Oh! Yeah, this is Karen from MSU—"

"If you'd like to leave a message, please press one. If you need immediate assistance, please press two for our administrative assistant. My office hours are Monday, Wednesday, and Friday from ten to—"

"Right," I muttered, trying to pull myself together enough to leave a somewhat coherent message. "This is Karen McDonald from MSU, returning your call about, uh, wolves."

I hung up the phone and rocked back in my chair, feeling more or less like an idiot. Someone cleared their throat behind me, and I turned to see Colin in the doorway.

"Yes?" I asked, mildly surprised to see him here before ten in the morning.

Colin nodded toward the lab. "Zeke's got something to show you."

"Zeke's here? This early?"

Colin grinned. "He thought he noticed something in the park and wanted to check it out. He called me this morning."

"Okay, you've got my attention."

I grabbed my water bottle and followed Colin to the lab. Zeke sat hunched over his workstation, surrounded by empty energy drink cans, Frito bags, and three computer screens, all filled with numbers.

"What's going on?" I asked.

Zeke spun around in his chair, frowning. "I just finished crunching the latest numbers. Something's weird."

He tapped a few keys and a map of Yellowstone came up on the screen. Glowing red triangles filled the map; the location of various packs.

"That's old data," I said.

"Yeah, I know," said Zeke. "Two years ago."

He bent over the keyboard, and the red triangles shifted around the map. "Here's last year. Now, look at what happens when I enter the data from our trip..."

The map changed again. Only now the triangles were spreading, or dispersing, leaving a ring of empty darkness in the center of the map.

"That...that doesn't make sense," I said. I tapped the blank space in the center of Zeke's screen. "That's prime territory in the middle of the park."

"No shit," said Zeke. "And look what it matches."

He pulled up another map. I took a deep breath. The bright red outline of the volcanic caldera, the super-volcano sleeping beneath Yellowstone, perfectly matched the pattern of red triangles.

"They're leaving the caldera," I whispered. "But why?"

"Maybe it's about to blow," Colin's soft voice said from behind me.

I shook my head. "Don't even joke about that."

Yellowstone National Park is the largest volcano in the world. The last time this volcano erupted, six hundred thousand years ago, it sprayed volcanic ash as far south as Mexico. It blotted out the sun. It may even have triggered the ice age.

"Well, maybe you should ask your friend what's going on," Zeke drawled, his eyes still fixed on the computer screen.

"Good thought," I said. "I'd bet Diana's noticed this...this bizarre migration pattern. But why didn't she say anything when—"

My voice faded as I realized Zeke was staring at me with a raised eyebrow. "Nah, I meant your, uh, your other friend. You know, Wolf Man."

I glanced to make sure the door of the lab was closed, then I shook my head and closed my eyes, pinching the bridge of my nose. "Zeke, what about, 'What happens in the park, stays in the park?'"

"Hey, all I'm trying to say is that sexy Mr. Wolf Man might have a unique and valuable perspective on this particular situation."

I turned to Colin for support, but he was nodding along with Zeke. "Karen - I mean, Professor McDonald - you should do it. This could be important. You can talk to him, right?"

I opened my mouth to respond and couldn't think of a single word.

Zeke leaned back in his chair and put his arms behind his head. "Boss Lady, I know you're all about pretending none of that crazy shit in the park ever happened, but seriously. What the fuck's going on with the wolves? These are not normal migration patterns. They're leaving primo habitat. There's got to be a reason."

I sighed and looked out the window. The leaves on the elms were already starting to change from deep green to a bright, sunny yellow. "I don't even know how to contact him," I said.

Colin and Zeke exchanged a look that worried me.

"Well, you could try—" Zeke started.

"And this conversation is over," I said, cutting him off and desperately hoping my cheeks didn't look as red as they felt.

"Okay," Zeke drawled. "But if the park is getting ready to blow, it might be nice to have some advance warning."

"Thanks," I said, backing out of the lab before either one of them could make another Wolf Man comment.

I bit my lip as I sank back into my desk chair. If the Yellowstone caldera blows, I thought with a numb, sinking feeling, we're all totally fucked.

CHAPTER TEN

"Vali Lokisen, huh? What kind of a name is that anyway? Japanese?" Susan looked up from her enormous white coffee mug, her brunette curls bouncing in the morning light.

"Uh." I pushed back from the table. "I think I'm going to get a scone. Would you like a scone? Or more coffee?"

Susan's smile widened, and my cheeks burned. I stood and walked away from the table with as much dignity as I could muster. We were having coffee at the Whole World Cafe, a vegan, gluten-free, co-op sandwiched between the bars and art galleries on Bozeman's Main Street. The place was packed with college students and dirtbag climbing bums. I rubbed my forehead; the headache nipping at my temples was getting worse, and the cafe's weird New Age electronica music wasn't helping matters.

Very stupidly, I finished an entire bottle of wine by myself last night as I tried to think of a plausible story to tell Susan. By the time I poured myself the very last glass from the overpriced bottle I bought after cashing Barry fucking Richardson's alimony check, I had a brilliant story. It was totally believable, not at all creepy, and didn't sound half as batshit crazy as the truth.

This morning, I couldn't remember a word of that story, and it didn't help that I woke up crying for some stupid reason. I'd walked to the coffee shop, trying to at least remember the premise that had sounded so appealing last night. Nothing. I showed up twenty minutes late. Susan was already on her second soy milk latte, and she looked suspicious.

The kid behind the counter had aggressively orange hair under his cowboy hat, gauges in his ears, and a barbell through his nose.

"Hi," I squeaked, feeling old and significantly lamer than everyone around me. "I'd like a scone, please."

He grunted something, and I handed him my credit card. After another five minutes someone shoved a blue plate at me with what must have been a scone on it. I took a deep breath and walked back to Susan's table.

Susan was beaming. "So, you met him in the park," she said. "This....Vali."

My mind raced as I took an enormous bite of the scone. It tasted like sawdust. I took a sip of coffee to force it down before I finally managed to stutter, "Yes, this last trip."

"With your grad students?"

I shook my head. "Before they showed up."

"And he was, what? Tall, dark, and handsome?"

"Well, he, uh—" I coughed and glanced at the front door. "He—"

Susan started laughing. "Oh, Karen! You had a real wildlife encounter!"

I stared at her. "Excuse me?"

"You've got no idea the kind of things that happen in the backcountry," she said. "That's what we used to call it when I was a park ranger. A real wildlife encounter."

I opened my mouth to disagree with her and then closed it again. *A real wildlife encounter.* Actually, that pretty much summed it up.

"So, did you sleep with him?" Susan's wide smile and sparkling eyes said she'd already guessed the answer to that question.

"Really, Susan? That's all you want to know? If I slept with him?"

Susan shook her head, and her wild curls bounced. "Nah, I don't really care if you actually *slept* with him. I was more wondering if you fucked him."

I rolled my eyes. That was Susan in a nutshell; she was not a euphemism type of gal. "Well, uh, kind of," I said, my voice hardly more than a whisper.

Susan made a face. "Kind of? How can you 'kind of' fuck someone?"

"Stop it," I hissed, casting a furtive glance around the coffee shop to make sure none of the kids in here were my students.

Susan leaned back and waved her hands in surrender. "Hey, good for you! I guess I don't need all the details." She sighed into her latte, her pained expression making her disappointment very clear. "So, did you get his number? You going to see him again?"

"I don't know," I said. "He doesn't exactly have a phone."

Susan sighed again, a dreamy look on her face. "Damn, do I ever miss being a backcountry ranger."

I choked on my coffee and coughed so hard Susan reached across the table to hit me on the back. After that, everyone in the coffee shop stared at us. Under the scrutiny of several dozen hipster twenty-somethings, Susan mercifully changed the subject.

"You coming fishing with us on Saturday?"

I shook my head. "I can't."

"What? You haven't been in ages. We're hitting up the Gallatin canyon, and there's a late stonefly hatch."

"I know," I said, running my fingers along the blue plate holding the scone. I did love the women's fly fishing group, but if I didn't get another grant this year, the whole tenure process might be in jeopardy.

"If you tell me you have to work, Karen, I swear to God I will force feed you the rest of that scone."

I winced.

Susan threw her hands up in the air. "Seriously? Did you move to Montana to work on a Saturday?"

Anger flared deep in my chest, hot and sudden, and I smacked my palms against the formica table, making my blue plate jump. "I moved to Montana to be a professor, damn it! So, yes, I suppose I did!"

Susan's eyes widened and she looked around the room. Everyone was staring at us again.

"Shit, I'm sorry," I sank into my chair, wishing I could hide behind my sawdust scone. "It's just...the semester just started, I've got a ton of data to analyze, and my latest grant proposal got rejected."

She smiled. "Hey, it's no problem. I wouldn't be your friend if I couldn't handle your crazy."

I grinned back and drained the last of my coffee.

"Maybe you just need another real wildlife encounter," Susan said, pushing back from the table.

"God, wouldn't that be nice," I said with a sigh.

IT WAS A BEAUTIFUL Saturday morning.

I tried not to think about the women's fly fishing group driving up the Gallatin Canyon as I watched the morning sun illuminate Hyalite Peak on the far side of the valley. I hated working on Saturdays, but there was no way around it. If I wanted money to fund my research, I had to get my grant approved this year. And that meant reading through all the feedback, finding out why they rejected me, and changing the entire proposal. Even if I thought they were all wrong.

Especially if I thought they were all wrong.

I parked my Subaru in the empty faculty lot and slammed the door shut. First thing Saturday morning, and I was already in a bad mood. Great. Just fucking great.

The lights in the science building hallway flicked to life as I walked through the echoing corridors, trying not to think of all the other things I could be doing with a beautiful Saturday morning in early fall.

The lights above me flickered and buzzed as I froze in the hallway. The door to my lab was ajar.

"I locked this," I whispered to myself. "I locked this Friday night."

My heart jumped as I approached the open door. My lab doesn't have a plethora of valuable equipment, but still. I've got a half dozen computers, and meth heads are always looking for stolen scales. If someone took one of our notebooks, we'd have no way to retrieve that data.

I stopped just outside the door and made a fist around my keys. The lab was totally dark, and a weird, labored rasping drifted through the open door, like a machine that had been left on and was starting to die. I eased the door open as quietly as possible.

Zeke. It was Zeke. He was sprawled across his desk, face down and snoring. Loudly. The lights flickered to life when I entered. He barely stirred.

"Zeke? You okay?" I called.

Zeke shifted and sat up, blinking bloodshot eyes. He smelled like cheap beer and cigarette smoke.

"Hey, mornin', Boss Lady!" he said with a wide smile, showing off his broken front tooth.

"Zeke, what the hell are you doing in the lab?"

He yawned, stretched, and wiped drool off his cheek. "Sleepin'."

"Yeah, I figured that part out on my own. But why? Don't you have an apartment in grad student housing?"

"Well. Funny thing about that." Zeke scratched himself and yawned again. "The missus wasn't too happy to see me last night."

"The missus? Since when do you have a girlfriend?"

He grinned. "Since August."

"Zeke, it's September. Early September."

"Yup," he said, twisting his neck to both sides. "She moved in last week. Then things kinda went downhill."

"Ah," I said, briefly wondering if I should try to look sympathetic. "Well, good luck with that. Listen, if you really need a place to stay—"

"Nah, nah. Although hell, sleepin' at a desk. Shit. I think you've got the right idea, Boss Lady, what with your whole long distance, inter-species—"

"Stop. Stop it right there," I said, holding up both my hands.

"Fine, fine." Zeke held his hands up in surrender. "But hell, what are you doing here? Isn't it Saturday?"

"Yeah. It's Saturday," I said, opening a window to air out the lab.

"Well, don't you know Saturday's are for cookin' a pound of bacon and nursing a hangover?"

I glared at him.

Zeke belched and shook his head. "Damn, Boss Lady, never mind," he said as he backed toward the door. "I'll just leave you to it, then."

He was gone before I could think of an appropriate response, leaving the whole lab smelling like cheap beer and unwashed male graduate student. Gross. I rubbed my temple, where the beginning of a headache was starting to coalesce. It looked like I'd be working in my office this fine Saturday.

MY CELL PHONE RANG from somewhere under the stack of papers on my desk. I shoveled them aside, grateful for the distraction. I was only halfway through the reviewer comments on my rejected NSF grant, and I'd already decided every single one of the peer reviewers could go to hell. Slowly, and hopefully painfully.

My phone was sitting face down in the middle of the textbook for my *Introduction to Ecology* class. I flipped it over, expecting Mom, then frowned. It was John Rodriguez. John studies the interactions between wolf and coyote populations in the park, and he's also just about the only member of my department I actually like. I swiped my finger across the screen to answer.

"Hey, John, what is it?"

"Karen. They've shot a wolf."

My stomach dropped out from under me. "Oh, no."

"It was just outside Yellowstone. I'm headed there now," he said. "Karen, it was... it was a rancher."

I shot to my feet. "Motherfucker!" I screamed into the phone. "Those goddamn rednecks!"

More wolves are killed by humans than all the other causes of mortality combined, which pisses me the fuck off. And that's why, ever since the press conference where I was asked to leave the room, John tries to be the public face of Montana State University's wolf research program.

"What the hell happened?" I asked, pacing to the window.

"That, uh, that's why I'm headed down. I'll let you know what I find."

"Wait a minute," I said, the sick feeling in my stomach growing. "What wolf? What wolf got shot?"

"I don't know. A big male, apparently."

The room spun. I closed my eyes. "What color?"

"Uh, let me check," I heard the phone shifting. My heartbeat felt very loud, and I tasted something bitter in the back of my throat.

"Doesn't say," he said, finally.

"I'm coming down," I said, slamming my laptop shut.

"No! Karen, no, I don't think that's a good idea," John stammered.

"West Yellowstone, right?"

John sighed loudly. "Just let me do the talking this time, okay?"

"Yeah, yeah," I muttered, glancing at the clock. I wouldn't be to West Yellowstone for at least ninety minutes. "John, when you find out what color the wolf is, you call me back."

"Okay... Are you going to tell me why?"

"Just do it!" I yelled, and I slammed the phone down on top of my computer bag.

A big male. I pressed my palms against my eyes.

Don't be Vali. Oh, for God's sake, don't be Vali.

HIGHWAY 191 WOVE IN and out of the Beartooth mountains, crossing the Gallatin river half a dozen times as it climbed toward West Yellowstone. It was a beautiful day. The sun sparkled off the dancing mountain river, and the tall grasses nodded with the full seed heads of early autumn. My stomach felt like a lead weight; tears bit at the corners of my eyes. I checked my cell phone every few seconds as I lost service, regained service, then lost service again. My phone found a single bar of cell service just as I drove past Big Sky Country ski resort, which was the kind of exclusive, ultra-expensive place Barry fucking Richardson would like.

My phone rang. For a second, I was afraid to answer.

I bit the inside of my cheek and swiped my screen. "Yes?"

"Gray," John said. "A gray male. No radio collar."

I let out the breath I'd been holding since Bozeman. "Thank you."

"Yeah, no problem," he said. "And Karen. I think it did kill a calf."

"So fucking what?" I yelled, my anger flaring again. "Don't they know they can be compensated for livestock losses? Stupid fucking ignorant—"

"You know it's not that simple," John said, cutting off what would have been a damn fine rant. "It's hard to prove the cause of death. You know that."

"Yeah, I also know that wolves are fucking sentient creatures, with more right to be here than the goddam cattle!"

John was silent. I could almost hear him shaking his head in erudite disapproval. "When's the last time you had a hamburger?" he finally said. "Where do you think that beef came from?"

I ground my teeth together to keep from telling him to shut the fuck up.

"I'm almost there," I said, hanging up the phone.

I took a deep breath and tried to loosen my death grip on the steering wheel. It wasn't Vali. But still, it could have been him. It could have been a lone black wolf who was shot this morning. I watched the mountains unfold through my windshield. I've got to warn him.

I've got to spend the night in Yellowstone.

IT TOOK ME A LONG TIME to find the ranch where the wolf had been shot. So long, in fact, I started to suspect John had given me the wrong address on purpose. I finally spotted the tiny, rusty address marker that matched my hastily scrawled notes and turned down a rutted dirt road.

This did not look like a prosperous ranch. The family lived in a trailer at the end of the road, surrounded by broken down vehicles. One of the pickup trucks had a fading bumper sticker that read "SAVE 100 ELK - SHOOT A WOLF!" I tried very hard not to kick the rust-spotted bumper as I left my car.

A dust plume rose in the distance, and the low whine of a four-wheeler filled the air. I shaded my eyes with my hand and watched two vehicles crest the nearest hill. The four-wheelers pulled into the yard, kicking up dirt and belching clouds of blue smoke. John was riding behind a young man, hardly old enough to be out of high school. I was guessing his father and grandfather rode the second four-wheeler. Their sun-lined faces were hard, and their eyes narrow.

"Thank you again for all your help," John said, dusting himself off as he came to his feet.

"Welcome," said the young man, curtly.

John nodded at me. "Mr. Leavenworth, this is my colleague from MSU," he said. "Karen, this is Gage, Rick, and Stan Leavenworth. They were kind enough to take me to the site."

John emphasized the word *kind*. I noticed a shotgun strapped to the back of the second four-wheeler.

"I'll be sure to put livestock loss in my report," said John. "And remember, you can file that compensation form."

The older man - Stan, I thought - snorted, demonstrating exactly what he thought of government compensation programs. Undeterred, John turned back to the young man, pulling a business card out of his dust-covered jeans.

"Gage, you remember what I told you about MSU. I'd be happy to give you a tour. We're always looking for bright, young students."

Gage smiled. He looked, for the first time, both very young and very shy. The expressions on the older men's faces softened somewhat.

I opened my mouth. John shot me a panicked look, shaking his head.

"Anything... I can do to help?" I asked, lamely.

"I think we're all done here," said John, positioning himself between me and the ranchers. "Thank you again for all your cooperation. We're all in this together."

The older ranchers just nodded, expressionless, but Gage smiled again, his dusty fingers curled around John's business card.

CHAPTER ELEVEN

"What the fuck was that?" I asked John over dinner in West Yellowstone. I'd pointedly avoided ordering beef, and now I regretted it. John's steak looked amazing.

"That's called recruitment," John said, with a sigh. "Also, being a decent human being. The calf that wolf killed probably cost the family eight hundred dollars, and you saw where they live."

"Not the wolf's fault," I snapped, stabbing at my chicken parmesan. "People shouldn't be ranching this close to the park."

"Right." John rolled his eyes. "You want to know how long that family's owned that ranch? Five generations, Karen. Five generations."

I took a bite of chicken. It was terrible. "And you want to know how long wolves roamed free in North America, before we showed up and slaughtered them all?" I said, jabbing my fork in the air for emphasis.

John shook his head. "I really don't want to have this argument again. Can we please fight over something else? Departmental politics? Anything?"

I sighed. John was kind of cute, in a vulnerable, nerdy sort of way. It really was a shame he was married.

"Listen," I said, "I don't mean to be such a—"

John raised an eyebrow.

"Well, I don't mean to be difficult. It was a rough week in the park. I think my nerves are still frayed. Can I get you another beer to make up for it?"

John shook his head. "Nah, I'm driving back to Bozeman. You too, right?"

"No. I'm staying here. I got a room across the street."

John raised both eyebrows at that.

"It's Saturday," I stammered. "And it's a—" I hesitated. I couldn't really say *long drive*. By Montana standards, a ninety minute drive is practically next door.

"Okay," said John, slowly. "You want to spend a rocking Saturday night hitting the bars in West Yellowstone. Got it."

I laughed. "Not quite. Actually, I'm going to bed early."

John looked even more confused. I ordered us both a second beer and tried to change the subject.

MY HOTEL ROOM WAS TINY, and it smelled bad, like someone burned a lifetime's supply of Ramen noodles in the sad, gray microwave. Since I decided to spend the night when I was already halfway here, I'd left Bozeman with just my purse. No toothbrush. No sexy pajamas. Not even a change of clothes for tomorrow. I took off everything but my underwear and my MSU T-shirt, pulled the paper-thin curtains shut, and lay on the bed, trying to will myself to fall asleep. And trying not to worry about whether or not this hotel room was even close enough to the Lamar Valley to reach Vali. Or if Vali was still around at all.

After an hour of tossing and turning I gave up and turned on the TV, flipping through channels until I settled on the most boring thing I could find, a televised bowling tournament. I turned to volume down low and leaned back, waiting for sleep.

MY EYES OPENED TO DELICATE spring sunlight, filtered through the pale green of aspen leaves. I was back in the dream forest. Finally.

I ran through the trees and burst into the meadow so quickly it surprised me. My legs staggered as I pulled up short to look around. The same flowers were blooming, that unrealistic mixture of wildflowers from every season. The sky was a clear, translucent blue, like the smooth curve of a robin's egg.

I was alone.

"Vali," I whispered, walking the edge of the meadow, staring through the trees. "Vali!"

I cupped my hands around my mouth, calling to the forest. "VALI!"

"Hello, beautiful Karen."

He'd entered the meadow silently. Now he stood directly behind me, so close we were almost touching. I clamped my mouth closed to stifle my moan. Of course, he was completely naked, and damn, he was so fucking hot. Relief crashed over me, flooding my body with heat and forcing the breath from my chest.

"Oh God, Vali, I'm so glad you're okay."

He wrapped me in his powerful arms and pulled my body to his. "Why would I not be?"

I met his eyes. "Listen, I have to warn you—"

He stopped me with his lips on mine. I opened my mouth to his hungry kiss, pressing my chest against his, my body shivering as his hands ran down my back to cup the curve of my ass. His scent surrounded me, and I was suddenly acutely aware of my thin T-shirt separating our bodies.

"Warn me later," he growled, dropping to his knees.

He yanked my underwear to my ankles, wrapping one arm around my hips as he buried his head between my legs. I hardly had time to gasp before waves of pleasure crashed over me, knocking me off balance. His moans rippled through my entire body, escaping from my lips. I sank my fingers into his hair, clinging to him for balance as my body burned under his touch.

"Oh, Vali, I'm—" I gasped, expecting him to pull back, to stop.

He did not stop. His fingers tightened around my hips as he pulled me closer, his tongue thrusting inside me as his lips devoured me, sending great red waves of pleasure soaring through my body, each one more intense than the last.

"I'm—" I panted, my hips rocking against his mouth, my hands digging in his hair.

He shook his head against me, his lips and tongue deep inside me. My orgasm tore through me like an explosion. I cried out, something loud and wild and animal, as my head rocked back and my mind drowned in a haze of ecstasy.

I was only dimly aware of Vali lowering me to the ground, and the tickle of grass against my thighs. My eyes slowly refocused to find Vali's full lips and high cheekbones, his dark curls against the cerulean sky.

"My woman," he said, his voice hoarse.

I opened my mouth to speak, but my lips seemed to have forgotten how to form words. He grabbed my hips, flipping me over. My face pressed into the ground, and I could smell the earth, and the green scent of broken wildflower stalks. He shoved my T-shirt down over my back to pool under my arms; then he pulled my waist up and spread my legs.

"Oh!" I gasped.

Vali moaned as he thrust inside me. He filled me so quickly it took my breath away, his hips hitting my thighs, his breath coming in quick pants above me. I dug my fingers into the dirt, grabbing for purchase among the thin, little roots as his thrusts rocked my entire body. He was so big, so damn big, he hit every pleasure center I had—

Vali leaned over my back and I could smell him, his wild, sweet scent. "My woman," he whispered.

His arm curved around my waist and his fingers traced the apex of my sex, sending shivers rocketing through my body. I opened my mouth to say it was too much, too soon, but all I could do was moan as my hips rocked against his and pleasure rolled through me like breakers against the shore. I let my cheek fall to the grass as my eyes closed, my vision swallowed by euphoria.

I came again, my body clenching around him as I moaned his name into the ground. His fingers pressed against my clit, drawing out my climax, until the pleasure was so sharp and intense it was almost pain. When I finally stopped screaming he released me, panting, and I collapsed onto my back.

His hands traced my breasts as I waited for my head to stop spinning. When I opened my eyes, his face was just above my chest. He grinned at me and kissed the hard tip of my nipple, then ran his tongue around the edge of my areola. I sighed at the flood of heat between my legs, surprised my body had any nerve endings left.

"My woman," Vali whispered.

"My wolf," I replied.

His laugh filled the aspen grove. Then his hips shifted, parting my legs, and he was inside me again, moving slowly and sweetly. I stretched my arms, letting the grass and wildflowers brush against my skin, my body rocking against Vali's without thought, without effort. This time the pleasure grew slowly, almost like a dance, until we were both gasping and panting as our bodies rose and fell, rose and fell against each other.

We came at the same time, both crying out as our hips crashed together, his cock spasming deep inside me. He fell forward onto my chest, his head pressed against my neck, his sweet, wild smell surrounding me. For a long time we lay like that, arms and legs entwined, our chests rising and falling together.

"What was it?" Vali finally said as his lips nibbled at my ear.

I blinked at the bright sky. "Hmmm?"

Vali rolled onto his side, one arm still resting across my stomach. "Your warning?"

"Oh." I tried to fight my way through the endorphins flooding my brain to form a coherent thought.

And I failed. Miserably. "Uh. I don't—"

Vali's laugh rolled across the meadow as he bent to kiss me. Our lips danced together for a very long time, and I wasn't sure there had been a warning. I wasn't even sure there was another world; all that seemed to matter was right here, pressing his naked chest against mine.

He pulled away, still grinning at me. "That can't be comfortable," he finally said.

"What?"

Vali glanced at my chest and I realized I was still wearing my blue MSU T-shirt, bunched up under my armpits. I felt my cheeks flush as I sat up, pulling off the shirt and tossing it into the grass. "I didn't even notice."

"I apologize for my haste," he said, his eyes on the crumpled mess of my discarded shirt. "I wasn't sure I'd see you again. I wasn't sure you'd want to return."

My heart surged. "Oh, I wanted to come back! I searched for you, Vali!"

"As I searched for you, beautiful Karen. Once I even thought I heard you."

Tears bit at the corners of my eyes. To cover them up, I leaned forward, kissing Vali's soft lips until I felt them curve into a smile.

"Oh, God, I've missed you," I said. And with that admission, the rest of the world came flooding back to me.

"Listen, I remember what I wanted to say," I said, shifting in his arms. "When you're...not here. Not dreaming. Look, you're safe as long as you're inside Yellowstone. When you're in the park. But outside of it, you need to know that humans are dangerous."

Vali smiled at me, his hand tracing the curve of my cheek. "Humans are always dangerous."

"Well, yeah, I suppose. But listen, please. Those ranchers, they've got guns. And it's not always clear where the park boundaries end, and—When I heard a wolf had been shot—"

Tears slipped down my cheeks, and I tried to brush them away discreetly.

"Beautiful Karen," he said, kissing the top of my head. "I appreciate the warning, but it is unnecessary. I can take care of myself."

I took a deep breath and tried to pull myself together. "Just...be careful. Please."

Vali shrugged and pulled me close to his chest. His back tightened under my arms and his breath caught in his chest. I had just enough time to wonder what I'd done wrong when he spoke again.

"I also have a warning for you," he said.

I pulled back, suddenly feeling cold. Vali hesitated; his wild, golden eyes looked lost. "I...I enjoy you, Karen. Very much. But you shouldn't come here again."

It was so far from what I expected him to say that I felt like I'd jumped in the stream in Yellowstone again. A dark, cold shock sank into my arms and legs, chasing away the post-orgasmic bliss.

"What?" I stuttered.

Vali stared at the sky. "I've appreciated the companionship. But it would be best if you did not come again."

"You're dumping me?" I started to blink furiously against a fresh flood of tears. "Wouldn't it have been better to dump me *before* you fucked me?"

Vali frowned in an adorable way that made me feel seriously pissed me off. "What do you mean? Did you not enjoy yourself?"

"That's not the point," I snapped, pulling away from his touch.

"Let me explain—"

"Stop. Don't even fucking say it. It's not me, it's you, right?"

"No," said Vali, sounding confused. "It's not me or you. It's—There's something wrong here. Don't you sense it?"

I wiped my cheeks and turned to him, my heart hammering against my ribs. "What are you talking about?"

"Not here. Not in dreams. Out there in...what do you call it? The ark?"

I took a deep breath as my heart stuttered. "The park? You mean Yellowstone?"

He nodded. "Something's gone wrong. I may be able to help, but Karen, it's very unstable right now. You should leave this place. Go somewhere far away."

"Vali, I can't leave. I live here. I work here. I mean, I study the wolves—"

My voice cut off as I remembered Zeke's charts with those overlapping circles. The black emptiness in the middle of the park, in what should be prime wolf habitat.

"Oh, shit." A cold shiver ran the length of my spine and the hairs on my neck prickled. "Vali, is this why the wolves are leaving Yellowstone? Is it the volcano?"

"It's more than that." His golden eyes darkened. "I've warned my brothers and sisters to leave this place. And now I'm warning you. If I can't correct what's gone wrong, I at least want you as far away as possible."

I tried to breathe as a maelstrom of conflicting emotions churned my heart and mind. "But...if you're still here, you're in danger."

"I've lived a thousand years. I'll be fine." His smile was not very convincing.

"Can you...can you change?" I whispered. "Come home with me?"

My head spun as I remembered his naked body in the Lamar Valley, pressing my lips against his as the thunderstorm rumbled over Druid Peak.

"I could find you in the park," I said frantically. "I could shoot you with another tranquilizer dart. I could be there by this afternoon, in the valley—"

"No. No, you don't understand."

"But, if you're in danger here, you would be safer—"

"No!" Vali leapt to his feet, backing away from me. "Karen McDonald, I don't want you near me!"

I felt like the air had been forced from my lungs. My head dropped to my knees, and I hoped Vali couldn't see my shoulders trembling.

"I—I apologize." His voice sounded oddly thin. "Karen, listen to me. If I can't stop this, I want to at least know you escaped. That you're safe."

His hand touched my shoulder, and I lifted my head. Vali crouched in front of me, looking pale and miserable.

"Karen, my beautiful Karen, I—"

His face began to fade, pulling away from me into a thick, white mist. I reached for him but my hand was caught, tangled in something rough and scratchy. I yelped, opening my eyes to see the mottled yellow of the motel room ceiling above me.

"Goddamn it!" I screamed, sinking my fist into the anemic pillow next to me.

What's crazier than having a boyfriend you can only meet in your dreams?

Losing him.

CHAPTER TWELVE

"So, when exactly are you coming to Bozeman?" I asked again. I was finally talking to Professor Laufeyiarson, from Stanford, and she was driving me insane.

"Arriving November nineteenth," she said. "Departing the twenty-second."

"You realize that's almost Thanksgiving?"

"Yes," she said, sounding impatient.

"And you want to see wolves?"

"Yes."

I sighed. "Listen, have you ever been to Montana in November?" I didn't wait for an answer; of course she hadn't been to Montana. "The weather is unpredictable. We could have a foot of snow that time of year, and almost all the roads in Yellowstone will already be closed."

"My talk is on Friday," she said, "and my flight leaves on Sunday. I thought we could go on Saturday—"

"Yes, I understand," I said. "But November - look, it's rare to see wolves in Yellowstone at any time of year. I just don't want you to set yourself up for a disappointment."

"You do track them, don't you?" she asked.

I balled my hand into a fist, crunching the curly cord of my office phone between my fingers. When I meet Professor Laufeyiarson, I told myself, I am not going to punch her in her smug face. I am not.

"Yes," I said, slowly. "Which is why I know it can be very hard to see them. But I'm happy to work with you, and with Stanford. We'll just do the best we can."

"I don't think it'll be a problem," she said. "I look forward to meeting you."

I took a deep breath before responding. "I look forward to meeting you, too," I lied, as calmly as I could manage.

I hung up my office phone and reached for my cell, scrolling until I found Diana's name. My finger hovered above her name as I tried to remember the last time I'd called her. It was a Tuesday now, so it must have been...Monday. Last Monday. Good. The last thing I wanted was to be so irritating I chased her away. I bit my lip and tapped her name. She answered almost instantly.

"Karen," she said, her voice breezy and light. "And how are you this beautiful morning?"

"Fine, thanks. Just checking on the pack. Any new movements? Anything unusual?"

"Nothing at all," she said. "The Leopold pack is still by Specimen Ridge. A few of our wolf trackers got to see the pack take down an elk on, oh, must have been Thursday. Quite a treat. You should check out the pictures on the website."

"Ah. Thanks."

"You have a further question for me?" Diana asked, sounding amused.

"Yeah," I said, shifting in my seat. "I'm wondering if you - I mean, if any of the wolf trackers - If anyone has seen that, uh, that big, black male. The lone wolf. From the Lamar Valley."

"Ah," she said, and damned if she didn't sound like she was smiling. "No, I'm afraid he doesn't want to be found at the moment."

My heart ached. "Well, thanks anyway. I won't keep you, then."

"It's no problem," she said. "You take care. Oh, and Karen, do be careful."

The line went dead before I had time to realize what a weird thing Diana just said. I shrugged, trying to ignore the dull ache in my chest. And wishing my one and only link to Vali wasn't some crazy hippie living by herself in the woods.

"WHO THE HELL COMES to Montana in November?" I asked my bowl of instant oatmeal.

I was due to pick up Professor Laufeyiarson in an hour, and I was running through a mental checklist of all the things I wanted to bring. The weather forecasts were not promising; already the sky outside my kitchen window was gray and heavy, and all the weather reports called for precipitation. Chances were good it would be snow.

I'd packed an extra pair of boots and a jacket. I didn't trust a Stanford professor to dress for a November trip to Yellowstone. She'd probably be wearing something fashionable and absolutely impractical that would provide zero protection from the elements. As always, I tossed in a few granola bars, my emergency flares, and an avalanche shovel to dig the car out of a snowbank in case things really went south. Although if that happened, I'd probably be ready to strangle Professor Laufeyiarson with my jumper cables.

As I started the car, I tried Diana one final time. I knew I was being ridiculous, but I really, really wanted to be able to spot some wolves. It felt like my professional reputation was hanging on it.

Diana's line went straight to voicemail, just like it had for the past two weeks. I bit the inside of my lip, trying not to add worrying about crazy hippie Diana to my already extensive list of reasons why I had trouble falling asleep at night.

"Satellite tracking says the Leopold pack is near Cooke City," I told myself as I backed out of my driveway. "We'll find them. We'll see the wolves."

I parked my car outside the Holiday Inn and walked to the lobby. Professor Laufeyiarson stood when I entered, folding her copy of the *New York Times* and tucking it neatly under her arm.

"Professor McDonald?" she asked, extending a hand.

Professor Laufeyiarson was not at all what I expected. She was young. Younger than she looked on her faculty webpage, and much younger than I expected. She must have been in her early thirties, maybe only a few years out of grad school. Around my age, actually.

"That's me," I said, shaking her hand. "Nice to meet you."

"Thank you so much for doing this." Her voice was more halting and awkward in person than it had been over the phone.

As I expected, she was wearing a stylish jacket that looked about as warm as tinfoil and a fashionable necklace with a strange, shimmery pendant. She turned to pick up her huge book bag, and I saw the swell of her stomach. Professor Laufeyiarson was pregnant. Very pregnant, by the look of her. My heart seized as tears prickled behind my eyelids.

That will always hurt, I thought. Always.

"Let me get that for you," I said, reaching for her bag. There was an awkward moment when we both held the straps, and then she let go.

"Thanks." She smiled, and her cheeks flushed.

"I'm sorry I missed your talk," I said as I navigated my Subaru out of the parking lot.

I had meant to make it to her talk, I really had, but I'd gotten carried away plotting Zeke's data. Over the past two months the trend had only gotten more obvious. The wolf packs really were leaving Yellowstone. It was enough to make me nervous.

"Can you give me the highlights?" I asked. It was a long drive to Yellowstone, and asking a professor about their research is usually a sure fire way to fill two hours.

"Of course!" She took a deep breath, and the car filled with a shrill metallic jangle. Her cheeks flushed again as she pulled her enormous book bag to her knees and dug around the side pockets, finally fishing out a bright pink iPhone. She tapped the screen and the ringing stopped.

"Sorry about that," she said, sliding her bag back to the floor.

"No problem."

"So, my talk was about the connection between the prose *Edda*—"

Her phone jangled a second time, and she sighed. "Ugh, that's my mom again."

It took another minute of awkwardly shifting the bag off the floor, onto her knees, and around her pregnant belly before Professor Laufeyiarson found her phone again. By then it had stopped ringing. She glanced at me.

"Wait for it..." she said.

Her phone rang again, and we both laughed.

"I think you'd better take it this time," I said.

She swiped the screen and held the phone to her ear. I could hear a shrill voice on the other end of the line, although I could only make out her side of the conversation.

"Hi, Mom—No, I'm fine.—Yes, fine. F.I.N.E. Dr. Singh said 'perfectly healthy,' remember?—No, Mom, he had a meeting.—Well, it was a meeting *at* a conference.—No, why would I even know that? I don't keep tabs on him.—"

I rested my elbow on the car door, bringing a hand to my mouth to cover my smile. I'll admit, I was intimidated by the thought of entertaining a Stanford professor. But driving together through the wide vistas of Paradise Valley, listening to her getting henpecked by her mother...well, it was almost enough to make me like Professor Laufeyiarson.

WE SAW THE FIRST SNOWFLAKES as we approached Yellowstone's Mammoth entrance. The two hour drive had flown by. It turned out Professor Caroline Laufeyiarson and I actually had a lot of common ground, and she seemed genuinely excited to see Yellowstone. It was a nice change. Usually the only people who come with me to Yellowstone have already seen it a thousand times. So those few, tiny flakes drifting out of the dark, low clouds made me feel irrationally irritated. I wanted to show off the wolves, damn it.

We both fell silent as my Subaru passed through the massive stone gates reading *For the Benefit and Enjoyment of the People*. I took a deep breath and decided to forge ahead with the question that had been bothering me for the entire drive.

Or since August, if I was being honest with myself.

"So...since you're a mythology expert. Are there any Norse myths about werewolves?"

"Werewolves?" Caroline asked.

"You know," I said, trying to keep my voice light and casual, "wolves turning into people. People turning into wolves. That sort of thing."

She was quiet for a moment as she stared out the window. The snowflakes increased, swirling silently outside our windows.

"Oh!" she said, suddenly. "Is that a hot spring?"

We'd crested the bluff, and the imposing pale pink and white terraced steppes of Mammoth Hot Springs rose before us like a medieval fortress. Steam filled the air above the springs, obscuring the top of the formation. I smiled. It was pretty damn impressive, after all.

"Yeah, that's Mammoth," I said.

"Can we stop?" she asked, leaning forward to peer out the windshield.

I tried not to grin at her enthusiasm. The streets of Mammoth were deserted, so it felt like we had the entire park to ourselves. I parked at the foot of the boardwalk circling the hot springs and tried to tell myself the snow wasn't getting heavier. We'd only gone a few steps when I noticed Caroline shivering in her fashionable California fake jacket.

"Oh, I'm sorry," I said. "I've got a jacket in the car for you. Hang on, I'll go grab it."

"Wait." She reached for her strange, shimmery necklace and wrapped her hand around it. Her eyes turned strange and distant. Then she shook her head. "No, let's go."

"Are you sure? Mammoth is pretty impressive. It's the biggest geothermal feature in the park, in terms of—"

"I'm sure." She walked past me, the snowflakes twirling in her wake.

I shrugged and followed her. It suddenly occurred to me she hadn't answered my question about werewolves.

Caroline seemed nervous as we left Mammoth to follow Route 212's lonely two lanes through the northern part of the park. The snow was getting thicker, but it wasn't sticking to the roads yet. Still, I supposed light snow might be more than enough to freak out someone from California. Light snow and being miles from civilization, in Yellowstone National Park, in late November. I tried to think of something I could say to put her at ease and drew a complete blank.

"Hey, we can turn around whenever you'd like," I said.

She was holding her necklace in both hands, and her eyes were almost closed. "No," she murmured. "Not yet."

"Okay. We'll keep looking for wolves, then."

I peered through my windshield at the thin black line of the road and the dancing snowflakes beyond. We were in the sagebrush flats of the Lamar Valley now, my research grounds, but the light was fading and our visibility was dropping by the second. At this point, we'd probably be lucky to spot a damn mule deer, let alone a wolf.

"Here," Caroline said, her voice loud in the small space.

"What?"

"Pull over!"

I turned to Caroline. "What? Why?"

"Just pull over!"

I guided my Subaru to the side of the road, put it in park, and turned on my flashers. Caroline leapt out of the car. Well, I thought, maybe she needed to pee. I gave her a minute of privacy before climbing out of the driver's seat. The wind was much stronger now, and biting cold against my cheeks. The road felt slippery too. I popped my trunk to pull out my binoculars and the extra jacket.

"Did you see something?" I asked, walking to Caroline's side of the car and handing her the jacket.

"Thanks," she said, pulling my jacket onto her shoulders. "Look for yourself."

I brought the binoculars to my eyes and stared through the falling snow, adjusting the focus. I glassed the tree line where the lodgepole pines met the sagebrush flats, figuring that was where the wolves would be seeking shelter from the snow. I didn't see anything, so I dipped my binoculars toward the far side of the river. There were several fallen logs, a jumble of bare willows branches, a man in a black suit—

"What the hell?" I gasped.

I dropped the binoculars and turned to Caroline. She was smiling at the horizon, a totally rapt, unselfconscious, blissful smile. Her arms wrapped around the swell of her pregnant belly. I picked up the binoculars again.

There he was.

There was a tall man with long, flaming red hair walking by himself in the middle of Yellowstone. In a snowstorm. And—I adjusted the focus on my binoculars—he was wearing a fucking suit. A black business suit. I blinked and lost my focus.

"Karen?" Caroline asked. Her voice sounded like it was coming from somewhere far away.

I turned my binoculars back to the river and jumped. The man was gone. But I could have sworn I just saw someone wearing a black suit in a snowstorm in the middle of the fucking wilderness.

"Um, Karen," Caroline said.

I shook my head, running my binoculars back across the tree line. He couldn't have just vanished. People don't just vanish.

"Karen, uh..."

I frowned as I turned to Caroline. "Did you just see a—"

The words died in my mouth. The man in the black suit was standing next to my car, smiling. He was tall, way too tall, with icy, feral eyes. I felt a surge of cold panic and stepped backward, banging my thighs against the hood of my Subaru.

"Karen, this is my husband," Caroline said, wrapping her arm around his waist. "Sorry about the, um, awkward introduction."

The man smiled at me, showing his teeth, and I was unpleasantly reminded of the alpha of the Leopold pack. 457M.

"What the fuck?" I hissed, pressing a hand against the hood of my Subaru to keep from falling backward.

"Hi," he said, nodding at me with that disturbing smile.

Then he bent to Caroline and their lips met. His hands ran along the curve of her stomach as they kissed. I turned away, took a deep breath, and brushed the gathering snow off my binoculars. When I turned back they were still pressed together, her arms around his hips. It was suddenly difficult to watch the way his hands caressed her stomach, the way their bodies bent together.

He had been good to me, when I was pregnant, I thought, and my heart ached. For all the shitty times we had before, and for all the shitty times we had after, Barry fucking Richardson had been good to me when I was pregnant.

I coughed discretely to get their attention. My phone rang. I blinked. I didn't even think I got cell phone service out here. It took me a minute of fumbling with the pocket of my flannel lined jeans before I could pull out my phone. The screen flashed *Diana*.

What the fuck?

I swiped the screen and bringing the phone to my ear. "Hello?"

"I don't want him here," Diana said.

"Excuse me?" I turned to Caroline and the fucking creepy guy in the black suit. They were both watching me with wide eyes. "I think you dialed the wrong number. This is Karen, Karen McDonald from MSU."

Diana made a sharp, impatient noise. "I know who you are!" There was a pause, and she exhaled loudly. "Bring him to me," she said, and she hung up.

Very slowly, I put the phone back in my pocket. I felt like the world had just begun to tilt. Caroline's husband laughed.

"She's charming, isn't she?" he asked.

"Who's charming?" I said, frowning at him.

"Forgive me," he said, extending his palm towards me. "I haven't even introduced myself. I'm Loki Laufeyiarson."

"Excuse me?" I did not take his hand. "Low... Key?"

"Loki," he said, dropping his hand. "You know, they used to name cities after me."

"One city," said Caroline.

Loki turned to her, smiling. "It's a nice city."

"More of a town, really," she said.

Loki brushed her cheek with his hand and then looked up, his eyes on the southern horizon. "You're right," he said. "Something's gone wrong here."

"Hang on," I said, raising my hands as I looked up and down the empty highway. "Where did you come from? How did you even get out here?"

"Let's talk about that in the car, shall we?" Loki said, opening the passenger door. "Diana is expecting us, is she not?"

The world tilted again as I climbed in the driver's seat. Caroline and Loki both sat in the back seat, their hands intertwined. Somehow that just made everything worse, more surreal and disturbing and impossible. I adjusted the rearview mirror so I wouldn't have to look at them as I guided the car onto the snow-gusted highway.

Loki.

Something about that bizarre name tugged at the edges of my mind. I reached for the thought, and it was gone.

Snow was coming down heavily now, coating the road, and my hands tightened on the steering wheel. The Absaroka Mountains loomed in front of me as my Subaru climbed toward Cooke City, and I had the distinctly uncomfortable feeling that I was driving into a box canyon. With no exit.

CHAPTER THIRTEEN

Diana's little log cabin nestled in the mountains outside Cooke City, a summertime tourist destination town that was almost entirely deserted in the winter, aside from a handful of survivalist nuts. Nuts like Diana. Conditions on Route 212 got progressively worse as my Subaru edged into the gloaming. At least the slick road conditions made it slightly easier to ignore Loki and Caroline whispering to each other in the back seat. In a language that didn't sound much like English.

It was completely dark when I reached Diana's long, windy road. Pine trees loomed over her driveway, dark and foreboding. I cut the engine, and my car flooded with the noise of Diana's hound dogs baying through the windows.

The cabin's front door swung open. Diana stood in the entryway, silhouetted in her yellow porch light. Her dark hair flowed over her shoulders, and her arms were crossed. She did not look happy to see us. I reached for my door handle and hesitated. I'd only been to Diana's house once before, and that was just a ten-minute stop to verify a reading on one of her satellites. We weren't exactly BFFs.

But hadn't she wanted us to come here? Biting my lip, I forced myself to open the car door and step out.

"Hi, Diana," I said, raising my hand in a tiny wave.

Diana turned to her dogs and made a noise like a small explosion deep in her throat. The hounds fell silent. My voice died in my mouth when I saw her hip. She was wearing a holster, with an actual gun.

And not a hunting rifle either. A real fucking pistol. I froze halfway between my car and her front door.

Loki walked past me and extended his hand toward Diana, his palm up. He said something in a language I couldn't understand. Diana shook her head, scowling.

"You do not enter my dwelling," Diana said.

"You'll entertain us in the snow, then?" Loki asked, sweeping his hand toward her driveway. "You're the one who requested my presence, after all."

"You showed up on my doorstep, Lie-smith," Diana growled.

Diana and Loki glared at each other. A low growl echoed off the trees, and I wasn't sure if it came from the dogs or Diana.

"Karen!" Diana called.

I jumped. "Me?"

"Do you know how to find Jake's Grill?" she barked.

"What?" I asked.

Diana tossed her hair over her shoulder. "Oh, for the love. Look, it's a restaurant on Main Street. There's only two restaurants on Main Street, and one of them is closed right now. I'll meet you there."

She turned her back to us, slamming the door closed behind her. Her porchlight snapped off, and I blinked as my eyes tried to adjust to the darkness. Then a low, deep rumble ripped through the night air, and I jumped again. Seconds later a single headlight split the darkness and an enormous motorcycle tore past me, headed down the road. I caught a glimpse of Diana's long hair streaming out from under the rider's helmet.

"Oh," I said, weakly. "I guess Diana has a motorcycle."

I followed Loki back into my car, trying to ignore how violently my legs were shaking.

"Jake's Grill," Loki said from the backseat. "Ah, now that sounds regal."

I started the car and edged out of the snow-covered driveway, drumming my fingers on the steering wheel as I followed the single tire track of Diana's motorcycle.

"So, is this where you tell me you'll answer all my questions at dinner?" I asked.

Loki laughed. "Oh, what fun would it be if all your questions were answered?"

Caroline's hand squeezed my shoulder, and she gave me a little smile through the rearview mirror. "I know this is all a little...much," she said. "I apologize. I wouldn't have done this if it wasn't important."

I sighed. "Let me guess. You're not really a professor."

Caroline huffed from the backseat, and Loki laughed again. "Yes, I am a professor," she snipped. "I wasn't referring to my career."

"And there is something weird here," Loki said. "There's certainly something *wrong*."

That's what Vali said, I realized. Suddenly, I felt very cold.

THE PARKING LOT AT Jake's Bar N' Grill was empty, save Diana's massive motorcycle. One sad, pale lamp flickered above the front door, its bulb already half obscured by falling snow.

"Regal," I muttered.

I swung open the door, and a tired, older waitress gave me a passing glance. "Meeting your friend, are ya? Go on in," the waitress said, hooking a thumb at the empty dining room.

Diana was sitting alone in the dining room under an impressive assortment of stuffed animal heads and a disturbingly graphic oil painting of Custer's last stand. The ferocity of her gaze made my steps falter in the doorway. Loki pushed past me and sat down across from her. I was reminded again of the Leopold pack's male alpha, 457M. The way he and Vali had bared their teeth at each other, circling and growling. The waitress followed me to the table, handing us plastic-laminated menus after Caroline and I sat down. Mine felt sticky.

"Drinks?" she asked.

"Just water for me," Caroline answered. She looked tired under the restaurant's fluorescent lights.

"I'm good with beer," I muttered. "Whatever's on tap."

The waitress nodded and turned to Loki.

"Do you happen to have a wine list?" he asked, with a wide smile.

The waitress frowned at him. "We've got both kinds," she said. "Red and white."

"Wonderful. I'll have a glass of the red."

Diana said nothing. The waitress shrugged and left. Aside from the faint sounds of country music drifting out of the swinging kitchen doors, the dining room was completely silent.

"You're making a mistake," Diana finally said, her voice low and threatening as thunder.

"Oh, I know," said Loki. "I'm sure the wine will be terrible."

I snorted a laugh at that and tried to turn it into a cough. "So," I said, turning to Diana. "You know this, uh, Loki?"

"Regrettably," Diana said. Her stony frown told me I wasn't about to get any more information out of her.

"Yeah, about that." I forced myself to turn to Loki. "How did you get here? I mean, did someone just drop you off in the middle of the Lamar Valley? Because that's not a safe stunt to pull. The conditions out there can be really dangerous, and if you're not prepared—"

Loki started laughing. My voice trailed off. He leaned back in his chair, and the air around him flickered and shimmered, like the edge of a candle flame. His face changed, shifted, became longer and more predatory. His red hair rose to float above his shoulders like fire, burning and dancing.

I shoved back against my chair. "Oh, my God," I gasped.

Caroline cleared her throat. "Norse, actually," she said. "Norse gods."

Oh, shit. I screwed my eyes shut. That's where I'd heard his name. The Norse gods. Odin. Thor.

"And Loki," I whispered, forcing myself to open my eyes.

Loki was looking more or less human again, thankfully. He raised an eyebrow at me. "At your service."

I tried to suppress my shudder. "I don't know what you're supposed to be the god of."

"Charm, good looks, and wit," Loki said. "Of course, you may wish to inquire into your friend's true nature as well."

"You're fucking kidding me," I hissed, turning to Caroline. She didn't look especially Nordic, not with her black hair and Roman nose, but what the hell did I know?

Caroline's cheeks flushed a deep red. "Oh, not me! I'm from San Diego," she stammered.

A shiver ran the length of my body as I turned from Caroline to Diana. She was tall, Diana. Tall and strong and beautiful. Perhaps a little too tall, too strong, and too beautiful.

"Diana," I said. "Ah, damn. That's the moon, right? The moon goddess?"

"Among other things," Diana said coolly. "The moon. The hunt. Childbirth. And all wild creatures are under my purvey."

Loki snorted. "I'm sure that's a great comfort to their barely sentient little brains. But don't fool yourself. He's no more a beast than you or I."

Another shiver worked its way down my spine. "Why are you here?" I said.

"Yes," Diana echoed. "Why are you here, Loki?"

"Because he broke free," Loki said. "In August. He escaped the prison."

Cold settled over my arms and legs as heavy as ice. August. Vali's face burned in my mind, his golden eyes and wide smile as the wind lifted his hair from his back.

You did this? he said. *I knew you were special.*

"I've been tracking him for ages," Loki continued. "This is the first time he's ever broken the prison."

Diana leaned forward. "And did it ever occur to you he's been running away from *you*, you selfish son of a bitch?"

"I'd say that's been quite obvious for at least the last century. And don't insult my mother." Loki gave Diana a smile that showed all his teeth.

"Who?" My voice sounded very small. "Who broke free in August?"

Loki and Diana glared at each other across the table. Caroline's cheeks burned, and she appeared to be studying the horrible oil painting very intently.

"Who?" I asked again. "Who are you talking about?"

"Salads," the waitress said from behind me, making me jump. She leaned across the table, handing out bowls of what looked like shredded iceberg lettuce. Then she gave us each a tumbler glass filled with ranch dressing.

"Dinners'll just be a minute more," she said.

Caroline took a few, tentative bites from her bowl of lettuce as the waitress retreated.

"It's no matter," Diana said, finally. "You won't find him."

"Of course I will," said Loki. "We've got something he wants."

All three of them turned to look at me.

CHAPTER FOURTEEN

"**I** have no idea who you're talking about," I stammered. "I'm just here because she," I gestured to Caroline, "wanted to see Yellowstone."

"Really?" said Loki. The air in front of him shimmered and rippled. His face shifted, flickering like a flame.

And then I was staring at Vali. Handsome, impossible Vali, with his long, dark hair and high cheekbones. His golden eyes. He was sitting just across the table, painfully close to me. I almost reached for him, almost sank my fingers into his hair and pulled those soft lips to mine—

"You've never seen me?" Loki's voice came through Vali's lips.

Adrenaline spiked, and my heart leapt, clattering against my ribcage. My muscles tensed as my whole body cried out to run.

"Who the hell are you?" I hissed, gripping the edge of the table as if I could somehow force reality to go back to normal by squeezing something really fucking hard.

"I am Loki, father of Vali. And I'm trying to free him." He paused. "It's time for him to come home."

"No." I forced myself to my feet. "I won't help you find him. If he's running from you, there's a reason."

Diana gave a smug smile. "Thank you, Karen. Lie-smith, you are most unwelcome here. I suggest you depart. Immediately."

Loki turned to me. For a heartbeat his face flickered; something deep and angry flashed in his eyes. "Please," he said, the word falling like a stone from his lips.

I shuddered. I'd run away from him too.

"No," I said.

Loki's expression did not change, but he seemed smaller somehow. Caroline took his hand. She was still staring at the painting, although it looked like she was about to cry.

"Karen, you may stay with me tonight," Diana said. "The road to Bozeman will be impassable."

"Thanks," I muttered. "But, Caroline - your flight leaves tomorrow morning, right?"

Caroline glanced around the empty restaurant before speaking. "I don't actually have a flight," she said. "I don't really travel that way anymore. And don't worry, we'll pay for your dinner." She turned to Loki.

And they fucking disappeared.

One minute, Caroline was sitting in front of me, saying something crazy about not having a flight home. The next, I was alone with Diana in the empty dining room of Jake's Bar N' Grill, staring at the glassy eyes of stuffed deer heads on the wall.

"Whoa," I said, sinking back into my seat. "This is quickly turning into the craziest night of my life."

Diana stood. "I'll see you shortly."

I watched as she disappeared through the front door. Snow swirled into the dining room behind her. The low growl of Diana's motorcycle thundered through the dining room and faded, leaving me listening to the clatter and hiss of the kitchen. Somewhere, someone was singing about whiskey for their men and beer for their horses.

"Hey, you want a to-go box or somethin'?" the waitress called.

I turned to see her standing by the kitchen doors with a tray, holding four untouched dinners and a pitcher of piss-pale beer.

I forced a big, happy smile. "Sure. Boxes would be great."

I REALLY DIDN'T WANT to drive back to Diana's house.

For a second, as I pulled my Subaru away from Jake's Grill, I thought there was a chance I could make it back to Bozeman if I just drove really slowly and carefully. But after skidding out at the one and only stop sign in Cooke City, I had to admit Diana was right. The road were impassable, and snow was still coming down. The Park Service had probably lowered the gates over Route 212, meaning I really did have nowhere else to go. I sighed and turned onto the road to Diana's house. The single tire track of her motorcycle was already filled with a thin layer of fresh snow.

Diana's door swung open when I pulled into her driveway, and a fresh round of barking and howling greeted me as Diana stepped into the driveway. She still looked angry, with her arms crossed over her formidable chest, but at least she wasn't wearing her gun this time. I glanced at the four take-out boxes on the passenger seat, had a brief vision of myself getting knocked into the snow by Diana's pack of enormous dogs, and decided to leave them in the car overnight. They'd probably freeze solid.

"Come in," Diana said, making it sound less like an invitation and more like a command.

I followed Diana through her front door, pushing the dogs aside. As I walked into her living room, it occurred to me she'd probably killed all the taxidermied animals in her house, from the black bear by the fireplace to the cougar over the mantle.

"There's pajamas on the couch," Diana said. "And you're welcome to use the shower."

"Thanks," I stammered.

"Tea?"

"Yeah, please."

She left the room without another word. I picked up the blue moon and stars pajamas from the couch and wandered down the hall. Once I found the bathroom, I took a very hot shower and tried to forget everything that had just happened in Jake's Bar N' Grill. Once I'd washed my hair and pulled on pajamas, I felt slightly more normal.

Diana was in the living room, sitting with her legs crossed in an enormous recliner. Two of her hunting dogs curled at her feet. She looked cold and regal in the silver moonlight pouring through the windows.

"Your tea," she said, gesturing to the coffee table.

"Thanks." I sat down and wrapped my fingers around the steaming mug.

We sat in silence for a few minutes. An Northern saw-whet owl called outside the window, sounding small and lonely in the darkness. Diana scratched one of her dogs behind the ear.

"I'm sorry you had to be involved with this," she finally said.

I wasn't sure how to respond, so I turned to my tea. It smelled good, like honey and mint. I took a few sips, and exhaustion settled over my arms and legs. The owl called again. I let myself sink into Diana's enormous couch. It felt very welcoming.

"Time for bed," Diana said. "He'll be waiting."

"Who?" I asked, blinking slowly. My eyelids felt very heavy. "Who's waiting?"

Diana smiled at me. It was disconcertingly similar to the smile she'd given the dog when she scratched its ear. "Sleep well."

With that, she left the room, her dogs trotting after her. I lay down and pulled a blanket over the couch, trying to relax. Diana's living room was not exactly calming. The pale moonlight cast strange shadows over her taxidermied animals, making it look like the black bear's head tilted at a slightly different angle every time my eyes wandered. And I could have sworn the mountain lion blinked at me. I shivered, telling myself sleep may just be impossible tonight.

And then I fell asleep.

SUNLIGHT DANCED ACROSS the nodding heads of grass and the delicate green aspen leaves, filling me with a wave of relief so strong it was almost ecstatic.

"Dreaming," I whispered. "I'm here. Dreaming."

I stepped forward and the aspen trees parted around me. A few more steps and I could see Vali, standing in our meadow.

I paused, frowning. Vali wore clothes, something dark and tight across his back and rear. Heat surged through my core as I stared at his backside, realizing exactly how tight those black pants were. Damn, he looked good dressed. I took another step, leaving the protection of the trees.

My heart plunged.

Someone else was in our meadow. With Vali. Someone tall and proud and beautiful, wearing a delicate blue dress.

"Diana?" I said.

Vali turned, a smile rippling across his face. "Karen!" he called.

I stumbled backward, into the shade of the aspen grove, my eyes stinging. He's wasn't alone. The realization burned. My vision blurred with tears as Vali's warm hands wrapped around my shoulders, his smell enveloping me.

"Are you well?" he asked. "I'm sorry, the last time I saw you, I was—"

"Don't!" I pulled out of his arms and pressed my hands to my eyes, trying to hide the tears. "Don't start. I just came here to warn you. Your...Loki is here. He's looking for you."

"Karen, I know. Diana told me."

I took a deep breath, but I couldn't quite force myself to open my eyes. Diana. Diana and Vali. Of course she's protecting him. They're lovers.

I've been such an idiot.

"Then I guess Diana's got everything you need," I snapped through gritted teeth.

His hand brushed my arm again, and I backed away. "I'm done!" I yelled. "I'm done here. I'm ready to wake the fuck up!"

"Karen, wait—"

But the aspen grove was already vanishing before me.

I gasped and sat up on the couch, facing the black bear in Diana's living room. His wide mouth was fixed open in a permanent grin; it looked like the old stuffed bastard was laughing at me. I wiped away my tears, furious with myself.

"He even told me," I hissed to the bear. "Vali said I wasn't the first to find him in dreams."

The bear grinned at my stupidity, and my heart ached. Of course Vali had other lovers. His father was a god, for fuck's sake. No wonder Vali had the body of a god. My stomach clenched violently and I pressed my hands to my eyes, trying to stop the new tears. Thinking about Vali's body was not a good idea right now.

The hallway flooded with yellow light.

"Karen?" Diana called.

I took a deep breath and briefly considered ignoring her. Then I considered punching her as hard as I could in her beautiful face.

"I'm here." My voice trembled far more than I'd have liked.

Diana stepped into the living room, followed by an undulating cloud of wagging tails and long, pink tongues. She looked strange in the low, blue light. In fact, she looked exactly the same as she'd looked in the dream. She was even wearing the same bizarre, shimmery dress.

"You really don't know much about mythology, do you?" she said, offering me a steaming mug.

"Excuse me?"

This was so far from what I expected her to say that I froze, forgetting to take the mug from her hands. After a moment she set it down on the coffee table and sank into the chair opposite me, crossing her legs in front of her like a closed gate.

"I have no lovers," she said. "Well, no male lovers, at least. And I kill those who try. So, even if Vali were so inclined, I dare say he'd know better."

I stared at her in the thin blue light, unsure how to respond. She gazed absently out the window to the dark, snow-covered forest. One of the dogs let out a long sigh, and she reached down to pat its head.

"Anyway," she said, "Vali, son of Loki, is yours alone."

"Really?" I squeaked.

"Really. And I have to say, you are rather appealing. If you ever change your mind about Vali..." Her voice trailed off and she gave me a slow smile.

I blinked. Did a Greek goddess just hit on me?

"Damn!" Diana yelled, slamming her mug down on the table. She exploded to her feet, the dogs howling around her. "Oh, that lying sack of shit!"

"What?" I asked. "What happened?"

"That bastard!" she hissed. "I know how to cover my tracks. But *you*—" Diana stared at me as if she'd never seen me before. "Of course! You and your little emotional outburst in Morpheus's realm. And Vali's reaction. By all the gods of fucking Olympus, we might as well have lit a signal fire for him."

"For who?" Fear coalesced in my stomach like a cold, hard stone.

"Loki's found him," Diana said. "Loki's got Vali."

My heartbeat surged. "What? How?"

"Through you, damn it. Loki must have tracked you through your dreams and used Vali's little emotional outburst to find his physical location. And now Loki's got him. Loki's finally trapped him."

My stunned brain snagged on something she said. "Vali had an emotional outburst?"

Diana ignored me. "Get your boots. I may be able to use you."

I jammed my feet into my duck boots and stood up, not bothering to lace them. "What can we do?"

Diana barely looked at me when she grabbed my arm. The room spun—

CHAPTER FIFTEEN

—And I was suddenly very cold.

Diana and I were outside, in a great, moonlit field. The air was very still, and the snow glowed with a silver light that shivered and undulated like a mirage. The cold air cut through my pajamas and stung my nostrils, making it hurt to breathe. My skin tingled all over. Something tall loomed before us, a blinding tower of snowflakes. It looked almost like a snow devil, those little tornados that sometimes flickered across the plains.

But it's wasn't moving.

"Lie-Smith," yelled Diana, her voice hard and cold. "I will kill you."

I turned. Diana stood next to me, her arms outstretched. She held a pistol with both hands. I followed the barrel of her pistol to see where she was aiming.

Loki.

He stood before the snow devil in his black suit, his flaming hair streaking out behind him. No, he wasn't exactly standing. He was staggering. His arms stretched in front of his body, with his palms facing the column of frozen, crystalline flakes. He looked very pale; a trickle of blood flowed out of the corner of his mouth.

He ignored us completely.

"Shit," Diana muttered.

A shiver of fear traveled along my back as I turned from Loki to the tower of snow crystals. Each flake held perfectly still, as if an entire storm were trapped between sheets of glass. And there was something *inside*. Something dark twisted and writhed within the column of snow. The flakes sparkled cold and hard in the moonlight as the dark shape whirled inside them, but they did not move.

The clearing filled with a harsh, animal cry, and I turned to see Loki falling to his hands and knees. The snow tower collapsed with him, sending a gust of crystal flakes dancing across my boots. The strange silver light vanished from the snow, and the moonlight grew colder. Loki's shoulders heaved as he spat blood onto the snow.

"Shit!" Diana yelled.

I looked up.

Vali stood in the middle of the field.

He was completely naked, with his arms crossed over his muscular chest and his bare feet planted in the snow. Loki's rasping breath echoed across the snow as he climbed to his feet. The air felt thick and heavy, like a thunderstorm, as the two men faced each other.

"Father," Vali said, his voice cold.

Loki smiled. Blood leaked from his mouth and dripped down his chin. "Come with me," he said.

"To stand in judgement for my crimes?" Vali asked.

Loki shook his head, still smiling. "No. No judgement. Just come home."

"You expect me to believe you?"

"I could force you," Loki said.

"Could you?" Vali asked, tilting his head at Loki.

Loki raised his hands, his palms facing Vali. A booming, echoing explosion ripped through the still air, and Loki collapsed against the snow.

"GO!" Diana yelled. Her gun still pointed at Loki. A thin trail of smoke rose from its barrel.

"Holy fuck," I whispered, staring at the crumpled mess of Loki's body on the snow. A dark stain radiated from his shoulder and crept slowly across the moonlit snow.

Snow crunched behind me. Vali, I thought, my mind spinning. Vali's naked. In the snow.

"Vali!" I yelled. He was almost to the trees, and he didn't look back.

"Diana!" I turned to her, screaming. "Vali, he's naked! He's naked in the snow!"

Diana walked past me without saying anything. Loki struggled to his feet, one hand clenched around his shoulder. Blood oozed between his pale fingers. They glared at each other. She did not lower her gun.

"Hello!" I yelled. "Vali is naked! He's *naked*! He'll freeze to death!"

Loki and Diana both ignored me. Oh, fuck, I thought. Oh, fuck. I turned and started to run.

IT WAS EASY TO FOLLOW Vali's footsteps across the frozen field. I sprinted after his tracks, the frozen air burning as I pulled it into my lungs. His footsteps turned once I reached the trees, and I followed. The snow was spotty on the frozen ground beneath the dark lodgepoles. Vali's tracks wove in and out of deep shadows.

"Vali?" I called, slowing to a trot.

My voice echoed strangely in the still, moonlit air, and the shivers in my arms and legs became violent tremors I struggled to control. Rubbing my hands over my thin cotton pajama top, I turned in a slow circle, searching for Vali's footprints.

I didn't see anything. My teeth began to chatter, and I crossed my arms over my chest. If I could just find my own footprints, I could backtrack until my trail met up with Vali's.

I turned in another circle. The trees were thick here, and there was hardly any snow. I didn't see anything that looked like a footprint. Or rather, everything looked like a footprint in the strange, stark moon-shadows.

"S-shit," I whispered, my teeth clanking together as my muscles contracted violently in an attempt to generate heat.

I took a few deep breaths and tried to think rationally. I was wearing pajamas. I didn't have a jacket. I didn't have a compass, or matches, or a map. I didn't even have a warm hat.

And I didn't know where the fuck I was.

"D-d-don't panic, K-Karen," I said, wishing my voice didn't echo so strangely across the frozen ground. "Just stay w-warm. Stay m-m-moving. You might get f-frostbite, but you can s-s-survive frostbite."

My hands already felt numb as I curled them around my shivering arms and started to walk toward the most familiar looking clump of trees, scanning the ground for any hint of human tracks. Or not-so-human tracks.

After a lot of staggering, I cleared the lodgepole pines and headed in what I desperately hoped was the right direction. I scanned the forest floor, but a thin scrim of clouds drifted in front of the moon, and my shivering was so violent my vision jumped and trembled. Everything on the ground was a blur, a great gray and white blur.

"D-doesn't m-m-matter," I said. "Just k-keep m-moving."

The ground tipped under my feet, and I found myself walking between sparse, snow-covered aspen. Moonlight gleamed off the fresh, trackless snow; it was beautiful and strangely peaceful. My shivering slowed and finally stopped, thank God. But then my body grew funny, and it was strangely hard to lift my legs.

"Dumb legs," I muttered to myself.

My voice sounded ridiculous, slurred and low, almost like I was drunk. Drunk in the snow. Funny. I started to giggle, weaving stupidly in and out of the trees. My giggles turned into laughs, making it even harder to move my dumb legs. A moment later the ground rushed up to meet me, and I got snow in my face.

It was warm. Warm snow.

I stretched out, spreading my arms through the magically warm snow. It was as welcoming as a feather bed. God, I was tired. I tried to remember what I was doing out here in the first place and drew a blank. It wouldn't hurt to close my eyes for a second, I decided. Just a second.

I into the snow, sighing in pleasure.

"Karen!"

Someone was calling my name. Some distant, male voice. I smiled. It was a nice voice. I should open my eyes for him, I thought, but it was too much effort.

SHIVERING WOKE ME. My entire body was shaking, jolting my head and forcing my eyes open. I blinked at the sudden rush of heat and light. I was staring at an enormous fire in a dark forest, with something soft and heavy over my legs and strong arms wrapped around my waist.

"Shhhhh, you're fine. You're safe."

"W-What?" I said.

Soft lips traced the back of my neck, and Vali's scent enveloped me. Warmth and sweetness.

"Karen," Vali whispered. His breath felt hot against my neck. "I asked you to leave. To go somewhere safe."

"I c-can't leave," I stammered. "I s-s-study the—"

"Wolves. I know." His voice was hardy more than a whisper. "But the wolves are leaving."

My body convulsed with shivers so violent my vision blurred. Vali's arms tightened around my abdomen.

"That's normal," Vali said. "Your body's warming up. You won't shiver much longer."

I nodded, not quite able to speak. I was covered in a dark fur, leaning against Vali's chest with his legs wrapped around mine. We were inches from a roaring fire. The flames danced hypnotically, and I found it impossible to tear my eyes away from them. I didn't think I'd ever seen anything so beautiful.

He kissed the back of my neck again. "What in the Nine Realms were you doing out here?"

"You w-were n-n-naked," I stammered.

He laughed softly. "Did you come to rescue me? You have that little faith in me?"

"N-No." I shook my head, trying to pull my thoughts together. Between the dancing flames of the fire and the heat of Vali's body, it was hard to focus. I grabbed at the soft furs around my body. "Where did t-this come f-from?"

"I've forgotten," he said, his voice soft against my neck. "It's been so long since I had a lover. Karen, any Æsir can pull a few items through the aether, weapons or clothes. Most of them can even travel that way." He sighed. "Not me, of course."

I didn't understand, but I was far too tired to care. I closed my eyes, leaning against the solid warmth of Vali's body. An image flashed through my mind, making me flinch. Loki, crumpled in the blood-stained snow.

"Oh! Vali, your dad! I think...I think Diana killed him."

Vali laughed again. This time there was no warmth in it. "No. He'll be fine, believe me. He's seen far worse."

Vali fell silent, and the flames in front of me caught my attention again. My mind drifted as I watched their scarlet and vermillion dance, heat and light coming together and falling apart, blending and fading and sending sparks to the heavens.

"There," Vali whispered. "Your shivering stopped."

I sighed and let my head fall back against his neck. Vali's hands tightened around my waist, and I realized for the first time we were both naked under the thick, dark fur covering my body. I flushed with a different kind of heat. I moaned and shifted, arching my back to press closer to Vali's chest. Vali flinched and scooted backward, but not before I felt the hard heat of his erection.

"I'm sorry," he said. "I'm not trying to seduce you. You were so cold, I thought the warmth of my body—" His voice cut off as I rocked my hips against his.

My stomach tightened in a familiar way and heat rolled down my body, coating the inside of my thighs. His cock pulsed against the small of my back, and his hands trembled against my stomach.

"Karen. I didn't mean to—I mean, we don't have to—"

I wrapped my fingers around his and pulled his hands up to cup my breasts. My nipples tightened under his palms. His hands were so warm; they left trails of smoldering embers across my skin, like my entire body ignited under his touch.

Vali groaned as his hands brushed my nipples. "Oh, you have no idea how hard it is to resist you," he said, his voice thick.

I pressed into his chest, my hips rubbing his cock. "Don't," I moaned. "Don't resist me."

His chest shuddered and he turned, lowering me to the furs. I spread my arms above my head, offering my entire body to him. Our lips met in a soft kiss as his hands followed the curve of my breasts and stomach, his touch setting me on fire. He was still kissing me when his hand spread my legs and pressed against my sex, his thumb circling my clit. I gasped into his mouth as my hips rocked against his hand.

Vali pulled back, smiling. "I really did only want to warm you," he whispered.

"I'm warm," I gasped.

"Are you?" His fingers pressed harder, and the waves of pleasure crashed through me, leaving me gasping for air.

"I'm warm!" I cried. "Oh, I'm warm!"

He grinned and lowered his body to mine, his chest hair rasping against my tight nipples as his hips pushed my legs apart. I moaned when his cock slid inside me, hard and hot, filling me almost to the point of pain. He sank his fingers into my hair and kissed me deeply, pressing me into the fur. I held still for as long as I could, feeling him pulse inside me, his heat and sweat covering me as our tongues intertwined and our bodies joined.

But it wasn't enough; I wanted more. I tilted my hips, pushing him deeper.

"Oh, yes," he groaned.

He caught my bottom lip in his teeth, then moved to my neck, nipping my skin and sending explosions of heat and pleasure skating through my body. I closed my eyes, surrendering to him, drowning in him. His hips matched my rhythm, first rocking slowly and then, as the heat between us built, moving faster and faster. The flames of the fire leapt and danced as our bodies came together, and oh God, he made me feel good, he made me feel so good—

I cried his name, sinking my fingers into his back as the orgasm burned through my body, blurring my vision and singeing every nerve ending. Vali stiffened above me, gasping as his cock shuddered deep inside me. A heavy, wet exhaustion rolled over me in waves as Vali shifted, wrapping his arms around my waist and pressing his body against my back, enveloping me in his warmth.

Closing my eyes, I let sleep take me.

I WOKE TO BIRDSONG, although it took my brain a moment to place the familiar sharp *de-de-de*.

Chickadee. It was a mountain chickadee.

I opened my eyes to the soft, gray light of early morning. A chickadee hopped from a low branch on the nearest lodgepole to the snow-covered ground, tilting its head at me. *What are you doing here?* It seemed to say.

I rolled over and pressed my palms to my eyes, trying to remember what I was doing in the woods.

"Something wrong?"

I turned. Val was lying next to me. My heart surged, and for a moment I thought I might actually cry. He was so damn handsome in the pale morning light, with his eyes soft and his hair messy from sleep.

"You're still here," I whispered.

He grinned. "Of course I'm still here. You didn't think I'd leave you, did you?"

I swallowed, not wanting to admit that was exactly what I'd expected. "But you're still...I mean, you're not a wolf."

The shadow of a frown passed across his face. "No. I'll not be a wolf again, I think."

"You can't change?"

He shook his head. "I've never been very good with magic. And that spell was...Well, it took three of them to cast it, and you saw what it took my father to break it."

I shivered as I remembered Loki falling to his hands and knees in the meadow with blood trickling from between his lips. And that was before Diana shot him.

"Your father," I said. "Is he going to find you, now?"

Vali shrugged. "Diana slowed him down. I'll have time to prepare. Don't worry about me."

An insane idea blossomed in my consciousness. "Come with me!" I cried. "Vali, if you're not going to be a wolf again, then come home with me! I've got plenty of room, I'd love to have you—"

He shook his head. Disappointment cut through my gut like a knife.

"It's not that simple."

"But you could hide in Bozeman," I said, knowing full well I had no idea what I was talking about. "I mean, there has to be a way to protect you from Loki. We could figure it out!"

"It's not just that. It's here, it's this place. Can't you feel it?"

His golden eyes met mine, and he looked almost pleading. I took a deep breath, closed my eyes, and listened. I could hear my heartbeat and Vali's deep, even breathing. The cold air smelled of snow and pine. And maybe something else, some flicker at the edge of my consciousness. Like a hint of smoke in the air.

"See," Vali said, lowering his voice until I could hardly make out his words. "There's a monster here."

I opened my eyes, and whatever I'd felt vanished in the sparkle of early morning sunlight on the snow.

"Isn't that a very good reason to leave?" I asked, trying to keep my voice light.

He smiled. "Perhaps. In another lifetime. But not now. Not when I have something to protect."

I reached for his hand and wove my fingers through his. Our lips met for a soft, lingering kiss. When he pulled away, his eyes glittered strangely in the growing light.

"I'm so sorry," he said. "I'm no kind of lover for you, beautiful Karen. I can't even offer you a proper meal."

My stomach cramped uncomfortably at the word *meal*. I tried to ignore it. "You saved my life last night."

He shook his head. "All I could give you was a moldering bear fur and a fire on the snow. Any proper Æsir could have done better. Shit, my brother would have brought a four-poster bed."

His voice cut off, and he sat up, turning away from me. Cold air rushed into the furs, filling the space between us, and I shivered.

"I wouldn't say the fur is moldering," I said, feeling stupid. "And the fire was nice, too."

Vali's dark curls swirled across his back as his head shook. "Diana," he called. "Diana!"

"I'm here."

Diana appeared at the foot of the bear fur. The train of her dress brushed the ashes of the fire. I jumped, pulling the furs up to my chin.

"Will you?" Vali asked in a low voice.

"Of course," Diana said.

Vali turned to me. His eyes shimmered in the pale light. "Karen," he whispered, "go somewhere safe."

"Wait, what? No! Vali, I don't want to lose you again—"

Diana knelt before me and touched my arm under the furs. The forest disappeared.

CHAPTER SIXTEEN

I opened my eyes in Diana's living room. I was on the couch, still clutching an enormous, black fur to my chin. A fire roared on the hearth, and several dogs sprawled across the floor, snoring. Diana stood next to me in her blue dress.

"You'll want breakfast," she said briskly. "Perhaps a shower first?"

I nodded, trying to keep my tears from splashing over my cheeks.

"Twenty minutes, then." Diana turned and left the room.

I couldn't quite force myself to say thank you.

My neatly folded clothes were waiting for me in the bathroom, next to a clean pink towel. I took a very long shower, trying to think of nothing more than the rush of hot water against my skin. When the shower began to sputter and turn lukewarm, I turned it off and wrapped myself in the pink towel. I stood in Diana's bathroom, naked and dripping wet, for a long time. It seemed like admitting defeat to put my clothes back on, as if I was admitting defeat by re-entering the real world, the Vali-less world, and pulling on my flannel-lined jeans. But as the steam dissipated and the bathroom slowly filled with the aroma of frying sausages, and I finally decided I was hungry enough to surrender to reality.

"Elk sausage, scrambled eggs, and coffee," Diana said, pointing to the counter as I entered the kitchen.

I nodded and filled a white plate with a mountain of eggs and sausages.

"You'll be tired today," Diana said. "Recovering from hypothermia does that. Take it easy, okay?"

"Sure," I said around a mouthful of sausage.

I ate in silence as Diana leaned against the kitchen counter, her arms crossed over her chest. "The roads are clear," she said, once I'd finished off my second helping of eggs. "You can go home."

I closed my eyes, willing myself not to cry again. "And Vali? Is he...Is he going to be okay?"

"I'll do what I can," she said.

"If you see him, can you tell him..."

My voice trailed off as I realized I had no idea what to say next. Tell him to forget about being chased by his father, and whatever's going on in the park? Tell him to come to my place so I can fuck him senseless?

I sighed and poured myself another mug of Diana's coffee. I already felt exhausted. The drive from Cooke City to Bozeman was going to take everything I had; I couldn't afford another stupid sobbing breakdown.

"I'll give him your regards," Diana said. She gave me a small, sad smile which made me feel about ten times worse.

"Thanks," I said, pushing back from her kitchen counter. "I'll see you around."

"I hope not," she muttered.

I decided to pretend I hadn't heard her.

FIRST THING MONDAY morning, I got an email from Professor Caroline Laufeyiarson.

Thank you so much for your help, she'd written. *I wish you all the best. If you need anything, please don't hesitate to ask.*

"Fuck you," I told my computer. "You used me, you and your creepy husband. You used me to get to Vali."

I hit the delete button so hard I hurt my finger.

"You okay, Boss Lady?"

I jumped in my chair and spun around to see Zeke leaning against the doorway to my office.

"Or do you always cuss out your computer on a Monday morning?" he asked, with a slow grin.

I smiled, feeling a little better now that Caroline's message was in the little electronic trash can of my inbox. "Honestly, me cussing at my computer's not that unusual. You've got something for me?"

Zeke's smile faded. "Yeah, in the lab."

I pushed back from my desk and followed him across the hall. Colin was sitting in front of a computer in the back corner, his feet on the desk in front of him and weird electronic dance music pouring from his headphones. There was an open Red Bull can and a half-eaten tuna sub sandwich on his desk, in direct violation of the "No Food or Drink" signs posted on every single wall. Zeke pulled a rolling chair to his workstation, sat in it backward, and typed frantically.

"Here it is," he said, tilting the monitor to show me the map of Yellowstone. A constellation of yellow dots appeared, ringing the edges of the map.

"Shit," I whispered. "Is that...?"

"Yup. Boss Lady, the caldera basin is officially empty. The wolves have left the building."

I sat down heavily in the chair next to Zeke. It squeaked in protest.

"They're headed out of the park," Zeke said. "All of them. We're looking at, hell, at least half the packs in Yellowstone are at or possibly even over the borders of the park right now. I mean, it's winter now and things are quiet, but once those fucking beef cattle start popping out babies and the wolves gobble 'em up, it's gonna be a double-D shitshow."

"What did your friend say?" Colin asked from behind me, making me jump. He was so damn quiet, I hadn't heard him leave his desk to join us.

Zeke took the bait. "Yeah, sexy naked wolf man. What's he got to say about the situation?"

"Nothing. He said nothing." I glanced from Colin to Zeke. They had almost identical grins plastered across their faces.

"Ah, you two don't do much talking, is that it?" Zeke drawled.

"Stop it," I said, standing up. "I do sign your paychecks, you know."

Zeke held his hands up in front of him, shaking his head. "It's cool, it's cool. I don't judge, Boss Lady."

I FLEW TO MAINE ON Christmas Eve, even though I could only spare three days for the visit. In our five years of marriage, Barry and I had never once spent a Christmas in Maine, and I felt like I owed my parents at least another five Christmases just to make up for that. Besides, the idea of spending Christmas by myself in Bozeman was just depressing. And my crazy idea of spending Christmas in a West Yellowstone hotel, hoping my dreams could still pick up on Vali, was even worse than depressing.

My dad met me at the airport in Bangor. He was on the sidewalk outside baggage claim, standing next to his ancient Chevy pickup with the wooden canoe rack on the top, his breath steaming above him. He hugged me with one arm and grabbed my suitcase with the other.

"Thanks for picking me up," I said as I climbed into the cab. It was warm and smelled vaguely of tobacco and motor oil, scents I would always associate with my dad and the afternoons I'd spent as a child in his mechanic's shop.

"Ayuh." He nodded as the engine started with a roar. "Didn't want you to have to rent a car."

I smiled. Barry and I had only come to Maine a handful of time, and he'd never quite understood my parents' obsession with saving us money on rental cars. He was appalled when Dad pulled up to Boston's Logan airport with a chainsaw and a pile of coiled, rusty wire in the bed of his pickup, and his entire face turned beet red when Dad thumped Barry's brand-new leather-sided suitcase on top of them. Barry fucking Richardson, I thought, would have made a shitty Mainer.

Unexpectedly, Vali surfaced in my mind. His high cheekbones and long hair. His sweet, animal scent, his soft touch and hungry eyes—

"You okay?" Dad asked.

"Huh?"

"You're awful quiet," he said.

I laughed. It came out sounding awkward and forced. "Yeah, I'm fine. It's just been a long semester."

My dad nodded in the fading December light. "Well, you're home now. You can sleep if you need to."

I yawned and leaned back against the headrest, cocooned by warmth, the rocking of the cab, and the dull and distant hiss of tires along the interstate. My eyes closed.

I DREAMT OF YELLOWSTONE. The sulfur smell of geothermal features hung low and heavy over the snow, and the bare aspen trees cast long shadows in the late evening light. I looked around, trying to orient myself. The sulfur in the air meant I must be in the caldera, the heart of Yellowstone's massive supervolcano, but I didn't recognize the slumped, rolling hills in the distance. They were stained red with the setting sun, like distant fire. I shivered. There was another scent beneath the sulfur and the swirling snow. Distant, acrid smoke.

Footsteps crunched across the snow behind me. I turned to see Vali. I tried to call to him, but my voice made no sound. His eyes glossed over me to focus on the distant red-tainted hills. He walked quickly, and a great, black cloak flared behind him. I followed, silent and distant. When he turned, I saw the sheath of a great broadsword strapped to his back, beneath his waves of dark hair.

Vali stopped before the great yawning black mouth of an enormous cave. His breath steamed into the evening sky. That acrid burnt smell was stronger here, so strong I almost choked. The last of the day's light flickered red and golden on the snow surrounding the cave.

Something is wrong here, I thought, my heart hammering against my chest. Something is very wrong.

Vali pulled the sword from its sheath on his back. The enormous blade glimmered blue in the fading light. He swung it in a great loop over his head, and it hissed through the frigid air. My stomach clenched violently. A sudden gust of wind swirled frozen crystals around Vali, lifting his hair from the back of his neck, filling the air between us.

I tried to scream, but the words caught in my throat. Vali strode into the darkness of the cave, his back straight, his head held high. He did not look back.

I JUMPED AS A HAND closed on my shoulder.

"You okay?" Dad asked.

"Yeah," I muttered, fighting the adrenaline surge flooding my body. "Sorry. Fell asleep."

Dad gave me a strange, measured look. The car had stopped, and I recognized the metal walls of McDonald's Auto Repair through the windshield. The yellow glow of the floodlight outside the garage made my dad look old and tired. I smiled to show him I was fine, but my entire body felt cold and my hands were trembling.

"It was just a dream," I said, half to myself.

But it was never just a dream with Vali, was it? I fumbled with the latch on my door. Cold air flooded the inside of the truck, stinging my cheeks.

"Let's go in," I said, trying to give my dad a big, reassuring smile.

Together, we picked our way up the ice-slick driveway from Dad's shop to the house. Christmas lights shimmered along my parents' porch railing. It was so cold the snow squealed under our boots. Dad held the door open for me. The house smelled exactly like I remembered, a heady mix of wood smoke and moose roast, and some of the panicked fear from the dream began to fade from my body.

"Dinner's ready when you are," Mom said, coming out of the kitchen to hug me. "It's moose and potatoes from the garden, but the biscuits come from the store."

I took a deep, shaky breath, trying to forget Vali's tall, graceful body swinging the shining blue sword in an arc above his head. And vanishing into the gaping black mouth of the cave.

"Thanks," I said weakly. "Sounds delicious."

I took a long, hot shower after dinner and headed downstairs to join my parents for a glass of scotch on the couch next to the glittering lights of the Christmas tree. Mom had hung ancient strands of big-bulbed multicolor lights across the mantle and all the way around her huge, gilded fleur-de-lis crest. Dad is Scottish, the great-grandson of a MacDonald from the Highlands, but Mom is French.

When I was growing up, Mom told me her grandmother Claire was descended from the royal Orleans who fled France during the Revolution. I never exactly believed her; our little log cabin deep in the Maine woods was a damn far cry from Versailles. But on my first date with famed literature professor Barry Richardson, after we opened our second bottle of wine, I told him I was descended from the royal French family Orleans. He seemed impressed. At least, he was impressed enough to invite me back to his house that night.

When I met Barry's family a year later, in their cavernous white home overlooking the Atlantic Ocean, Barry introduced me as Karen McDonald, related to the royal Orleans family of France. As if that would make up for the log cabin, the Maine accent, the fact that I could operate a chainsaw and change the oil in my pickup truck. His parents were not particularly impressed by me. Not then, and not in the years that followed.

I shook my head and took a healthy sip of my scotch to get rid of Barry Richardson. "Mom," I said, "you can go ahead and fill the stockings."

Mom was sitting by the winking embers of the fire, knitting. She looked at me with shock. "You know Santa doesn't come until you're asleep!"

I laughed. "Mom, I'm thirty-seven!"

She smiled at me but didn't move to fill the stockings. "So, honey, are you seeing anyone special out there in Montana?"

I managed to stifle my groan with another mouthful of scotch. At least she waited until after dinner to bring this up. "Uh, no, not really."

"Not really?" she asked. She'd stopped knitting, which was a bad sign.

I finished my scotch in one gulp, trying to pick my words carefully. Of course I wasn't *seeing* Vali. I hadn't seen him in a month, not since the morning I woke up in his arms, wrapped in furs in the middle of Yellowstone. My chest tightened. I asked him to come home with me.

And he said no.

"That's the end of the story," I whispered.

"What's that?" Mom asked. Now both my parents were staring at me.

Blood rushed to my cheeks. "I think I'm going to bed," I said, standing with a really exaggerated stretch. "You know, so Santa can come fill the stockings."

Mom frowned, and I felt a twinge of guilt for letting her down.

But honestly, what the hell could I say to explain Vali?

CHAPTER SEVENTEEN

Three days later I was back in the airport, heading home with a brand-new hand-knit hat, scarf, and mittens, plus an emergency survival kit for my car, thanks to Santa. Not that I was complaining. I gave my folks gift certificates to their favorite diner and a subscription to a Portland microbrew-of-the-month club. The McDonald family was nothing if not practical.

I had to take three separate flights to get from Bangor, Maine to Bozeman, Montana. Of course, I got stuck at O'Hare, and I spent my entire four hour layover frantically emailing John my notes for the faculty meeting I was now going to miss. Then I had to sprint through Denver International Airport to make it onto the tiny propeller jet headed to Bozeman. It was the last flight of the day, and everyone in the plane looked either pissed off or exhausted. Or both.

I leaned back in the seat and closed my eyes—

—I WAS STANDING IN YELLOWSTONE. It was night, and there was no moon. Even the stars looked faded, as if the darkness spilling from the mouth of the great, looming cave before me was somehow sneaking across the sky, blotting out the sparks of light.

"Vali?" I whispered in the darkness.

There was no response. The burnt smell hovered in the air, stinging my nostrils. I took a step closer to the cave.

"Vali?" I said.

My voice echoed across the open space, sounding far louder than it should have been. The world seemed to be trembling, holding its breath.

Waiting.

I woke shivering, and I spent the rest of the joltingly bumpy flight to Bozeman staring out the window, trying to convince myself there was nothing blotting out the icy pinpricks of stars above me.

IT WAS TEN BELOW ZERO in the Bozeman airport parking lot, and my goddamned car wouldn't start. I left my suitcase in the trunk and walked back inside, blowing on my fingers in the baggage claim, waiting for Courtesy Services to give me a jumpstart.

By the time I made it home it was just past midnight, which meant it was two in the morning in Maine. I'd been traveling for twenty hours. There was a sparkly gift bag wedged behind my screen door, but I didn't see it until I'd kicked it halfway across the living room.

"Shit," I muttered under my breath.

I turned on the light to see what I'd just sent skidding across the floor. It was a bottle of Glenlivet single malt scotch, from Susan. *To Karen,* she'd written. *For all the odd goods.* I smiled for the first time since I left the Bangor airport twenty hours ago. The scotch went on the kitchen counter, and I collapsed into my bed.

But my dreams were unsettled and disturbing. I woke tangled in the sheets, my heart racing, certain I'd been running from something low and dark and close behind my back.

Headlights swept my bedroom ceiling in a cold, pale arc as I stared at the ceiling. My heart knocked frantically against my rib cage. The alarm clock on my dresser said it was barely past three in the morning. I sighed and kicked off my blankets. If I wasn't going to sleep, I might as well answer some emails.

I heard someone in my kitchen.

It was impossible, but I heard the soft *tsh* of a cabinet drawer closing, and then the low hiss of the kitchen faucet.

I froze. My muscles tensed and my fingers knotted into fists. Was it Susan? Who the hell else had a key? I looked around my darkened bedroom for something I could possibly use as a weapon. I didn't own a gun, and all my knives were in the kitchen. I needed something solid, something heavy... I finally settled on a lumpy, oversized coffee mug I'd gotten from a local artist at the farmer's market.

I came to my feet as silently as possible and wrapped my hands around the coffee mug. The back of my mouth tasted metallic and bitter. Taking a deep breath, I crept toward the kitchen, trying to see what I could make out in the dim glow of the streetlight outside my window. Someone was standing at my kitchen stove. Someone tall, dressed in black. My fingers tightened around the coffee mug as I prepared to bring it down on his skull.

But I hesitated. What I saw didn't make any sense. The man in my kitchen wasn't going through my stuff, trying to steal God knows what from my cabinets. He was just standing there, at my stove, watching the red glow of the burner under my tea kettle. I frowned.

The dark figure turned to me.

"Karen," he said. "Lovely to see you again."

The light switch clicked on, and I flinched at the flood of white light. The man smiled. He was very tall, with red hair. And he wore a dark suit.

Loki.

The last time I saw him, he'd been pulling himself out of the blood-stained snow in Yellowstone.

"What the *fuck* are you doing in my kitchen?" I yelled.

He looked from my stove to the counter next to my sink. Three mugs stood in a neat row on the speckled countertop. "I'm making tea. Or would you prefer the scotch?" He gestured to the Glenlivet bottle on my kitchen table.

I shook my head. "No. What the fuck are you doing here? Now?"

"Making tea," he said again. He gave me a disarmingly handsome smile, and I had to fight the urge to smash the coffee cup into his face.

My tea kettle whistled, and Loki moved to the stovetop, pouring hot water into the three empty mugs. My kitchen filled with steam and the scent of lavender and chamomile. Loki picked up my white coffee mug with MAINE written on the side in bright red lobsters and offered it to me. I shook my head. Then I stared back at the kitchen counter, and my heart jumped.

"Why are there three?"

Loki smiled, grabbed the remaining two coffee mugs, and walked past me into the living room. "Come on," he said. "We've got something to discuss."

There was a soft rustling noise in the living room. I followed Loki through the door. He bent over my couch, handing a mug to a dark figure sitting on my couch.

"Caroline?" I asked.

"Hi," she said, somewhat apologetically. The swell of her pregnant belly was enormous; she looked pale and tired in the half-light from my kitchen. "Sorry about this. I didn't want to wake you."

"What are you doing here?" I demanded. "I mean, shouldn't you be..." My voice faltered as I made a vague hand gesture around my abdomen.

"It's fine," she said, waving her hand dismissively. "I'm on sabbatical this semester."

"That's not exactly what I meant," I said, trying not to stare at her stomach.

She laughed. "Oh, right! No, the baby's not due for another two weeks. And besides, it's not like getting to the hospital is going to be a problem." Her eyes flickered over Loki, and she smiled.

Loki did not smile. I felt the first small tendril of fear creep along my back, and I wrapped my arms around my chest. "What's this about?"

Loki met my gaze. "Vali," he said.

The fear gathered in a hard knot, low in my stomach. "No way. No fucking way. I'm not going to help you. You tricked me this fall. Both of you. You set me up so you could catch Vali."

Caroline held her hands up. "I'm sorry about what happened in November. If there had been another way—"

I laughed, but it came out as more of an angry bark. "Oh, screw you! You knew *exactly* what you were doing. You wanted to find a wolf, right? Well, you could have told me you were looking for Vali! You could have told me—"

"And what, exactly, would you have said to that?" Loki said, his pale eyes flashing.

I fell silent. The soft tick of the clock in my study filled the room. The refrigerator hummed. Finally, I shook my head and stepped back.

"Vali doesn't want to be found," I said. "So, I'm not helping you. And there's nothing you can say that will change my mind."

Caroline sighed. Loki's hand moved to cup her shoulder, but his eyes didn't leave my face. The clock in my study ticked again.

"There's the front door," I said, pointing. "Shall I open it for you?"

"Karen," Caroline said. "Let me explain—"

"No." I stalked to the front door and opened it. A blast of cold air rushed into the room, ruffling the stack of Christmas cards on my coffee table. I tilted my head toward the door.

Loki followed me, stepping onto my front porch and offering Caroline his hand. She stepped outside, wrapped her arms around the swell of her stomach, and shivered. Ice crystals shimmered on the sidewalk, reflecting the light spilling out my windows.

"Well," I said, reaching to close the door, "it's been a pleasure."

"He loves you," Loki said.

My hand froze above the doorknob. Loki reached out and pulled the door closed between us.

CHAPTER EIGHTEEN

The clock in my study ticked. My refrigerator hummed and then clicked off. I swallowed, trying to force myself to turn around and walk away from the door.

He loves you.

"It's a trap," I whispered. "It's another goddamn trap."

I closed my eyes and saw Vali, his back straight, his head held high. Vali holding that great, blue sword. Vali walking into the looming darkness of the cave.

With a sigh, I opened my front door. Loki smiled at me in the dim light.

"Come on," I grumbled. "We can talk."

I walked to the kitchen, grabbed the bottle of Glenlivet and three glasses, and carried them to the living room. I poured three generous servings; if I was going to face Loki again, I at least wanted a stiff drink. I handed out the scotch and sank into my couch without a word. Caroline took a tiny sip while Loki and I both drained our glasses.

"Tell me what you want," I said as the scotch burned its way down my throat.

Caroline sighed, handing her scotch to Loki. "How much do you know about Norse mythology?" she asked.

I snorted. "You mean, do I know your husband is the God of Lies?"

Loki rolled his eyes; Caroline ignored me. "Do you know about Yggdrasil?" she asked. "The World Tree?"

I shook my head. My Google searching had stopped at Loki. Caroline straightened her back and somehow managed to look professorial, despite the fact that she was sitting on my couch at three in the morning, wearing what might have been pajamas. "According to Norse myth, there's a great Wyrm named Níðhöggr coiled in the roots of the World Tree."

"A what?" I asked.

"Dragon," said Loki, his voice low and cold. "Níðhöggr is a dragon, perhaps *the* dragon. It lives in the roots of the World Tree, and it has slept for millennia. Now it sleeps no more."

"Hang on a minute," I said. I grabbed the Glenlivet off my coffee table and poured myself another glass. After a moment's hesitation, I refilled Loki's glass too. He drank it in one swallow and then exhaled jaggedly.

"My son does not trust me," Loki said. "He would not see me, and he would not speak to me of his plans. We all sensed the Wyrm's awakening, but now it's grown stronger, and the entire area is heavily warded. I cannot travel there, not through the aether."

He paused, and his gaze lingered on the Glenlivet bottle. I poured him another glass, which he drank in one slug.

"And I can no longer sense my son," he said.

"Wait, what about Diana?" I said. "She's not exactly your biggest fan. And she said she'd protect Vali. Did she make it so you can't travel there or, uh, sense him? Is she hiding him?"

Loki shook his head. In the pale light spilling from my kitchen, he looked tired and sad, with strange shadows creasing his lips and the corners of his eyes. "This is not her doing. This magic is older and more powerful than either of us."

"Okay," I said, taking a deep breath. "So, there's a dragon in the roots of the World Tree. But what's it doing here? In Montana?"

"This is an odd place," said Loki, rolling his empty glass in his palms. "There are some places where the Nine Realms are far-flung, and there are some places where they are stacked tightly, one against the other. Where the borders between them are thin."

I leaned forward and poured him another glass of scotch. Odd goods, indeed.

"Thank you," he said. Then he raised an eyebrow at me. "Didn't you ever wonder why boiling hot water pours from the ground in this place?"

"Well, that's because in Yellowstone the earth's crust is—" I paused.

"Thin?" Caroline asked.

I took a deep breath and decided to just let this debate between science and mythology go. "There's a...dragon," I said. "And Vali, what? He went after it? He went to stop it?"

"I don't know," Loki said. There was a sharp edge to his voice. He raised his glass to his lips and drained it.

"Look," I said, "I hate to disappoint you, but it's not like Vali texts me or anything. I haven't seen him since November."

Loki stared at me. For a heartbeat something flashed in his pale eyes, something dark and feral and howling. My stomach clenched painfully, and I turned away, my breath catching in the back of my throat, the words I was about to speak dead in my mouth.

"I saw him," I said. My voice sounded choked and thin, as if it came from far away. "I dreamt of him. On Christmas Eve. He had a blue sword, and he...He went into a dark place."

Loki closed his eyes. "So, he's found Hrotti," he muttered. "Vali has claimed the ancient sword of heroes."

I felt cold as I remembered the dark mouth of the cave and the burned tang in the air. "What do we do?" I said.

Loki shook his head and ran his fingers through his hair. Caroline wrapped her arm around his shoulders.

"What do we do?" I said again. "You came here for a reason. You want something from me. What do you want?"

For a long time neither of them moved. The refrigerator kicked on again with a hum; the clock ticked softly in my study. Finally, Loki sighed and reached for the Glenlivet. He divided the last of the scotch into our two glasses.

"Take us there," he said, raising his glass to clink against mine. "Maybe it's not too late."

I WAS ALMOST TO MY kitchen to make a pot of coffee when something caught my eye. It was a slender, red book, tucked in the far corner of my shelf. *The Red Dragon: Reexamining the Subverted Self in Early Medieval Literature.* By Barry R. Richardson.

Wondering for the hundredth time why I hadn't just thrown the damn thing out, I set the empty scotch glasses in the sink and flicked on the coffee maker. *The Red Dragon* was Barry fucking Richardson's sixth book, the one he'd dedicated the me. That goddamn book was the reason we had our honeymoon in Wales, where I spent most of my time getting quietly drunk in quaint little pubs while Barry spent all day doing some sort of research in obscure libraries.

I laughed. At first, I tried to hide it, but the more I tried to stop, the harder I laughed, until I finally had to sit down at my kitchen table, my face buried in my arms and my shoulders shaking. When I was finally able to breath without dissolving into giggles, I saw Caroline standing in the doorway with a deeply concerned expression on her pale face.

"Is everything all right?" she asked.

"Oh, fuck," I said, wiping my eyes on the sleeves of my pajama top. "It's just...It's my ex-husband. He would love this."

For once Caroline looked completely lost. I stood and took the glasses from her hands, putting them in the dishwasher.

"Barry Richardson," I said. "My ex. He's a professor at Northwestern. He studies medieval literature. And he just—" I had to stop as my words dissolved into a fit of giggles. "He just loves dragons. I mean, he had a fucking dragon tapestry in his office. He probably still does."

"Oh," she said. "That's... funny?"

I snorted another laugh and grabbed a few coffee cups from the cabinet. "It is funny," I said. "Can I get you some coffee?"

I filled a mug and turned to her. A bolt of panic shot through my chest. Caroline was hunched over against the counter, her hand pressed to her side and her face contorted in pain.

"You okay?"

"Yeah. Yeah, fine." Her back straightened and she exhaled sharply. "It's just, uh..." She waved her hand, looking around the kitchen.

"Braxton-Hicks?" I asked.

"That's right. Just false contractions." She smiled, but her voice wavered.

I glanced toward the living room. Loki was still sitting on the couch, staring out the darkened windows.

"Listen," I whispered, "I don't mean to be insulting, but is there a reason you need to be here? Because the park, right now... it might not be the best place for someone who's about to have a baby."

She shook her head. "Vali won't talk to Loki. But he talked to me. Once. Besides, I'm not due for another—" She gasped and bent over again, hand pressed against her side.

"How far apart are they?" I whispered.

She shook her head. "They're not... contractions. They're not consistent." She stood back up and turned toward the living room, her eyes softening as she stared at Loki. "Do you know how long he's been looking for Vali?"

"I don't even want to know," I said, and I handed her a cup of coffee.

CHAPTER NINETEEN

W e were out of my house, coffee in hand, by four in the morning.

As I locked the front door, I had a sudden, irrational urge to call someone and tell them where I was going and what I was doing. I couldn't tell John, of course. I'd lose my job if the other Natural Science professors at Montana State heard I was looking for a dragon in Yellowstone. And Susan would think I'd lost my mind.

Strangely enough, the one person in the entire world I actually wanted to call was Barry fucking Richardson. I pulled my phone out of my pocket and stared at it as my breath escaped my lips in billowing white clouds. I hadn't talked to Barry since we'd finalized the sale of the condo in Florida. What time was it in Chicago? Almost five in the morning? He'd be awake, I bet. He'd be at his desk, hunched over his computer.

Would he answer the phone?

"Is there a problem?" Loki asked.

I shook my head and shoved my phone back in my pocket. "Sorry. No problem."

WE WERE THE ONLY CAR on the highway.

The moon set over the horizon as we left Bozeman, and the winking stars felt very close, almost pressing down against the windshield of my Subaru. Loki and Caroline sat together in the backseat, and the driver's seat felt like its own little world as my

Subaru crested the pass through the Gallatin mountains and began to drop into Paradise Valley. I remembered Vali, and the way the wind lifted his hair off his neck. He'd looked so strong and proud the last time I saw him. The familiar slow heat of arousal spread through my body.

"Don't," Loki growled from the backseat.

"Excuse me?" I said.

"Don't think about it," he said. "We don't want to draw its attention."

"Oh, come on! How the hell would you know what I'm thinking?" I checked my rearview mirror, but it was too dark to make out Loki's expression.

"I don't, of course," he said. "But I can smell you."

"Smell...?" My voice trailed off as his words registered. I shifted, suddenly painfully aware of my damp underwear.

"Unless you were thinking about someone else when you got so turned on?"

"Loki!" Caroline hissed.

"And if you're thinking of Vali, you'd also be thinking of Níðhöggr, no?" Loki murmured. I didn't need to see him to know he was smiling.

A cold knot of fear settled low in my stomach. "Fine," I muttered. "I won't."

"I cannot read thoughts, but Níðhöggr can," Loki said. "And it would be best not to warn it of our approach."

I tried to bring my mind back to Vali, to his strong body and easy smile. Not to the monster who might be waiting for us in the wilderness, just past the black, yawning maw of that cave.

And I was thinking about the dragon again.

I smacked my steering wheel in frustration. "Damn it, you can't say, 'Don't think of something!' Then it's all I can think about!

It's like telling someone not to think of an elephant. Boom! Now everyone's thinking of a fucking elephant!"

Caroline laughed from the backseat.

"Talk about something," I said. "Please. Let's talk about something that's not batshit crazy."

"Fine," Loki said. "What would you like to talk about?"

"I don't know!" I snapped.

"Do you want to hear how I met my wife?" he asked.

"Oh, don't you dare," Caroline said.

"No!" I said. "No, God, no. Just tell me something, I don't know. Something happy."

Loki sighed. And then he told a story. I tried to remember it, even as he was telling it and the miles spooled away beneath my tires and the stars shivered above my dashboard. It was a story about elves and dwarves, wickedness and heroism, sacrifice and love. But even then, even as I drove my Subaru through the sweeping vastness of Paradise Valley, between the great mountain ranges, I couldn't quite grasp it. Somehow I knew, even then, that parts of the story would come back to me, over and over, for my entire life. Sometimes even now, when I'm falling asleep or just upon awakening, I swear I've remembered it. But then I blink, and the story vanishes again.

By the time Loki fell silent, we'd been traveling through Yellowstone National Park for over an hour. The sky was an opalescent gray above the Absaroka mountains, and only a handful of stars remained in the indigo sky to dance above us. Thick silence rippled from the backseat, filling the car.

"Is that the end of the story?" I asked, finally.

Loki laughed. I realized I could just make out his reflection in my rearview mirror. "Of course not," he said. "No story ends. Now pull over just up here."

My tires crunched over the snow as I slowed and turned off the road.

"Hey, I remember this place. This is where I picked you up in November," I said.

I turned to the back seat. Loki gave me a distracted smile. Caroline's eyes were closed, and her pale, furrowed brow gleamed with sweat.

"You go ahead," she said, leaning her forehead against the door frame.

I shrugged and opened my door, bracing myself against the cold. The snow underfoot squealed in protest as I followed Loki to the edge of the highway. We'd parked in front of a low sagebrush-dotted rise. Loki took off, climbing the slope despite the knee-deep snowdrifts. I was panting by the time I caught up with him, and the cuffs of my jeans were frozen.

He stood at the top of the rise, his arms outstretched, his palms up. The clouds above us were streaked with pink; the cold air tore at my throat.

"It's too far," he muttered. "We'll never make it on foot."

"What's too far?"

Loki turned to me, narrowing his odd, pale eyes. "Can you sense it?"

I tried to ignore the cold and remember the last time I'd seen Vali. Can't you feel it? Vali had asked me. I closed my eyes, reaching for that feeling, that sense of something gone wrong.

Yes, there it was. The frozen air held an angry, burnt scent. It was the same acrid smell that had drifted from the looming darkness of the cave in my dreams.

"There," I said, opening my eyes and pointing into the gloaming. "What direction is that? South, south-west?"

Loki nodded. "Very good. I was right about you. But it's miles away, and I can't travel with these damn wards—"

He froze and turned back to the road. Then he ran down the hill, vanishing faster than I would have thought possible. By the time I made it halfway down the hill, he was already at my car. Caroline leaned against the roof with Loki at her side. As I crunched through the snowdrifts on my frozen feet, I heard Caroline's wavering voice. Counting. My stomach lurched, and my legs felt painfully heavy.

Caroline looked up as I approached. Her eyes seemed very large in her pale face. "I'm sorry," she whispered. "I think...I think my water broke."

My chest tightened. I remembered that fear. Before the pain, before my contractions felt like anything more serious than a runner's cramp, there was a cold, hard fear. And the struggle to keep fear from turning to sheer panic.

"Hey, it's okay," I said, putting my arm around her shoulders. She felt very small under my huge down jacket. "You're going to be just fine. I can help."

She took a deep breath. "They're still a few minutes apart."

"Great," I said. "Let's get in the car."

Loki helped her to the backseat and closed the door gently. Then he turned to me, his pale eyes wide.

"We're at least three hours from the nearest hospital," I whispered. "Can't you whoosh her away?"

"No, I cannot," he snapped. "These are the most powerful wards I've encountered."

"She can't have a baby in Yellowstone, Loki!" I hissed, squeezing my fingers into a fist.

"Damn it." Loki shook his head. "Take us to Artemis. Please."

"What?"

"Oh, whatever you call her. The moon. The huntress. The one in charge of childbirth."

"Diana?"

Loki nodded and I climbed in the car, trying not to listen to Caroline's low, animal whimpers.

"Just hang in there," I said as the engine revved to life. "We're not far."

My knuckles blazed white on the steering wheel as we climbed into the jagged Absaroka mountains. Away from the hospital.

"Fuck," I muttered under my breath. "I hope you know what you're doing, Loki."

CHAPTER TWENTY

The sun crested over the snow-capped mountains just as we pulled into Diana's driveway. Loki opened the backseat door before I'd even slammed my Subaru into park, and he was on Diana's doorstep before I could unbuckle my seatbelt.

Diana's front door opened slowly, spilling golden light into the cold, early morning air. She looked enormous and unforgiving in the doorway, with her arms crossed over her formidable chest. I couldn't believe I'd ever mistaken her for human.

Loki fell to his knees on the hard-packed snow. "Artemis," he said, his voice jagged. "Help my wife."

The car door opened behind me and Caroline stepped out, resting heavily against the roof of the Subaru. None of us moved or spoke. Diana's eyes traveled over me to Caroline, hunched and panting behind me, and finally came back to Loki, kneeling in the snow.

"Please," Loki said. The word sounded like it had been ripped from his lips.

Diana's expression grew even colder. "If I do this, you will be in my debt," she said.

"Of course," Loki said, through gritted teeth.

Diana stepped around him to Caroline, extending her arm. The barest hint of a smile flickered across her lips, although I couldn't tell if it was welcoming or victorious. "My dear," Diana said, "please come inside."

Caroline hesitated. Her eyes darted to Loki. When he nodded, she took Diana's arm. Together they walked toward the cabin. Loki stood and stepped out of their way, but Caroline stopped in front of him.

"My husband comes too," she said.

Diana shook her head. "That's ridiculous."

Caroline dropped Diana's arm and reached for Loki. Their hands locked together. "Then I don't want your help," she said.

There was another long silence, broken only when Caroline gasped and doubled over, grabbing her side. Loki wrapped his arm around her waist. His fire-red hair rippled as a gust of wind shook a glittering cascade of ice crystals from the pines.

Diana spat a long stream of thick, greasy words that could only have been curses before shaking her head and opening her front door. "Fine," she hissed. "Come in."

Loki and Caroline walked in together, arm in arm.

Diana turned to me. "You too," she yelled. "I'm going to need all the help I can get."

Trying to ignore the sinking feeling in the pit of my stomach, I followed Loki into Diana's cabin.

"Karen, to the kitchen," Diana barked when I walked through her front door. "There's food, water, juice. Bring it all."

I nodded and turned down the hallway. Diana's fridge was disturbingly well-stocked, especially for someone who lived two hours away from the nearest grocery store. I filled a few plates with cheese, crackers, and grapes, poured glasses of water and juice, and arranged them all on a gleaming silver tray I found leaning against Diana's coffee maker.

An enormous fire roared on the hearth when I entered the living room. The huge glass-eyed taxidermied animals stood sentinel as Caroline and Loki embraced by the fire, their bodies rocking together. Her arms wrapped around his shoulders and his hands pressed into the small of her back. I had to turn away.

I stood like that with Barry. With that thought I was back in Chicago, back in the sterile hospital room, surrounded by the beep and glow of machinery, holding my husband and trying to breathe as the birthing contractions ripped my body apart.

"Thank you, Karen," Diana said, taking the tray from my hands.

I shook my head to clear the memories. "No problem. Anything else I can do?"

Diana glanced at Caroline and Loki. They could almost be lovers, slow dancing in the middle of Diana's living room. "Stay close," she said. "The baby's coming fast."

I leaned against the doorway and felt rather useless as Diana held a glass of orange juice to Caroline's lips. Caroline drank it in hesitant little sips, then collapsed against Loki, her eyes closed and her head resting on his chest.

Diana knelt in front of them, closing her eyes and running her hands over Caroline's stomach. She nodded, stood, and whispered something to Loki. A moment later Caroline's back stiffened and she moaned, burying her face in Loki's chest.

"Breathe," Diana said. "Try to relax." Then she turned to Loki. "Get her out of her clothes. I'll bring a robe."

Caroline whimpered, and Diana walked back to me. "Get the towels," Diana whispered. "Down the hallway. Second door on the left."

"Yeah, sure. How many?"

"All of them!" Diana snapped.

I stumbled into the hallway. It felt absurdly good to be away from the heat of the fireplace, so I leaned against the wall and took a few deep breaths, trying to process this crazy morning. When I felt slightly closer to normal, I looked for the second door on the left. It turned out to be a linen closet smelling vaguely of cedar and stacked with a rainbow of towels. I grabbed as many as I could carry and around.

Then I heard the first scream.

When I got back to the living room, Caroline was on her hands and knees on the polished wood floor, a long, dark robe draped over her back. Loki knelt next to her, their faces so close they could be kissing. Diana was rubbing her back. I suddenly felt embarrassed. I was trespassing, after all; I hardly knew these people. I had no right to be here—

"Towels!" Diana barked.

I jumped to obey, dumping my armful of towels next to Diana. The air in the living room now carried the iron tang of blood mixed with wood smoke from the fire, the heavy scent of sweat, and the thick, animal smell of amniotic fluid.

"Here," Diana grabbed my wrist and pulled me to my knees. "You. Rub her back. Right here."

She guided my hand to the base of Caroline's spine and pushed. I followed her lead, digging my knuckles into the soft fabric of the robe and pushing on the knotted muscles beneath. Caroline's body was shivering in long, slow waves.

Diana rocked back on her heels and reached between Caroline's legs. "The baby's posterior," she said, "but she'll flip around. In the meantime, it's going to be... uncomfortable."

Caroline whimpered again, almost a sob. Loki leaned close to her, their cheeks pressed together, and whispered soft and low in her ear.

"This wasn't...the plan," Caroline panted. "I wanted...painkillers. All the painkillers."

Despite myself, I laughed out loud. Even Diana smiled.

"You're going to be okay," I said, pressing my hands into the hard muscles of her lower back. And, for the first time since I saw Caroline doubled over against my kitchen counter at two this morning, I actually believed it.

"I'm repositioning the baby," Diana said. "It's going to feel a little strange."

Caroline nodded, her long, dark hair sticking to her forehead. Diana moved her strong hands quickly over Caroline's stomach and between her legs, pressing in ways that were uncomfortable to even watch. Caroline winced but didn't cry out. Once Diana declared the baby properly positioned, she told Caroline to stand up and walk.

Loki helped Caroline to her feet, and together they made a slow circle around the living room, pausing every few seconds while Caroline's body stiffened and rippled with another contraction. After about ten minutes, Caroline fell to her knees in front of the fireplace with a low, grunting moan.

"It's time," Diana said. She spread towels across the floor and helped Caroline roll onto her back.

Loki knelt behind Caroline, his arms around her chest, her face resting in the hollow of his neck. Caroline's breathing was fast and shallow, and her eyes were glazed.

"Karen, get over here," Diana ordered. "Hold her leg."

I knelt on the towels, trying to avoid the pool of blood spreading from beneath Caroline's body as I braced her leg against my shoulder. I tried to find somewhere to look that wasn't the mess of blood and hair between her legs, or her face pressed against Loki's cheek, his lips touching her forehead.

"Good," muttered Diana. "Very good, Caroline. Now, push when you feel the—"

Caroline's body tensed, and she screamed in a high, animal cry. Her leg bucked and kicked against my shoulder. Then she fell back against Loki's chest, whimpering.

"I'm here," he said. In the flickering light of the fire his lips and cheeks looked odd, like they were covered with thin, pale streaks. "I'm here with you," he whispered.

"Good, very good," Diana said, running her hands along the curve of Caroline's stomach. "Keep pushing."

I glanced down, following Diana's hands, and I saw the baby's bright pink scalp beneath the dark mess of wet hair pushing to enter the world.

"Once more," Diana coaxed.

Caroline cried again as her leg kicked hard against my shoulder. The baby's head emerged, pale, waxy with vernix, and streaked with blood; for a heartbeat the world held still as I stared at the tiny, squished little face and thought how odd, how incredibly odd it is to have life, any life, anywhere.

Caroline moaned, and the baby's shoulders emerged. Diana wrapped her fingers around the child as the rest of the tiny body slid into the world, wet and wrinkled and purple. The infant filled her little lungs and shrieked. Her cries of protest reverberated off the walls and filled the world.

"A girl," Diana sighed.

She placed the child gently on Caroline's chest and rocked back on her heels, wiping her hand across her face. I lowered Caroline's leg and watched the infant, the tiny new life who just entered this world.

The baby girl's sobs turned to gasps and grunts as Caroline and Loki wrapped their arms around her tiny body. The blood-streaked umbilical cord stopped pulsing, and the baby stared groggily around the room, her cloudy blue eyes unfocused in her wrinkled face.

Loki bent to wipe the blood from her hair with his palm and kiss the furrows of her tiny forehead. "Adelina," he whispered.

"Adelina Lokisdóttir," Caroline said.

I looked up. They were both crying. I wiped my cheek and realized I was crying, too. My stomach lurched violently. It was far too hot in this room. I turned away from the new family and stumbled to my feet. The room spun around me, and I braced myself against the wall. *Don't. Don't think about—*

No good. I ran down the hallway, ripped open Diana's front door, and staggered outside. The cold hit me like a sledgehammer, bringing fresh tears to my eyes. My vision blurred as I staggered to my car, doubled over in the snow, and vomited.

I fell to my knees, sobbing, my body doubled over and heaving, the cold air ripping my throat with each ragged gasp, an ocean of tears cascading to the snow.

Meredith.

Her name burned in my chest. Meredith Richardson.

My girl. My baby girl.

CHAPTER TWENTY ONE

By the time I could breathe again, my legs were numb. I wiped my eyes and nose on my sleeve, and noticed with a detached sort of interest that I was shivering. The top half of my shirt was soaking wet from my tears, and my jeans were frozen from kneeling in the snow for God knows how long. The sunlight falling through the lodgepole pines behind Diana's house seemed very bright. I dropped my head to my chest and took a deep breath before reaching for the bumper of my Subaru and pulling myself to my feet. My chest felt raw and hollow, like the inside of a vast, echoing bell.

"I'm so sorry for your loss."

I turned to see Loki several steps behind me, a white coffee mug in his outstretched hands. "I'm also deeply grateful for your assistance," he said.

He walked toward me, and I took the mug. My hands trembled as I brought it to my lips, taking a long sip of something rich and smooth.

"What's this?" I asked. My voice was ragged.

"Mostly Bailey's," Loki said. "With a shot of coffee."

I took another sip. Heat slid down my throat and into my stomach. "How did you know about my... loss?"

He shrugged. "You wear it on your face. It makes you very beautiful."

"That's the most fucked up thing I've ever heard," I rasped. Then I paused, remembering our conversation about the dragon. "Well, one of them, at least."

I drained the coffee mug in silence. My shivering finally subsided as warmth from the drink spread throughout my body.

"Vali had a brother," Loki said, softly. I turned to him, but his eyes were far away, somewhere above the jagged treetops.

Somewhere over the mountains, a red-tailed hawk cried, sharp and lonely. The sun vanished behind a cloud, and I shivered again.

"Do you want to talk about it?" I asked.

He turned to me with a smile that did not quite reach his cold eyes. "Do you?"

A hard knot tightened in my chest. "We had maybe twenty minutes," I said. "Maybe half an hour. With our girl, with Meredith. Twenty minutes to hold her, to feel like this would actually work, like all the problems between us were somehow...manageable. That we could pull together and make a family."

I reached up to wipe the fresh tears from my raw cheeks. "The arteries to her lungs never fully developed. She survived for almost a week, inside a ventilator. By the end they were giving her blood transfusions hourly. And then she just—"

My throat tightened, and I waved my hands in the air. As if I were describing a bird, taking flight. I stamped my feet in the snow and coughed to clear my throat.

"I haven't talked about this in five years," I said.

Loki nodded, his eyes on the mountains. I wrapped my arms around my shoulders and took a deep breath of cold air. Somehow, I felt better.

"Vali is the second born son of my wife Sigyn," Loki said, his voice as soft and cold as the snow. "Our firstborn was named Nari. He took after me, in almost all respects. He was small, cunning, gifted in magic. But Vali...I suppose Vali was all the things I once wished I could be. Strong. Bold. There was no doubt Vali was one of the Æsir, even from the day of his birth."

Strong and bold. I remembered Vali's blue sword glinting in the light as he walked into the cave, his head high. Absurdly enough, I smiled. Strong and bold sounded about right.

Loki shifted in the snow. "Listen, Karen. I've something to tell you. Not because I seek absolution, but because it may prove important, to you and to Vali."

He took a deep breath and turned away, running his fingers through his hair. "I've done many things I lived to regret. And I expected punishment. When Óðinn, Thor, and Skadi led me underground, when I saw the great snake. Well, I wasn't exactly surprised. But when they brought in Sigyn and my sons—" He shook his head. "I thought I was being given a chance to say goodbye."

Loki fell silent.

"You didn't get to say goodbye?" I asked.

"You have to understand," Loki continued, as if he hadn't heard me, "Óðinn couldn't kill me. Óðinn and I have sworn an oath of brotherhood, and it's no small thing to kill your brother. But I pushed him too far. I expected to be shut away, locked up and forgotten until they all had a chance to cool down. I thought it would be a simple thing. Even as they led me into the ground, I was imagining how easy it would be to escape."

The white mug in my hands had turned cold. "So, is that when you escaped? When they brought in your family?"

"That was when they turned Vali into a wolf," Loki said, the words falling from his lips like cold, hard stones. "It was a brutal spell. Complicated. Painful. I've never heard anyone scream like that."

I shivered again, although this time it had nothing to do with the cold.

"When the spell was over, Vali was trapped inside the wolf's body. He was terrified, mad with pain and rage. And Nari...I believe

Nari wanted to help, actually. He ran to his brother's side." Loki paused. Somewhere in the distance, a red-tailed hawk cried, its call slicing through the frozen air like a knife.

"Vali ripped him apart," Loki finished.

I opened my mouth but could find no words. *I am dangerous,* Vali told me, again and again.

"But...why?" I whispered.

"To bind me. I can travel the aether better and faster than any of them. I can take almost any form: animals, insects, all the members of the Æsir. The only thing that could bind me in that pit, and truly hold me, was a part of myself."

Understanding dawned slowly. My body rippled with a low, sickened tremble. "They used your son?"

Loki nodded. "His small intestine, specifically. Óðinn and Thor bound me. The very men who taught Nari and Vali how to fight. They couldn't kill my children themselves, of course. Shedding the blood of another Æsir, an innocent Æsir, is a serious offense, almost as unforgivable as violating the oath of brotherhood. Hence the spell to transform Vali."

"Holy shit." The coffee and Baileys turned over in my stomach.

Loki cleared his throat, and I turned away as he wiped his eyes. "My wife Sigyn died in that pit, after a millennium of imprisonment. I promised her I would find Vali, undo the spell, somehow heal the damage inflicted on our son. Because of me. Yet here I am, and again Vali is gone." His voice made a strange sound as he said *gone*, almost like ice cracking on a frozen lake.

"Hey," I said, wrapping my hand around his arm. "It's okay. We'll figure this out."

He turned to me. Something raw and painful flashed deep in his pale eyes. I smiled. Never in my life had I tried so desperately to look confident.

"We'll figure this out," I said, leading him toward Diana's cabin. "We'll find Vali. I promise."

I pushed open Diana's front door and led Loki into the hallway. He hesitated on the doorstep, just long enough for me to worry what the hell I'd do if he started crying. A small, hiccuping shriek sounded from the living room and Loki stepped past me, his face once again perfectly composed.

DIANA'S KITCHEN WAS filled with the steam and sizzle of cooking sausages. She stood at the stove, poking a metal spatula into an enormous frying pan.

"Anything I can do?" I asked.

Diana turned to me, her eyes serious and dark. "I know what he's going to say. I want you to know you can ignore it. You can just go home."

I shrugged, figuring it would do absolutely no good to ask Diana what in the holy hell she was talking about.

"Maybe some breakfast first?" I asked.

Diana sighed, and I felt a pang of guilt, like my decision to stay and have sausages and scrambled eggs with the woman whose baby I'd just helped deliver had somehow disappointed the goddess of childbirth. Then she handed me a tray filled with coffee mugs and ushered me into the living room.

Caroline smiled at me. She was propped up on cushions on Diana's dark blue couch. Adelina was wrapped in a white blanket and curled against her chest. Loki sat next to her, his eyes on his daughter. Now that she had been cleaned and dried, Adelina's hair was a brilliant shock of red. Even the tiny eyelashes casting delicate shadows over her full cheeks were red.

"She's gorgeous," I whispered, and I meant it. She looked like an illustration in a storybook: the perfect baby girl.

"Thank you," Caroline said. "Thank you for everything."

I nodded. My chest felt hollow and wrung-out, echoing with old memories. I suddenly felt restless. Maybe I should take Diana up on her suggestion. Maybe I should just leave.

Diana snorted as she entered the room, balancing an enormous tray filled with plates of sausages and scrambled eggs. "That child has a lot of her father in her," she said. It did not sound like a compliment.

"Thank you," Caroline beamed.

Diana rolled her eyes as she set the tray down. I took a plate and glanced toward the door, wondering when it would be socially acceptable for me to leave. Being in Diana's house with Caroline and Loki was making me strangely uncomfortable. I'd been single for a long time; I'd gotten used to living alone and answering to no one. It wasn't often I felt this aching loneliness, this vast, white need for someone with strong arms around my waist, and a sweet, wild scent, a muscular body rippling under mine—

With a start, I realized everyone in the room was staring at me.

"Sorry," I said, wiping my eyes with the back of my hand. "It's been a long night, I guess. What did I miss?"

Diana turned to Loki. "I suppose you were right," she said.

The infant on Caroline's chest wiggled, grunted, and fell silent. Everyone stared at me again. I shifted uncomfortably.

"Will someone please just tell me what's going on?" I said.

"You love Vali," Loki said.

I opened my mouth, but nothing came out. The dull ache in my chest intensified. The last time I'd seen Vali came back to me in a flash, the early morning sunlight on his sleep-soft eyes and tousled hair.

Come home with me, I'd said. *Please.*

My chest tightened as another memory percolated through my consciousness. My first year in Montana, I'd woken up almost every morning sobbing. At the time I hadn't understood what the hell was happening to me, and I'd spent that entire year terrified of slipping back into the depression that sent me crawling to my parents in the first place.

But now it seemed obvious. My dreams of Vali stopped when I moved out of my parents' cabin. I'd lost the man I loved, and I woke up every morning missing him so deeply it hurt.

I swallowed hard and nodded at Loki.

"I love him as well, obviously," Loki said, continuing the conversation as if I hadn't just been emotionally gutted and hung to dry. "But our relationship is...complicated. Still, I'm willing to go after him."

"No." Diana shook her head. "That's a terrible idea, and you damn well know it. Even if you didn't have a newborn child to care for."

"That's not an issue," said Caroline, locking eyes with Diana. "I'm perfectly capable of caring for Adelina until he returns."

"Of course it's an issue. Don't be obtuse. But it's not even the worst part of that idea. The dragon—"

"Níðhöggr," said Caroline.

Diana waved her hand dismissively. "Whatever you call it. That monster can sense magic from miles away. Loki would never be able to find it."

Loki smiled. "So what exactly do you propose? Abandoning Vali to his fate?"

Diana scowled. "You know, you're a real asshole sometimes."

Loki spread his arms wide, looking quite innocent. Aside from the sharp gleam in his pale eyes.

I bit back my frustration. "Could someone please tell me what's going on? For once?" I pleaded.

To my surprise, Diana spoke. "We all felt the dragon awaken. That's why I came here, to monitor the situation, and I believe it's what drew Vali to Yellowstone as well."

"Oh," I said. My voice sounded small and pinched. "Is that why he went in the cave? To, uh, monitor the situation?"

Loki cleared his throat and leaned forward. "No. I think he went in the cave to be a hero."

The room fell silent.

"You mean he's trying to stop the dragon?" I said.

"Well, we can't really tell," Caroline said, glancing at Loki. He nodded, and she continued. "I've only talked to him once, but he said the situation was getting worse. And he said he wanted to do whatever he could to protect you. So, we think—"

"Wait, what?" My head was spinning. Suddenly the room felt very warm and far too small.

Loki gave an exasperated sigh. "Vali's in love with you. If Níðhöggr decides to destroy this place, you'll be killed. That's not a bad reason to be a hero."

My heart hammered against my ribcage as his words sank in. "But... he hasn't stopped the dragon, has he?"

"No," said Loki. "Vali has not stopped Níðhöggr."

An even worse thought took shape in my consciousness, and my gut twisted. "Is Vali... Is he still alive?"

Diana and Caroline both shifted uncomfortably.

"I cannot tell," Loki whispered, his voice low and rough. "I do think...That is, I believe, if he died, I would know. I would feel it. But I can offer no guarantees."

"You think you would know?" My voice had a ragged, sharp edge I couldn't hold back. "You *think?*"

"Even my magic has limits," Loki said. "And Níðhöggr's wards are strong. Until you told us of your dream, I wasn't even certain Vali had approached Níðhöggr's den."

"So, what can we do? How do we get to Vali?"

Loki fell silent. Diana cleared her throat.

"You don't have to do anything," Diana said. "You can go home."

"And leave Vali?" I couldn't sit still anymore. I jumped to my feet, my restless energy forcing me to pace the room. "No, I can't. I won't. I'm not going to leave Vali if there's a chance he's—"

My voice cracked and broke apart. I squeezed my hand into a fist, holding my breath until I stopped trembling.

Caroline cleared her throat. "We don't really know much about the Níðhöggr," she said. "But only someone who has a very strong bond with Vali could hope to find him. Even then, the experience is probably going to be extremely dangerous."

I straightened my shoulders. It didn't feel like much of a decision. Dangerous hardly mattered when weighed against the possibility of losing Vali forever. "Okay. So. Where do I go?"

Diana looked out the window, her brow furrowed in the pale morning light. "I've tried to find that cave for five years. The dragon moves. It hides its den."

"I've had similar experiences," Loki said. "Artemis and I can both sense Níðhöggr's presence, although we can't get close." He raised his eyebrow at me. "But you can also sense it."

I sighed. "Yeah, I guess. I can smell something, at least."

"Then you may be able to find Vali," Loki said.

"But didn't you say it's far away?" I asked.

Loki shrugged. "I'd guess it's at least ten miles from the road."

"Great," I muttered. "So, I have to follow the smell of smoke for ten miles. Across the backcountry of Yellowstone. In January. Piece of fucking cake."

CHAPTER TWENTY TWO

I sat down heavily at Diana's kitchen table and reached into my pocket for my phone. Exhaustion pressed down on me as I scrolled through my contacts, and I reached for my coffee mug, scowling when I discovered it was empty. Ten miles through the backcountry is a big deal. The snow could be five feet deep in the valley, and I'd never make it on foot. I'd need my skis, warm clothes, food, and water. Damn, I might even need my tent and sleeping bag. I shivered. Diana's house was at least three hours from Bozeman; if I drove home, got my skis, and came back to Yellowstone, it would almost be dark.

No. I couldn't wait; Vali needed me now. So I needed someone in Bozeman, someone I could trust to grab a few things and meet me in Yellowstone. Susan was the obvious choice, but she was in Wyoming with her family until the semester started. I bit my lip. John? No, I had no way to explain what I wanted that didn't make me sound like a lunatic. Well, damn. That really only left one choice.

I sighed and tapped my phone.

Dialing Zeke, the screen read.

"Boss Lady!" Zeke was pretty damn cheerful for nine in the morning. "What's up?"

"I need a favor," I said. "A big one."

"Yup, no problem." He didn't even hesitate.

I took a deep breath. "Okay. My spare keys are under the flowerpot on the front porch of my house. I need you to go into my garage and bring me a few things. My cross-country skis and boots, my down jacket from the hall closet, my backpack, a couple of water bottles." I paused for a breath. "Are you writing this all down?"

"Oh, I got it." He sounded disturbingly cheerful. "You going somewhere?"

"Uh, yeah. Do you think you can get that for me this morning? Don't worry about getting any work done, okay? Just call me when you leave Bozeman, and I'll meet you in Mammoth."

I paused. This was going well.

"Awwwww, hell yeah!" Zeke cheered. "This is about Wolf Man, isn't it?"

I groaned.

"You know why the wolves are leaving the park, don't you? Well fuck me sideways and call me Betty, Boss Lady, you're gonna do something about it, aren't you?"

"Just bring me my stuff. Please. And I'll..." I took a deep breath. "I'll explain when I see you. I'll *try* to explain."

Zeke whooped over the line. "Fucking yeah, this is awesome. Just wait till I tell Colin. Don't worry, Boss Lady, we've got your back. One hundred percent."

"Colin? No, you don't have to—"

But the line had already gone dead.

"Shit," I muttered, cupping my head in my hands. The dull thud of a coffee mug on the table made me look up.

"Got you a refill," Diana said.

Diana set a coffee mug on the table as I shoved my phone back in my pocket.

"Thanks. I guess this could be my last cup of coffee for a while," I said, trying to sound like I was joking.

Diana gave me a small, sad smile. I turned away, not wanting her sympathy. Or anyone's sympathy. Exhaustion hovered somewhere on the edge of my consciousness, like a black cloud just beyond the horizon. But I couldn't afford to rest, not right now. Not when Vali needed me.

The surprisingly loud cries of newborn Adelina filled the kitchen in sharp and angry bursts as I finished my coffee and Diana turned on the tap, filling her sink with hot water and lemon-scented suds. Adelina's sobs felt like little needles across my skin, pulling my heart in strange directions. I pushed back from the table and walked to Diana's coffee maker, biting my lip as I refilled the mug yet again. God, I missed Vali. What I wouldn't give to curl up in his strong arms right now, to forget about dragons and babies—

I jumped as my cell phone buzzed against my leg. It was a new message from Zeke: *Boss Lady - headed out. See U @ Mammoth.* My heart jolted sharply against my ribcage.

"Well, shit," I muttered. "That's the first time Zeke's ever been early. For anything."

"Your companion?" Diana asked.

I shook my head.

"No. Just my graduate student. He's meeting me in Mammoth with my gear."

Diana nodded thoughtfully. "Good. It's easier when you aren't alone."

I took a deep breath and then another long sip of hot coffee, hoping caffeine and adrenaline would counteract the sleepless night. "Guess I'd better get going, then," I said.

Diana nodded once, curt and professional, and my heart gave a strange twinge. I hadn't realized how much I'd been hoping she would have some last minute plan.

But that's me, of course. I was the last minute plan.

I set my mug in the sink and left Diana to the dishes.

CAROLINE GAVE ME A wide smile when I walked into the living room. She was breastfeeding Adelina, and I was surprised I didn't feel uncomfortable at the sight of her bare breasts. Maybe watching her give birth had moved us past the awkward discomfort stage. Or maybe my growing sense of impending doom was drowning out any squeamishness about nipples.

"Well, that was a hell of a way to have a baby," I said, running my fingers through my hair.

Caroline laughed. "Yeah. I just wish I could think of some way to explain it to my mom. She's going to kill me if she finds out I'm in freaking Montana."

Adelina grunted loudly, and we both smiled.

"It's hardly the first thing in my life that's failed to go according to plan," Caroline said, shrugging as she adjusted her arm under Adelina's tiny body. "I'm so sorry I'm not more help. I wish I knew more about Níðhöggr. I wish I could do something."

I opened my mouth to say *don't worry about it,* and then shook my head. "Honestly, I don't know if anything would help at this point."

"Still," Caroline's cheeks flushed. "Listen, about November. I'm really sorry. I never should have... I mean, I should have been straight with you. From the beginning."

Diana's black coffee churned uncomfortably in my gut, and I shook my head. "It's okay. I can understand. I mean, you could hardly tell me you were looking for the son of a Norse god."

She smiled. "Still, for what it's worth. I'm sorry."

My throat went dry. This all sounded uncomfortably like what you told someone you didn't expect to see again. "It's fine," I said, swallowing. "We're cool."

Adelina grunted and squirmed, and Caroline shifted to pull the robe back over her breasts. She gave me an apologetic smile as she moved Adelina to rest on her shoulder.

"You know, I don't have a lot of, well, friends," she said, her voice low. "But, after everything that's happened, with November and yesterday, I'd like to consider you a friend. If you, um, don't mind."

My shoulders relaxed somewhat. "Listen, if we survive all this, there's a great wine bar in downtown Bozeman. I'll take you out."

She grinned. "Good plan."

THE ROADS WERE CLEAR and empty, so I figured I'd arrive in Mammoth at least thirty minutes before Zeke and Colin. It was the off-season, and the whole town would be shut down, but if I were mildly lucky I'd be able to buy a topographical map at the Visitor's Center. It couldn't hurt to get a few maps, even if what I was looking for was almost guaranteed not to be on any of them.

But, forty-five minutes later, the Visitor's Center was closed, and Zeke's banged up Camaro was parked at the base of Mammoth hot springs. I pulled up next to him and saw Colin in the passenger seat. Also odd. Both of them jumped out of the car, smiling. They were wearing snow pants.

My heart jumped, and I tried to tell myself that snow pants didn't necessarily mean anything. Zeke wore a wool hat six months of the year, indoors and out. And Colin wore long underwear to work because he went skiing in the Bridger mountains before coming to lab.

"Hey, Boss Lady!" Zeke called.

I raised an eyebrow at his filthy Camaro. "You've got my skis in there?" I asked.

"Hell yeah," Zeke replied. "We've got everyone's skis in this rusty baby."

I shook my head and pinched the bridge of my nose. "No," I said. "No. No. No. What the hell are you talking about?"

Zeke walked over to me and put an arm around my shoulders. "Boss Lady, listen to me," he said. "Colin and I talked it over, and we cannot, in good conscience, let the woman who signs our paychecks head off into the wilderness of Yellowstone, in January, by herself."

I shook my head. "I said *no*. You've got no idea what you're dealing with. I mean, I hardly know what I'm dealing with."

Zeke gave me a huge grin. "You're saving the world," he said. "And we're coming with you. Can you deal?"

Zeke and Colin followed my Subaru out of Mammoth. Zeke's Camaro backfired as we left and terrified an entire herd of elk. An hour later, when we pulled off the side of the road and parked along the hill Loki and I had climbed at daybreak this morning, I still had no idea what kind of story I could possibly tell Zeke and Colin.

Thankfully, they didn't ask. Both Zeke and Colin just grabbed their backpacks and strapped on their skis, moving with the smooth efficiency of people who've spent much of their life outdoors. My fingers fumbled with my ski bindings in the cold air, and Colin spent his first fifteen minutes gliding across the snow telling me exactly how much I needed to upgrade my cross-country ski gear.

By the time Colin had finished lecturing me about various backcountry ski bindings, we'd crested the hill. I could no longer see the highway; the frozen plains of Yellowstone stretched before us, bordered in the distance by the lodgepole pine forest. The cold knot of fear in my stomach spread thin tendrils to my spine, legs, and finally my heart.

Zeke cleared his throat and spat loudly into the snow. "Well, Boss Lady, where now?"

I smiled, and the fear in my gut retreated a tiny fraction. "Just a sec."

Closing my eyes, I tilted my head back and tried to open myself like I'd done when Vali asked if I could sense it.

Vali... The winter sun caressed my face, warming me in spite of the cold air. I remembered his touch, the sweet, wild tang of his scent, his hungry mouth against mine.

There. I'd found the smoky, burnt smell in the air. And, hiding somewhere within the smoke, was a hint of Vali's wild scent. My heart stuttered as I opened my eyes.

"That way," I said, pointing with my ski pole.

"North-northwest," said Colin. He'd pulled a compass from his chest pocket, and he was studying it intently.

Zeke and Colin skied into line behind me, and for a long time we said nothing as we traveled over the snow. It was a perfect day for cross country skiing. The sky was clear, and the temperature hovering just below freezing. It was warm enough to be comfortable, if you kept moving, but cold enough to keep the snow slick and fast.

An enormous herd of buffalo ambled across the far end of the valley, using their massive shoulders to clear snow from the frozen grass. I sniffed the air again. Above the rank, animal smell of the buffalo was the thick, burnt scent of the monster I was tracking.

"We'll have to go around them," I said, staring at the buffalo herd. They looked much bigger out here, so far from the safety of my car. I tried not to imagine how easy it would be for one of their sharp horns to tear through my jacket, and my skin.

Colin took another reading on him compass. "Still north-northwest?" he asked.

I nodded. "It's in the forest, I think. Past the buffalo."

Zeke gave me a crisp salute. "Roger that, Boss Lady. Ten-four and around the buffalo."

"What does that even mean?" I asked as Zeke pushed off, sliding across the snow with an odd level of grace for such a burly man.

Colin grinned at me. "I don't understand what he's saying at least half the time."

Then he slipped off, following Zeke's trail and leaving me shaking my head.

CHAPTER TWENTY THREE

We didn't speak again until we were past the buffalo herd and under the fringe of the lodgepole forest.

"Okay, guys," I panted as I skated to a stop under the trees. "Let's take a short breather." My legs were shaking, and I felt giddy after coming so close to the buffalo herd, although I'd never admit that to Zeke and Colin.

"Good plan, Boss Lady," said Zeke.

He pulled off his backpack and took out what looked like a chunk of Swiss cheese wrapped in tin foil. They he pulled out a dried salami, took a bite out of both, and handed them to Colin.

"You guys didn't bring a knife for that?" I asked, raising an eyebrow.

"Why'd we need a knife for this?" Zeke asked around a mouthful of salami.

I shook my head and gave up yet another futile attempt to civilize my graduate students. When Colin handed the block of cheese to me, I tore a chunk off with my teeth.

"Don't worry, Professor," Colin said. "What happens in the backcountry, stays in the backcountry."

Grinning, I felt a surge of gratitude so sudden, unexpected, and fierce it brought tears to my eyes. "Thank you," I said, the words catching in my throat. "I'm glad you're here."

Colin shrugged. Zeke let out a tremendous belch.

"Let's keep moving," I said, zipping up my jacket. It felt colder under the trees.

Zeke frowned. "Isn't, uh, Wolf Boy going to meet us? Or something?"

I sighed. "Okay, first, he has a name. It's Vali, not Wolf Boy. And second, he's not a wolf anymore."

"And is Vali going to meet us?" Colin asked, gently. "To explain why the wolves are leaving Yellowstone?"

I glanced into the woods. They seemed dark, as if the trees were somehow swallowing the bright sunlight falling across the valley. The burnt scent was stronger now; I could sense it even with my eyes open.

"Can you smell that?" I asked, ignoring Colin's question.

Zeke and Colin glanced at each other. They were silent long enough for me to worry they'd both decided their doctoral advisor had completely and totally lost her fucking mind. Then Colin nodded, and raised his arm.

"It's coming from there," he said, pointing into the trees. "And it's getting stronger. We're following it, aren't we?"

My chest tightened. "I'm following it," I said. "You don't need to. I don't know what it is, exactly, but it's probably seriously dangerous. And no, Vali isn't coming to us. I'm going to him."

Zeke grinned. "Hey, Boss Lady, don't worry about it. We've gotcha covered. And Wolf Boy, too." He winked as he pulled his backpack off the snow and shrugged in onto his shoulders.

IT DIDN'T TAKE LONG for the forest to become strange. The trees grew tall and dense. Too dense. Yellowstone doesn't get much rain, and the volcanic soil in this part of Montana is thin and nutrient poor. It's not an ecosystem that can support dense vegetation. But those trees...

"I don't even think these are lodgepole," I said, pressing my mittened hand against the dark trunk of an enormous pine.

We'd stopped again to pick our way around a windfall of dead logs, which meant taking off our skis, climbing over tree trunks larger than any I'd ever seen in Montana, and then knocking the ice off our boots to put our skis back on. It was slow, cold, tedious travel. My calves spasmed with cramps, and my arms trembled with the effort of lifting my skis. Even my shoulders ached from pulling myself over fallen logs.

"No, they're not lodgepole," said Colin. His voice was soft and hushed in the darkness of the forest.

Zeke clambered over the tree trunk and stood next to us. "You think that's weird," he said. "Check this out."

He unzipped his pocket and pulled out a small compass. I leaned toward him to look. The red compass needle ticked and swung wildly, making a full circle in his hand. It settled for a moment between E and S, skipped, and spun again. Colin whistled.

"You should go back," I said. "You should both go back. Now."

Zeke shook his head. "Are you kidding? This is the coolest shit I've ever seen. Colin, did you get a load of this?"

Colin nodded. "I don't think this place is exactly normal."

I knocked a clump of ice off the bottom of my ski boot and hesitated. My foot hovered in mid-air as I watched Colin and Zeke stare at the still-spinning compass needle. My chest ached. I was torn between telling them to get the hell away from here as fast as they could, or tearing up again as I thanked them for coming this far.

Colin met my eyes. "I think we should keep moving. This way, right?" Colin asked, raising a ski pole.

I nodded, my mouth dry. The scent was so strong now I could almost see it, like a dark haze hovering over the snowy ground, snaking between the massive trees. Shaking myself, I clicked my boot into my ski binding. By now I could have followed the scent blindfolded.

"I think we're getting close," I said.

I pushed my skis through a narrow gap between two pines so tall their crowns were lost in the gathering darkness. Beyond those pines was a meadow. The last of the day's light was just fading from the periwinkle sky above the trees, leaving the clouds streaked with pink. Snow lay thin on the ground in the clearing, and there was another scent in the air, the low, sulfur tang of geothermal features.

On the other side of the meadow was the cave.

My heart hammered in my mouth as I turned around, wondering what I could possibly say to Zeke and Colin to explain that looming, dark maw. Zeke pulled himself through the trees and skidded to a stop next to me.

"Hey, sweet," he said. "Hot springs!"

Of course. Now I noticed steam rising in the air like white ghosts against the darkness of the trees ringing the clearing. At least a dozen small, translucent blue pools, glimmered softly in the meadow. I heard the swish of skis on snow as Colin slid next to me.

"Huh," Colin said, sniffing the air. "I've lost it."

Zeke scratched his head. "Yeah, me too. You, Boss Lady?"

I stared past them at the mouth of the cave. The darkness inside the entrance seemed almost palpable, like a heavy oil slick, waiting to spill across the meadow.

"There," I said. It came out a rough whisper; my voice had fled.

Colin and Zeke turned to the cave.

"Through those woods?" Colin asked. He raised his ski pole, jabbing it at the cave.

"You don't see it?" I whispered.

Colin's brow furrowed under his knit wool hat. "See what?"

I swallowed. "That cave," I hissed. "That giant freaking cave!"

Just looking at the dark entrance made my skin crawl, but I was afraid to turn away. As if something might come out of that inky void the moment I turned my back.

"Cave?" Colin echoed. "I don't see a cave."

"All I see are more goddamn trees," Zeke said.

A slow shiver ran the length of my spine. I'd wanted to send them away earlier, but I'd hesitated. Now I had no choice; that cave entrance must be for me alone.

"Then I guess you're not coming with me any more," I said, clearing my throat to hide the waver in my voice.

"Hey, I didn't wanna give you the wrong impression," Zeke said. "I mean, it's more goddamn trees, but that's not a problem. Hell, I love skiing through this creepy ass forest!"

"I know," I said, smiling in spite of myself. "But I don't think you can come any further. I think this next part is just for me."

Colin shrugged. "Well, we can certainly try."

"Sure. Of course you can," I said.

I slid my backpack off my shoulders and let it rest against my skis, sighing with relief. For a second my entire body felt like it was floating. I clipped out of my skis and propped them against a tree, wedging my backpack between them. There wasn't much snow on the ground between the opalescent, steaming pools, and I seriously doubted skis would be very useful against a dragon. Zeke and Colin watched me. Their eyes seemed wide in the fading light.

Squaring my shoulders, I turned to face the cave. It looked exactly like it had in my dream on Christmas Eve, when I saw Vali for the last time.

"No, it's not quite right," I muttered under my breath. I'd been standing slight closer to the entrance, and a little to the right.

I took a few steps to the right.

"That should be about right," I whispered as I forced my eyes off the steam-dappled ground and back to the mouth of the cave.

The darkness in the mouth of the cave moved. It surged slightly, then lay still. As if it were breathing. As if it were waiting for me.

"Boss Lady?" Zeke's voice sounded strange and far away.

I turned around, my heart hammering wildly against my chest. I'd left the meadow; I was already at the mouth of the cave. Zeke and Colin stood a good twenty yards away, beneath the trees, next to my skis and backpack. They seemed very far away, almost in another world.

My gut tightened, and my skin prickled with a long, slow shiver. From the corner of my eye, the darkness in the mouth of the cave shifted and undulated.

"Colin and Zeke," I called, cupping my hands around my mouth to carry my voice. "Do not wait for me! You pack up, and you head home."

Both of them shook their heads simultaneously. Insolent little shits, I thought.

"No," Colin called. His voice echoed strangely in the clearing. "We'll wait for you."

Zeke pushed himself forward on his skis, and Colin followed. It seemed to take a very long time for them to cross the small meadow. Even when they stood almost next to me, Colin and Zeke still looked oddly distant and distorted. Like they were on one side of a mirror, and I was on the other.

"You, uh, need anything?" Zeke asked. He looked uncertain.

I had never, in four years, seen Zeke look uncertain about anything. The hesitant, caged expression on Zeke's face terrified me even more than the shifting, churning darkness behind me, more than the spinning needle of the compass or the strange trees that didn't fit the ecosystem or the low, acrid burnt smell in the air.

I shook my head. My hands trembled, and I tried to hide them behind my back. "I'm fine."

"You want a ski pole?" Colin asked. It sounded like a joke, but his face was pale, and his lips were drawn tight.

"Bear spray?" Zeke offered.

I closed my eyes, remembering the enormous blue sword Vali had pulled from his back and swung in a wild, hissing arc before he entered the cave. I pictured myself swinging one of my thin, little white ski poles through the cold gloaming, and I couldn't stop my laugh. Colin and Zeke looked even more concerned, and even further away, when I turned back.

"I don't think it's that kind of cave," I said. "I'm going in. Please don't wait for me."

I turned from their pale faces and stepped into the darkness.

THERE WAS A SMALL, battery operated headlamp in my pocket. I fumbled in the darkness for a few seconds before I found the headlamp and pulled it over my forehead. For a brief second after I switched it on, the lamp flared, and I could almost make out my ski boots. Then it dimmed rapidly, until I couldn't even see my hands. I pulled the headlamp off my head and examined it, seeing only a dim flicker of orange deep in the bulb. Then the darkness flowed over my hands, and that flicker was gone.

Damn. I stuffed the useless headlamp back in my pocket and started shuffling forward slowly, my arms raised so I didn't crash into anything. The ground under my feet felt smooth and hard, almost like concrete, and it sloped gently downhill.

"Hello?" I whispered. My voice bounced and echoed in the darkness, amplifying until it seemed to be coming from everywhere. *Hello? Hello? Hello?*

My skin crawled at the reverberating crash of my own voice. So much for subtlety.

I walked for a long time. Long enough to realized I was hungry and thirsty, in addition to cold and sore. Long enough to regret leaving my backpack with my skis. Slowly, I realized I could see the pale flash of my fingers in front of me. A few more steps, and I could see my white ski pants, and the dark, hard ground beneath me. A few more steps—

My breath caught in my throat. The hum of fluorescent lights and the beep and chirp of medical equipment rushed into the cold air of the cave. My nostrils filled with the harsh, sterile smell of bleach. The murmur of voices grew behind me. Three nurses wearing matching light blue scrubs emerged from the darkness and brushed past me, vanishing a few steps to my right.

"What the fuck?" I whispered.

I recognized those nurses; they worked in the Neonatal Intensive Care Unit at Chicago's Children's Hospital. And they were working the day—

I blinked and turned slowly, expecting to see the darkness of the cave behind me. No. I faced a blank, white wall and a massive bulletin board covered with reports, forms, and schedules. And a huge, impassive, white clock. Ticking down the seconds.

"Time of death," said a man's voice.

I turned again.

CHAPTER TWENTY FOUR

I saw myself.

I wore a pale green hospital robe, and my disheveled, greasy hair hung lank down my back. My shoulders were hunched and my head was down as I sat in the hospital's dark wooden rocking chair, next to the empty incubator. Barry Richardson crouched before me, his hand on my arm, his head tilted forward.

I was not crying.

That part I remembered; I did not cry. Not then. Not when Dr. Patterson announced the time of death in his soft, almost apologetic voice. And I had not cried that morning, just a few hours earlier, as he explained why they needed to remove the life support systems. As he'd said the words, "zero chance of survival."

My stomach clenched violently, and my vision doubled. My breath came in great gulps, tearing at the sterile hospital air, and I fell to my knees.

"God, no," I hissed, squeezing my eyes shut.

The machines of the hospital hissed and clicked and beeped. I opened my eyes and the blue and white pattern of the hospital's linoleum floor swam into view.

"I am so sorry for your loss," Dr. Patterson said in that same measured, level voice. I remembered wondering if he'd learned that in medical school, the perfect tone for condolences.

Barry's voice caught in a ragged sob. I stared at him. Tears streamed down his face, leaving dark wet splotches on his white Oxford shirt. That part I didn't remember. I had forgotten his tears.

I took a deep breath and forced myself to look at the hunched figure in the rocking chair. My younger self.

The Karen in the chair did not move. She did not acknowledge Dr. Patterson's words. Meredith sat in her lap, locked in her trembling arms, her small, still body wrapped in the pink and blue stripes of the hospital blanket. I'd rocked her against my chest all morning as the machines keeping her alive were turned off, slowly, one by one. There were still needles in her tiny arms and bands around her ankles. But she was turning cold. I remembered that, how quickly her small body grew cold.

Karen Richardson was not crying. Not the woman sitting in the rocking chair, the woman who was still married to Barry, who had just become a mother and then suddenly, horribly, not become a mother.

But I was sobbing, sitting on the floor of the cave, watching myself. Watching my daughter.

Dr. Patterson reached for the Karen in the rocking chair, his arms crossing the space between his rolling office chair and her hunched shoulders.

"No," I heard myself say, my voice choked and thick. "Don't take her!"

Barry knelt beside me, pressing his forehead against mine. "Karen," he said. "She's gone."

There was a low, animal sound, a sort of deep howl, from the woman in the rocking chair. And then a choked, wracked sobbing. The word no.

No. No. No.

They had to pull her from my arms as Barry held me back. And I hit him. My hand lashed out, following Meredith and slamming into my husband's face so hard I knocked his glasses to the floor.

The round tortoiseshell frames skittered across the cold linoleum, coming to rest just in front of my dirt-stained knees, as a nurse finally pulled Meredith's cold little body away from the screaming, hysterical woman in the rocking chair, the woman they would soon be sedating. I tried to turn away as the nurse walked past me, but I saw everything. I saw my once-husband's very expensive glasses glinting on the floor. I saw Dr. Patterson whisper to the nurse, ordering a sedative.

And I saw my daughter's perfect little face. Her dark lashes. Her scattering of downy hair.

My Meredith.

I collapsed on the floor of the cave, shaking, pulling my knees to my chest.

"Go away!" I heard myself growl.

My eyes squeezed shut as my cheek pressed against the cold dirt of the cave's floor. I remembered this part, too.

"Karen, please," Barry said. His voice trembled. He knelt in front of me, I remembered. He knelt in front of me, and he opened his arms. "Please."

I heard the rocking chair scrape across the floor as the woman who had been me pulled away from her husband. "No," she said. Her voice was almost a shriek. "Don't touch me! Just go away!"

I opened my eyes enough to see Barry's shoulders shudder as his head dropped to his chest. My heart ached with a sharp, empty throb. You could have found some comfort in each other, I realized. What an idiot you are, Karen McDonald.

What a great, fucking idiot.

The voices fell silent; the smell of disinfectant and baby powder was gradually replaced by the heavy burnt scent of the cave. The hospital room slowly faded, and I was alone in the vast, pressing darkness, curled on the cold floor of the cave. I crammed my fist in my mouth to silence my sobs.

EVENTUALLY, MY TEARS ran dry, and my stiff, cold legs began to ache. I pushed myself off the dirt, rubbing my palms across my eyes.

"What now?" I whispered to the darkness. My own voice bounced back to me.

Now? Now? Now?

I stood and tried to shake some warmth back into my body before I raised my hands and turned in a slow circle in the darkness. I felt nothing. The air in the cave was perfectly motionless. The back of my mouth tasted bitter, and I swallowed hard.

It was impossible to judge time in the cave. I moved forward one shuffling step at a time, inching along the smooth, downward-sloping floor, breathing deeply and trying not to think. Perhaps I'd been walking for five minutes. Or fifteen. Or fifty.

Slowly, the darkness enveloping me began to lift. Once again, I realized I could see my fingertips, ten pale dots floating in front of my eyes. My stomach clenched. I froze as my ears throbbed with the wild pounding of my heart. What the hell would I see this time?

But I knew.

I already knew.

CHAPTER TWENTY FIVE

The first thing I saw was the bottle of pills. The empty bottle of pills.

I should have thrown that bottle in the trash. That was one of my many regrets, in the first few days of my hospital stay. I should have thrown the bottle in the pink bathroom trash can, with the cotton balls and crumpled Kleenex, or buried it under the coffee grounds in the kitchen trash.

But I didn't throw it away. I left it on the bathroom sink. I didn't even replace the cap.

"Karen?" Barry's voice rang through the house.

He shouldn't be home right now. He should be teaching his class, his two hour long senior seminar on Chaucer. It was a Wednesday morning in late March, and Dr. Barry Richardson should be teaching his Chaucer class for at least another hour and a half.

"Karen?"

There was a desperate note to his voice. A touch of panic. I turned around, slowly, and saw that I had left the door open.

I should have closed the door to the backyard.

I didn't.

Something crashed behind me, and I turned. Barry had dropped the briefcase carrying his brand new Macbook laptop, and it smashed against the floor. Of course. His computer screen was cracked when I got home from the hospital. He was always so careful with his things. I never knew how he had cracked the screen of his precious laptop.

"Karen!" he screamed.

I followed him, knowing what he was about to find.

I HADN'T WANTED TO die indoors.

Even though it was a cold, dreary day, the kind of gray spring day that makes the word "summer" sting like a cruel joke, I did not want to die indoors. So, I took the pills and I left the bottle on the counter. I opened the door to the backyard, and I left it open.

And I went outside to die.

There I was, my body slumped on the pale green grass under the crabapple tree, looking weirdly small in the overcast light. I hadn't realized I'd fallen forward. My face was streaked with mud when Barry pulled me into his arms. My eyes were open; a thin stream of white foam leaked from the corner of my mouth.

Barry fumbled in his pocket, reaching for his phone. But he was talking already. Talking to me.

"Oh, my God, Karen, no," he said, his voice low and hushed, like a prayer. "Karen, please don't. Please."

Barry wrapped his arm around me, and he rocked me like a child as he pulled his phone from his pocket. His hands shook as he swiped the screen.

"I need an ambulance," he said. "Immediately. My wife—"

His voice broke, and he began sobbing. His face pressed against my hair and his chest heaved so violently it shook my motionless body.

The sting of tears filled my eyes again, and I brought my hand to my mouth. Watching my husband sob into my hair with his arms wrapped around me, I felt something cold and hard, something deep within my chest, begin to dislodge.

I had been angry at Barry Richardson for a very long time. Longer than we'd been divorced. Longer, even, than we'd been

married. I had loved Barry, and I'd been angry at him, and the two
had seemed inseparable.

But standing there, on the hard floor of Níðhöggr's cave, in the
thin, gray light of the Wednesday morning when I decided to kill
myself, I felt the anger breaking up, dislodging. Floating away.

"I'm sorry," I whispered. "Barry. I am so sorry."

There was no reply. There was no sound at all, save his desperate
sobs, and the thin echo of a woman's voice coming from his cell
phone.

"Hello? Sir? Can you tell me if she has a pulse?"

The ambulance arrived quickly. Two young men and one woman
loaded me onto a stretcher with hurried efficiency. The woman
turned to Barry, putting a hand on his arm as she led him back into
the house. I followed, mute and unseen, my heart throbbing in my
chest.

"I knew she was unhappy," Barry said. His voice sounded strange
and distant. "I just didn't realize—I didn't—"

"Sir, do you have any idea what she may have taken? Do you
know how long it's been?"

Barry shook his head. "We lost our baby. Our little girl. And
she's, she's really been struggling..." He stumbled past me, through
me, to the bathroom.

"Here," Barry said. He held the empty bottle toward the woman
like an offering. "This must be..."

The EMT picked up her radio and said something in a rapid
staccato before turning back to Barry. "That's good," she said. "That's
very helpful. Do you want to come to the hospital?"

Dr. Barry Richardson, the world's foremost authority on dragons
in medieval literature, looked lost and broken. His hair stuck up on
one side, and his glasses were crooked. There was a streak of black
mud down the front of his suit jacket. "I...I don't..."

The EMT put an arm around his shoulder. "You've done everything you could," she said.

"No!" I yelled, crashing forward. "Barry! I'm sorry!"

The fragile early spring sunlight shattered around me; the living room I'd shared with Barry Richardson swirled and faded like mist.

I screamed. I screamed into the void for a very long time.

WHEN I CAME BACK TO myself, my body was curled into a tight ball against the cold of the cave's floor. My forehead pressed into the dirt and my shoulders heaved with dry sobs. I coughed, inhaled dirt, then coughed again. My head throbbed with a heavy, red ache, and every muscle in my body screamed. I rocked back on my legs, wiping my cheeks and blinking in the absolute blackness of the cave.

God, I'd been such a shitty wife.

I hid my head in my hands as if there were someone who could see me, judge me, and find me hopelessly wanting. My stomach cramped as I exhaled slowly. The burned air of the cave made my eyes water. It slowly occurred to me I might never find my way out of this cave. A long, slow death by dehydration and starvation might be the only thing waiting for me in this damn cave. I shivered. What a shitty way to go.

Suddenly I wanted nothing more than to just collapse on the floor of this cave, to curl up in a ball and forget everything, all the horrible mistakes I'd made, my entire life with Barry Richardson. My stupid, wasted year in Maine after my suicide attempt, where the only bright spot had been my dreams of Vali.

I raised my head, staring into the darkness. I'd felt something, like the delicate whisper of a moth's wing brushing my cheek. And now the blackness of the cave held an infinitesimal hint of Vali's sweet, wild scent. My heart jumped, and I forced myself to stand.

"Vali?" I asked, raising my voice just above a whisper.

I heard nothing but the bounce and echo of my own words. Still, he'd been here. Vali had made it this far. I inched forward, whispering his name.

Eventually I could see my hands again, although this time the darkness in the cave wasn't lifting. Rather, it was shifting, becoming thicker and picking up a red tint. My fingers pushed through phosphorescent smoke, leaving trails of red light where they disturbed the air.

I heard something, a low, soft rustling, like the rattle of dry leaves across bones. I froze, and the red light swirled around my body. The sound continued, a long, low hiss. It moved, reverberating around the cave, until it was impossible to tell if it was coming from behind me, in front of me, or if it was passing right next to me.

The noise stopped, and the cave was once again perfectly silent. My mouth went dry, and my heartbeat seemed very loud.

There was a sudden flare of light ahead. I jumped backward. It vanished and reappeared, vanished and reappeared. My arms and legs trembled with the effort of suppressing the overwhelming impulse to run.

The light flashed on once more, and this time it stayed on. It was an enormous, perfectly round circle of flaming red, with a vertical black slit down the middle. As I watched, the slit expanded and then narrowed, like a symmetrical crack in the sphere of flame.

It's not a light, I realized. My entire body went cold.

It's an eye.

CHAPTER TWENTY SIX

" Well. Aren't you interesting?"
The voice came from everywhere and nowhere, from
the empty space behind me, from the walls surrounding me. It was
thick and rich, and it sounded almost amused.

My head spun as I tried to remember how to breathe. The
enormous eye rolled in its socket. I was dimly aware of another, larger
movement. Something almost incomprehensibly huge shifted in the
empty blackness of the cave. A dull, red glow came from somewhere
far above me.

"And have you come to stop me, Karen, daughter of Elizabeth,
granddaughter of Claire, of the line of Orleans?"

The red light pulsed and swam around me. For a moment, it
seemed like I could almost see them, my mother and her mother and
her mother before her, a line of women stretching away into the dark
distance of the cave. I shook my head and dug my fingernails into my
palms, the sharp pain clearing my vision.

"No," I said. My voice sounded very small. "I haven't come to
stop anyone."

The creature shifted, its massive body making a sound very much
like a sigh. "Then begone." The enormous eye began to close.

"Wait! Níðhöggr!"

The eye opened wide, once again focusing on me. The air
warmed as the enormous *thing* stared at me.

"I'm here for—I mean, I'm looking for—" I stammered.

There was a thrashing, scraping noise somewhere far behind me. "Yes. I know why you're here."

It fell silent. My pulse pounded in my ears.

"Is he—Is Vali still alive?"

That shifting sigh again. The eye narrowed. "I cannot kill the bearer of Hrotti, enjoyable as that would have been."

Relief flooded through my exhausted body. Vali was alive. Thank all the gods, Vali was alive.

"Where is he?" I whispered.

"Oh, there's not much left of him, Karen of the line of Orleans."

My stomach dropped. "Where is he?" I said.

The eye rolled back to focus on me, and the air between us grew even warmer. "You," Níðhöggr said. "You, I could certainly kill."

Well, shit. I remembered Zeke offering me a ski pole, and then I imagined myself swinging my puny little duct-tape-covered ski pole over my head before this massive flame-colored eye. It was such a stupid idea, I actually laughed.

The eye narrowed. The air in the cave was growing uncomfortably hot. I remembered Colin offering me bear spray, and I snorted another laugh. Karen McDonald, off to slay a dragon with a ski pole and grizzly bear spray.

I'm going to die wishing I had a fucking ski pole and a can of bear spray.

I lost it. I started laughing hysterically, uncontrollably, a desperate barking, coughing laugh that sounded almost like it hurt. I laughed harder than I'd laughed in years, until tears rolled down my cheeks and my sides ached.

"Most people scream," the voice rasped, once my frantic laughter had calmed enough for me to catch my breath. "They beg me for mercy. Yet, you laugh. You are a bizarre little creature, Karen of the Orleans."

I wiped the tears from my cheeks, my ribs aching. "Oh, I've been called much worse," I said. "Now, aren't you going to kill me?"

The eye shifted, and the air grew somewhat cooler. "Perhaps," Níðhöggr said.

The darkness flared suddenly, becoming a blaze of red and orange, and I squeezed my eyes shut, raising my hands to cover my face. Nothing happened. After a few slow breaths, I opened my eyes.

Someone stood in front of me, a human figure dressed in dark jeans and a tight red shirt. At first, I thought it was a woman, but then he turned to face me and I realized I'd made a mistake. His chest was flat and muscular, his hips narrow.

"Or maybe we can make a deal," Níðhöggr said.

I nodded, my mouth dry.

Níðhöggr put his finger to his lips, a gesture that gave me an odd shiver down my back. "I suppose I can give you what you want. But—" He gave me a predatory grin, full of teeth.

Then Níðhöggr spun on his heels, took a step backward, and turned to face me again. I blinked, my mind spinning. I was staring at a woman. How could I have thought she was a man? Her face was round, and her chest curved unmistakably with the swell of her breasts.

"You have to try to stop me," she said, her voice smooth as honey.

"Okay," I stammered. "How do I—"

She smiled, and the world went black.

I GASPED. AIR TORE at my throat, making me cough. Panic surged through my gut and I gagged as something hard pressed against my nose.

"Easy now," said a deep, male voice. "Easy."

Firm hands grabbed my shoulders, and someone rolled my body onto my back. Hospital, I thought, panic surging through my body like an electric current. Am I back in the hospital?

It took far more effort than I'd expected to force my eyes open. I took another heaving breath, my frantic heartbeat subsiding as I filled my lungs. I was staring at a pale turquoise sky streaked with high, delicate cirrus clouds. The roar and crash of waves echoed in my ears. The air was cold and heavy with a sharp, briny tang.

Was I dead? Was there an ocean in the afterlife?

"There. You'll be fine."

I turned toward the voice and saw a rocky beach stretching out beneath me. A man sat next to me, staring at the waves. An old man. No, wait, maybe not an old man. Perhaps he was my age, floating in that odd limbo of middle age which could be anywhere from late twenties to early fifties.

"Where—" My voice scratched at my throat, and I started to cough violently. The man ignored me until my coughing was over, and I lay shivering on the stones.

"Well, now," he said. "I suppose you'll be going after him."

I pushed myself up to sitting. "What?"

The man turned to face me. I noticed with an unpleasant shock that his right eye socket was empty. "He went that-a-way," he said, pointing over his shoulder. "I imagine he'll stick close to the water. Do what you can. I don't expect much, but if you can get that sword away from him, you'll be rewarded."

"Vali." My heart surged like the waves. "He's here? He's still alive?"

The man grinned at me, his lone, pale blue eye sparkling. Then he was gone. One second, I was staring at his empty eye socket; the next, I was alone on a rocky beach, listening to the crash of waves along the shore and the lonely cries of seagulls far overhead. I shivered. I was cold, hungry, and very, very tired.

Feeling hungry convinced me that I wasn't dead. I could understand being tired or cold if I were dead. But it was just too much of a stretch to think the dead would be *hungry*. After a few deep breaths, I staggered to my feet. The ocean stretched before me, gentle undulations of green and slate gray stretching to the mist-obscured horizon. A faint rainbow twinkled in the clouds skating above the waves. I turned and saw vibrant green, rolling hills climbing to meet a dark pine forest.

And there was... *something*. I squinted, bringing my hand to my forehead to shield my eyes. Yes, there it was again. A quick, reflective flash of light somewhere on the hillside. My heart tugged in my chest.

"Vali?" I whispered.

I shook my head and stared down the beach. *He went that-a-way*, the man said, and it seemed true, somehow. It felt like Vali was there, between the crashing surf and the jagged rocks.

"Vali," I told the waves and the thick, salty air. "Hang in there. I'm coming."

My feet hurt as I limped across the rocky beach. Every muscle in my body ached with a dull, pervasive pain, like I'd tried to run a marathon the day before. An enormous cliff loomed in the distance, severing the ocean from those emerald green hills. I appraised it silently for several minutes before deciding to stay on the beach. The sun sank toward the distant forest and, with every step, a hard knot of apprehension in my chest tightened. Níðhöggr's words echoed in my mind.

There isn't much left of him.

CHAPTER TWENTY SEVEN

B y the time the sun fell behind the trees I was seriously regretting my decision to stay on the beach. The rocky strand had narrowed to a thin strip between jagged cliffs and crashing breakers, just perfect for twisting an ankle, and I was growing increasingly certain the damn tide was coming in. From the looks of the littoral zone along the cliffs, the water at high tide would be well over my head. A wave surged over the rocks and up my ankles, dumping cold seawater into my boots.

"Fuck this," I muttered, struggling to keep my balance while the wave clattered back to the ocean. "Vali must've climbed the cliffs."

A low, soft moan echoed across the dark rocks. My heart stopped. I stared at the slick, seaweed-covered strip of rocks in front of me. An enormous, half-submerged boulder blocked the way.

"Vali?" I called.

There was no response. In the still air, my heartbeat seemed loud enough to drown out the constant murmur of the hungry tide. Slowly, I scrambled across the rocks to the boulder. It was too slippery to climb, and I'd get drenched going around it.

That low, pained moan came again, rippling across the water. Adrenaline shot through my body, and my exhaustion evaporated.

"Vali!" I called. "Hang on, I'm coming!"

I edged into the waves. My hands scrabbled across the seaweed covered boulder, looking for purchase. The ocean was freezing. The shoreline dropped off quickly, and I sank up to my waist before I reached the other side of the boulder. The waves rose to my breasts, making my jacket puff and float around me. My teeth were chattering violently by the time I dragged myself around the rock and out of the water. Behind the boulder was a small, sheltered cove of broken rocks and strange echoes, already knee-deep in water. It seemed deserted in the fading light.

"Vali?" My voice trembled.

"Leave."

I saw him the moment he spoke. He was sitting chest-deep in the water, the scabbard of his great sword Hrotti across his folded knees. His hair was drenched, and his red-rimmed eyes were wide and wild.

"Vali, oh God, I'm so glad—" I stumbled toward him.

He exploded to his feet, leaping backward until his body pressed against the cliff face. In an instant Hrotti was in his hands, its blade glowing a soft blue as it pointed directly at my heart. Some distant, rational part of my brain noticed his motions were quick and smooth; physically, he looked fine.

But Níðhöggr doesn't hurt you *physically*.

"Don't touch me," he growled.

"Vali, it's me. Karen."

"Go. Away!" His eyes burned as he stared at me down the length of his sword.

I swallowed and stepped closer to him. The water in the sunken cove rose to my hips. Vali's sword remained level, its wicked blade inches from my chest. I held my hands up at my side.

"I'm not going to hurt you," I said.

"I'll hurt you," Vali said. His voice was strange and distant, as if it were coming from far away.

"Vali, I know about your brother Nari. I'm so sorry. It wasn't your fault."

"I killed him," he hissed, his voice low and thick. "I kill the ones I love. I'm a monster."

"No. Vali, stop it." I tried to ignore the way Hrotti's blade trembled in his hand as it moved closer to my heart. "You're not a monster."

"Of course, I'm a monster. I was imprisoned as a monster." His sword touched my chest and sank silently into the center of my jacket. "And, when the sea claims me, I'll die as a monster."

I had a sudden vision of Vali's body claimed by the sea, his long hair drifting in the current, his beautiful, golden eyes darkened forever. Hot, righteous anger surged through my frozen body, choking whatever reasonable argument I was about to make. After all I'd come through, after literally facing down a dragon, I was not going to watch Vali drown.

"Oh, stop it!" I yelled.

I grabbed the point of Vali's stupid sword and pushed it away, although it burned my palm. My jacket ripped open with a low growl. I ignored the sting of pain in my hand and stalked toward him, cold sea water swirling and gurgling around my waist.

"You think you're a monster? You? Because you were trapped? Because you were tortured, and forced to do something terrible? That doesn't make you a monster, Vali! That makes you the victim of monsters!" I screamed over the dark rumbles of the ocean.

Vali trembled. He stared at the sword in his hand like he'd never seen it before.

"I've killed people," he said. "Men. Women. I killed those who helped my father." His voice echoed off the rocks. Tears streaked his cheeks, shimmering in what little remained of the day's light.

"So what?" I yelled. "So fucking what? You want to know what I did? You want to know what Níðhöggr showed me?"

Vali stood silent and motionless. His eyes looked very large in his pale, tear-streaked face.

"I killed myself!" I screamed.

I paused, shoulders trembling, my breath catching in my throat. Vali stared at me with his mouth open.

"You killed your brother, but you were under a spell. You'd just been transformed, and you killed Nari as a wolf. But me... I planned it out. I planned it for weeks. I calculated the lethal dose myself, then doubled it just to be sure. And I was not under someone's goddamn spell."

My vision blurred. I wiped the back of my hand across my eyes, but it just encouraged a new flood of tears. Barry's face filled my mind, the way he'd held my shoulders in the mud under the crabapple tree with his glasses askew and his shoulders heaving.

"Don't you dare tell me you're the monster," I said, although my voice was already half strangled with tears. I closed my eyes, blocking out Vali's wide eyes and open mouth.

An enormous, cold wave slammed into my shoulders, driving me face-first into the ocean. Seawater stung my eyes and my knees sang with pain as they crashed against the rocks. I shoved off the bottom and gasped as my head broke through the water. Saltwater stung my eyes. My feet clattered against the rocks, trying to find purchase. The wave was receding, dragging me into the black ocean with it.

Strong hands grabbed my shoulders, pulling me to my feet. Vali's tear-streaked face came into focus.

"Karen, you have to leave. You'll die here."

I threw myself against his chest, digging my fingers into his hair. "No," I growled.

Some distant, rational part of my brain noted that leaving wasn't much of a possibility. Vali and I were pressed against the enormous cliff face, hemmed in by boulders whose tops already swirled with white-capped breakers. Even if I were a strong swimmer, and I wasn't, the icy waves would smash me against those rocks if I tried to get back to shore. A broken femur would probably be the best-case scenario.

The ocean surged again, lifting my entire body, and I wrapped my legs around his waist.

"I'm not leaving without you," I said.

His arms tightened around me. "Karen, no," he moaned. "You can't. I—I don't want to lose you."

The next wave hit the back of my neck, lifting both of us. My mouth filled with cold salt water. Vali staggered backward, somehow managing to keep his balance on the slick rocks. I closed my eyes and pressed my face against his neck, feeling his pulse pound against my lips. Oh, damn, I'd missed him! The wild, dark desperation I'd felt in the cave swelled again inside me, and I held him so tightly my arms ached.

"I won't leave you," I said as the freezing wave receded. "Vali, I love you!"

His entire body trembled. The air began to tremble as well, whistling and pulling at our clothes. I squeezed my eyes shut and clung to his strong body as the world around us was ripped apart.

We fell together.

CHAPTER TWENTY EIGHT

Vali laughed.

The world stopped spinning, and the salt tang of the ocean faded. I opened my eyes hesitantly, although I didn't release my death grip around Vali's shoulders. Grass. I saw green grass, and gray clouds trimmed with delicate, opalescent pink. I blinked, taking in the steep cliffside beside us. The ocean rolled over itself in dark furrows, far below us.

"What the hell?" I whispered.

Vali's eyes flashed above his tear-stained cheeks. His grip around my waist tightened and he spun us in a circle. "I did it!" he screamed. "I did it, Karen!"

"Did what?"

"We traveled through the aether!"

He pressed his lips against mine, kissing me. He tasted like the salt of the ocean, the salt of tears, and my body responded with a flood of heat and fierce arousal. I'd never needed someone so suddenly or so desperately. I crushed his face to mine, tilting my head as I opened to him. He responded to my sudden need, his hands tightening around my hips. When he pulled away, I gasped, my heart racing.

"I love you," Vali said.

My eyes stung, and my vision blurred with fresh tears. "Oh, Vali—"

"No, listen."

He ran his hand along my cheek, forcing me to meet his gaze. "My entire life I've tried to use the aether. I was the biggest failure in the Nine Realms because I lacked magic. It was a joke to the rest of the Æsir. I was a joke! But when I thought of losing you to the ocean..."

Vali crushed me to his chest. "You saved my life a second time, beautiful Karen."

I tried to speak, but my voice came out a strangled sob. Vali's fingers traced the jagged rip Hrotti left across the front of my jacket and through my clothes. His hand found my skin, sending jolts of electricity dancing across my skin. My body pulsed with need, tightening my stomach. I grabbed the waistband of his pants, shoving them down over his hips as I pressed my lips to his, devouring him with hungry kisses. We sank together into the soft grass, our tongues embracing as our lips crushed together.

Damn, I wanted him! I wanted all of him, right now. He struggled to pull my ski pants down my hips as I pressed my shoulders against the grass, arching my back, offering myself to him. When he finally slid my pants over my ankles, I gasped, digging my fingernails into his shoulders as my hips moved against his, needing to take him into me, needing to destroy the space between us.

Vali's hand grabbed the side of my jacket, ripping it, my silk turtleneck, and my bra wide open. My skin prickled as cold air danced over my breasts. Vali's golden eyes flashed in the fading light.

"Don't you dare stop now," I gasped. The heat of his erection pressed between my legs and, oh God, I wanted him. No, I needed him, needed his hard length inside me the way I needed to move, to breathe.

"Vali, please," I whimpered.

His fingers tightened around my ribs, and he pulled us together. We both cried out as he entered me, forcing my hips deep into the grass. For a moment we held still, his cock buried deep within me, my heartbeat drowning out the distant crash of the waves, pleasure searing a path through my body.

"Oh, Karen," he panted, his breath hot against the curve of my neck. "I'm glad you're alive."

"So am I," I gasped.

His hips began to move against me, releasing waves of heat that crashed through my body. I reached for his neck, losing my fingers in his long hair. Our lips met, and I could no longer speak. So am I, I thought, before my conscious mind dissolved in the rhythm of our bodies moving together.

So am I.

"WHERE ARE WE?" I ASKED.

"We're in Asgard," Vali said.

We were curled together in the soft grass at the top of the cliffs, his arm around my shoulders, my head resting on his chest. The tide seemed to be retreating, and the stones of the beach where I'd found him glimmered in the faint light far below. An enormous orange moon was slowly rising over the rolling ocean.

"This is where I was a child," Vali said. "But it's... strange right now. It's too empty. There should be people here."

"There are people here," I said.

Vali laughed. "Not just us, beautiful Karen. And not exactly people."

"No, there is someone else here. Didn't you see him?"

Vali propped himself against the grass and looked at me. "Him? You saw someone?"

I shifted, suddenly uncomfortable. "I talked to someone when I first arrived. He was... I guess he was about my age. He told me to..." I swallowed. He had told me to get Vali's sword. "He told me to find you. And he only had one eye."

"Ah. Right." Vali bent down and kissed me again, slowly and deeply. My body ached under his touch, already hungry for more, and I moaned into his mouth.

He pulled back and shook his head. "No, we'd better get dressed. He's going to be expecting us."

"Who?"

"Óðinn," Vali said. "The All-father."

"The one who turned you into a wolf?" I whispered.

Vali's face darkened, and he lowered his voice to a rough whisper. "I'm sure he's already watching us. Best not to run from him."

I shivered as Vali shifted away from me to pull on his shirt. We dressed quickly and silently. My silk turtleneck was ripped down the middle, so I tried to wear it backward. I pulled what was left of my jacket over the turtleneck.

"Well, I must look fucking fantastic," I muttered, running my fingers through my hair. It was still wet from the ocean.

There was just enough moonlight for me to see Vali's smile.

"What?" I asked. "Is the backward turtleneck that bad?"

"By the Nine Realms, you are beautiful," he said.

I felt my cheeks blaze as he reached for my hand, pulling me into his arms. He kissed my damp hair as he crushed me to his chest.

"And I think you were right," he said. His voice was strangely thick.

"Right about what?"

"Perhaps I'm not a monster." He took a deep breath. "Monsters don't love."

My heart clenched as his meaning sank in. I ran my hand along the strong curve of his neck, feeling the flutter of his pulse against my palm. "You were never a monster, Vali. You were just a small part of a larger plan. Óðinn used you to trap your father."

He sighed, his entire body rippling against mine. "And you saved me."

"Vali, I just—"

He pressed his finger to my lips. "Shhhh. We should go. We're being watched."

I shivered. Vali stepped back but didn't let go of my hand, so we walked across the grass together, hand in hand, as if we were young lovers going for a stroll under the enormous moon. Once we crested the nearest hill, I realized what I'd seen sparkling on the grass when I first arrived.

Windows. An enormous building sunk into the hillside. Its hundreds of black windows winked in the moonlight. There was something deeply unsettling about that stretch of darkened windows, and my skin prickled with the sudden urge to walk away. Quickly.

"What's that?" I asked.

"It's Val-Hall." Vali smiled at me. "Would you care to accompany me to the hall of the All-father, my love?"

I couldn't quite force myself to return his smile. "Of course."

As we approached the massive building, I was able to slowly make out more features of Val-Hall. The windows were dark, but orange torches flared behind a pair of open doors, casting a flickering illumination across a looming staircase. The smell of roasting meat drifted toward us, and my stomach clenched painfully, reminding me I hadn't eaten since breakfast. In a different world.

The man I'd seen on the beach stood at the top of the staircase, his arms crossed beneath his broad-brimmed hat. His empty eye socket was even more disconcerting this time around, and his expression was stony. He didn't acknowledge us until we'd climbed the steps to stand next to him.

"All-Father," Vali said, bowing low before him.

"Lokisen," Óðinn said. "I thought Níðhöggr broke you."

Vali frowned. "I—"

"Well, well, well. If it isn't Karen McDonald," Óðinn said, cutting off Vali completely. "You didn't bring me what I wanted, woman. But you know what they say. Don't expect anything from mortal women, and you'll never be disappointed!"

I stood, frozen, with my mouth hanging open. For some reason, his words made me want to cry.

"I assume you have a reason for bringing us here," Vali said.

Óðinn laughed. "Oh, I didn't bring you here. This is just where you washed up. Wreckage on the tide, you and your whore."

Blood rushed to my cheeks, and I took a deep breath, ready to tell Óðinn exactly what I thought of him and his stupid hall, but he cut me off.

"So, I expect you two are hungry. You need a place to spend the night. And I do happen to have a few ideas which may interest you."

Vali glanced at me, then back to Óðinn. "We're willing to listen to your ideas," he said.

Óðinn clapped his hands together. "Lovely! Well then, do come in."

We stepped across the threshold and entered Val-Hall. I followed Vali and Óðinn through a vast, echoing room filled with long tables and benches. I could still smell food, although these tables were all empty, and the fireplaces looked dark and cold. The torches cast odd shadows along the walls. It felt like someone, or something, moved in those shadows, and I grasped Vali's arm a bit harder than was perhaps necessary.

"What happened here?" Vali asked, his voice low.

Óðinn gave a hard, bitter laugh. "Your father happened."

The hallway narrowed, then opened into a small room. A fire blazed in the corner, and a neat, circular table in the center of the room was set with golden plates which glimmered in the candlelight. A basket of rolls sat in the middle of the table, and my stomach rumbled.

Óðinn sat, then gestured to the table. "Please. Do join me."

I pulled back a seat and joined Óðinn, reaching for a roll. This had to be a trap of some kind, but I was too damn hungry to care. Vali removed Hrotti's sheath from his back and leaned the hilt of the sword against the table, within easy reach.

Food filled the golden plates as soon as Vali sat down; piles of ribs, stacks of small, roasted potatoes, and what looked like a purple sort of coleslaw. Heavy wooden goblets appeared soon after the food. I sniffed my goblet before trying a tiny sip of whatever was inside. The drink was amazingly light, with a gentle bite and a hint of carbonation.

"Wow," I said. "What's that?"

Vali laughed. "It's mead."

"Right. I should've guessed." Our eyes met across the table, and my heart surged against my rib cage. This was almost certainly a trap. But, damn, at least I was trapped with him.

Vali cleared his throat. "You had ideas to discuss?" he said.

"Right," said Óðinn, wiping his mouth with a thick, ivory napkin. "All business. I appreciate that about you, boy. You are so much like your mother."

A shadow flickered over Vali's face.

"You did hear about your mother, didn't you?" Óðinn said. "Such a tragedy."

"Yes, I heard," he said, his voice low and even.

I reached for Vali's hand under the table and wrapped his fingers in my own, squeezing gently.

"The ideas?" Vali said.

Óðinn scratched the side of his cheek and turned to look absentmindedly around the room. "It's a nice place, Val-Hall. And, as you can tell, it's significantly less crowded than it used to be."

"What did my father do?" Vali asked.

Óðinn cleared his throat, looking from me to Vali. "Listen, boy. You've been with the wolves a long time, but this you should remember. There's a way things began. And there's a way things need to end." Óðinn smacked his palms together in front of his face, making me jump in my chair.

"You're talking about Ragnarök?" Vali asked. His voice was hushed, almost as if he was afraid someone might overhear us.

"Exactly!" Óðinn boomed. "The last great battle. The Æsir riding across Vígríðr to meet the Jötunn. The way the Nine Realms were supposed to end, damn it." He smacked his hand on the table so hard the basket of rolls jumped in the air.

"Excuse me," I said. "Ragna...what?"

"Ragnarök," Vali answered. "The battle that ends all Nine Realms."

I shivered. "The end of the world?"

Vali and Óðinn nodded as if the end of everything was no big deal.

"Wait," I said, turning to Óðinn. "You wanted the world to end?"

Vali leaned back in his chair and crossed his arms over his chest. "You had a plan."

Óðinn laughed. It made my skin crawl. "Of course, I had a plan!" he said. "But your idiot father had a plan, too. And now, instead of a nice, clean break and a brand new world, we've got a damn mess. The Nine Realms fractured. Níðhöggr awake, my warriors scattered, the Æsir washing up all over the place."

Óðinn tossed a bone over his shoulder, wiped his hands and mouth on a napkin, and raised an eyebrow at Vali. "Listen, boy. I didn't invite you here to talk about what happened. We survived. We're starting over. The Æsir are coming back to Asgard, son. The armies are rebuilding."

Óðinn smiled, and the hairs on the back of my neck prickled. "Vali Lokisen," he said, "would you like to come home?"

The room was so quiet I could almost hear the constant thudding of my heart.

"Come...home?" Vali's voice sounded very small, as if it were coming from far away.

"Why not?" Óðinn spread his arms, a magnanimous gesture that seemed to encompass the room, the vast, empty hall, the dark and restless ocean. "I'll give you the house you grew up in. You remember that place? With the rose bushes?"

"On the beach," Vali murmured. "Yes, I remember."

"Well, come back to Asgard, then." Óðinn's one eye flickered over me, like an afterthought, and he cleared his throat. "You can even bring your woman."

"Wait, wait, wait," I stammered. "You want Vali to come back and, what, help Níðhöggr? Blow up Yellowstone? End the world? Is that it?"

Óðinn didn't even look at me. "What do you think, boy?" he said.

Vali cleared his throat. "What's the price?" he said.

I turned to the great hilt resting against the table. Hrotti. The sword Óðinn asked me to bring back. There it is, I thought. There's your price.

I was so focused on Hrotti that, when Óðinn finally spoke, I was certain I'd misheard. Vali nodded, then turned to me and raised an eyebrow.

"I'm sorry, what?" I asked.

"It's my father," said Vali. "Óðinn wants Loki."

"You want us to bring Loki here?" I asked, still not sure I'd heard him correctly.

"Not at all," said Óðinn, his blue eye sparkling jovially. "I just want you to kill the bastard."

CHAPTER TWENTY NINE

Óðinn led us back down the hallway in silence, stopping to open a narrow wooden door. "I'll see you in the morning," he said, in a way that gave his words the force of a threat.

Shivering, I followed Vali through the door into a small, dark room. A bed loomed in one corner, and the remains of a fire smoldered on a hearth in the corner.

"I don't trust him," I said after the door closed behind us. "And I don't like him, either."

Vali laughed. "That's very wise of you."

He bent to blow on the embers glowing in the fireplace, and the flames leapt back to life. I sat on the edge of the bed and sank into the soft mattress as Vali fed kindling to the fire.

"What do you think?" I asked, trying to stifle a yawn. "What are we going to do?"

Vali turned to me, his eyes sparkling in the firelight. He pulled Hrotti off his shoulder and propped it against the wall. "I think I've never fucked you properly."

A slow shiver of arousal slid through my body. "Properly?"

Vali grinned. "Yes, properly. On a bed."

He pulled off his shirt, and a low moan slipped from my lips. Suddenly I was no longer tired.

"So, I think," he continued, "right now, I'm going to fuck you properly. On a bed. And after that, I think we'll both sleep very deeply."

I shivered again, but this time not from the cold. Vali reached for his pants, sliding them over his hips and muscular thighs, and I completely forgot about being stranded in Asgard. His eyes flashed as he crawled onto the bed.

I pulled the shreds of my silk turtleneck off my chest and scrambled to shove my pants down my hips, but Vali stopped me.

"Oh no," he whispered, bringing his lips to my hands and kissing the inside of my wrist. "I said I'm going to fuck you *properly*."

Our eyes met in the flicker of firelight.

"Lie down," he said, his voice thick and low.

I did as he said. Vali followed me, the weight of his body pressing against mine. I could feel the heat of his erection against my thighs and I moaned, cursing the layer of clothing between us. Vali's chest shook against mine as he laughed.

"Be patient," he whispered. "I haven't gotten to enjoy you on a bed yet."

I bit my lip and tried to be patient as Vali kissed my neck, moving slowly from my ear to my collarbone. His tongue flickered across my chest, tracing the curve of my breast to circle my areola. When he drew my nipple into his mouth I gasped out loud, rocking my hips against his. His hands moved over my arms until his fingers laced with mine, pressing me into the soft mattress while I writhed under him.

"Oh, Vali, please," I moaned.

He turned to smile at me. "What is it?" His hips moved slowly against mine, making my entire body tremble. "Do you want me to stop?"

"No!" I pleaded.

He grinned and moved down my body, his lips kissing a trail across the curve of my stomach. He hesitated at the waistband of my ski pants, and I moaned again, pleading wordlessly. Vali pulled my pants over the rise of my hips with agonizing delicacy, stopping to kiss every inch of newly exposed skin. When he reached my knees, I bent legs, forcing my pants off. He laughed again.

"Is it that hard to slow down?" he asked, spreading my legs before him.

I tried to respond, but he slid his fingers up my inner thigh, and all I could manage was a low, hungry moan.

"I don't think you realize," he said, bending to kiss my thighs, "how hard it was to stay away from you."

I whimpered as his lips moved across my skin, closer to the curl of hair between my legs.

"How many nights I lay awake, thinking of all the things I wanted to do to you," Vali murmured, his breath sending sparks across my skin.

With a jolt, his fingers reached my sex, sliding inside. I shivered as his lips touched the apex, his tongue pressing delicately on my clit as his fingers curled inside me, unleashing a wave of pleasure.

"Now that I have you," Vali said, his voice raised so I could hear his words over my own pants and gasps, "I'm going to do it all."

Vali's tongue pressed harder, and his fingers moved faster. My orgasm crashed through me like an explosion, sudden and overpowering. I had enough time to cry out before my mind dissolved in a red haze.

I sank into the pillows, my eyes slowly re-adjusting to the flicker of firelight on the ceiling. Vali usually liked to tease me, to bring me just to the brink and then pull back, ebbing and retreating until I'm out of my mind with need, and the final orgasm burns through my body so powerfully it's like dying. But here I'd just come so hard and fast I barely had time to register what was happening.

"Oh, I'm sorry," I gasped. "I just-I was so ready."

"Don't," Vali murmured, his breath warming my thighs.

My oversensitive skin sang with his touch as he moved from between my legs to press his lips against my neck. My body responded to the press of his weight, my back arching instinctively to meet his hips. His hand slipped between us, caressing the inside of my thighs. His fingers reached my labia, sending electric currents through my core.

"Vali," I moaned. "I just-I can't again-"

"Shhhhh," he hissed, his breath hot against my collarbone. "Properly."

My hips ignored my protests and began rocking against the heat of Vali's body as his thumb circled my clit, pressing harder and harder, while his fingers curled inside me, rediscovering the spot that had just sent me over the edge. I barely had time to register what he was doing when my second orgasm rocked through my body, sending my head spinning and making me scream his name.

I collapsed onto the bed, barely aware of where I was. Or who I was. Dimly, I realized Vali was parting my legs, pressing his stiff cock against the heat of my sex. I moaned, and he entered me with a sudden thrust, filling me completely, jarring me out of my post-orgasmic haze.

"Oh, God," I moaned as my legs wrapped around his hips totally of their own accord.

Vali knelt above me, his head back, all the muscles in his neck tense. He cried out, something guttural and animal and entirely victorious, before returning his fingers to the smoldering ember of my clit. His touch wasn't exactly gentle, not this time, but my body responded in a way I'd never experienced, the pleasure scorching my thoughts and memories, destroying my rationality, until all that was left was our two bodies, coming together as one, flickering and surging and burning, burning, burning in the firelight.

CHAPTER THIRTY

I woke to the sound of crashing waves and, for a few disorienting seconds, I had no idea where I was. The wall opposite me was a warm, creamy white, shimmering with the golden sunlight of early morning, I heard the low rumble of the ocean in the distance, and I was wrapped in what may very well have been a bearskin.

Clearly, this was not my bedroom.

I sat up, pushing the dark fur off my chest. Where the hell was I? An enormous fireplace dominated the wall opposite the bed, and a row of sunny windows behind me opened to the ocean. The fireplace brought back some memories. I ran my fingers over the thick fur next to me, then leaned into the pillow. It smelled like him, warm and wild.

So, I really had found Vali.

I stood up, pulling my shredded silk turtleneck and long underwear pants from the tangled mess of clothing on the floor. Something hard smacked the floor, and I bent to see my cell phone, still wrapped in its clear plastic drybag.

"Shit," I whispered. "Colin and Zeke."

The last time I'd seen my two graduate students, they'd been outside Níðhöggr's cave, looking scared and worried. I pulled the phone out and slid my fingers across the screen. My phone flashed *No Service*. Of course. Feeling like an idiot, I slipped it back into my pocket, trying to tell myself that Colin and Zeke had the common sense to ski back to their car after I vanished into thin air. I leaned against the door with a heavy sigh.

"The second I find cell reception," I muttered to myself, "I'm calling Zeke."

I opened the door beside the fireplace and stepped through. Vali stood in the next room, facing an open doorway. The rising sun illuminated the lines of his very beautiful, very naked body. I froze. This is what I wanted, I realized. Vali, with me, when we woke. This is what I've always wanted, ever since I'd first dreamt of him.

He turned and smiled. "Good morning, beautiful Karen."

"Good morning." My voice sounded shaky and uneven. "Where are we?"

The room appeared to be a small kitchen, with a sunny sink and a little wooden table. The doorway beyond Vali opened to a small, sheltered beach. I could just see the stones of a pathway leading through what looked like a tangle of wild rosebushes.

"This is where I grew up," Vali said. "Although the house was different then."

I met his eyes. "Different?"

"It was bigger," he said, his voice soft and thoughtful. "The great hall was much grander, Nari and I had our own rooms..."

A shadow crossed his face, and he fell silent. Nari, the brother he killed. I could picture them with painful clarity, two boys racing down that stone path, through the wild rose bushes. Playing together on the beach. Crashing through this beautiful little house, breaking its silence with shrieks and laughter. God, how bittersweet it must feel to be here again. I crossed the room to wrap my arm around his waist.

Vali turned to me, cupping my chin in his hand. "Do you like it here, Karen?" he asked, his golden eyes hooded and solemn.

My breath caught when I tried to answer him. "I - I don't really know," I said. "I haven't exactly seen much of this place."

His shoulders relaxed, and the ghost of a smile played across his lips. "Shall I give you a tour, then?"

The house was perfect. It was, in fact, disturbingly perfect. Every room opened to the ocean, from the cozy kitchen to the bathroom with an enormous brass tub. It was exactly the right size for two people.

"But I don't understand," I said, slowly. We'd come back to the cozy little kitchen, the room where I'd first seen Vali leaning against the door.

"What don't you understand?" He pulled back a chair and sat down at the table.

The wooden table suddenly filled with what appeared to be blueberry pancakes, sausages, and steaming mugs of coffee. I jumped, banging my head against the doorway to the bedroom.

"What the hell?" I yelped.

Vali smiled. "Oh, that. It's just breakfast. When you're hungry, you sit down, and you eat."

I shook my head and took a deep breath. "Not that. Okay, not just that."

The pancakes smelled amazing. I pulled up a chair and sat down across from Vali. "Last night," I said, reaching for a coffee mug, "Óðinn left us in - ah!" I flinched and pulled my hand away from the mug.

Looking down, I saw parallel red gashes across my palm. Hazy memories from last night surged through my mind. I remembered Vali's glowing blue sword, Hrotti, pointed at my chest. And I remembered pushing it away, ripping the hell out of my clothes in the process.

"Let me see," said Vali, his eyes dark and serious.

"It's nothing."

Vali frowned and reached for my hand. Reluctantly, I unfurled my fingers. He exhaled sharply, shaking his head.

"You're quite brave," he said.

I snorted and picked up the coffee mug with my uninjured left hand.

"Hrotti is no ordinary weapon," Vali said. "I'm afraid you may always bear a scar."

"What is Hrotti?" I asked.

Vali took a bite of his pancake and chewed contemplatively. "It's magic. It's the sword Sigurðr used to slay the dragon Fáfnir. Of course, Fáfnir was just an enchanted little shithead dwarf. He wasn't a real dragon."

Vali went back to his pancake, as if talking about dragons and enchantments was an ordinary breakfast conversation. Maybe it was, in this place. I opened my hand and stared at my palm. Two little red lines stared back at me, like parallel paper cuts. They didn't seem like much for pushing a weapon of myth and legend off my chest.

"And you're right," Vali said, as I attempted to pick up my fork without re-opening the cuts from Hrotti.

I stared at him.

"Óðinn left us in Val-Hall," Vali continued. "All the houses in Asgard connect to Val-Hall, whether you want them to or not. That's why they say Val-Hall has five hundred and forty doors."

"How exactly does that work?" I asked.

Vali shrugged. "I have no idea. Óðinn and Loki built Val-Hall together, back before they hated each other."

I blinked in surprise. "Your dad built this place?"

"Of course. Óðinn and my father are the most powerful magic users in the Nine Realms." His eyes darkened. "You can imagine what a disappointment I was."

"Oh, Vali—"

"Loki's own son couldn't even cast a simple illusion. I couldn't travel through the æther. Karen, even the mortals laughed at me."

I frowned as the last conversation I'd had with Loki percolated up through my memory.

"But that's not what he said." I paused, trying to remember Loki's exact words. "He said...you were everything he once wished he could be."

Vali barked a hard, sharp laugh. "Well, they do call him the Lie-smith."

He turned to face the window, and I decided to drop this particular subject. Vali had probably re-lived quite enough painful memories for one morning.

When he spoke again, his voice was lighter and softer. "Nari was always trying to find ways around it, that link to Val-Hall," Vali said. "Time was different as a wolf. Nari's been dead for over a thousand years, I think. But to me, it still feels like yesterday. I keep expecting him to walk through those doors, telling me he's created another passage to Sif's private chambers."

I reached across the table and took his hand. Vali smiled, but his eyes glistened with tears.

"I don't think the pain ever goes away," I said. "Not really. Not when you lose someone you love that much."

"Your daughter," he whispered.

My heart rose to my throat. She would have been six this year, my beautiful Meredith. She would have started first grade.

"How did you know?" I asked.

"You used to talk about her, in the pine forest. On the moss."

I shook my head. "I don't remember that."

"I don't think you wanted to remember."

I looked up to meet Vali's golden eyes. He looked especially handsome in the soft morning light, and I was suddenly so happy to be alive, my chest ached.

"I love you," I said. I hadn't meant to say anything; the words tumbled from my mouth unbidden.

"I love you too, beautiful Karen." He squeezed my hand once before letting go and returning to his pancakes.

We finished breakfast together, in comfortable silence, as the rising sun flooded the little kitchen with bright, golden light. Afterward, I tried to pull what was left of my clothes together in the bedroom. My jacket was totally destroyed; Hrotti had ripped the front completely open. My fleece top was also ripped down the middle, as was the thin silk turtleneck I wore against my skin.

An enormous wooden wardrobe stood in the corner, next to the bed, with an old, fly-speckled full-length mirror on the front. I stood next to the mirror and examined my torso in the sunlight. Sure enough, there was a thin, red scrape across my chest, from my collarbone to the swell of my left breast. I ran my fingertips across the tender skin and smiled at my reflection. Now that was a scar for pushing a weapon of myth and legend off my chest.

But how was I going to cover it?

This morning I'd worn my same long underwear pants and ripped silk turtleneck, but the shirt was little more than tatters at this point. I wasn't exactly looking forward to facing Óðinn again under any circumstances, but especially not wearing a few shreds of dirty maroon silk.

I cracked open the door to the kitchen. Vali leaned against the counter, already dressed in the dark leather he'd worn in Yellowstone.

"Um, I've got a slight problem," I said.

Vali's brow furrowed.

"Nothing bad," I said. "It's, uh, I guess I don't have anything to wear."

He smiled. "Just check the wardrobe."

"Okay..."

I closed the door again and narrowed my eyes as I approached the wardrobe. It was, by all appearances, a perfectly ordinary wardrobe. Still, I opened the door a tiny crack at first, afraid it was going to magic me away to someone else's bedchamber.

The wardrobe was full of women's clothing, mostly frilly, fancy gowns. I pulled out a pale blue dress with lace trim. It felt like it was made of velvet. I pressed the fabric to my chest and glanced in the mirror. It looked like it should fit, so I tugged off my wrecked turtleneck and stepped into the dress.

It was my size. No, not just my size; it fit me exactly, as if it had all been custom made to hug my body, even my big hips and short arms. I twirled in the mirror, admiring the way the pale dress made my waist look slender and my tits look freaking enormous. Then a dark green dress caught my eye, and I figured I'd better try that one as well.

I ENDED UP TRYING ON a few more of the dresses than was strictly necessary. They were all ridiculously comfortable and hopelessly flattering. I'd never looked so good, I thought, not even during that formal engagement photo shoot Barry's parents insisted on buying for us. I was wearing a sleek, red sheath dress and admiring a dark blue ballgown when Vali knocked on the door.

"Everything okay in here?" he asked.

I laughed. "Oh, damn! I'm sorry, I got a little distracted. Come in."

Vali gasped, and I turned to make sure he wasn't hurt.

"What's wrong?" I asked.

He gave me a hungry smile, wrapping his hands around the tight waist of the little red dress. "You," he whispered, his breath soft against my neck, "look amazing."

His breath was soft against my skin, and it filled me with a low, hungry ache.

"I guess I got carried away," I said, gesturing to the pile of dresses I'd tossed on the enormous bed.

But Vali wasn't paying any attention to the pile of dresses on the bed. He ran his lips along my neck in a way that made my skin flush with heat. Then he grabbed the skirt in his fist and lifted it to press his hands into my thighs. I rubbed my hips into his, unable to stop my moan when I felt the hard heat of his arousal.

"I thought you liked the dress," I said. "And now you're trying to take it off."

"No," he growled. "I want you to leave it on."

AFTER A SECOND HELPING of breakfast, which turned out to be smoked fish and what tasted like blood sausage, Vali and I walked along the stone pathway to the beach. I'd finally chosen to wear the most normal-looking outfit in the wardrobe, soft black pants and an elegant, long-sleeved, low-cut sapphire top. At least the pants had pockets, and the top was almost the sort of thing you might see at a Renaissance Fair. I hated to leave the short red dress behind, but I couldn't see facing Óðinn in anything quite that sexy.

Besides, it needed a wash after what we'd done in it.

Vali's golden eyes grew dark as we crested a small rise at the end of the beach. From the top, I could just make out the distant windows and sweeping wooden staircase of Val-Hall.

Vali turned to face me. "Before we see Óðinn again," he said, "please tell me what you think. Do you like this place?"

I took a deep breath, searching for the words. "It's very beautiful. I mean, the house is perfect. The clothes are, uh, very nice. And breakfast showing up by itself, well, that's a plus."

Vali tilted his head. "You hesitated."

I looked past him to the slow undulations of the waves, and the white crests of the breakers crashing against the pale beach. "Well, it's just—" I stopped, worried I'd sound like an idiot.

Vali watched me. The wind off the ocean lifted his dark hair, and it danced around his shoulders.

I sighed. "Well, what exactly would I do all day?" I asked

Vali laughed. The sound rang off the green hillsides.

"No, I'm serious," I insisted. "I mean, it's beautiful, but I don't know how long I could stare at this ocean without losing my freaking mind."

Vali raised an eyebrow. "You don't think I could entertain you?"

"Oh, hell yes, you could entertain me. I mean, I'd love to stay here and do nothing but fuck you for days. For weeks, even. But don't you think we'd eventually, I don't know, want to do something..." My voice trailed off. Now I really was sounding like an idiot.

"I remember my mother did embroidery," Vali said, with a soft half smile on his full lips.

Something in my face must have betrayed what I thought of embroidery, because Vali held up his hands in surrender and laughed. "So, beautiful Karen, I take it you prefer the chaos of Midgard?"

"I do," I whispered. "I like my job, Vali. I like my chaotic, stressful life in Montana. I don't want to give that up. Is that...okay?"

Vali grinned. "Of course, that's okay."

"And I—I want you to be a part of it," I stammered.

Vali brought my fingers to his lips and kissed them. "Beautiful Karen, I wouldn't have it any other way."

I felt a hard knot in my stomach begin to unfold as some nameless fear I hadn't even known was there finally let go.

"Now, my darling," Vali said, "shall we meet with Óðinn and find our way back to Midgard?"

"Yes, please," I said, taking his arm and turning my back on the little cottage by the sea.

Óðinn met us in the fields. Very suddenly. One minute Vali and I were walking, our fingers interlaced, staring at the winking windows of Val-Hall or the crashing surf against the stone beach. The next, Óðinn stood in front of us, his single blue eye sparkling.

I jumped. I might have stumbled backward, if Vali's arm hadn't steadied me. Vali bowed slightly. The sunlight winked off Hrotti's hilt nestled in its sheath across Vali's broad shoulders.

"All-Father," Vali said, his voice low and formal.

"Lokisen," Óðinn said, nodding briefly. "The house isn't quite like it used to be, but we can change that. If you're willing to pay the price, of course."

Vali said nothing. Óðinn's broad smile did not seem to reach his eye.

"I take it you're ready to go?" Óðinn said.

"We are," said Vali, his fingers tightening around my hand.

Óðinn nodded. "Heimdallr usually handles this. But he hasn't come back yet, so you're stuck with me. Hold on tight."

The world spun. With a start, I noticed a rainbow over the ocean. A very vivid, very straight rainbow. It was enormous, as big as the ocean, as big as the sky. It was all I could see—

—and then it was very cold, and very bright.

So bright it hurt. My eyes squeezed closed reflexively. Glare, I realized. I was staring at the brilliant glare of bright sunshine on ice. I moved my hand to shade my eyes and found my fingers were still knotted with Vali's.

"You okay?" he asked.

Slowly, Vali's golden eyes came into focus. I nodded and felt his arms wrap around my chest.

"Where are we?" I asked.

It was so cold the words bit at my lungs. I looked up and saw bare tree limbs glistening with ice.

"I know this place," Vali said.

My eyes focused on the trees beyond his shoulder. We stood on a tiny frozen stream, in an ash grove. The trees gleamed with ice, refracting the sunlight in a thousand frozen sparks. The ash grove and the frozen stream both seemed deeply familiar, yet I couldn't quite place them.

"Yes," Vali said. "I know it now. This is where I first met you."

"What?"

Vali pulled back, smiling. "Over there," he said, moving his hands to my waist and turning my hips. "Do you remember?"

I followed his gaze through the ash trees and up a small hill to a woodpile.

My father's woodpile.

The world spun again, and I fell backward.

CHAPTER THIRTY ONE

I opened my eyes slowly. Vali's face hovered in front of me, his brow furrowed, his golden eyes dark with concern.

"Karen?"

I shook my head. I was now sitting on the ice instead of leaning against Vali's chest, and the air was so cold my nose stung with every breath. "Shit, I'm sorry," I said.

Vali offered me his hand, and I took it. He wrapped his arms around me as I stood and gave me a long, sweet kiss that made my body flush with heat, despite the cold air.

"Do you not remember?" he whispered.

"I remember. The black wolf, by the wood pile. Of course, I remember." I pulled away and ran my hand along his cheek. "I just can't believe it was you. I thought—I honestly thought I invented you, as something to cheer me up during the worst time of my life."

Vali laughed. "My beautiful Karen, I thought the same. And then, when I found you again, I thought it must have been the happiest day of my long life."

"Found me?" My breath caught in my throat as I realized what he was saying. "Oh, Vali! Did you follow me? Did you follow me to Montana?"

His arms tightened around my waist. "I did. I'm not sure I even realized what I was doing, but yes. I searched for you. I spent years searching for you."

His lips were on mine before I could say anything, his tongue deep inside me, his hands running the length of my back. I moaned in his mouth as my hips rubbed against his, my body trembling under his touch. When he pulled away, the cold air burned my lungs as I tried to catch my breath.

"Karen," he growled.

I put my finger on his lips. "Vali, any other time, I would fuck your brains out right here. But it's goddamn cold, and I'm freezing already."

He sighed and kissed my finger so slowly and sensually that I started to seriously weigh the risk of frostbite if I ripped off my clothes.

"Fine," he sighed. "What now?"

I shivered in his arms, trying to press more of my body against his warmth. Something hard bit into my hip. My cell phone.

"Oh, crap," I yelped. "Colin and Zeke!"

"Who?"

Vali frowned as I dug into my pocket and pulled out my cell phone. The low battery icon flashed weakly in the top corner, but at least I had two bars of cell signal. I pressed Zeke's name as my stomach tied itself in knots. The phone rang hollowly against my ear. Come on, Zeke, I thought. Please at least have the sense to get out of Yellowstone in the middle of winter...

"Boss Lady!" Zeke cheered.

"Thank God," I gasped. "You're okay?"

"Uh, yeah, considering. How the hell are you?"

"I'm okay—"

"Did you find him?" Zeke asked, cutting me off.

"Yes," I said, smiling at Vali's hopelessly confused expression. "I found him."

"Well, nice. That's good and all. But, uh, Boss Lady, I got some news. And it ain't good."

My phone gave a sad little ping, warning me that my battery was dying. My heart sank. "Is it Colin? Or our funding?"

"Nah, none of that. Colin's just fine, and the NSF's got our asses covered for the next two fiscal years. Boss Lady, it's the park."

Zeke took a deep breath over the phone as my phone pinged again. My mouth went dry.

"I take it you haven't exactly been keeping up on the news?" he said.

"No." I frowned. "Actually, I'm not even sure what day it is."

I thought that might make Zeke laugh, but his voice was deep and serious. "There's a new hot spring bubbling up in West Yellowstone," he said.

"What? Zeke, that's not even within the caldera boundary!"

"Yeah, I know that. It's swallowed half the goddamn town. And the grizzly bears are coming out of the park. There was one walking right down 191 into Big Sky, middle of the day and everything."

I shook my head. "They should be hibernating right now."

"It's legit, Boss Lady. It's been all over the news. People are freaking the fuck out. There's, like, twelve different TV stations in Bozeman right now. John Rodriguez was interviewed by NBC, CBS, and the motherfuckin' BBC, trying to argue that all this crazy cat crap could be part of a natural migration cycle, or some other bullshit."

I did my best to ignore the absolutely irrational pang of jealousy that I wasn't being interviewed by the BBC.

My phone pinged, and Zeke continued. "Uh, Boss Lady, I'm guessing you know what's actually going on, don't you?" he said.

"Maybe," I said. "Listen, I've got to let you go. My phone's losing it. Be careful, okay?"

Zeke's response was cut off as my cell phone died in my trembling hands. I met Vali's eye. "We've got a problem."

"Níðhöggr," Vali said.

"We didn't stop him."

"Of course we didn't," Vali said. "I doubt we even slowed him down."

My gut clenched into a hard knot of fear. "What the hell are we going to do now?"

"We need to get you somewhere warm," Vali said, taking my cold hands in his.

"Shit," I whispered. There was an obvious solution to that problem, at least. "Do you want to meet my parents?"

MY FEET CRUNCHED THROUGH the ice-crusted snow as we climbed out of the ash grove and up to the woodpile behind my parents' house. A thin column of white smoke rose from the chimney above the two bay garage at the bottom of the driveway. The McDonald's Auto Repair sign glistened beneath its icy casing. I pictured Dad bent over the open hood of some ancient rust-bucket held together with salvaged parts and sheer willpower. Smoke rose from the chimney of the house behind as well, so they must be here. In one place or the other.

I faced Vali. He looked very tall and wild, dressed entirely in black leather, with Hrotti's enormous sheath strapped across his back. He could not possibly be more different from Barry Richardson.

"Here goes nothing," I muttered under my breath.

"Let's try the shop first," I said, turning toward the garage.

Vali nodded. He looked quite stern, and possibly just a little intimidated.

We picked our steps carefully down the ice-slicked driveway, trying to stay on the patches where Dad had scattered ashes from the woodstove for traction on the ice. The little silver bell above the door to McDonald's Auto Repair jingled as I pushed the door open, and the smell of oil, exhaust, and rust enveloped me. An ancient Chevy pickup squatted in the first bay, and a space heater clanked away in the corner. I coughed to clear my throat.

"Hello?" I said.

Mom stood up from the desk. She met my eyes, then sat back down again very quickly.

"Karen?" she asked, almost to herself. "Scott! Come here!"

The old duct-tape-encrusted creeper seat squealed and clattered as Dad slid out from under the Chevy. He sat up and stared at me, wiping his hands reflexively on the rag tucked in his belt.

"Karen?" he said. "Is everything okay?"

I opened my mouth, but nothing came out.

"Mr. and Mrs. McDonald?" Vali said from behind me.

Shit! What the hell was I going to say about the enormous fucking sword on his back? I took a deep breath.

"I'm Vali Lokisen," he said. "I'm so pleased to meet you. Karen's told me so much about you."

Vali stepped around me to shake my mother's hand, and I stared at him, trying to keep my mouth from falling open. He was wearing dark jeans and a pressed chambray shirt. His long, dark hair was pulled back into a neat ponytail. He looked entirely... normal. I hardly realized he was still talking.

"I offered to surprise her with a New Year's vacation to anywhere she wanted," Vali said. My parents were staring at him with their mouths open. "And she told me she wanted to see you."

"Oh, Karen!" Mom pushed away from the desk and walked over to me, grabbing my arms. "Oh, honey, you didn't need to do that!"

"Uh..." I coughed, trying to tear my eyes off of Vali.

The room filled with a sharp electronic trill. I frowned.

"That sounds like my phone," I said. "But the battery just died."

With everyone staring at me, I pulled my phone out of my pocket. A name flashed across the glossy black surface.

"It's... it's Caroline," I said, meeting Vali's gaze. "Caroline Laufeyiarson."

He shrugged. "Take it."

"Just a minute. Sorry!" I said to my parents, who were still gaping openly at Vali.

I pushed open the door, listening to the bell chime as I stepped back into the cold. Once the door was safely closed behind me, I swiped the screen, raising the phone to my ear.

"Hello?"

"Hello!" Caroline's bright voice came over the line, somehow transmitting clearly despite my phone's dead battery. "Karen, are you okay?"

I rubbed the bridge of my nose. "Yeah. I'm fine. Listen, this isn't a great time, actually—"

"Oh, right," she said. "I know. I just thought it'd be a bit, you know, abrupt. Not to warn you."

"Warn me?" Something cold danced up the back of my neck.

Caroline coughed delicately over the phone. "Behind you," she said.

Very slowly, I pressed *End Call* and slipped my phone back into my pocket. Then I turned around.

Loki stood next to the door of McDonald's Auto Repair, his arms folded over his chest and his bright red hair shimmering in the icy air. He raised an eyebrow.

"Hi," Loki said.

CHAPTER THIRTY TWO

I opened the door to my dad's shop and heard laughter. My parents were both smiling at Vali, their faces happy and relaxed. Well, damn, it certainly hadn't taken long for Vali to win over my folks.

"Hey," I said. "Vali, I need a minute."

Vali walked over to me and put his arm around my waist. "What is it?"

"Loki," I whispered. "Outside."

"Take me to him," Vali growled under his breath.

I spun to face my parents. "Mom, Dad, we've got to go."

I hesitated, slowly realizing how freaking weird that sounded. "I mean, we're going to head into town. I really want to show Vali the, uh—" I paused and tried desperately to think of something, anything, in downtown Pinevale that would be worth showing off.

"The gazebo," I said, finally. "I want to show him the gazebo. So, we'll just be going. Now. Right now."

Mom smiled. "Well, what do you two want for dinner? We have plenty of moose, and I'll start on the bread right away. You could get some ice cream from Plourde's, maybe? And some wine?"

I tried very hard to smile at my parents like a normal person. "Yeah. That sounds great. We'll get ice cream and wine."

Vali opened the door, the silver bell chiming above him, and I followed, bracing myself for the blast of cold air. As I stepped onto the ice of my parents' driveway and pulled the door closed behind us, I heard the hiss of metal against leather. I turned and saw Hrotti gleaming in the winter light.

"Father," Vali hissed, staring down the length of his blade at Loki, who was still leaning against the cold metal wall of McDonald's Auto Repair.

"Welcome back, son," said Loki.

"Wait!" I yelled, pressing my hand to Vali's chest.

The world spun—

—And it was no longer cold. I blinked as my surroundings swam slowly into focus. We were in a warm, brightly lit room, with huge, open windows. The sparkle of light on water filled the windows, almost blinding me. I turned away to face a back wall covered with books. The floor was a jumbled mess of bags, blankets, and baby accoutrements.

"Karen!" Caroline cried.

She was sitting on an enormous, round bed in the center of the room, surrounded by a deep nest of pillows, books, and what looked like every toy the Baby Einstein company had ever made. Tiny Adelina nestled against her chest. Loki walked to the bed, kissing Caroline's cheek as he took the white-swaddled infant from her arms. He picked a careful path around boxes of diapers, fuzzy pink blankets, and black-and-white checkered toys to stand in front of Vali. Hrotti hovered in the air between them, gleaming a cold blue in the odd, warm light of the room.

"I should have told you," Loki said, smiling at the baby in his arms. "Vali, you've got a sister."

Vali did not respond, and a knot of fear settled in my stomach.

Caroline nodded formally at Vali. "It's an honor to see you again," she said.

Vali shifted, his body tensing as he brought Hrotti over his head. The sharp metal hissed as it slid into the sheath across his back. I dared to breathe again. Vali stepped away from my side, walking slowly around the room. He stared out the windows, then paced to the back wall, running his hands along the bookcases. Loki, Caroline, and I watched him silently.

"This place has changed," Vali finally said.

"Much has changed," Loki replied.

Vali moved to stand directly in front of Loki. He was taller than his father, I realized with a jolt of surprise. The air between them seemed to thicken somewhat, almost like a thunderstorm was approaching.

"Father," Vali began.

Baby Adelina hiccupped once against Loki's neck and began to scream in her high pitched and piercing infant voice. Vali's eyes widened, and he took a step back.

"Oh, is she hungry?" Caroline asked. "I can take her."

Loki frowned. "No, I don't think she's hungry. I think she just wants to move." He pressed her tiny body against his chest and began to walk, bouncing Adelina in his arms. Her shrill wailing continued.

"Hold on," Caroline said, pulling her phone from somewhere in the sheets of the vast, white bed.. "Her last feeding ended, uh, twenty-three minutes ago. So, yeah, she's probably not hungry." Caroline's forehead creased. "But she hasn't slept in almost five hours, and the book says she should be sleeping every ninety minutes. Loki, I think we should call Dr. Singh again."

Loki sighed. "If you wish."

Caroline turned to me with an apologetic smile. "I'm sorry. Apparently, Adelina doesn't exactly sleep."

"Of course, neither do I," said Loki.

He'd made a full circuit of the room, and he now stood next to the bed, bouncing Adelina's white-clad body gently in his long arms. Adelina's cries finally settled to hiccupping chirps as she nestled against the hollow of his neck.

I wrapped my hand around Vali's arm. "Can we talk?" I whispered.

Vali nodded and turned toward the bookcases. I followed him through a small doorway into a bathroom with another wall of windows open to the vast, glittering sea. What looked like a very expensive breast pump balanced precariously on the copper rim of an enormous bathtub, and almost every surface was cluttered with baby-related detritus.

Vali snorted as the door closed silently behind us. "This place is nothing like it used to be," he muttered. "What the hell is he getting at, changing it like this?"

I took a deep breath, trying to find a place to sit that wasn't covered with empty baby bottles or tiny pink clothes.

"Maybe your dad's not like he used to be, either," I said.

Vali stared at me. "What are you trying to say?"

"Look, I've gotten to know Loki a little more, and—" I stopped, struggling to find the right words. I couldn't exactly say I liked Loki; there was something about him that made my skin crawl. But—

"Don't kill him," I said, feeling ridiculous. "Please."

Vali's brow furrowed.

"I know you're angry," I said, haltingly, "and you have every right to be. And I understand why you'd want to go live in that house on the beach, like Óðinn offered. I just...I think it's a bad deal, killing your dad."

My shoulders slumped. That had to be the worst argument against killing someone in the history of the universe.

Vali laughed. His warm voice echoed through the small room. "Karen, I have no love for Óðinn."

I blinked.

"Óðinn imprisoned me," Vali said. "I have no plans to do his bidding, like one of his mindless dead warriors. There may be little love lost between me and my father, but I promise you, I'm not going to kill him."

A wave of relief swept through my body so suddenly it made tears prick my eyelids. "Thank you," I whispered.

Vali raised an eyebrow as the corners of his mouth twitched into a smile. "Did you really think I'd kill someone holding my baby sister?"

I opened my mouth to respond, but Vali turned and left the bathroom before I had the chance. I followed, trying to decide if he'd meant that as a joke.

"I'm afraid we still have something to discuss," Loki said. He was sitting on the edge of the bed with Adelina gurgling and chirping in his arms.

Vali nodded, his face dark. "Níðhöggr."

Loki handed a grunting Adelina and a glass of water to Caroline. She gave him a grateful smile before pulling open her white robe and bringing Adelina to her breast. I turned away, but not before noticing Caroline had very nice, full breasts. My eyes flickered to Vali. He smiled at me, oblivious to the half-naked woman on the bed.

"Yes, Níðhöggr," Loki said. "Artemis told me the wards are growing stronger. I assume the beast is not defeated?"

"I tried," Vali said. "I couldn't touch it. Remember, Hrotti was used to kill Fáfnir. And he was an enchanted dwarf, not an actual dragon."

"Yes," Loki said. "Yet, I would have chosen the same weapon, and the same path."

Vali stiffened. He looked stunned by this offhand compliment.

"Dragons," Loki muttered, turning to his wife. "What do you know of dragons, my love?"

Caroline sighed and shook her head. Her dark hair fell over her shoulders. "No more than you, I'm afraid. I'm hardly a dragon expert."

A dragon expert. My mind whirled as something unexpected fell into place.

"Oh, shit," I said. "I know a dragon expert."

CHAPTER THIRTY THREE

"A shame you have to leave tonight," my dad said.

"And all the way to Bar Harbor!" Mom chimed. "You watch out for moose on the road, you hear?"

I cringed, wishing I hadn't just lied to my parents about where we were going. And why we had to leave tonight.

"It's been such a pleasure meeting you," Vali said, slipping between me and my parents. "Next time will be a longer stay, I promise. And I want the recipe for that moose roast!"

My mom laughed as her cheeks darkened. "Oh, it's just garlic and salt. Nothing fancy."

She turned to hug Vali, her eyes bright. Vali was so tall her head barely came to his chin. I stared, trying not to let my mouth fall open. In all the time I'd been married to Barry, I could never once remember my mother hugging him. Not even at our wedding.

"You need anything for the drive?" Dad asked as we opened the front door. A gust of frigid air swept between us.

"We'll be fine," Vali said. "Thank you so much for your hospitality. It's been a real pleasure, Mr. and Mrs. McDonald."

My parents beamed as I stepped through the front door. They love him, I thought, shaking my head. One dinner, and they love Vali already.

"See you again soon," I said, trying to ignore the shimmer of tears in Mom's eyes as she closed the door behind us.

We walked down the driveway and around the bend of McDonald's Auto Repair's small parking lot. As soon as we were out of sight of the house, the air around Vali rippled slightly, like a heat shimmer. Then he was once again wearing his black leather and fur, with Hrotti strapped to his back. I reached for his hand, and our fingers interlaced.

"For fuck's sake, don't wear that in Evanston," someone growled.

I jumped. Loki was standing under a tree next to the driveway, his arms crossed against his chest. Vali scowled; Loki ignored him.

"Are you ready?" Loki asked.

I nodded and tried to look confident. My throat suddenly felt very dry.

"Good." Loki clapped his hands together and walked to us. "I need you to picture it."

"237 Monticello Place," I said. "Evanston, Illinois."

Loki shook his head. "No, not the address. Picture it. Close your eyes, and take us there."

I clenched my hands into fists. 237 Monticello Place was the last place in the world I wanted to picture. It had been Barry's house before it was mine. Well, before it was ours; it had never actually been mine. A trim Victorian, walking distance to the University, the kind of elegantly pretentious home most professors could never hope to afford. Of course, most professors weren't Barry Richardson, with his illustrious family history and multiple vacation homes.

A Japanese maple grew in the front yard, shading the sidewalk and the wrap-around porch. In the summers I had put hanging ferns on that porch, but at this time of year the porch would be empty, the wicker rocking chairs and their pastel pillows in storage. The sidewalk would be clear, neatly shoveled by the company Barry paid every winter. There would be an orange bucket of salt by the front steps...

"Good enough," Loki said.

A tingle of electricity moved through my body, and a gust of wind blew back my hair—

—I opened my eyes.

Vali, Loki, and I stood on the sidewalk of Evanston, Illinois, in the fading light of early evening. We were staring at 237 Monticello Place.

"Damn," I whispered.

"Do you want me to join you?" Loki asked.

I shivered. Loki looked perfectly normal, aside from the flaming red hair and unnaturally pale blue eyes. He wore a black suit with a thick jacket, a perfectly acceptable Chicago businessman outfit. Still, there was something disconcertingly feral about him.

"That's okay," I said. "I think this is going to be weird enough with just the two of us."

"Very well. Call Caroline when you're done here," he said.

Without another word, Loki vanished. I blinked, staring at the spot where he'd been standing. A few pale ice crystals shimmered in the empty air. "That's...very disturbing." I said.

"Tell me about it," Vali muttered.

With a deep breath I pulled away from Vali and squared my shoulders. "Well, let's do what we came to do."

I hoped I sounded braver than I felt.

Salt crystals crunched under my boots as I crossed the sidewalk and walked toward the front porch. I held my breath as I stepped past the orange bucket to climb the front steps, trying to tell myself he might not even be home.

My hand trembled as I pressed the doorbell, releasing a cascade of melodic chimes on the other side of the frosted glass. The world began to blur a bit at the edges; I forced myself to breathe, trying to slow the runaway thrumming of my heart.

The hallway light flickered on, and Barry's silhouette appeared in the doorway. A sharp pang lanced through my chest at the sight of those familiar, slightly stooped shoulders. How many years had it been since I'd seen Barry fucking Richardson?

The door swung open, and warm air billowed out.

"Hello?" Barry said.

Our eyes met, and his mouth stayed open, his lips moving soundlessly.

He looked older, I realized with a shock. He had more gray hair around his temples, and he wore a different pair of glasses. Could those possibly be bifocals?

"K-Karen?" he stammered.

I realized with a flash of panic that I had absolutely no idea how to explain what we needed. "Hi, Barry. I, um—"

"Come in," he said. His hand trembled slightly as he pulled away from the door. "Come in, please, it's freezing outside."

"Thank you."

I stepped over the threshold. Vali followed and stood next to me in the entry hall of the home where I'd spent three years of my life. Barry pulled the door shut behind us.

I coughed slightly to clear my throat. "Barry, this is Vali Lokisen."

Barry and Vali shook hands. Then they both turned to me.

"We, uh, we need your help," I said. I took a deep breath and slowly realized I knew exactly what to say. "It's a 'Brown Eyed Girl' thing."

When Barry and I were first dating, we heard the song "Brown Eyed Girl" everywhere we went. At first it was almost a joke. We'd pull up to a gas station to fill his Lincoln, and "Brown Eyed Girl" would be playing over the loudspeakers. We'd go out to the North Avenue Beach on a sweltering summer day, and we'd overhear "Brown Eyed Girl" at the hot dog stand. Barry would turn on the radio as he made me breakfast after the first night I spent at his house, and sure enough, Van Morrison came over the airwaves, singing about making love in the green grass.

At some point it moved from funny to disconcerting, and then it became a joke again. Eventually "Brown Eyed Girl" grew to become shorthand for anything we couldn't exactly explain, or any time things got a little crazy.

Barry's eyes widened behind his unfamiliar glasses. "Sure, Karen. Of course, I'll help. What do you need?"

I shifted uncomfortably on the Persian rug that had once belonged to his great-grandmother. "I promise I'm not crazy," I said, "but I need to know something about dragons."

Barry blinked and adjusted his glasses. "Dragons?" he asked, as if perhaps he hadn't heard me correctly.

I could feel my cheeks flush. "Yeah. I, uh, need to know what they're after. Typically, I mean. And how to stop them."

It was very quiet in the entry hall of 237 Monticello Place. Barry's enormous grandfather clock ticked hollowly in the living room.

"Hypothetically speaking, of course," Vali added. His confident voice filled the narrow space.

Barry shook his head. "Yes, of course," he said. "Let me just get a few things from the study. I'll meet you in the dining room."

He adjusted his glasses again and backed out of the hallway.

"So," Vali whispered, "that's Barry fucking Richardson."

I brought my hand to my mouth to cover my smile. "That's him."

Vali nodded. "He's a good man."

"He is."

I remembered what the dragon showed me, remembered Barry's laptop hitting the floor as he ran to the backyard to save my life.

"He's just not the man for me," I whispered.

"He most definitely is not," Vali said, with a smile.

BARRY RICHARDSON WAS in his element. He'd spread books and charts across the dining room table; he even pulled in his whiteboard from the study. Vali, Barry, and I had been talking for hours, and I was embarrassed to discover how little I knew about his life's work, even after being married to him for almost three years.

"So, it's not just about a hero with a big sword?" I asked, catching Vali's smile out of the corner of my eye.

"Oh, heavens, no," Barry said, running a hand through the wild tangle of his graying hair. "In fact, most of those 'dragons' were not, properly speaking, Wyrms. Instead, they were things like, oh, enchanted dwarves, or the like. The actual Wyrms, the Foes of Old, well, it took more than some knight in shining armor to pacify them."

Vali leaned across the table, his face resting on his hands. "So, what did they want?"

Barry raised an eyebrow. "The story is a virgin, right? The sea-dragon Cetus demands the maiden Andromeda. The dragon of Saint George wants the local princess. But—" Barry stopped to scribble the circle-and-cross symbol for *woman* on his whiteboard, "—the older stories don't specify *young* women. Just women. And not only women, women of nobility. Of certain lines, you know, ancient lineages."

The room suddenly felt much colder. Níðhöggr's words echoed in my head. *And have you come to stop me, Karen, daughter of Elizabeth, granddaughter of Claire, of the line of Orleans?* Shivering, I tried to force myself to pay attention to the conversation.

"And what happens to the women?" Vali asked.

Barry shrugged. "Well, they get eaten, presumably. Metaphorically, or literally, I suppose. They're a sacrifice, the sacrifice that saves or sustains the world, if you like. But it's interesting to note they're not just *maidens* - that's a modern twist on the stories. In the older versions they're grown women, sometimes even queens..."

Barry's voice faded into a pleasant background hum as I stared out the window. The sun had set hours ago, and Barry's small backyard was lit with the golden glow of the streetlights which gilded the tips of the branches on the crabapple tree. Sacrifice, I thought. The sacrifice that saves the world.

The sacrifice that keeps Yellowstone from erupting.

My head spun. The room was too damn hot, then too damn cold. I felt like I was about to pass out.

"Excuse me just a minute," I said, pushing my chair back from the table.

Before I could stand, a familiar grumble filled the dining room.

"Is that—" I paused. "Is that the garage door?"

Barry's cheeks flushed before he cleared his throat and regained his composure. "That will be Danielle," he said. "Excuse me."

Barry left the room, and I turned to Vali.

"Vali," I whispered. My voice trembled. "That's it. Níðhöggr wants a woman. That's what will keep Yellowstone from erupting."

Vali frowned. "But how the hell do we find the right woman?"

I opened my mouth to tell him what I knew, the certainty that ran through my body like an electric current, when Barry cleared his voice from the doorway.

"Karen," Barry said, "this is Danielle. My fiancée."

Danielle was slight and blonde, with close-cropped hair and an athletic build. She wore a tailored pea coat which looked expensive, and her pink lips curved into a nervous smile. She wasn't quite as pretty as I would have expected, and she exuded an air of nervous energy which spoke of an affluent upbringing. She looked, I had to admit, like a very good match for Barry.

"Very pleased to meet you," I said, extending my hand. "We were just getting ready to leave."

"Oh, you're welcome to stay!" Her words bubbled out in an almost frantic stream as she gave me a delicate handshake. "I just picked up dinner. If I'd known we had guests—" She looked up to give Barry a slightly accusatory glance. "Anyway. It's nothing particularly special, just one of those roast chickens from Whole Foods. But you are welcome."

Vali came to his feet with a very charming smile on his handsome face. I tried to catch his eye and shake my head. He ignored me. "We'd love to join you," he said.

"YOU'RE SURE I CAN'T give you a ride somewhere?" Barry asked as we stood together in the entry hall. Wind rattled the storm door, drowning out the cozy splash and hum of the dishwasher. Dinner had gone surprisingly well, for a meal shared with my ex-husband, his fiancée, and my current lover. That had been almost as disconcerting as talking about how to stop a dragon.

"No, we're fine," I said. "We've got a ride."

"In fact, I'll go meet them now," Vali said. He turned to shake Barry's hand. "Thank you so much. For everything."

Vali slipped out the door, a blast of cold air following in his wake, and I was alone with Barry in the foyer.

"He seems like a good man," Barry said, nodding toward the door.

"He is." I smiled. "He said the same thing about you."

Barry nodded again, thoughtfully. "You seem to be doing well, Karen. I read your last article, in *Nature*."

I tried to keep my mouth from falling open. "You read my article?"

"Of course. *Nature*'s a big name. That's quite an accomplishment."

"Thank you." I glanced toward the kitchen. "I like her. Danielle. She's...very nice."

Barry wore a thin, private smile. "Yes. She is."

Silence fell between us, heavy and thick. I glanced at the darkness outside the front door, where Vali waited for me.

"I never thanked you," I said. "I want to thank you now."

Barry stared at me, his brow creasing.

My cheeks burned. "You cancelled your class. Your favorite class. To come home and be with me."

Barry tilted his head slightly to the left, like he always did when he was confused but didn't want to admit it.

"Barry, you saved my life," I said, the words tumbling out in a rush. "I never thanked you for saving my life."

"Oh." His cheeks reddened slightly, and he ran a hand through his hair.

I looked down at my hands. "I'm glad," I said. My voice was so pinched it was almost a whisper.

Barry cleared his throat. "Oh, Karen. There's no need to thank me. The world is a better place with you in it."

I blinked the tears from my eyes and leaned forward, hugging him. The familiar contours of his body stiffened in my arms. "You take care," I whispered, patting his back.

He cleared his throat. "You too."

We stepped apart, shifting awkwardly.

"And thanks for your help," I added, pulling open the heavy front door.

"Anytime," Barry said.

His head was still tilted to the left. Barry used to look like that a lot when we were together, I realized; head tilted and slightly confused, as though we never could quite manage to speak the same language.

I pulled the door closed behind me and walked toward Vali.

"SO NÍÐHÖGGR WANTS A woman," Loki said, leaning back in his chair.

We were back in the strange, airy room, with its wall of windows opening on a sparkling sea, sitting around the table with Loki and Caroline. Little Adelina lay swaddled in what looked like an enormous white shell, which hovered and swung several feet off the polished floor. Three translucent balls spun in the air just above the shell. I was trying not to stare at them, which wasn't easy.

"But not just any woman," Vali said. "Someone special, someone with a specific lineage. How the hell are we going to find some random woman of ancient lineage?"

Loki fixed me with his oddly pale blue eyes. Despite the warmth of the room, I felt cold.

"Karen," Loki said, "what exactly did Níðhöggr say to you?"

I hesitated, my throat suddenly dry.

"Níðhöggr doesn't talk," Vali said dismissively. "And neither of us got close enough to talk, anyway."

"No." My voice sounded very small. "Níðhöggr talked to me."

Vali's face fell. "What? But you told me you saw—" His voice faltered.

My heart clenched. "I did see...things. Horrible things. From my past." I took a deep breath, trying to banish the mental image of Barry's tear-stained face and crooked glasses. "But after that, yes, I saw Níðhöggr. We...talked."

Loki tilted his head. "And you got what you wanted," he said.

I shivered. An inescapable cold feeling was pooling in the pit of my stomach. "Yes. I got Vali."

"In exchange for...?" Loki prodded.

"No!" Vali cried, jumping to his feet. "I know what you're getting at, but you're wrong, damn it! It can't be Karen! Look, if Níðhöggr wanted her, Níðhöggr would have taken her when she was there!"

"Shush." Loki waved a dismissive hand at Vali. "Let your woman speak." He turned back to me with those burning pale eyes. "What exactly did you and Níðhöggr discuss, Karen?"

I couldn't bring myself to look at Vali. "He—or she—called me 'Karen, daughter of Elizabeth, granddaughter of Claire, of the line of Orleans.'"

Vali groaned and sank back into the chair, his head in his hands.

"Go on," Loki said.

"And then she, or he, asked if I'd come to stop it. When I said no, Níðhöggr said..." I tried to swallow around the growing lump in my throat. "Níðhöggr said we could make a deal."

The room was absolutely silent. Even Adelina's shell cradle made no noise as swooshed rhythmically through the still air. Loki arched an eyebrow at me, and I felt my cheeks burning.

"I got Vali," I said, softly. "Níðhöggr said it might as well give me what I want, as long as I..." The breath caught in my throat.

"As long as you what?" Loki pressed.

My shoulders slumped. "As long as I try to stop it. At the time, I-I didn't know what that meant. But I guess Níðhöggr wants me to come willingly. Knowing what I'm doing."

Vali smacked the table with his open palm. The sharp crack reverberated through the room, making me jump.

"No." Vali said, his dark hair swirling as he shook his head. "Karen, no. You can't do this!"

Tears swelled behind my eyelids, blurring his handsome face. "I'm sorry," I stammered.

"There's got to be another way," Vali said, frantically looking from Loki to Caroline. "She can't be the only woman of that line!"

Loki's eyes met mine in the gentle sunlight filtering through the open windows. "Karen. Is this something you're willing to do?"

I closed my eyes, thinking of Yellowstone. I remembered the first time I'd seen the wolves of the Leopold pack sprinting together across the vast Lamar Valley, their powerful bodies rippling as they wove through the sagebrush. I remembered my first summer hiking in Yellowstone, when I'd come around a bend in an aspen grove and startled an entire herd of elk, their shaggy black necks rising simultaneously to gape at me. I pictured the high, vaulted ceilings of the lodge at Old Faithful, echoing with the shrieks of children.

"Yes," I said. "If it's what it takes to stop Níðhöggr, then I'm willing."

"No!" Vali hissed. "There's got to be another way! Let's find someone else!"

Loki pushed back from the table. "Stop it. You know there's no one else. And you know time grows short. Time was already short when you decided to face Níðhöggr on your own."

Vali and Loki stared at each other. The air between thickened. I stood and wrapped my arms around Vali's broad shoulders, pressing my face against his neck and inhaling his rich, wild scent. He trembled in my arms.

"Vali, if Níðhöggr blows up Yellowstone, it's going to be a worldwide ecological disaster," I said. "There'll be four inches of ash covering the corn fields in the Midwest."

Vali pulled away from me and staggered to his feet. "So what? You and me, we could run. We could go somewhere else. Another Realm, even."

"No. Vali, people would die. Millions of people would die," I said.

Vali grabbed my shoulders. His golden eyes burned in his pale face. "I don't care about millions of people! I care about you! You're worth more to me than millions of people."

I took a deep, jagged breath and leaned into his broad chest. His heartbeat thundered against my cheek. "I can't," I whispered. "I can't."

Vali's arms wrapped around me, crushing me to his chest. "Oh, damn it!" His voice cracked. "I love you, Karen."

Loki cleared his throat. "We should go," he announced. "The wards have only grown since I saw you last, but I can still reach your house. And I can drive you from there."

I nodded against Vali's trembling chest and tried to blink away the tears threatening to spill down my cheeks. "Okay," I whispered.

"Stop," said Caroline, looking at Loki. "Karen, do you have any idea when Níðhöggr wants to, uh, destroy things?"

"What?" I asked.

"Do you think it's going to be tonight?" Caroline asked. "Or did you get the sense Níðhöggr was waiting for you?"

I frowned, trying to remember Níðhöggr's words. "Waiting, I guess. But I don't get the feeling Níðhöggr is especially patient."

"And the point of this is...?" Loki asked, raising an eyebrow at his wife.

Caroline smiled at him. "Darling, you could at least give them a night together."

"Ah. Of course," Loki said. "I'll see both of you in the morning."

The room swirled around me. I closed my eyes, clinging to Vali's chest—

—and it was again very cold.

I opened my eyes and saw the front porch of my own little house. The light above my front door shone bravely against the darkness.

"Where are we now?" Vali asked. His arms were still tight around my shoulders.

"Home," I said. "We're home."

CHAPTER THIRTY FOUR

The front door to my house was unlocked. I muttered thanks for small favors, because I had no fucking idea where my keychain ended up. If I ever made it back to Montana State University, the Security Department was going to be furious with me over losing all the keys to my labs and office. The utter banality of that thought made me smile as I fumbled for the light switch.

My living room light flashed on, and I pulled the door closed behind Vali. He watched me as I glanced around the room, trying to see it through his eyes. It looked shabby and small after Barry Richardson's house, with my tacky decorations and Ikea rugs instead of oil paintings and Persian carpets. I glanced at the messy stack of BIO 101 exams on the front table, the half dozen fleece jackets heaped in my rocking chair, and the line of coffee mugs propped against the window. Damn, I really should have picked up the house a bit before I charged off to Yellowstone to chase a dragon with a Norse god and his wife.

"So, here we are," I said, making a vague, half-hearted gesture around the room.

Vali stepped closer to me, so close I could see the red ringing his golden eyes. He wrapped his fingers around my wrists. My heart sank.

"Don't," I whispered. "Please...don't try to talk me out of this. I-I just can't—"

Vali shook his head, although his eyes never left my face. "No, beautiful Karen. I will not try to change your mind."

My shoulders sagged. I leaned against Vali's broad chest, trying not to cry as I stared at my living room wall. I painted that wall bright red, Sedona Sunset red, during my very first winter in Bozeman, as I listened to cheesy country music on the radio and drank Trout Slayer beer. I loved that red wall, damn it. My heart shuddered in my chest. I didn't want to leave this house.

I didn't want to die.

Vali pushed me back gently, forcing me to face him. His lips pressed together, making a hard, thin line. When he spoke, his voice trembled.

"If you don't do this, and if Níðhöggr destroys your park, you'd never be able to escape it. No matter where we may run, you would be haunted by the devastation. You'd never be able to forget that you might have prevented it."

His face swam, and my tears escaped down my cheeks. I tried to speak, to tell him he was right, but my voice broke apart in my throat.

Vali reached for my cheek and tilted my face to meet his eyes. "Karen," he said. "I would make you my wife."

His words were so utterly unexpected that I laughed.

Vali frowned. "I speak the truth."

I shook my head, pulling out of his arms. "Vali, I...This is..." I walked backward and collapsed on the couch before my knees could give out.

Vali sat next to me, taking one of my hands in his and gently bringing it to his lips. He kissed each of my fingers before speaking again.

"If you'd have me as your husband," he said, softly.

My stomach twisted. I remembered Barry Richardson sinking to his knees in the mud of our backyard with my limp body in his arms.

"Vali. It's not you. It's—I'm not—I don't make a very good wife."

He shifted on the couch, exhaling slowly. "Are you implying I'm beyond reproach? Because we both know what I've done."

"It's not that. It's just—" I stopped speaking, unable to form any further words. Barry's tear-stained face floated in my mind. I remembered the sick crunching sound his laptop made as it crashed to the floor, and my chest tightened.

"Vali," I choked. "I'm not—I'm not really wife material."

He reached for my cheek, his fingers brushing my face until my eyes met his. "Isn't that for me to decide?"

I smiled in spite of myself. Vali leaned in and kissed me, slowly and tenderly, his lips brushing mine as our fingers intertwined. Something dark and hard and cold slipped free as our lips danced, melting away under the heat of his embrace. When we pulled apart he was smiling.

"Karen McDonald," he said, "I would make you my wife."

"Vali, even if I say yes, tomorrow, I'm going to—" My voice cracked, and I couldn't bring myself to finish that particular sentence. "It's not like we'll have much time together," I said.

Vali's eyes shone. "Karen, you're not the first woman to share my dreams."

He paused, and I tried to ignore the cold, irrational stab of jealousy piercing my heart.

"But you are the first woman, in all my long years, I have wanted to marry."

As I struggled to think of something to say, Vali leaned toward me again, tilting his face to meet mine. Our lips touched, and he kissed me gently, waiting for me to yield to him, to open myself to his advances. His hands moved through my hair and the world fell away, tomorrow's obligations disappearing in a red haze as Vali's lips and hands absorbed my attention.

"Karen McDonald," he growled as we pulled apart. "I would be your husband, regardless of what comes tomorrow." He paused. "If you would have me."

Yes, my body cried, leaning into him as my heart raced, and my sex pulsed with his heat.

"You'd marry me for one night?" My voice sounded pinched and narrow.

Vali laughed softly into my hair, his strong chest rising and falling against my breasts. "My love, if all we had together was one more heartbeat, I'd still marry you."

I pulled in breath, trying to force my voice to work. My lips seemed to have forgotten how to form words.

"Is that a yes?" Vali asked, running his hand up my thigh.

"Vali," I gasped as his hand began to stroke the seam of my pants. "Yes. Yes, I'll marry you!"

Vali's eyes danced. "Tonight. Now."

I laughed. "It's the middle of the night. We can't possibly get a marriage certificate right now."

He grinned. "All we need are the words, my beautiful Karen."

My chest tightened as Vali turned on the couch to face me directly. He took both my hands in his.

"I am bound to you," he whispered, his voice thick with emotion. "You are a part of me."

I swallowed hard. My heart hammered against my ribcage as his words reverberated through my mind. Vali watched me with burning eyes. The air in my living room seemed thicker, somehow, almost crackling with electricity. For a heartbeat I hesitated, biting my lip as I wondered if I was really ready to do this again.

Vali's lips curved into a gentle smile, and my breath caught in my throat. My dream lover, the man who was there for me during the darkest time of my life, was sitting on the couch in my living room right now, asking me to marry him.

"I—I am bound to you," I said. The words seemed to echo, growing and filling my living room. "You are a part of me."

My entire body tingled when I fell silent, and Vali's arms closed around my shoulders, crushing me to his chest. He pressed his face against my hair, my neck, my cheeks, kissing me again and again. "My wife," he whispered, his voice trembling. "My beautiful wife."

I lay back against the couch, pulling Vali's warm hands with me. "I love you," I said. "I love you, husband."

CHAPTER THIRTY FIVE

It took me a long time to rise through the misty half-world of my dreams. Even after I'd forced my eyes open and found Vali lying next to me in the soft light of early morning, I thought for a heartbeat I was still dreaming.

Vali snored softly, and my heart swelled. I smiled and closed my eyes, breathing in his sweet, wild scent and remembering last night, all the ways we'd come together on this bed, making love to each other as husband and wife.

And here I'd been so damn certain I would never marry again.

"Vali Lokisen," I whispered. "I am bound to you. You are a part of me."

There was an odd sort of rustling noise behind me. I frowned and turned over.

Loki stood in the corner of my bedroom, his arms crossed over his chest. He raised an eyebrow just as I realized I was completely naked, and the blankets were pooled around my ankles.

"Good morning," Loki said amicably.

"What the fuck are you doing here?" I yelled, yanking the sheet over my chest.

The mattress shook as Vali sat up behind me. "Father," he growled over my shoulder.

"You're a real asshole," I said, glaring at Loki.

"You know, I get that a lot," Loki said. His pale eyes sparkled, and he looked like he was trying not to smile.

"I can't imagine why," Vali said.

"Damn it, Loki, we are going to have some serious discussions about boundaries," I grumbled.

Loki turned and pulled my curtains wide open. Golden sunlight fell across the floor of my bedroom in thick bands, and my body suddenly felt as though it had been plunged into cold water.

It was morning, and my time was up. I wouldn't need to have that conversation with Loki, because this was the last morning I'd ever spend in my little house. My entire body shivered. Vali wrapped an arm around my shoulders, as if he could tell what I was thinking.

"Well, now that we're all up, I suppose I'll make breakfast," Loki said as he turned to leave the room. He did not shut the door behind him.

"Seriously!" I yelled after him.

Vali laughed softly and pulled me closer. "I'd apologize for my father," he said, "but you're the one who told me not to kill him."

I sniffed. "I'm beginning to regret that."

"Hmmmm," Vali murmured against my neck. His kisses grew more insistent. I leaned into his chest as his heat filled my body, burning away my cold fear. His hands cupped my breasts, and my nipples grew hard as the sheet fell to my waist.

"My wife," he whispered, his lips and tongue tracing the curve of my collarbone.

Heat surged between my legs, and I bit my lip to keep from moaning. "Vali," I whimpered. "The door is—" I gasped as Vali's hand moved between my legs.

"Forget the door," he growled.

My hips rocked as his fingers danced across my sex, brushing my clit in slow, rhythmic circles. I arched my back and felt the heat of his erection pressing into my thigh.

"Unless you want me to stop?" he whispered as he dragged his teeth along the sensitive skin of my neck.

"No," I gasped. "No, don't stop. Make me forget the door. Make me forget everything."

His low laugh brushed my skin, sending shivers of electricity through my body. "When I'm done with you, wife, you won't even remember your name."

His touch grew more urgent, and the room vanished as I closed my eyes, letting him embrace me, letting his fingers and lips chase away thought and memory. He eased me back onto the bed, kissing a path down my breastbone as his fingers caressed my nipples. He moved slowly, running his hands over my nipples and his lips across the curve of my stomach until my sex was aching in low, dull throbs.

"Vali," I pleaded.

He moaned, his breath soft against my navel. "My wife."

His hands finally dipped to my thighs, and I groaned with relief. His fingers brushed the curls between my legs, and I arched my back, pressing my thighs up to meet his hand, desperate for his touch. His golden eyes sparkled wildly in the soft light of early morning as he moved up my body, his lips closing around my nipple as his fingers finally entered me.

My eyes rolled back in pleasure, and I cried out something that I'd intended to be his name but that came out as a guttural, animal moan. Vali's thumb circled my clit and waves of heat cascaded through my body. Just when I felt I would lose control, he backed off, curling his fingers inside me and filling me with a different heat, a different ecstasy. His breath came faster now against the swell of my breast, and his long hair fell across my chest.

"Worried about the door now?" he panted.

"D-door?" I stammered. His thumb was on my clit again, pressing hard, then backing off, and it was inordinately hard to get my mouth to form words.

He shifted to kneel above me, his fingers still curling inside me. Oh, damn, the sight of his naked, muscular chest above me almost sent me over the edge.

"What's your name?" he whispered. His fingers were moving faster now, and my hips rocked along with them, my body trembling as swells of pleasure carried me closer and closer to the abyss of orgasm. "What's your name, wife?"

"N-n-n," I panted, unable to get the words out. Name? My mind was a red wash of pleasure, unable to focus on any one word. What the fuck did names matter now?

Vali gave me a victorious smile and drove his fingers into me, thrusting hard. I came like an avalanche, screaming as my body stiffened beneath him, my back arching and my head driving into the mattress, my name completely and utterly forgotten.

I lay still for a moment, panting as the room circled above me. Slowly, I realized Vali was still kneeling between my legs, the stiff length of his cock glorious in the early morning light. I moaned softly as a fresh shiver of arousal lanced through me.

"More?" Vali asked, arching an eyebrow.

I hooked my legs around his hips. "More."

I ALMOST FELL ASLEEP again as I sank back into my mattress in a soft red haze of satisfaction. The bone-deep exhaustion of the past few days settled over my body like a gentle weight, pushing me onto the sheets. Vali shifted next to me, sighing contentedly, and I closed my eyes. If I could just keep from thinking, just freeze the past and the future and keep them out of this bedroom, then everything would be perfect.

Something metallic crashed from the kitchen, followed by a sharp ceramic clank. My eyes flew open as the peaceful serenity of the morning evaporated.

"Goddammit, Loki," I growled to my ceiling.

The bed shook slightly as Vali laughed next to me. "Want me to go punch him?" he offered.

I shook my head. "If anyone's going to punch him, it's going to be me. But not before a shower."

Vali propped himself up on his elbow, his forehead furrowing. "Shower?"

"Yeah. I really don't want to punch anyone until I can at least wash my..." My voice trailed off as the expression on his face registered with my cloudy brain.

Shower. Shit. Vali spent the last two thousand years imprisoned as a wolf. I assumed he'd seen cars and buildings, from the outside, at least. But a shower?

"You don't know what a shower is, do you?" I asked.

"It's...rain?" Vali said, hesitantly.

I grinned as I pushed myself out of bed. "Come here, sexy. Let me show you something."

Vali trailed me, looking puzzled.

"So, this is the bathroom," I said, gesturing at the white tiled walls and wishing I'd cleaned the floor this week. Or last week, for that matter.

"Yes, that much I was able to discern," Vali said, still frowning slightly.

"Ah. Just wait," I said, pulling my tea-rose shower curtain back with a flourish. "You twist these silver knobs here," I said, demonstrating. A rush of water roared through my shower nozzle. "And just give the hot water a minute—"

"Oh!" Vali's eyes widened.

He stepped forward cautiously, extending his hand toward the falling water as if he were afraid the drops might bite.

"It's...it's warm," he said, looking at me with such wonder I felt like he was giving me personal credit for the invention of indoor plumbing.

"Nice, huh?" I smiled, stepping into the tub. "Just pull the curtain back when you come in, or you'll get water all over the floor."

I moved to the far end of my tub, giving Vali room to join me. He stepped over the white porcelain lip of the bathtub and arched his back like a cat, groaning with pleasure as the hot jets of water made a halo of steam around his head.

"Oh, Karen," he moaned, stretching under the water, his face blissful.

I giggled with my back pressed against the wall. It was a small shower, even for just one person, and Vali's muscular frame took up a lot of room. But squashing myself against the wall was worth it to see that look on his face.

"I'll just leave you to it, then," I said.

His arms were around my waist in a heartbeat, pulling me into the steam and heat of the shower jets.

"Don't you dare leave," he growled, his lips and teeth tracing my neck.

Our hips rocked together, and I gasped as he reached down to part my legs. I had time to wonder how he could possibly be so hard again before he lifted me, pressing me against the tiled wall while hot water streamed down my face and hair. Our wet chests slipped against each other as I hooked my legs around his waist, opening to him. He entered me with a moan of pleasure, and the world held still as we embraced, our bodies joined, our hearts racing together.

"Yes, this is nice," he panted.

I tried to answer, but his lips pressed against mine as his hips drove me into the water-slicked tile. Water poured off my hair and shoulders, forcing me to close my eyes. My drenched body was pinned against the wall by Vali's muscular chest, and he was deep inside me, stretching me, filling me, hitting some pleasure center buried so far within me it must have been at my very core.

I pressed my legs into his waist, driving him deeper. My short, gasping breaths turned into sharp cries of pleasure, and my head knocked against the tiled wall as water poured down my face in rivers. I dug my fingers into his broad shoulders, wanting to be closer, wanting to be a part of him.

Vali slipped and hand between our water-slicked bodies and traced the curve of my stomach, dropping to brush his thumb over my clit. Lightning raced through my body, searing my nerves, and my cries became screams, echoing off the walls and filling the steamy air. I dissolved in ecstasy, losing myself in the heat and the feel of his body in mine. Vali's back and legs stiffened a moment later, crushing me against the wall as his orgasmic cry joined mine.

He held me against the wall, his forehead pressed to mine, our chests rising and falling together as hot water coursed down our bodies.

"Shower," he whispered. "I like it."

I moaned when he slipped out of me and lowered me to the floor of the bathtub. My head spun in the steam. The hot water hitting my over-sensitive skin was almost too much to bear.

"I'm getting out," I said. "Stay as long as you like."

Vali caught my shoulders before I could pull back the shower curtain, and gave me a long, slow kiss. When he pulled back, smiling at me through his wet hair, my heart felt like it might burst.

"Damn, I love you," I whispered.

"I should hope so, wife," he said, turning back to the shower.

CHAPTER THIRTY SIX

It took my orgasm-clouded brain a second to recognize the tall, red-haired man sitting at my kitchen table. Loki. Of course. Vali had distracted me so thoroughly this morning, both in bed and then again in the shower, that I'd almost forgotten I woke up to find Loki in my bedroom.

"I have a doorbell, you know," I snapped. My voice came out a bit harsher than I intended.

Loki looked up from the *New York Times* he was reading and raised an eyebrow.

"I also have a phone," I said, pushing my wet hair from my eyes. "Or you could have just waited in the goddamn living room. Really, anything would have been better than standing in my fucking bedroom, you creep!"

Loki gave me a sly sort of half-smile, and I felt blood rising to my cheeks. Exactly how loud had Vali and I been this morning?

"If you're quite done," Loki said, although it was unclear whether he was talking about me reaming him out or my morning activities with Vali, "I made blueberry pancakes. That is your favorite, no?"

My eyes widened. "How the hell did you know that?"

"You have the recipe taped to your fridge. Also, you're welcome."

I tried to think of something snarky to say to that, but I came up empty. Instead, I grabbed two pancakes and a cup of coffee. The pancakes were actually pretty good, but I certainly wasn't going to tell Loki that.

"So, you've married my son," Loki said, leaning back in his chair and crossing his legs.

I coughed and choked on my pancake. After a few minutes of gasping in a very undignified manner, I took a sip of coffee and nodded. "I did."

Loki sighed and turned to the ceiling. "I wasn't expecting that," he said, softly.

"Yeah, well, me neither. Honestly, I wasn't exactly expecting any of this shit."

"I'm sorry about this, Karen. Truly. If there were another way..." His voice trailed off.

I took another sip of coffee and found my anger at Loki slowly evaporating. It was hard to stay mad at him. Which was just one of the many intensely irritating things about him.

"Karen?" Vali's voice echoed from the bedroom.

"Here," I answered. "In the kitchen."

Vali walked into the kitchen, smiling at me. He was completely naked and dripping wet. Water ran from his long hair and down his muscular chest and legs to pool at his feet on my kitchen linoleum. And, despite two orgasms already this morning, his gorgeous cock was semi-hard again. I tried to ignore the sudden rush of heat soaking my underwear.

"It's the, uh, shower," he said, rolling the word *shower* around in his mouth. "It's gone all cold. I turned the little circle thing, but I can't get it to work."

I bit my lip to keep from laughing. "Oh! I think we probably used all the hot water."

Vali gave me a blank stare.

"I mean, that's normal. You didn't break anything," I said, trying not to gape too openly at the way the V of the muscles across his lower abdomen led down to his cock. Damn, he looked good naked.

Vali turned to Loki, and his smile vanished. "Father. You will respect the bedchamber I share with my wife."

"Of course. My apologies, and it won't happen again. There's breakfast on the stove." Loki fixed us both with a level stare. "We should get going. Soon."

My stomach clenched, and my appetite evaporated. The plate in my hands clanked against the kitchen counter. Vali turned to me, his hair still dripping. For a heartbeat I wished he'd ask me again to run away with him.

Because I'd say yes. God help me, I'd say yes.

"I'm not hungry," Vali said, shaking his head and spraying the kitchen with a fine mist of water droplets.

Vali stretched as the air in front of him shimmered. A heartbeat later, he was fully dressed. Black leather and fur stretched across his chest and pulled tight over his thighs, hardly disguising the bulge between his legs. I repressed the sudden urge to run my hands over those pants. Damn. He looked good fully clothed, too.

Loki folded his newspaper, pushed his chair back from the table, and stood. "If you're both ready?" he said.

My mouth went dry; my arms and legs suddenly felt like they weighed a thousand pounds. Vali crossed the kitchen and took my hand, his eyes searching my face.

"Karen?" he whispered.

I leaned against his chest, feeling the warmth of his skin through his leather shirt, hearing the rhythm of his heartbeat. His arms wrapped around my chest, and the world stood very still as I breathed him in, the sweet, wild scent of my husband.

"I'm okay," I whispered, bracing myself on his arms. "I'm ready."

Vali held my arm as we walked through my living room, the clock in my study ticking in counterpoint to our steps. I pulled the door shut behind me, not bothering to lock it, and we walked down the front porch stairs together. Sunlight sparkled off the snow in my front yard; it looked like it was going to be a glorious day.

I wiped my eyes on the back of my hand and turned toward the driver's side of my Subaru, but Vali pulled me back. "Sit with me," he said. His lips curved into a smile, but his eyes brimmed with tears.

I nodded and handed my keys to Loki. "You can drive, right?" I asked.

Loki raised an eyebrow and managed to look somewhat offended. I coughed, refusing to apologize to someone who had appeared in my house in the middle of the night without permission. More than once.

"What do you think I'll need?" I asked Loki. "Skis? Snowshoes?"

He shrugged. When he spoke, his voice was low. "I don't think you'll need anything."

My heart sank. I hadn't realized I'd been looking forward to a few extra minutes with my house, one final trip to the garage to gather my ski gear.

The Subaru's engine purred to life, and Loki began backing out of the driveway. I held my breath as I watched my front door shrink and recede behind us. The front porch light was still on, shining valiantly against the dawn.

Vali pulled me close, kissing the top of my head and running his fingers through my hair. I closed my eyes, trying to think only about the feel of his fingers on my neck, the soft rush of his breathing, the rise and fall of his chest.

I SAT UPRIGHT WITH a jolt, woken by the slam of a car door. I was surrounded by sunlight so bright it was almost blinding, and a sharp lance of pain shot through my neck as I stretched. It took a second for my brain to process where I was, and to remember what the hell I was doing in the backseat of my own car. I must have fallen asleep as Loki drove us to Yellowstone.

The door creaked open with a blast of cold air, and Loki's face leaned in. Panic shot through my chest, and my heart surged as though it wanted to break free of the cage of my ribs. My fingers trembled as I unbuckled my seatbelt. Vali appeared at my side as I climbed out of the car. Tears streamed silently down his cheeks, and he leaned to kiss my forehead. His hands wrapped around my waist, tight and trembling. I tried to breath, but my nostrils stung with the burned scent of the cave. I could feel Níðhöggr's dark, brooding presence. Fear rose in my chest, tasting bitter in the back of my throat.

Loki cleared his throat. "I doubt you'll have far to go, this time."

I shivered violently in Vali's arms. His grip tightened, and I suddenly wondered if I could do this. I wasn't sure I could even stand without Vali's arms around me.

Loki continued. "I believe it's just over that—"

"Yeah, I know," I said, irritation flaring in my chest.

I wiped my eyes and turned to the hill. Níðhöggr's scent was so strong the dragon might as well have been screaming to me. Vali's arms shook as he released my waist. He caught my hand in his and brought it to his lips, kissing my palm. Then he pulled my hand from his lips and pushed it against my chest, to the space above my heart. His hand slowly left mine as he stepped away, smiling through his tears.

My vision blurred, and I turned away, afraid to look at him any longer. Loki offered me his arm. Feeling numb, I took Loki's outstretched hand. His cold fingers closed around mine, pulling me toward the hill.

"Don't look back," Loki whispered.

I opened my mouth to say yes, I won't, but the words froze on my lips. Shivering, I pulled away from Loki and stepped off the highway's shoulder. My feet crunched against the snow. The effort of the climb helped calm the raging mess of grief and anger in my heart. With every step I thought of another thing I should have done, or said, before I left my house. My car. My husband. A scurry of ice crystals blew across my black boots, falling like tiny stars.

The snowpack changed under my feet, becoming thicker and softer. My boots sank into the snow, first up to the laces, and then all the way up to my ankles. I glanced up, expecting to see the sagebrush flats I'd crossed on skis with Zeke and Colin.

The sagebrush was gone. Everything that had once looked like Yellowstone National Park was gone. A coil of cold panic began to spool inside my gut. A forest loomed before me, dark and primordial. The trees would have been massive even in the redwood forest of California, and the snow under them seemed strangely dark, as though it had been dusted with ash.

So close to the road, I realized with dull horror. Níðhöggr is this close to the road, to the rest of Yellowstone. To the human world. I felt dizzy and weak, as if my legs were about to give out and spill me across the gray snow.

"No," I said, although it was hardly more than a whisper. "No!"

My voice echoed strangely off the trunks of those massive trees, and a cold shiver flowed down my back. Everything about this place was *wrong*. I squeezed my eyes shut, fighting the urge to turn and run.

Vali's voice echoed through my mind. "If Níðhöggr destroys your park," he told me last night, "you'd never be able to forget that you could have prevented it."

I bit the inside of my cheek, concentrating on those words. Leaving my eyes screwed tightly shut, I sniffed the air, following the dragon's burnt, acrid scent.

"I can prevent this," I whispered. "I can."

Arms outstretched, I stumbled through the snow, following the dragon's track.

THE SECOND TIME I TRIPPED, I allowed myself to open my eyes.

I was surrounded by massive tree trunks, trunks like the pillars of a cathedral for giants. The light was strange and dim, as though it came from some distant, dying star. My arms and legs felt strangely numb, and I realized slowly I was no longer even certain I was on the Earth. The snow that crunched under my feet certainly didn't look right; it was too dark, too heavy.

Something faint and golden flashed on in the distance. It was almost like a streetlight shining through the gloom.

"Oh," I said. "You left the light on for me."

My footsteps sounded very loud as I wove my way through the trees, following the light. For an infuriatingly long time, the light grew no closer. In fact, it seemed to retreat with every step I took, remaining maddeningly out of reach. A desperate, wild sort of hopelessness began to bloom in my chest. Did I really come all this way just to lose myself in some alien forest, to die on this dark snow, beneath these monster trees?

The light surged, growing stronger. My legs ached, and my feet throbbed. I forced myself to stumble forward, urged on by the light. It grew stronger again, and then again, until I pushed through a tangle of dense branches and found—

No.

My own heartbeat pounded in my ears, throbbing through my temples. I pressed the palms of my hands to my eyes and forced myself to count slowly to ten. Taking a deep breath, I pulled my hands away from my face.

"See what's there," I whispered. "See it, Karen."

I opened my eyes.

There, nestled beneath the heavy canopy of the dark forest and illuminated by one slender silver streetlight, stood 237 Monticello Place. I was staring at the home of Barry Richardson, the world's foremost authority on dragons in medieval literature.

His trim Victorian sat in the middle of the wilderness, between drifts of gray-tinged snow. The sidewalks on either side ended in untouched snow fields, but the house itself looked exactly like it had yesterday evening, when I knocked on the door to ask my ex-husband how to defeat a dragon. The bare limbs of the Japanese maple cast odd shadows across the dingy snow; I could even see the bag of salt by the front steps. My skin prickled and my stomach curled strangely, as though it was trying to pull me backward through the forest.

The door swung open with a familiar squeal. I jumped as adrenaline surged through my body. My aching muscles tensed to run.

"Stop it," I hissed to myself. "This is Níðhöggr. Barry Richardson's house is not really sitting in the middle of this fucking forest."

Still, it was a struggle to force my feet to move. My legs seemed to have turned to stone, and some deep, primal part of my brain kept screaming for me to run away. I clenched my fists, ignored my survival instincts, and forced myself to walk across the snowy fields to the sidewalk in front of 237 Monticello Place.

CHAPTER THIRTY SEVEN

The lights in the hallway flashed on, shedding their bright light across the Persian rug in the entry way, as I took the last steps to the wrap-around porch. I heard the tick of the grandfather clock in the living room. I could even smell a faint trace of artificial lemon from the cleaning solution Barry's housekeeper always used.

Closing my eyes, I stepped over the threshold. Warmth wrapped around me like a thick blanket. Behind me, the door swung shut with a disturbingly final thud. I jumped, biting my lip so hard I tasted the quick, metallic flash of blood across my tongue. The grandfather clock ticked and fell silent. My breath hissed in and out of my lungs.

Something rustled, low and soft, in the back of the house. My mouth went dry. Without realizing what I was doing, I took a step backward. My thighs hit the closed front door with a loud smack.

I heard the low whine of a cabinet door opening, followed a moment later by the soft click of its closing. The kitchen, I realized. It's in the kitchen.

"Are you coming?"

The thick, rich voice echoed down the hallway, at once deeply strange and intimately familiar. Panic crept up my spine like a small animal with cold claws. I glanced backward and saw the front door no longer had a knob.

No escape, then.

I cleared my throat.

"Yes," I said. "I'm coming."

My own breath echoed strangely as I walked down the hallway. The door to the kitchen was ajar, and a dark shadow lay across the white tiles of the floor. Whether it was human or otherwise was impossible to tell. It was less than a dozen steps from the front door to the kitchen in 237 Monticello Place, but it seemed to take me a very long time to cross that distance. I hesitated at the kitchen door, mouth dry and muscles aching.

"Don't keep me waiting," the voice sang.

My jaw clenched as I entered the kitchen.

A very tall man leaned against the pale gray of the kitchen's granite countertop, wearing dark pants and a tight shirt so red it seemed obscene. His hair was the same shade as his shirt, the vivid color making the rest of the kitchen look pallid in comparison. He cupped a white coffee mug with long, delicate fingers.

He should not have been attractive. Somehow that was the worst part of the entire scene, that Níðhöggr had stolen 237 Monticello Place from somewhere deep in the recesses of my memory, or maybe even from Evanston, Illinois itself, taken it to some cold, alien planet and then dared to fill the kitchen with this tall, gorgeous man who oozed sexuality. My core flared with the heat of anger, and the dull, insistent, wholly inappropriate throb of arousal. The man raised an eyebrow, as if he could tell what I was thinking.

"Welcome back, Karen, daughter of Elizabeth, granddaughter of Claire, of the line of Orleans," Níðhöggr said.

My heartbeat surged in my ears, but my body felt frozen. Níðhöggr shifted his lean frame, somehow crossing the kitchen floor without seeming to actually move. He held the white coffee mug up to me. Without thinking, I took the cup from his outstretched arm. It was pleasantly warm against my palms, and I raised it to my face, inhaling deeply.

It was Emerald Spring tea, from Intelligentsia Coffee in Chicago. My very favorite kind of tea. Barry used to joke that I should thank

Emerald Spring tea in the acknowledgements section of my doctoral thesis.

I took a sip. It was perfect. Níðhöggr had even added half a spoon of sugar, and I guessed he'd even done it properly, layering the sugar on top of the tea bag before he added the hot water.

"Thanks," I stammered.

Níðhöggr nodded briskly, his body shifting and flickering somehow. Curves appeared on Níðhöggr's chest and hips, and his face softened. By the time Níðhöggr spoke again, I was staring at a tall woman who wore a tight red top and a long black skirt.

"Of course," she said. "It's important you're calm."

Something inside me jumped at that, sending a red flash of panic through my exhausted body. The panic died almost as quickly as it had appeared, replaced by a dim sort of wonder. I took another sip of the tea, trying to determine if it had been drugged. Or if I gave a damn one way or the other.

"And have you figured out why I call for a woman?" Níðhöggr asked.

I shook. My body ached, and I felt very tired, the sort of bone-deep exhaustion I'd felt just after defending my doctoral dissertation. Or after packing up everything that was mine inside this house before moving to live with my parents in Maine. For a moment, a stack of white paper flashed through my mind with the black, italicized title: *This Certifies the Dissolution of a Marriage.*

Níðhöggr sighed. "I always expect women to understand. You know all about cycles, after all."

She smiled at me, a forced sort of smile which showed all her teeth, and I realized with an unpleasant jolt her eyes were red, as unnaturally red as her shirt and hair, and her pupils were dark, vertical slits in the middle. They were exactly the same as the giant eye I'd faced in the cave a lifetime ago. My skin crawled and the mug jumped in my hands, spilling tea across my fingers. I hissed as the hot water seared my knuckles.

Níðhöggr shook her head with a gentle sound of disapproval. "Well, I suppose I can hardly expect one of you mortals to put all the pieces together. Even if you are a professor." She drew out the last word, slowly and painfully, just in case I hadn't understood I was being insulted.

I set my cup down on the kitchen counter before I could spill any more. "Thanks for the tea," I muttered.

When I looked up again, Níðhöggr was male. The tight red shirt rippled across his flat, muscular chest and the hint of a smile played around the corners of his lips. It was a disturbingly human expression, and one that made him even more sexual.

"So, Karen," he said, bringing his fingers together in front of his lips, "have you come to stop me?"

The air between us felt thick. Despite the warmth of the tea, my body felt cold. The grandfather clock in the living room ticked. I swallowed hard, trying to remember why I was doing this.

To save Yellowstone. To save all the kids running around in the Old Faithful lodge. To save the wolves of the Lamar Valley.

Vali's beautiful body flashed through my mind, naked and sprawled across the grass of the Lamar Valley with my tranquilizer dart in his thigh.

To save Vali.

"Yes," I said. "Yes, I have."

His smile widened. "And how exactly do you plan to do that?"

My shoulders sagged. "I have no idea. I have no weapons. I can't even fight. It's pretty clear I can't touch you."

"Oh?" Níðhöggr's eyes flashed and he stepped closer to me. Uncomfortably close. His shirt was open across the neck, revealing the curve of his collarbones, the pulse flickering in his neck. He was so close I could smell him; acrid smoke and darkness. The scent I'd chased across Yellowstone.

I flinched, and my hips hit the kitchen counter. Níðhöggr leaned over me, one arm on either side of my waist, trapping my body.

"You can touch me," he said in a low growl.

I gritted my teeth against the heat of arousal surging between my legs. "That's not what I meant."

His fingers traced my cheek, forcing me to meet his eyes. They flickered and burned in shifting waves of scarlet and vermillion which swirled around his thin, black pupil. "You came here with no plan," he whispered. His lips almost touched mine as he spoke. "No idea what was expected."

His fingertips dropped to dance across the skin of my neck. I trembled and screwed my eyes shut, blocking out his intense eyes which made me feel like I was about to melt.

"I'm here," I forced myself to say. "Whatever it takes. I'm here."

Níðhöggr laughed, and the floor creaked as he stepped back. The room felt colder after he moved away; I tried to suppress my shiver. When I opened my eyes, Níðhöggr was female again, and she was watching me carefully with one hand on her chin.

"You have good hips," she said. "You're strong. You're of the correct lineage. Yes, you'll do nicely."

I blinked, thinking I must have misheard her. Did the dragon who lives in the roots of the World Tree just mention my *hips*?

Níðhöggr pressed her full lips into a tight line. "Don't tell me you still haven't figured it out?" Her melodic voice was thick with disapproval.

My mouth was dry, so I just shook my head.

"Cycles," Níðhöggr sighed. "We sleep, we wake. We eat. We watch the worlds spin into being and fade into nothingness."

I nodded once, very slowly, trying to give Níðhöggr the impression I was following along.

"And then we plant our children," she said, smiling widely. It was such an affable smile I felt the corners of my own mouth turning up in response. My mind felt slow and fuzzy, as if it were wrapped in thick wool.

Níðhöggr became male again, quite suddenly, and his smile turned feral and hungry. He moved strangely, his hips undulating like a snake, until there was almost nothing between us. I tried to turn away from his burning eyes, but the effort was too great. My mind drifted back to the last words he'd spoken, something about a child. It made no sense. It made no difference, either; I'd come here to die, hadn't I?

Níðhöggr leaned over me, pressing me against the cool granite of the countertops. "You," he whispered. His teeth very close to my neck, his breath was hot, and my skin prickled. The air between us burned. "You will carry our child. And then we will sleep again, until she comes of age."

"Wait, what?" I yelped.

I jumped backward. My head whacked the kitchen cabinet. Hard. White spots exploded across my vision. Níðhöggr pressed himself closer, his lips tracing my earlobe. His hips shifted, rubbing the full length of his enormous erection against the heat between my legs. My body responded with a flood of hot arousal, soaking my underwear so thoroughly I was certain he could feel it.

"How—How does that even work?" I stammered.

Níðhöggr laughed against my neck. "You're a biologist, are you not? Don't you know how babies are made?"

I closed my eyes, trying desperately to think. A baby. That's something else I'd lost when I signed that stack of white paper, wasn't it? Those pages were the dissolution of a marriage, and the dissolution of any hopes of having a family. And now—

Níðhöggr's hands pushed my shirt up and grabbed at my thighs, destroying my train of thought. The heat of his body surged against mine, urgent and undeniable. This didn't make sense - nothing about this made sense - but it was damned hard to think about anything except how good his lips felt against my neck, and how much I wanted those long fingers to close around my nipple.

Níðhöggr ran his tongue down my neck. I clamped my teeth together to keep from moaning. There was something wrong here, something desperately wrong, but goddamn it, my body was screaming for him. Níðhöggr pushed a hand into my pants, his fingers pressing against the throbbing swell of my clit. Electricity shot through my body, exploding across my brain like summer lightning. My mind cleared for a heartbeat, long enough for me to bring my hands to his chest and push back. It was like pushing a rock.

"No," I whimpered. "No, I'm—I'm married."

Níðhöggr laughed. His finger moved against my sex, faster and harder. I dropped my hands from his chest and clutched the counter, trying to fight the flames of ecstasy burning through my body. My hips began to rock against his hand. I tried again to protest, and my breath caught in my throat. The crest of my orgasm was coming, hard and fast. I could sense it swelling behind his touch, waiting to envelope me.

"Married," Níðhöggr said. "Virgin. Harlot. I care not. You're fertile, and I'll plant the seed."

His voice was cold and calm while I gasped and writhed under his touch. He pinched my clit between his fingers, and I drowned, the room vanishing in a hot, red haze as the muscles of my exhausted body seized and trembled.

Níðhöggr's hand retreated, leaving me shaking.

"Take off your clothes." He sounded almost bored.

"I—" My heartbeat thundered in my ears, and my entire body ached. I felt filthy. Vali, I thought. Dear God, I'm sorry.

"You came here prepared to die, did you not?" Níðhöggr asked.

He began unbuttoning his red shirt, revealing an absurdly sculpted chest with a trail of thick, dark hair leading down the hard lines of his stomach to the bulge in his dark pants. The very large bulge.

I tore my eyes away from his body, trying to focus on the kitchen. But the room felt thin and unsubstantial, and it wavered like a heat mirage. My stomach twisted with vertigo, as though I stood on the precipice of some unimaginably tall cliff.

"Yes," I whispered. "I came here to die."

Níðhöggr met my gaze, his strange red eyes glowing in his inhumanly handsome face. "I could still kill you," he said, casually, as though we were discussing the weather.

I felt as though the room had grown colder, pulling all the warmth from my body. "But would—would that save Yellowstone?"

His lip twitched upward in what might almost have been a smile. "Well, you'd never know, now would you?"

"No," I said, my voice coming out a pinched whisper "No, I don't want to die."

"And you do want a baby, don't you, Karen McDonald?" His voice carried the slightest hint of amusement.

My mouth was dry and papery, making speech impossible. I nodded. Yes, I wanted a child. I have always wanted a child.

And, far worse, I wanted him. I wanted those hot hands on my body again. I wanted to feel his muscles against my skin and run my fingers down that trail of hair to grasp that massive bulge in his pants. God help me, I wanted to fuck him.

Níðhöggr made a sound that may have been a laugh, and then his arms were around me again, filling my body with a second wave of heat as he yanked at the waistband of my pants. A low, thick rip echoed across the kitchen as the zipper pulled apart. He forced my pants over my hips, and the undeniable coil of arousal tightened deep inside me. I tried desperately to think of Vali, my husband, my love, but Níðhöggr's hands forced my legs apart, and my hips surged forward to meet his.

"No," I gasped. "Not—not in the kitchen."

Níðhöggr laughed, low and thick in his throat. "We were never in a kitchen."

CHAPTER THIRTY EIGHT

I opened my eyes wide and flinched. We were in the cave, of course. The ceiling and sides stretched away into darkness. Huge, thick candles guttered on the stone floor.

"Down," he said, pushing on my breastbone. "Take off your shirt."

I shivered, glancing around the cave. There were candles, thick, red pillars flickering in the gloom, but there didn't seem to be a bed. Or even a blanket.

"Down," Níðhöggr growled. His eyes burned.

I obeyed him, pulling off my shirt and sitting down hard on the cold stone floor. Rough pebbles jutted into my shoulder blades as I lay down and closed my eyes. I am not going to enjoy this, I told myself.

Níðhöggr's long, elegant fingers closed around my ankle. I braced myself to have my hips rocked back with his thrust, but instead his lips fluttered against my ankle, kissing me so gently he barely brushed my skin. My eyes flew open and I stared at him, trying to make sense of his movements.

He was fully naked now, with the largest erection I'd ever seen erupting from a nest of thick, red hair between his legs. His strange, burning eyes were closed. He'd rocked back on his heels, his cheek pressed against my ankle, his lips moving softly over my skin.

He shifted as his lips moved up my calves, becoming more insistent. Now his teeth scraped against my skin, making me shiver and burn, although each flash of pleasure was followed by a wave of guilt. Níðhöggr's eyes opened as he reached the underside of my knees, and he gave me a smile so wickedly handsome I moaned out loud.

"No," I whimpered, trying desperately to remind myself that Níðhöggr was not my husband.

I shouldn't enjoy this.

Níðhöggr's lips danced along the inside of my thighs, followed by the drag of his teeth. I bit the inside of my cheek to keep from crying out, begging for more.

Then his lips found my sex, and my restraint evaporated. I screamed with need, reaching for his head and burying my fingers in his hair. My hips rocked against his mouth, demanding him, taking him. He moaned into me, his tongue buried deep inside me, and my body responded with wave after wave of ecstasy. The hard stone beneath me fell away, the guilt and shame fell away, and all that was left was the burning heat of his lips on my sex and his tongue inside me, filling me, devouring me.

My entire body arched under his touch, and my screams filled the cave as I came, hard, against his mouth. I moaned as he pulled away—

And he was on me again, clenching my hips as he forced my legs apart. Panic flared in my pleasure-clouded brain as I remembered the size of his massive erection, remembered his hard heat against my thighs, and then he was inside me, thrusting against me, and for a moment I felt I would be ripped apart. He was enormous, far too big to fit in my body. But somehow he did fit, although it burned as he stretched me almost to the breaking point. Then the burning ebbed, retreating before a tremendous surge of pleasure, and I was filled, completely and utterly filled.

Níðhöggr laughed above me, triumphant. His hips rippled against mine, moving his massive length inside me. I trembled, expecting pain, but the pain didn't come. It didn't. My entire body burned, aflame with the heat of desire and ecstasy, but there was no pain.

"No," I gasped, trying to remember why I couldn't enjoy this, why this was so wrong.

My own body ignored me as it pressed my hips up to meet Níðhöggr's thrusts. Oh, damn, he felt good. It was as though his cock filled every part of me, my entire body, driving away anything that was not raw pleasure. I wanted it, some dim, distant part of my mind realized as my body matched Níðhöggr's rhythm. I wanted him to fill me, to fuck me, to pound me into the ground and obliterate me.

My second orgasm took me by surprise, cresting before I fully realized what was happening. The climax forced the air from my lungs as my body stiffened against Níðhöggr's, my hips smashing into him, my vision blurring and going dark as my mind flooded with dark heat.

He didn't stop. I moaned and whimpered against his onslaught, his thrusts almost painful against my super-sensitive clit. Níðhöggr's hips drove into mine mercilessly, forcing my body to respond, while he smiled coolly above me.

"I think you like this," he said as I came again, my body crumbling, my voice moaning and crying out as another orgasm hurtled through my mind and body, destroying me.

I lost track of how many times I came against his hips, screaming into the oblivion of the cave, my naked body thrashing against the dirt and stones as he pounded me, steadily, rhythmically, his eyes watching mine with cool amusement. I forgot why I was there. I forgot who I was. The entire world narrowed to one cave, to one man. To the place where our bodies came together, sparking fire and oblivion.

And then, finally, after I'd lost all thought and rationality, all sense of myself, Níðhöggr's expression shifted. His eyes flashed. The rhythm of his hips faltered and then sped up, and his breathing hitched. He thrust into me even harder. By then I was so swollen and sore I cried out, my voice as sharp and hard as the rocks beneath me.

He ignored me. His fingers tightened around my shoulder, grinding into my skin. His back arched, driving his cock so deep inside me it seemed to pierce the very core of my being, and he screamed something guttural and fierce in a language I did not recognize. The buried length of his cock thickened and jerked as he came inside me. The heat of his semen burned my abdomen.

His eyes met mine as he pulled out, panting. "It's done," he said. "You make a nice little whore."

I took a deep, jagged breath. My entire body sang with pain. Scrapes burned on my hips and thighs and shoulders where my body had clenched and pounded against the stone. When I pushed myself up to sitting, I winced at the very deep ache between my legs.

"What now?" I asked. My voice was ragged from screaming.

Níðhöggr rocked back. She was a woman now, naked and gloriously perfect. "We're done with you," she said.

"But—" Tears stung the back of my eyelids. Some tiny, still-functional part of my brain realized what an absurd reaction that was.

Níðhöggr picked up her red shirt and came to her feet, towering over me. From this perspective, her perfectly round breasts looked enormous, their dark nipples almost red. She pulled the shirt over her head and turned away. For a horrible moment, I thought I had been entirely dismissed.

"Now you bear our child," Níðhöggr said, without turning around. "When the time is right, the child will come to us. We have no further need for you."

I wrapped my hands around my stomach. Somewhere deep inside me, the heat of Níðhöggr's semen coursed toward my womb. I could almost picture it, thick and white, streaking through the inside of my body like a comet through the soft darkness of the night sky.

"The baby..." I whispered. "She won't be human?"

Níðhöggr laughed. "As if you would have had human babies anyway. Look who you married!"

Married. My stomach lurched.

"You know, Vali's mother was a goddess," Níðhöggr said.

I nodded as a wave of nausea tore through my body.

"They imprisoned her, the Æsir. Killed her son in front of her and then stuck her in a cave with nothing but her bound and gagged husband and a venomous snake for company."

Níðhöggr knelt next to me, her red shirt stretched tight across her ample chest. She smelled good, somehow, like a dark, exotic flower. "And do you know what the real surprise is?" she asked.

I clenched my teeth and shook my head, dreading where this story was going.

"She stayed," Níðhöggr whispered. "For one thousand years, Loki's wife Sigyn stayed with her husband. Vali's mother stood next to Vali's father, catching poison from a snake in a bowl so it wouldn't fall on her husband's face."

I felt Níðhöggr's soft, warm fingers on my cheek, and I opened my eyes to meet her beautiful face. "Sigyn," Níðhöggr said, softly. "To the mortals of Midgard, she was the goddess of fidelity. That's the example your dear Vali has for a wife. That's his standard."

I rolled to my side and vomited onto the cold floor of the cave for a very long time.

CHAPTER THIRTY NINE

When I finally returned to my senses, I expected to be alone in the darkness, with my guilt burning hot and low in my gut. *And my baby*, some distant part of my mind chimed. My hands crept to my stomach, scraping across the stones like small, scared animals.

The cave slowly swam into focus. The candles were still guttering, casting a pale, shifting light across the rocky floor. Something dark sat in front of me, waiting patiently in the gloom of the cave.

Níðhöggr.

I flinched as the face came into focus. Níðhöggr wore the woman's form. She sat cross-legged just past the dark pool of my vomit, watching me with a slightly bored expression. Our eyes met, and my stomach curled up and rolled over.

"Typically, we give our vessels a choice," she said, as if we were continuing a pleasant conversation.

I wiped the back of my hand across my mouth, trying to comprehend what she was saying. "Choice?"

"What to do next. Where to go. Whom to see. That kind of thing." She flicked her hair back, watching me with the same cold, distant expression Níðhöggr had worn as a man, while he fucked me, as my body came over and over again under his. I shivered. The motion made the dozens of raw scrapes across my back and legs sing with pain.

"We can, for example, send you back..." Níðhöggr's voice trailed off.

"To Vali," I whispered.

Níðhöggr brought her hands together in front of her full, rosy lips. "Ah, yes. Vali. The husband to whom you were so faithful. For almost twenty-four hours. Won't he be delighted to find you with child, and not by him?"

My jaw clenched so tightly I felt my teeth might crack. "No. No, I can't go home."

"Good," Níðhöggr said, brightly. "That's ever so much easier for the child. Fewer attachments. Fewer complications."

She clapped her hands. The room spun. For a second I thought I'd be sick again. Then the roar of breakers filled my ears, and a rocky beach came racing forward to meet my face.

EVERYTHING HURT.

My arms and legs lit with pain as shivers wracked my body. My throat hurt, my stomach hurt, the raw space between my legs hurt. Something deep inside my abdomen ached and throbbed. Even the sunlight hurt my eyes, making me curl over on my side. Rocks clattered and shifted beneath me as I struggled to make sense of what I was seeing.

Waves. Row after row of dark furrows, rippling beneath leaden skies before breaking against a rocky beach. I pushed myself to sitting and the headache hit me, the kind of sharp throbbing pain that comes after a very long crying fit.

Two revelations arrived alongside the stabbing pain of the headache. First, this was the beach where I'd found Vali shivering against the cliffs with Hrotti on his knees. And second, I was completely naked.

"Shit," I said.

My voice echoed across the rocks, flowing out to sea and returning to me as a faint whisper. My legs looked strangely pale against the smooth gray-black rocks. My poor body, I though. The body I've tried so damn hard to keep in reasonable shape was now bashed and scraped, impregnated and then discarded on the beach like worn out garbage. Hot, red anger welled up from somewhere deep inside me, giving me a surge of energy. I staggered upright, my bare feet slipping on the cold stones.

"Naked?" I yelled at the ocean. "You left me naked!"

The ocean rumbled and fell over itself, ignoring me. Rage spilled out of me, coursing through my body like the dark twin of sexual arousal.

"Fuck you!" I screamed, and the echoes of my rage bounced back to me. "Fuck you, Níðhöggr!"

I stepped closer to the ocean, slipped, and crashed down on my knees. Pain shot through me. My vision blurred with a sudden explosion of white dots. I whimpered, rocking back onto the stones and pulling my knees to my chest. Scarlet blood welled out of fresh scrapes on both my knees, but nothing seemed to be broken.

What exactly would I have done if I had broken my kneecap? I shivered. The hot rush of angry energy seeped out of my body like water running into sand, replaced with a numb, cold dread. Those breakers seemed to be getting closer. Some distant part of my mind noted this must mean Asgard has tides. And a moon, to pull the oceans back and forth.

Asgard. Vali's childhood home. Níðhöggr fucked me and dumped me here, in the former home of the husband I'd just hopelessly, irreversibly betrayed. And Níðhöggr left me buck-ass fucking naked to boot. At least there was nobody else around to see.

Someone coughed. I jumped, trying to cover everything at once and failing miserably.

Óðinn stood behind me, his one blue eye sparkling. He was staring openly at my naked back with a raised eyebrow.

"You're looking a bit worse for the wear, my dear," he said.

I tried to cover my breasts with my bloody knees. Óðinn sat down next to me on the rocks, leaned uncomfortably close to my neck, and inhaled deeply. My skin crawled.

"Ah, knocked up, too! And not by one of us! Well, that's certainly interesting."

I opened my mouth, but no words came out. Seagulls cried and dove into the waves as long, slow waves of shivers wracked my body.

"So, what are you doing here?" Óðinn asked conversationally, as if he found bloody, naked women on this beach every day.

"I...I don't even know. I didn't mean to... I mean, you can send me..." I stopped myself. Home, I'd almost said. As if that word still had any meaning.

"Fine." Óðinn sighed heavily.

He shifted on the rocks, and for a second I was horribly convinced he was going to leave, just vanish into thin air like Loki. I hadn't exactly been pleased to see him, but the thought of being left alone on this beach, naked, sent a bolt of pure panic through my exhausted body.

"No!" I gasped.

Óðinn raised his hand, waved it in a rapid, intricate pattern—

—And we were suddenly inside, sitting across from each other at a sturdy wooden table. Stubby candles flickered warmly between us. Behind Óðinn, a row of windows showed the same dark ocean, throwing itself against the shore beneath heavy skies.

I glanced down at my chest, worried I'd still be naked with my breasts totally on display. But no, I was wearing a soft green dress with long sleeves and a high neckline. Óðinn handed me a steaming mug filled with what smelled like coffee, which he had apparently conjured from thin air.

"Start at the beginning," he said.

I hesitated as I wrapped my fingers around the warm mug. I had no reason to trust Óðinn; he was, after all, the one who imprisoned

Vali. And Loki. My heart clenched like a hard, cold fist beneath my breastbone.

It wasn't like I had much of a choice.

Óðinn listened to my story without a single change of expression as his pale blue eye focused somewhere just above my head. I glossed over the sex part, but blood rushed to my cheeks as I fumbled to find the right euphemism. When I finally finished my stammering, disjointed narrative, Óðinn leaned forward and stared at me, his face carefully neutral.

"So, you're carrying Níðhöggr's spawn. And the dragon sent you here," he said.

"Pretty much."

He laced his fingers carefully in front of his chin. The gesture made him seem like an old man. "This puts me in a delicate position."

Óðinn rocked back in his chair, his eye returning to the space above my head. Waves crashed outside the windows, and I realized it had grown quite dark while I talked. I wondered if Loki and Vali were back at my house, if they were perhaps making dinner in my kitchen, and my eyes stung with sudden tears. Suddenly, I wished Óðinn would say something. Anything.

Just as I opened my mouth to break the silence, Óðinn rocked forward, pressing his hands against the smooth wood of the table.

"Very well," he said, as if we'd just reached some sort of agreement. "I can't exactly shove you off on anyone else. And having you here will be helpful, in a way."

"Helpful?" I croaked. Was he about to ask me to start scrubbing the floors? And would I be in any position to refuse?

Óðinn's lips curled, although his smile didn't reach his cold eye. "He'll come looking for you, of course."

"Vali?" My heart leapt as shame and hope flared somewhere deep inside me.

He laughed. "Vali? Are you kidding? He didn't have enough talent to find the Bifröst, not even when the gate was wide open. No, that idiot isn't going anywhere."

Óðinn stood. He seemed very tall in small room.

"But Loki will come," he whispered.

The air crackled and thickened, and Óðinn vanished. Candles on the table guttered as the air in the room swirled to fill the empty space where Óðinn had stood. I pushed away from the table and staggered to my feet, feeling numb and clumsy. The room was suddenly too hot, and the soft beeswax scent of the candles was cloying. I stumbled to the door and shoved it open. A fat gibbous moon hung heavy over the black waves. The thin, sweet perfume of wild roses wove with the briny tang of the ocean. The landscape before me was entirely dark, and entirely deserted; I may as well have been on the moon.

But I knew this beach, I realized with a bolt of shock that turned my entire body cold. I knew this place. This is the house Óðinn promised Vali in return for killing Loki. It's the house where my husband was a child, where his mother Sigyn was so very faithful to his father.

That's what Óðinn wanted, after all. It's what he asked Vali to do: kill Loki, and you can come home. And now here I am, in this very house.

"I'm a trap," I said.

Trap, said the echo of my solitary voice. *-rap. -ap.*

But that wasn't exactly the truth. The house was the trap. Hell, Asgard itself was the trap, for all I knew.

I was just the bait.

My stomach surged in protest, and bile rose in the back of my throat. I had just enough time to think *morning sickness* before bending over and vomiting into the tangle of wild rose bushes.

"I'm pregnant," I said, as if saying the words would somehow change the situation. "Pregnant, and bait in a trap. What the hell am I going to do?"

I wrapped my arms around my abdomen, cradling the small spark nestled within, that tiny, silvery life. All at once the answer was painfully obvious.

Because Níðhöggr was right. I was a fucking biologist, and I knew how babies were made. Half of this little life came from Níðhöggr, but if the dragon could make a baby alone, he would never have asked for women. No, he needed me, both my womb and my genetic material. That meant the baby growing inside me was my child too.

And I loved her already.

I wiped the back of my hand across my mouth.

"Live," I told the night. "I'm going to live."

CHAPTER FORTY

"Shit," I muttered to myself.

I'd been living in Asgard for over a month, and the way the afternoons faded so quickly to dusk still surprised me. After spending half the day under the heavy shade of the thick pine forest, I should have guessed I'd have trouble estimating the time. The sun was already hovering just above the slow, dark undulations of the Asgardian ocean. Frowning, I held my hand to the horizon, counting the fingers between the sun and the sea. Just my index and pointer. Damn, that meant I only had thirty minutes to make it home.

Home. I snorted under my breath. Funny how that little word adapts to fit the circumstances. Just one month ago I'd never have believed anywhere but my little house in Bozeman could be home. Now Asguard, and Vali's childhood cottage, were not exactly home, but the closest I was going to get.

Gritting my teeth against the slow burning muscle cramps in my calves, I forced myself to walk as fast as I could without actually running. I couldn't remember the exact wording of the American Academy of Pediatrics recommendations about exercising while pregnant, but I thought the gist was don't push yourself too hard. And something about not getting out of breath.

I huffed loudly. If I hadn't been so distracted by that damn bird. Today was only the second time I'd seen that species, with its flash of brilliant blue beneath a drab gray underwing, and I couldn't resist trying to sketch it. I'd followed it for hours through the forest, jotting down observations and making almost a dozen quick drawings. I wasn't much of an artist, but for all I knew I might be the greatest wildlife biologist in all of Asgard. Snorting another laugh, I paused to adjust the shoulder strap of my leather bag, which was digging into my collarbone.

"My kingdom for a proper backpack," I said, with a sigh.

Getting this shoddy shoulder bag had been a days-long struggle between me and the bedroom wardrobe. That damn wardrobe was slightly psychic, or at least able to sense my needs in very broad terms. But it seemed to lack imagination. For the first week, all it had given me was velvet dresses and what I guessed were embroidery supplies. Finally, I started standing in front of it with my eyes closed and concentrating very hard on exactly what I wanted.

A backpack, I told the wardrobe. A small, fabric bag with two shoulder straps and a clasp on top.

I opened the wardrobe and found brightly colored thread, hoops, and pale silk. Again, and again. Finally, I kicked the damn thing, hurting my toe in the process.

The shoulder bag arrived the next morning. That night I started asking for paper and pens. A black and white composition notebook. Ballpoint pens or, failing that, regular old number two pencils.

I finally got thin sticks of what must have been charcoal, and reams of thick, tea-colored parchment. Good enough for field work, I told myself.

Several leaves of the parchment were stuffed into the shoulder bag, which was currently cutting into my collarbone, next to the empty leather wine skin I'd filled with water this morning. I hadn't planned to be gone all day, or I would have brought more than two biscuits from breakfast. Originally, I'd planned on mapping the far side of the river this morning, but then that damn bird alighted on a cattail, and my day took a totally different turn.

The thick, springy grass finally gave way to sand, and I sighed in relief. Almost home. I glanced at the sun, which was now burning red against the dark ocean. I'd been tracking the sunsets since my third day here, when I decided I had better do something other than cry and vomit if I was going to survive. In the past thirty-two days I'd spent on Asgard, I'd only missed two sunsets, and that was due to rain so heavy it obscured the light. I really didn't want to mess up that streak.

The peaked thatch roof of the little cottage came into view, and I let myself slow down. My legs burned, and my stomach grumbled in protest.

"Sorry," I murmured, rubbing my belly reflexively. "Dinner's coming, little one."

I risked another glance to the ocean. The sun hadn't yet started to dip below the waves, so I had time to pull open the cottage's heavy door and shrug off my bag. The candles on the kitchen table sprung to life as I stepped through the door, and the room filled with the smell of rich, roast meat. My mouth ached as I watched my plate fill with food. As always, it was accompanied by a glass of mead. I sighed. I was sticking with the American Academy of Pediatrics strict "no alcohol while pregnant" guidelines, but damned if I didn't regret it every night. With another glance out the open door, I grabbed a roast carrot and nibbled it slowly, waiting to see how my stomach would react.

My first bite was met with a familiar wave of nausea. I took a few deep, steadying breaths. If I could make it through the first few bites without throwing up, I was usually in the clear.

My stomach contracted sharply, and bile rose in the back of my mouth. No such luck today. I sprinted across the kitchen and emptied the carrot, and what was left of breakfast, into the sink, coughing and gagging.

"Gross!" I said, splashing water over my lips. "Got it. You're not a fan of carrots, baby girl."

Feeling shaky and weak, like I always did after throwing up, I staggered across the kitchen and back out the door. I'd set up my observation post on top of the nearest dune, next to an enormous rose bush. The burning orange sun was halfway submerged in the ocean when I sank to my knees and then, after brushing away the twigs, lowered myself to my stomach, shifting slightly around the hard knot in my abdomen. I was still too early in the pregnancy to notice any external differences, but I could feel the hardening of my uterus when I lay like this.

"You get any bigger, baby girl, and I'll have to dig a pit for my tummy," I said.

I forced myself to settle down and align my gaze with the flat stone I'd buried here last month. Then, blinking frantically, I stared at the sun as I drew a straight line in the sand with my finger, connecting the position of the setting sun to the flat stone.

"Done."

I pushed myself back up to sitting. The sun flickered once as it vanished beneath the waves, and I felt an unexpectedly strong pull of loneliness at the arrival of the night. Was this the worst time, then? Just after sunset?

"Stop it," I muttered, shaking my head. "There's still work to do."

I'd left the door to the cottage wide open. The candles flickered happily just inside the open door, making the place seem almost welcoming. Almost like something other than a pretty little trap, with me as the bait. I bit my lip, trying to think about something else. Like where I'd put the parchment tracking the sun's motion.

"This place could use a bit more storage," I told the kitchen as I rifled through the stack of papers on the counter. The kitchen smelled better than ever, and my now totally empty stomach groaned in protest.

"Not now," I told my stomach.

There it was! I pulled one of the largest pieces of parchment from the stack. An array of dots, vectors, and dates lay scattered along the jagged top edge. Insects were singing from the rose bushes as I walked back to my observation post. I lay the parchment atop the flat stone, aligning the dark spot in the center of the parchment with the notch I'd made in the stone. Then I took my charcoal pencil and traced the line I'd made in the sand onto the paper. I dated it *1/31?* and stood back, holding the parchment at arm's length.

Even accounting for human error, my lines marking the sun's descent marched steadily across the page. Each day, the sunset shifted about an eighth of an inch westward on the horizon. Without my phone, watch, or any other timepiece, it was hard to tell if the days were growing shorter, but this felt like irrefutable evidence that the axis of this planet was definitely tilted.

"And there you have it, baby girl," I said, wrapping an arm around my belly. "I'll have to submit my findings to the *Asgardian Journal of Science*. Maybe I'll get another publication out of it."

Smiling at my own stupid joke, I turned back to the candlelit cottage. Dinner was waiting.

CHAPTER FORTY ONE

I ate slowly, partially to avoid another vomiting spell, and partially to fill my time. If I was being honest with myself, filling the time was the bigger challenge. During my first pregnancy I'd had my doctoral dissertation to finish, with the very real deadline of childbirth to inspire me. It seemed like every time I blinked, another trimester had flown by. But here on Asgard, I had exactly zero obligations.

I hated it. Feeling useless was fucking miserable. I'd spent my first week on Asgard huddled in a thick blanket, sitting on the beach as my body slowly healed. The scrapes and bruises closed and faded while I watched the ocean, the shifting lines of foam, the dance of the waves, and the brave little seagulls, diving into the cold and emerging with tiny, silvery fish in their beaks.

Once I could move without wincing in pain, I realized I had to find some way to fill my time before I went completely insane. First, I tracked the setting sun, trying to determine if its position on the horizon was static or in flux. Two days later, after the wardrobe provided some reasonable supplies, I started mapping.

I began with the beach. The mouth of a large river was about two hours' walk from the cottage, and dedicated myself to mapping its progress. That was where I saw river otters for the first time. Transfixed, I spent an entire afternoon sitting on the broad banks of the slow, wide river, watching two otters leap and dive in the stony rapids.

That night I'd started another project: Asgardian wildlife inventory. The inventory was, by and large, quite satisfying. I'd noted almost one hundred species, mostly birds, and almost all of them were new to me. In lieu of any colored writing utensils, despite my repeated mental pleas to the wardrobe for pastels or oil paints or even a good old box of Crayola crayons, I had forced myself to pick up the discarded embroidery hoops and spools of colorful thread. I was halfway through a pathetic embroidered rendition of a strange orange and purple song bird which liked to hang out around the rose bushes. Sewing, I had to admit, wasn't a bad way to pass the long evening hours between darkness and sleep, that time when the normal humans back on my world were doing the dishes, or watching TV, or reading a book.

Or making love.

My chest clenched. I set down my fork. The plate before me was still half-full, but my appetite had faded with the sunlight. I glanced at the windows, now filled with darkness and the strange, smudged reflections of candlelight, and a familiar stab of anxiety shot up my spine, making my heart race uselessly.

Yes, this was the worst time. This, and first thing in the morning, when I roll over in the bed I once shared with Vali and find myself alone. Again.

Goddamn it, I missed people. I missed hearing about Zeke's bar fights, and telling Colin he'd have to take a shower at least once a week if I was going to let him teach the freshman biology lab. I missed my job. I missed—

"Stop it," I said, slamming my palms down on the table. The plate jumped, then vanished.

"That's all over and gone," I hissed to myself. "Over. Gone."

My voice fell flat in the empty room. I shivered. Not a great habit, talking to yourself. Almost as bad as letting myself think about

Montana State University, or Zeke and Colin. It was almost February now, if time tracked here the same way it did in our world.

Almost February. I was halfway through the first trimester of my pregnancy, assuming a half-dragon gestated like a normal human baby. And I'd been entirely alone now for over a month.

I sank into the rocking chair by the hearth and closed my eyes. Well, not entirely alone. I'd seen Óðinn exactly once since he brought me to this very kitchen before enigmatically and somewhat rudely vanishing. It was just after I decided to map the coast. I'd walked south until I discovered the massive cliffs where, a lifetime ago, I had found Vali after Níðhöggr tortured him with memories of his brother.

That place sucked me in. I'd spent all afternoon pacing those great, dark cliffs, lost in a fog of despair. It was late at night when I finally found my way back to the cottage, and I'd crawled under the covers still in my clothes, trying desperately not to think about how terribly much I still loved Vali. The next day I was too nauseous and depressed to eat; I hardly left the bed. Some distant part of my mind began contemplating the best way to leap from the ocean cliffs, and I didn't seem to be able to stop those images. How easy it would be to walk to the border where the green grass faded to a sheer, dark wall. And then to take one more step. A little step, even. Like a move in a dance.

Óðinn appeared in the bedroom that night, scaring the ever-loving shit out of me. I screamed and jumped back so hard I bashed my head on the wall

"What the fuck?" I demanded, yanking the covers over my chest although I was still wearing the blue dress I'd put on the previous morning.

"You're not eating." Óðinn said. He frowned and folded his arms across his chest, looking like the world's most disapproving father.

"I'm pregnant," I growled through clenched teeth. "It's called morning sickness, you fucking idiot."

Óðinn pursed his lips and furrowed his brow. For a heartbeat, he looked like a very old man. Then, without warning, he vanished, leaving the air in the room swirling. As I stared at the empty space where he had been standing, my heart seized so violently I felt like a chasm had opened in my chest, a vast, dark crevasse of loneliness.

I sobbed until my entire body hurt. Sleep finally claimed me, curled up like a kitten in the heart of the great bed I had once shared with my husband. The nauseous churning in my stomach woke me hours later and forced me to vomit thin, acidic bile for twenty minutes before I could stomach any of the scrambled eggs, hard biscuits, and smoked fish the kitchen table offered me.

That night was the worst. My first night here was pretty bad. The second night, the night when I realized no rescue was coming, or even possible, was worse. But the night when Óðinn appeared and vanished, teasing me with the possibility of companionship, was the new record for Worst Night on Asgard.

I did not return to those cliffs. Once I started mapping the northern coast, and tracking the wildlife, it was slightly easier to forget those high walls, with their whispered promise of a swift, painless death. I curled an arm around my waist, pressing slightly to feel the ripening bulge of my uterus.

"Stop it," I whispered to myself.

I had considered not eating again, just to bring Óðinn back. But my thoughts hadn't gone any further than idle speculation. Even if I did bring Óðinn back, what the hell could I say? Would I beg him to stay and chat with me for a few hours? To take me back to wherever it was he lived?

"Stop it," I said again, more forcefully this time. The candles flickered slightly.

I bent over and grabbed the stupid embroidery supplies. Usually trying to do a freeform needlepoint of a new species took all my mental effort, leaving plenty little time for feeling sorry for myself or fretting over the impossibility of what came next. Squinting, I threaded my smallest needle with bright orange thread. The little bird had a brilliant orange chest with a purple-capped head. Right now, I was trying to fill in the breast, although it was already slightly lopsided. I jabbed my needle into the silky fabric, pulling the thread taut.

The candles on the table flickered again. I frowned. The windows were all closed. My skin crawled, shivering with the delicate prickle of electricity. The hairs on the back of my neck tingled.

"Hello?" I said.

The air in the room shifted, as if a door had opened behind me.

Loki stood before me, almost touching the kitchen table. His wild red hair fluttered and settled around his shoulders. His cold, blue eyes widened when they met mine.

"No!" I screamed, jumping to my feet. Spools of threads and embroidery hoops went flying. "Loki, it's a trap!"

The air swirled. The candles sputtered. Thin gray wisps of smoke rose from the few candles whose flames had just vanished, overwhelmed by the sudden motion. My entire body shivered, and my skin felt like it wanted to crawl away from my body.

"Loki!" I screamed.

Another figure appeared behind Loki's tall body. Loki's pale eyes widened even further, and his lips parted silently. A bloom of red appeared in the center of his chest, spreading across the dark green fabric of his shirt. I stared, transfixed, as the green of Loki's clothes turned black.

There was a smell, I realized numbly, a sharp, coppery tang which overlaid the omnipresent brine of the ocean and the sweet beeswax of the candles. I opened my mouth to say something, but nothing came out.

Loki slumped forward, falling to his knees. His head tilted upward, almost pleadingly, but his eyes were strange, soft and unfocused. A thin red tendril of blood leaked from the corner of his mouth, streaking across his pale skin. I had an absurdly strong urge to wipe it away.

I tore my eyes away from Loki's face. Backcountry first aid lesson one, my stunned brain chimed. Assess the situation.

A thick, red pole rose from the center of Loki's back. No, it wasn't red. It was wood. It only looked red, and shiny, because it was so covered with blood. The coppery tang in the air thickened, and my stomach clenched.

The slick, red stain vanished and the pole became wood just below the two strong hands. I forced myself to look at the person behind those hands, although I knew who it was. Who it had to be.

Óðinn did not meet my eyes. He stared at Loki's crumpled body as if he expected it to run away, as if he was pinning it to ground instead of twisting a weapon in what was clearly already a fatal wound.

"No," I said.

I meant it to come out as a shout, but it was little more than a whisper. The whole scene felt like a nightmare, one where you can't find your voice to scream. Blood poured from Loki's chest, just about where his heart should be. It coursed down the shaft of Óðinn's spear in thich red ribbons of blood and pooled on the tiles of my kitchen. Some of his blood was soaking into my embroidery hoops. Damn, I thought. I'll never get that out.

Something flashed in the corner of my vision. I looked up. A bright line of electric blue was shivering in the air, almost level with my face. I watched with a numb, detached interest as the hissing blue line pressed against Óðinn's exposed neck. Óðinn's hands relaxed around the shaft of his spear as he stood straight.

I knew that blue. I'd seen that exact shade before. For some reason it was deeply comforting. It even had a name, didn't it? A nice name.

"Hrotti," I whispered.

CHAPTER FORTY TWO

Óðinn took a step backward, almost hitting the closed front door. I blinked, following the buzzing glow of Hrotti's length. Someone was holding that blade. Someone I knew, or someone I should have known. I frowned as my mind struggled to process what I was seeing.

It couldn't be him. Loki was lying at my feet, silent and still in a pool of his own blood. But the man holding Hrotti against Óðinn's neck was—

"Loki," Óðinn growled.

Loki's eyes narrowed. His grip on Hrotti's hilt was so tight his knuckles were turning white.

"Bullshit," Loki spat.

I jumped at the sound of his voice, glancing at the crumpled body on the floor. Blood still flowed down the shaft of Óðinn's spear, although it now was a slow trickle, not the gushing flood it had been at first. The pool of blood surrounding Loki's lifeless body had devoured all my embroidery, and was now seeping around my feet.

"Never, not even on your worst day, would you have fallen for that trick," Loki hissed.

Óðinn's lone eye twinkled cheerfully as if Loki wasn't holding a blade against his Adam's apple. "I guess you got me," he said.

Loki sheathed Hrotti on his back and stood straight. With a smooth twist, Óðinn pulled his spear free from the body on the floor, hefting it toward the ceiling. The corpse collapsed against the stone floor with a disturbing wet thwack, and the scent of blood grew thicker.

"No." Loki frowned. "You got exactly what you wanted, as always. But what the hell is that?"

Óðinn raised a bushy eyebrow over his black, empty eye socket and tilted his head in my direction. "She's pregnant."

My cheeks burned with a rush of shame. I felt tears, my constant companions for the last month, simmering just behind my eyelids.

"I can smell that," Loki said.

I flinched as my numb brain processed his words. It was like I was an exhibit in a museum.

"Naturally. But who's the father?" Óðinn asked. He looked pretty damn cheerful for a man who just killed someone.

Loki closed his eyes and tilted his head back, taking a deep breath. The pale flash of his neck looked hopelessly vulnerable. The room was so quiet I could hear the distant rumble of breakers crashing against the shore. It couldn't have taken longer than a few seconds, but it felt like a very long time.

"Oh," Loki finally said. "I see. Interesting."

I choked out a sob as the tears broke free. Too humiliated to make eye contact, I turned to the floor. Where I found an ocean of blood climbing the skirts of my long, blue dress. I screamed and jumped backward.

Loki made a strange sound. It was so horribly out of place that my shocked brain couldn't make sense of the noise. Then Óðinn made the same sound, and it clicked into place.

Laughter. Loki and Óðinn were laughing at me.

I balled my hands into fists. "What. The. Fuck!" I snarled, glaring at both of them.

My fury seemed to make them laugh harder. The fucking bastards, both of them. For a moment they were almost indistinguishable, with the same bright blue eyes, and the same nasty low chuckle.

"Get the hell out of my kitchen!" I yelled. "And take that fucking *body* with you!"

Óðinn shook his head, wiping a tear from the corner of his eye. "They are entertaining, these mortal women. I'll give you that."

Loki finally caught his breath, although he still wore a shit-eating grin. I wanted to smack it off his face.

"But you don't want her here," Loki said. "You're rebuilding Asgard, you old fool. You can't have Níðhöggr's spawn here."

"And I can tell Níðhöggr that I did try to stop you," Óðinn said. "You know, that was actually fairly convincing." He gestured at the broken body at my feet.

Loki sighed. "Another mess for me to clean up, then?"

Óðinn gave him an odd sort of smile. "We each do what we're good at, no?" He glanced at me, then back at Loki. "I'll give you an hour."

Óðinn vanished, making the air swirl around my kitchen. It was enough to extinguish the flicker of the remaining candles. The room plunged into darkness, with only a glimmer of starlight from the windows.

"Amateur," Loki muttered.

All the candles suddenly flared back to life. I staggered backward, trying not to notice the way my feet squelched in the pool of blood congealing on the stones of my kitchen floor.

"Well," Loki said, bringing his hands together in front of him. "Let's go home, shall we, daughter?"

There were so many things wrong with that sentence I hardly knew where to begin. Trying to avoid the rapidly congealing pool of blood on the floor, I walked to the kitchen table and sank into a chair, my eyes still fixed on Loki.

"Back up for a second," I said. "How about you tell me who you just killed?"

Loki's smile widened. He looked at the crumpled body on the floor and raised his eyebrows, as if he were just noticing it. "Oh, this?"

"Yes, this," I spat. "What the hell?"

He met my eyes and a shiver danced along the length of my spine. The first two people I'd seen in over a month had to be the fucking creeps Loki and Óðinn.

"You didn't think this was real, did you?" Loki asked.

I frowned. "Loki, there's a dead body on the fucking floor. I can see it. I can even smell the thing."

Loki pulled a chair back and sat down across from me, resting his chin in his hands. "Yes. Yes, there is a smell. I'm quite proud of that, incidentally."

A slow shudder rippled up from my gut. "You're...proud? Of killing someone?"

Loki appeared to be examining his fingertips. "Occasionally."

My mouth went dry. For the first time, it occurred to me to wonder what exactly the Norse god of lies was doing here. And what the hell had just happened between Loki and Óðinn? It sounded worryingly like an agreement, but I had no idea what had just been resolved.

"Fine," Loki sighed. "I'll clean it up, and we can talk."

"How—"

The words died in my mouth. A gust of wind swept through the room, sending the candles dancing, and the body vanished as suddenly as Óðinn had disappeared. I blinked at the pool of blood on the floor.

"Now," Loki said, leaning back in his chair. "Time to go home."

"There's...There's still blood. On my floor."

"No, there isn't."

"It's right there!" I pointed, as if Loki couldn't see the dark puddle that had ruined my embroidery.

Loki grinned. "This is not your floor, daughter."

"Stop calling me that!" I snapped.

He ignored me. "Your floor happens to be in Bozeman, Montana. And it's hardwood, not slate."

"Shut up!" I pushed back from the table, rocketing to my feet. "Just shut up! And get the fuck out of my house!"

Loki didn't move.

"Or...the house! Get the fuck out of the house where I am currently living, okay?"

The air in the kitchen gusted again, rustling the hem of my dress. My embroidery hoops clattered as the pool of blood vanished. I had the surprisingly strong urge to pick them up and examine them for any stray rust-colored stains, followed by the urge to thank Loki. I resisted both of them.

"So, we're good," I said. "You can leave now. Just, out the way you came in."

"Daughter..."

"I am not your daughter," I growled.

Loki's smile vanished. His eyes were cold, and his lips pressed together to form a tight, pale line. "You married my son. Or have you forgotten?"

He may as well have punched me in the gut. My stomach clenched so tightly I doubled over. A soft, terrible whimper slipped from my lips. Horrified, I clamped my hands over my mouth.

"But I apologize," Loki continued. "I should have said, daughter-in-law."

I opened my mouth, but the words refused to come. All those weeks by myself, longing for someone to talk with, and now my speech had fled. Silently, I shook my head back and forth.

"Vali misses you," Loki said. "It's time to come back."

For a second, I felt like my legs really would collapse beneath me. Trembling, I sank into the kitchen chair before my treacherous body could spill me over the slate floor.

"No," I said.

Loki shifted in his chair, crossing his legs. He said nothing.

"I mean, are you deaf?" I asked. "Did you not hear what Óðinn just said?"

He raised an eyebrow over his disturbingly pale eyes.

"I'm—" My throat narrowed. The flickering candles blurred as I tried to blink back the tears. "I'm pregnant."

"Yes. Interesting, that. We all assumed Níðhöggr wanted death. Yet, the dragon longed for life instead."

"It's...what?"

Loki raised an eyebrow. "Interesting. Níðhöggr surprised me. And I'm not easy to surprise."

"Interesting?" Anger flickered somewhere deep inside my chest. "I betrayed your son, and you think it's interesting?"

"Yes," he said, as calmly as if he were discussing the weather. "It's interesting. And now, it's time to go home."

"I can't go home," I said, spitting the word *home* as if it were a curse.

"I don't see why not." Loki fixed me with his intense, pale eyes.

"B-because..." My voice trailed off.

I'd done my best not to think about what happened in the cave with Níðhöggr. Or what I'd done to my husband. But here it was, laid out before me in black and white, as stark as blood spilled across the stones of the floor.

"I slept with Níðhöggr," I said. My voice wavered, flickering like a candle flame.

"Yes. That much I figured out on my own."

I shivered, then wrapped my arms around my chest. For a heartbeat, I tried to think of someone more unsympathetic and asshole-ish than Loki. Just Óðinn, I supposed.

"But, I—" I lowered my voice, trying to force the words out. "I enjoyed it."

Loki's expression didn't change. His hand twitched, as though he were considering reaching for me, then settled back on his knee.

"Of course you did," he said. "I don't think any of our species would have survived if the act of reproduction wasn't enjoyable."

I balled my fists in frustration. Damn it, this wasn't complicated. Was he just trying to piss me off?

"But I'm..." I couldn't even bring myself to say the word *married*. "To Vali," I whispered.

"And he's the reason I'm here," Loki said, taking a deep breath. The candles surged. "I assumed you died. Everyone assumed you died. That irritating Southerner—"

"Zeke?"

He nodded. "He's the one. He was especially broken up about it. He wanted to hold a funeral. Wouldn't shut up about it, actually."

I smiled in spite of myself. Zeke was broken up about my death? Who would have guessed?

"Vali stopped me," Loki continued. "He wouldn't let me contact your parents. He swore on all Nine Realms you were still alive, and he begged me to do something."

"So, here you are," I sniffed and wiped my hand across my cheeks.

"Yes. Here I am."

Our eyes met over the candles. In this light, he looked oddly tired. The candles threw strange shadows over his face, making it look scarred and distorted.

"This is the fourth realm I've searched," Loki said. "I thought you'd be in Múspell, if you were anywhere. Finding you here, on Asgard. Well, that's interesting."

Something Loki said came back to me, tugging at the edge of my mind. "My parents? Did... did someone contact them, eventually?"

He shrugged. "Taken care of. They think you're in a coma."

"They what?"

"Everyone thinks you're in a coma. Vali insisted. He said you'd want to come back to your old life, once I found you. So, there's now an illusion in the Bozeman Memorial Hospital who looks quite a bit like you, if I do say so myself. It convinced everyone but the Southerner."

"Zeke," I croaked, too shocked to say anything else.

"The doctors are a bit suspicious, but I visit them frequently enough to refresh the illusion." He fixed me with a level stare. "It won't last forever, though."

"Damn." I dropped my head to my hands.

"Indeed." Loki stared out of the windows as if there were something to see other than darkness and the faint glimmers of the rising moon, casting a weak illumination over the undulating sea.

"You have to get rid of it." My voice cracked. "Me, I mean. You have to get rid of that illusion. Let everyone think I died."

Loki brought his fingers together in front of his lips. "And what exactly would that accomplish?"

"They could...They could all move on. Get over it."

"Your parents? Get over the death of their only child?"

I shook my head. "No. Okay, maybe not them. The others. Everyone else, I mean."

"Vali, you mean."

I moaned before I could stop myself. Even hearing his name hurt.

"You expect him to get over the loss of his wife?" Loki said. "I've lost a great many people in my long life, daughter. I haven't yet gotten over one of them."

I clenched my hands in my lap, forming fists. "I'm no kind of wife."

"Surely that's for him to decide."

Staring at Loki's calm face, my loneliness and fear crystallized into rage. Who the hell did he think he was, barging into Asgard to make me feel like shit? To slap me in the face with all the horrible things I'd done to his son? I slammed my fist into the table.

"I betrayed him, damn it! Why is that so fucking hard for you to understand? I promised to be faithful, and then boom, I turned around and fucked someone else!"

"Yes," Loki hissed. "You fucked someone else. So what? You stopped Níðhöggr. You did what you had to do to save your realm."

"Do I have to spell it out for you?" I growled through gritted teeth. "I'm not a good wife! Vali deserves better! He deserves... Shit, he deserves someone like his mother."

For once, Loki reacted to something I'd said. His eyes widened in surprise, then narrowed again in a surprisingly predatory expression. "Are you talking about Sigyn?"

"Níðhöggr told me all about her. She was faithful. She stayed with you in that cave for, what? A thousand years? And look at me. I was his wife for less than a day before I agreed to have someone else's baby."

Loki's laugh echoed through the kitchen, sharp as a cold knife. "You think Sigyn stayed with me out of love? Because she was faithful?"

My body felt numb. I couldn't even force myself to speak; I only nodded miserably.

"Karen, Sigyn was trapped!"

"She wanted to leave?" My voice trembled as I asked.

"Yes, damn it. She tried to leave. She tried every way we could imagine. I used so much magic trying to break those wards that the earth shook, but the cave was impenetrable."

I stared at my hands. "That's not what I heard," I whispered.

"Of course not. My wife was innocent. Óðinn couldn't very well say he'd imprisoned one of the Æsir for no reason, so he told everyone it was her decision." He laughed again, a hollow ring that bounced uncomfortably off the kitchen walls. "As if anyone would make that decision."

We sat in silence as the echoes of that strange, pained laugh faded. In the distance, I heard the constant thrum of the waves smashing themselves against the stony shore. I tried not to think about how empty and strange this place must feel to Loki, the home he once shared with Sigyn. Who was trapped, not faithful.

But she didn't choose to betray him, either.

I shook my head as if I were waking up from a spell. "I can't," I said. "Not with..."

My voice faded. I wrapped my arms around my waist, cradling my womb and the little spark of life within. Tears welled up from somewhere deep inside, spilling across my cheeks.

"I betrayed Vali to have this baby," I whispered. "I can't do that to him. I can't ask him to live with a child who isn't his, to look at her face every day and know—"

"Oh, by all the idiots in Asgard." Loki leaned back in his chair and rolled his eyes dramatically. "Did you even have one single conversation with Vali, or did the two of you just spend all your time fucking?"

My mouth fell open; there was nothing I could do to stop it. "Excuse me?"

"Do you honestly think your husband would be anything but delighted to welcome you back? And to raise your child?"

I tried to close my mouth and failed. I'd been in Asgard for over a month. In all that time, I'd never once stopped to consider how Vali might react to my return. Returning was impossible, so I built a neat little wall in my mind around my old life. It was over and gone.

Loki shook his head. "Honestly," he muttered, almost to himself.

The door swung open. I gulped, expecting Óðinn's scowl.

It wasn't Óðinn.

It was Vali.

CHAPTER FORTY THREE

His hair was pulled back, and his great black robe swirled around his legs. His arms crossed over his chest, holding a bundle of white cloth tight to his body. He raised his golden eyes to meet mine, and the world held still.

I was on my feet before I realized what was happening. Someone was making odd, choked little cries, and it took me a moment to realize it was me. I was crying, or laughing, or some combination of the two. Vali smiled at me. My body flooded with a heat I'd almost forgotten, the kind of white hot rush of arousal and comfort that made me think *home*. Yes, with him, in his arms. That's home.

I walked around the table, my legs trembling. Vali shifted, raising the bundle of white cloth in his arms. My breath caught in my throat.

Vali held a baby.

There was an infant in his arms, as tiny and perfect as Caroline's newborn daughter. The baby had dark hair and light skin, with perfect curving pink lips and little fists squeezed tight against its pudgy cheeks.

"Tell me you wouldn't take them in," Loki said.

His voice shot through my chest like a lance. I'd almost forgotten Loki was here. I shot him an irritated glare, then turned back to my husband, standing in the doorway. Vali hadn't moved.

An uneasy shiver raced down my spine. Vali hadn't moved at all. I stared at the figure in the doorway. Vali didn't so much as blink. His shoulders didn't rise and fall with the rhythm of his breathing. The constant wind off the ocean didn't twist a single hair on his head. I took a step backward on legs that felt as though they'd just turned to stone.

This wasn't Vali. My husband wasn't here, on Asgard, standing in the doorway of his childhood home. This was just some cruel trick.

"You tell me it would matter that you weren't the mother of that baby he's holding," Loki said. "Just tell me you couldn't open your heart to them. Both of them."

I tore my eyes away from the vision in the doorway. Loki had his feet on my kitchen table, and his arms crossed behind his head. His eyes sparkled.

"Oh, fuck you," I breathed. The weight of his cruelty settled on my chest like a stone. "How dare you!"

Loki didn't respond. He looked like he was struggling not to smile. My hand itched to punch his pale, arrogant face and knock him to the floor.

"How dare you create this...this thing," I waved my arm at the heartbreaking imitation of Vali standing completely motionless in the doorway. "Just to make a point? Fuck you! You insensitive asshole!"

"Would you turn him away?" Loki arched a delicate eyebrow at me.

"Go to hell," I spat, sinking back into the kitchen chair. "I don't know how Caroline can even stand to be around you."

The corners of his lips twitched up, the exact opposite of the reaction I wanted. "Me neither. But we're not here to discuss my marriage."

My shoulders slumped. I leaned forward and dropped my head into my hands as if my body could no longer support its own weight. Seeing Vali again, even just for a moment, and even if it had only been an illusion, left me drained and exhausted. For those few precious seconds before I realized it was all a trick, I had almost felt like my world could be whole again.

Now it was over. I sensed the black weight of my grief and loneliness waiting for me, just outside the ring of candlelight. Or rubbing its shoulders against the window panes, biding its time until Loki vanished, and I was alone again. Only this time, I would be alone forever.

"You're crying," Loki observed.

I rubbed my palms across my cheeks, trying to destroy the evidence. "Fuck you," I said, wishing I could think of a more colorful expletive. Zeke always had at least half a dozen brilliant insults ready to drop at a moment's notice, but my stupid brain seemed stuck on the f-bomb.

Loki sighed. "You're going to make me spell it out for you, aren't you?"

I tried to glare at him, but looking at his face made my vision blur with tears again. He had Vali's high cheekbones, and Vali's soft lips.

"If you would accept Vali, with a strange, new baby in his arms, and find it in your heart to love that child—"

"Stop it," I said. "It's not just that, and you damn well know it. This child...I mean, my child...she isn't going to be...normal."

He laughed softly. "Karen, you married one of the Æsir of Asgard. Surely, you don't believe Vali expected to have normal children?"

My throat tightened, and my heart fluttered like a hummingbird's wings. A distant memory resurfaced through the haze of my emotional exhaustion. It was a dream, or what I thought had been a dream. One of the early dreams, back in the pine forest, when Vali and I made love on thick, green moss next to a little stream. Back when I thought Vali was just an expression of my subconscious, a lifeline created by my brain to keep me tethered to this world.

Only we weren't making love that night. We were talking. Or, more specifically, I was talking. About Meredith. I was describing her perfect little hands, and how long and delicate her fingers looked against her baby blanket. Barry held her tiny fingers and said she'd grow up to be a piano player.

I cried, of course, as I told Vali things I would never once share with another person in the six long years since Meredith's death. But Vali was crying too, even as he held me to his chest and ran his fingers through my hair. His entire body shook as he mourned the loss of a baby he'd never met. A child who wasn't even his.

Vali told me once that I had talked about Meredith, and I said I didn't remember. I don't think you wanted to remember, Vali had replied.

I bit my lower lip so hard the metallic tang of blood filled my mouth. Why would I want to remember that now?

Loki took his feet off the table, and the front legs of his chair returned to the floor with a resounding bang. He took a deep breath, ran his fingers through his bright red hair, and leaned forward.

"Look. Karen. If you don't want to go home, fine. But you can't stay here. Even if Óðinn wanted you here, which he most certainly does not, this is a bad place for you. Surely, you can see that?"

I nodded, too numb to think of a response.

"I can set you up somewhere else. Not Midgard, of course. I think even if you were in the Australian outback, Vali could sense it." Loki's eyes drifted to the windows again, and his fingers drummed on the table. "Maybe Jötunheimr. It's cold, but you're used to that. I could give you money and land. Set you up as a wealthy widow."

A thick coil of anxiety wrapped my chest, tightening around my heart. Loki was offering me a fresh start, some safe haven for me to raise my child. Why did it taste like ashes in my mouth?

Loki's chair scraped the stones of the floor as he pushed back from the table, coming to his feet. "Well, that's it," he said. "Those are your options: home or Jötunheimr. You choose."

I closed my eyes, burying my head in my hands. My cheeks were hot and damp with tears. That horrible, beautiful vision of Vali in the doorway refused to leave my mind. His smile. The way his eyes danced when he saw me, how his entire face seemed to brighten. And how ready I'd been to fall into his arms. Home, I'd thought.

"I—" I hesitated, trying to swallow. My mouth had gone completely dry. "I'm scared."

"Karen." Loki hesitated. I looked up to see a strange expression on his face, one that made me think of Caroline and the baby.

"We are, all of us, scared," he said.

My entire body shivered, and I pressed my palms against the table, as if I could use the furniture to steady myself. For a heartbeat, as I came to my feet, I seriously thought my legs would refuse to hold me up. Loki waited while I closed my eyes, took a deep breath, and then walked to him and took his hand.

"So, what's it going to be?" he asked. "Love or fear?"

I tried to force my lips into a smile. "You're right," I said, my voice cracking. "This isn't my house. My home is in Montana. With my husband."

Loki nodded, the air around us shifted—

—And I was staring at a red wall in a dark room. I blinked as my eyes adjusted. It was a familiar red. Sedona Sunset red.

My heart hammered at the cage of my ribs. This was my wall, in my living room, the one I'd painted myself. I turned very slowly. The windows were dark, and my house smelled good, like caramelized onions and spices. Low music drifted from the rectangle of light falling through the kitchen door, and it was suddenly hard for me to breathe.

"Have fun," Loki whispered. He let go of my hand.

"No," I hissed. "You can't just leave!"

Loki grinned at me in the darkness. Then the space beside me was empty, and I was alone in my own living room.

"Hello?" Vali's voice called from the kitchen.

My legs trembled, and my thoughts scattered like snowflakes. I opened my mouth but no sound came out.

"Loki? Was that you?"

The living room light flashed on, almost blinding me. Something crashed to the floor with a sharp, metallic clang that reverberated around the room. I glanced down to see one of my little saucepans on the floor and burgundy splatters across the carpet.

Vali stood in the kitchen doorway, frozen, his eyes so wide they seemed to take over his face. He gave a sharp, strangled sort of cry, then ran across the room to crush me in his arms. My legs gave out, and I fell against his body. I pressed my head against his neck, breathing in his wild scent, feeling his heartbeat race against my lips. Nothing had ever felt so good. Nothing had ever felt so much like home.

I opened my mouth to explain, or to apologize, but all I was able to say was, "I love you."

EPILOGUE

"Please tell me it stopped raining," I said.

I saw Susan's reflection roll her eyes behind my back. I'd been basically strapped into this seat in the middle of the guest house's luxury bathroom for damn near an hour while Randy, my hairdresser, struggled to turn my strictly utilitarian haircut into something sexy and romantic.

"Karen, for the hundredth time, it's not raining," Susan answered.

"But the weather forecast said seventy percent chance of showers after two—"

"Trust me. It's absolutely gorgeous out there."

"Relax," Randy admonished me, through a mouthful of hairpins.

Sighing, I tried to relax my shoulders before I met Susan's eyes in the mirror. "You're sure?"

Susan flicked her hair back in annoyance. "Look, why don't I go take a picture?"

She stomped out of the room, and Randy made a valiant attempt to turn his laugh into a cough. For the thousandth time, I tried to angle my head just right to catch one of the kitchen windows in the bathroom mirror. Impossible. It could be a freaking hurricane out there, and I'd never know.

"I'm not being a Bridezilla about this, right?" I asked Randy.

"Course not," he said, this time with a tiny white rose clamped in his lips. He pinned the rose to something in the back of my head and smiled. "But you know what they say about Montana. If you don't like the weather, wait five minutes."

I closed my eyes, trying to picture clear blue skies. Vali and I picked June because it's my favorite time of year in Montana; the hills are green, the wildflowers are exploding, and the jagged mountains are still dazzling with snow. I hadn't even considered the goddamn capricious weather. When we woke up to a gray drizzle this morning, I wanted to scream.

"Can't we get Loki to fix the weather?" I asked, standing in front of the bedroom's bay windows and watching the aspen grove where we were supposed to exchange vows in seven short hours. It was surrounded by a haze of mist.

Vali walked up behind me, kissing my neck. "He doesn't do weather. And besides, I like it."

"You like rain?" I asked. "On our wedding day?"

His hands dropped to cup the swell of my pregnant belly. "In Asgard, rain during a wedding is considered lucky."

I turned to face him, catching his grin. "Is that true?"

"Maybe." He pulled me into his arms. "Is it true I don't get to see you again until the ceremony?"

"Maybe," I answered.

"Then you'd better come back to bed now," he said. "I promise, when I'm done with you, you'll forget all about the rain."

I caught my reflection in the bathroom mirror and blushed. I'd been smiling like an idiot beneath the piled curls of Randy's masterpiece as I remembered how many time Vali made me scream this morning. Thank God I'd insisted on getting my parents a separate cabin.

"And you're free to stand," Randy said, tapping me on the shoulder. "Just try not to touch it for the next couple of minutes, and it'll stay fabulous all night."

I stood, suppressed the immediate urge to touch my hair, and spun to the kitchen widow. A thin scrim of high, white cirrus clouds drifted through a bright blue sky. The aspen leaves flipped and danced in the breeze.

"Oh, thank God," I sighed.

"She did tell you it wasn't raining," Randy said as he packed up his arsenal of supplies.

I opened my mouth to reply, and Susan squealed from behind me.

"Oh, you look fantastic!" she said. "Turn around, look!"

Randy and Susan spun me in front of the bathroom mirror so I could examine myself from every angle. My dark hair spilled from the rose-bedecked swirls on top of my head into an avalanche of tight ringlets that reached to my shoulders.

"Wow," I said. "This looks even better than the first time I got married."

Randy nodded appreciatively, and I told myself to send him an enormous tip first thing tomorrow. Or, maybe not *first* thing.

Susan giggled. "Your mom's got the dress in the bedroom. You ready?"

I nodded, trying to ignore the flutter of nerves in my chest. We were already married, for God's sake. Why the hell was I nervous?

My wedding dress was easy to put on, at least with two grown women helping me. I worried it wouldn't fit perfectly; my last meeting with the seamstress was almost a month ago, and my pregnant belly had grown considerably since then. But the dress fit just right, tight across the stomach and chest with an eruption of white lace below my waist. I told myself to send an extra tip to the seamstress, too. Second thing tomorrow morning. Or third.

"Oh, you look so lovely!" My mom's voice trembled. Her eyes were wide and shiny, almost as if she were—

"Mom, are you crying?" I couldn't believe it. My stoic New Englander parents are not given to many displays of emotion.

Her cheeks reddened, and Mom dabbed at the corners of her eyes. "I'm just happy for you, dear."

I turned back to Susan, figuring I'd give my mom a minute to collect herself. "And the flowers?"

Susan gave me a thumbs-up. "All set. Your bouquet is down there, with your dad."

"The music?" I asked, frantically trying to think of anything else I may have missed.

Susan wrapped her arms around my shoulders, somehow managing to give me a hug without touching my hair. "Shut up," she whispered. "Everything is fine. Just enjoy yourself."

My stomach fluttered again as I turned back to the mirror, checking my lipstick. Now that I was wearing it, the dress felt slightly ridiculous. Barry Richardson and I had gotten married at the courthouse. I hadn't even worn white. I don't think his parents ever forgave me for depriving them of an opportunity to throw a huge wedding gala.

This wedding had been Vali's idea.

"Don't you mortals have a custom of celebrating a marriage with a ceremony?" he'd said.

His eyes had danced as he asked that question, and I guessed he knew all about weddings. It had only been a week, or perhaps not even a week, since Loki had dropped me, without warning, into the middle of my own living room.

"Perhaps," I said. "Why? Do you want a wedding?"

His smile widened. "Of course I want a wedding! Do you think we can pull it off before the little one shows up?"

He ran his hands over the tiny but growing lump in my belly as he spoke. Damn it all, I thought, Loki had been right. Vali hugged me so tight it almost hurt when I told him I was pregnant. When I asked if he would want to be the father to my child, he'd said he was hurt I felt like I even had to ask.

"You do look amazing," Susan said, pulling me back to reality. "And so does the aspen grove. Everything is perfect, I swear. Ranger's honor."

Tears started to well in my own eyes, and I blinked them away. "Thank you."

I hugged Susan, then my mom, then both of them at the same time. Someone coughed from the doorway, and Susan gave me a conspiratorial little smile.

"We'll see you down there," Susan said, taking my mom's hand and leading her from the room.

I took a deep breath, held it, and let it out. "I'm ready," I whispered, running my hands over the bulge of my stomach. "Let's do this, baby girl."

"You are the most beautiful woman in Midgard," Vali said from the doorway.

"Vali!" I squealed. "You're not supposed to see me before the wedding!"

He entered the room with a grin. "Couldn't resist."

Damn, he looked handsome! He wore a dark blue suit and a brilliant white tie, with a boutonniere of wildflowers pinned to his lapel. He had offered to pull his hair back, or even cut it off, but I balked. I wanted to say my vows to the man from my dreams, with his long, dark curls framing his face and spilling down his back.

Suddenly Susan's sneaky little smile made sense. "Susan put you up for this, didn't she?"

"I bribed her," Vali said, leaning close to nibble my ear. "With promises of the true story of how we met."

"Oh, you can't!" My yelp of protest dissolved into a sigh of pleasure as Vali leaned down to kiss me. His lips tasted smoky and rich.

"Is that whiskey?" I asked.

"Just a sip," he said. "Zeke told me it's a human tradition."

"I don't remember actually inviting Zeke to this wedding," I muttered.

"You didn't. He's here as my guest."

I groaned. "Did you invite Colin too?"

"Of course!"

I should have guessed. Colin and Zeke had shown up on my doorstep last week, uninvited, with a beat-to-shit van packed full of other graduate students I barely recognized. Zeke told me they'd come for Wolf Boy, and that it would be an affront to our common humanity to let him marry without a proper bachelor party. I thought about telling them to get lost, but Vali shrugged and said he would love to learn more about modern human customs.

Ten hours later, I was on the verge of calling the police - or Loki - when the van backfired into my driveway at daybreak. Vali staggered out of the back, vomited on the front steps, and collapsed on the couch for the rest of the day, smelling like he personally drank half the whiskey in the great state of Montana. When he finally woke up, he told me only that he'd been sworn to secrecy about the entire night.

Since then Colin, Zeke, and Vali had been disturbingly close.

Vali kissed me again, before I could protest. "And how's our girl?" he asked, dropping his hands to the curve of my stomach.

I smiled. "She's fine."

Vali was with me when I got my first ultrasound. I held his hand so tightly I left small, purple bruises on all his fingers, like little rings. I'd cried when the OB told me she looked perfectly healthy, and Vali held me on the hard plastic of the doctor's examining table for a very long time.

Vali tilted his head, looking at my stomach. "Is she kicking?"

"Don't worry. She was moving all morning."

Vali dropped to his knees, resting his head against the white satin of my dress. "Hello, baby girl," he whispered. "Daddy's here."

"Oh, there she goes!" Our daughter turned inside me, making a slow ripple of motion across my abdomen as she responded to Vali's voice. "I don't know how you do that. She won't move for me."

He grinned, his hands pressed to my womb. "You stay in there a little longer, sweet girl," he whispered. "Mommy and Daddy have some plans for the next few nights."

Vali stood and gave me an incendiary smile, leaving no doubts about the nature of those plans. We were going to spend our honeymoon in British Columbia, hiking at Lake Louise, although I doubted we'd end up doing much actual hiking. I didn't remember feeling sexy at all during my first pregnancy, but Vali treated each new inch around my waist as an aphrodisiac, and his constant arousal only turned me on more.

"I thought pregnancy and marriage were supposed to be a turnoff," I said.

"Nothing about you is a turnoff," Vali whispered, leaning close to run his lips down the curve of my neck.

I closed my eyes. Unzipping my dress was starting to seem like a very good idea. The rest of the wedding party could wait—

"If you're quite done."

I jumped. Loki stood next to us, close enough to touch.

"Goddamn it, Loki!" I said. "You have got to stop doing that!"

Vali didn't even move. "I'm not done," he muttered, his face on my neck and his hands tight around the small of my back.

I sighed, allowing myself to relax in his arms for one last kiss. We made it last a long time.

"What are you doing here?" I asked Loki, once Vali and I pulled apart.

"The pathway to the aspen grove is a bit muddy. Vali thought you might like to be transported to the ceremony."

I blinked at my husband. Just when I thought he couldn't surprise me, he considers things like mud and dresses.

"That would be great," I said, smiling at Vali. "Thank you."

Vali kissed me one more time on the curve of my jaw, and I closed my eyes, feeling the heat of his body in my arms, breathing his wild scent. Our eyes met as he pulled away, saying all the things I could not find the words to express. He took my hand and raised it to his lips, kissing my fingers gently.

"See you there," he whispered.

I watched him walk through the door, waiting for my heartbeat to return to normal. Some part of me wondered if there would ever come a time when our kisses didn't leave me gasping for breath, or shot through with arousal. God, I hoped not.

Once I heard the front door close, I turned to Loki.

"May I ask you something?" I whispered.

"Of course."

"Is everything—" I paused, wrapping my arm around the swell of my belly. "Is everything going to turn out all right?"

Loki raised an eyebrow. "Oh, I've absolutely no idea. But we've all managed so far." He gave me that odd smile again, the one that made me think of him holding a newborn.

"Are you ready?"

I took a deep breath and nodded. "Yes."—

—And the two of us stood together in front of the aspen grove. The Gallatin River chattered behind us as aspen leaves shifted and rustled in the breeze. The soft notes of George Winston's *Montana* album, drifting from the little speakers nestled in the aspen grove, mixed with the gentle chatter of subdued conversation. A baby shrieked, and I turned to see Caroline standing under a cottonwood, bouncing Adelina in her arms. Caroline's entire face changed when she saw Loki; it was like watching the sun rise over the mountains of

Asgard. My chest clenched as I realized how close I'd come to never smiling like that again.

Loki shifted against me, but I grabbed his arm. His pale eyes met mine.

"Thank you," I whispered.

He nodded, then joined his wife and child under the cottonwood. Adelina screamed with laughter as I stepped closer to the aspen grove. There was John, sitting with his wife and three kids on the white folding chairs under the trees. Diana sat on the other side of the aisle, somehow managing to make a flannel shirt look elegant and regal. Zeke was in the back row, his legs spread wide. He grinned at me beneath a pair of absurdly enormous aviator glasses. Next to him, Colin raised one hand in a small salute. He at least had the decency to look somewhat sheepish about crashing his boss's wedding. Sitting in the front row, my mom was still dabbing her eyes. Susan stood in front of the makeshift aisle of folding chairs, wearing what she'd insisted on calling her "bridesmaid jeans."

And next to Susan, smiling in the dappled June sunshine, stood Vali, his wildflower boutonniere nodding in the gentle breeze. *Husband,* I thought, my breath catching in my throat. *Home.*

My dad walked and handed me the tightly wrapped bouquet of wildflowers Susan and I had picked that morning. Bright scarlet penstemon, purple lodgepole lupine, and the brilliant blue-and-white shooting stars of columbine. Just like in our dream meadow.

Dad smiled, and somewhere, someone started Wagner's *Bridal Chorus.*

"Are you ready?" he whispered.

I nodded and took his arm. On the other side of the aspen grove, Vali's golden eyes rose to meet mine.

"Yes," I said.

LOKI AND CAROLINE RETURN IN THE TRICKSTER'S SONG[1]

"**D**o you really think she'll be all right?"

I glanced up from the mirror in our bedroom, where I was fumbling to jab a sparkly earring into my earlobe, and saw Loki's shoulders straighten. If I had to guess, I'd say the Norse god of fire and lies was stifling a sigh.

He turned and gave me a glorious smile. "Yes, darling. I think she'll be fine."

"But we've never left her alone before..."

I glanced toward the closed door of the nursery where Adelina was sleeping, for now, and fought the urge to check on her just one more time.

"You leave her with me every day when you go to work, do you not?"

"Well, that's different," I protested. "You're her dad. And you're a god."

"You did interview twelve candidates for this babysitting position, my darling."

I sighed. "I know. But—"

"And Stephanie was here for two hours yesterday. I think you showed her how to operate the Diaper Genie at least five times." Loki looked like he was struggling to suppress a smile.

"But what if—"

He wrapped his arm around my waist and pressed a finger to my lips. "Wife, when was the last time we went out?"

"Uh—" I stammered. "Before the semester started?"

He shook his head, and I tried to think. It was difficult to remember what life had been like before Adelina was born. And it had only been— Wait, how long had it been?

"Four months," I said. "Didn't we go out to dinner just before she was born?"

His arm tightened around my waist. "Five."

"Really?"

"Five."

Loki started to nibble my ear. I almost pushed him away, but his lips actually felt...*good*. I leaned against him and tried to remember what it felt like to be turned on, to crave the sensation of his body pressed against mine.

"I took you to Bali," he whispered. "We had dinner on the beach."

"Oh!"

Heat raced to my cheeks. I remembered that dinner. I also remembered what we'd done afterward, on an isolated stretch of white beach, as the moon rose over the gently phosphorescing waves. I'd been supremely, hugely pregnant. Everything about me had been round and swollen, from my cheeks to my ankles. I felt revolting.

But my husband made me feel like a goddess.

I had so many orgasms under that tropical moon I thought I'd pass out. In fact, I must have passed out, because the last thing I remembered about that night was waking up naked in our bedroom, in sheets filled with the fine, white sand of Bali's beaches.

And then Adelina showed up, two weeks earlier than anticipated. And things had—

Well, they had changed, of course. What did I expect?

The doorbell rang, and I jumped out of Loki's arms. A second later Adelina's shrieking cry pierced the air, slicing through my chest like a cold knife. My brief flicker of arousal vanished with my Bali memories, and I rushed to her bedroom.

My daughter was red-faced and wailing in her crib. She'd broken free of her careful swaddle wrap, and her tiny fists railed at the world. Her face was a contortion of rage beneath her flaming hair.

I loved her so much it hurt, like a kick to the gut.

"Shhhhh, Mommy's here," I whispered as I wrapped her in my arms.

Adelina arched her back in response to my pathetic attempts at comforting. Like she always did. A month ago, Dr. Singh diagnosed her with colic, shrugged, and told me some children are just more difficult than others.

Lucky me, I'd thought. I couldn't just have a nice, normal baby.

Find The Trickster's Song[2] on Amazon

THANK YOU!

Y ou're amazing!
 Thank you so much for reading and supporting independent artists. Without you, I wouldn't be writing.

Now that you've finished Vali and Karen's story, please do consider leaving a review. Reviews make or break the careers of independent authors like me, and I really do read every single one.

You can leave a review on Goodreads[1], Amazon[2], or the retailer of your choosing. Also, click here to join my mailing list[3] and I'll send you *Honeymoon*, the free Loki and Caroline novella that's not available anywhere else.

---

1.   https://www.goodreads.com/book/show/37847743-the-wolf-s-lover

2.   https://www.amazon.com/dp/B078VNWKT3/
    ref=sr_1_7?s=books&ie=UTF8&qid=1515327655&sr=1-7

3.   https://dl.bookfunnel.com/nxonrreiwu

ACKNOWLEDGEMENTS

This book would never have happened without the support, encouragement, and occasional harassment, of many lovely people.

First, as always, thank you to my wonderful husband. I would have given up on "the Vali story" without his ceaseless cheerleading. He also makes a fine beta reader, among other things.

The talented Bronwyn Green provided invaluable feedback, and made this story much, much stronger. I am so deeply grateful, my friend.

Thank you also to Jayne Ingram-Shover for the beta reading and the encouragement!

Teresa Conner made the cover, and all the teasers, for this book. If the cover caught your eye, it's thanks to her!

I am still thankful, every day, to be part of a network of amazing fellow authors. Cora Cade, Jessi Gage, Jessica Jarman, Mira Stanley, Kris Norris, Torrance Sené, and Janine Ashbless have given me more encouragement, advice, and support than I could ever repay. You ladies are the best! (They're also fabulous writers, and you should check them all out.)

I'm grateful for my former co-workers at Montana State University. Any details that help bring this story to life are thanks to them; the mistakes are mine alone.

And finally, thanks to my fine Montana skiing partners Mark, Jake, Greg, and Lars. Wishing you much gnar to shred, my dear friends.